PRAISE FOR

Cindi
Myers

"Charming. The protagonists' chemistry and Lucy's spunk
keep this fluffy novel grounded."
—*Publishers Weekly* on *Life According to Lucy*

"The story is rife with insight and irony,
and the characters are just plain fun."
—*Romantic Times* on *Detour Ahead*

"Ms. Myers will definitely keep readers sighing with delight."
—*www.writersunlimited.com*

Dear Reader,

The editors at Harlequin and Silhouette are thrilled to be able to bring you a brand-new featured author program for 2005! Signature Select aims to single out outstanding stories, contemporary themes and oft-requested classics by some of your favorite series authors and present them to you in a variety of formats bound by truly striking covers.

We want to provide several different types of reading experiences in the new Signature Select program. The Spotlight books offer a single "big read" by a talented series author, the Collections present three novellas on a selected theme in one volume, the Sagas contain sprawling, sometimes multi-generational family tales (often related to a favorite family first introduced in series) and the Miniseries feature requested previously published books, with two or, occasionally, three complete stories in one volume. The Signature Select program offers one book in each of these categories per month, and fans of limited continuity series will also find these continuing stories under the Signature Select umbrella.

In addition, these volumes bring you bonus features...different in every single book! You may learn more about the author in an extended interview, more about the setting or inspiration for the book, more about subjects related to the theme and, often, a bonus short read will be included. Authors and editors have been outdoing themselves in originating creative material for our bonus features— we're sure you'll be surprised and pleased with the results!

The Signature Select program strives to bring you a variety of reading experiences by authors you've come to love, as well as by rising stars you'll be glad you've discovered. Watch for new stories from Janelle Denison, Donna Kauffman, Leslie Kelly, Marie Ferrarella, Suzanne Forster, Stephanie Bond, Christine Rimmer and scores more of the brightest talents in romance fiction!

The excitement continues!

Warm wishes for happy reading,

Marsha Zinberg

Marsha Zinberg
Executive Editor
The Signature Select Program

SPOTLIGHT

Learning Curves

Cindi Myers

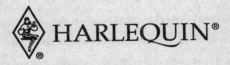

HARLEQUIN®

TORONTO • NEW YORK • LONDON
AMSTERDAM • PARIS • SYDNEY • HAMBURG
STOCKHOLM • ATHENS • TOKYO • MILAN • MADRID
PRAGUE • WARSAW • BUDAPEST • AUCKLAND

ISBN 0-373-83675-9

LEARNING CURVES

This edition published by arrangement with Harlequin Books S.A.

® and TM are trademarks of the publisher. Trademarks indicated with
® are registered in the United States Patent and Trademark Office, the
Canadian Trade Marks Office and in other countries.

www.eHarlequin.com

Printed in U.S.A.

For Jim,
with much love

Liar. Shelly tugged at the ruffled neckline, trying to pull it up over her cleavage. The designer apparently hadn't considered that some women had real breasts, either.

"Emma and Stacy loved the dress," Yvonne said.

Emma and Stacy were liars, too, Shelly decided. They were also sizes four and six respectively. They needed all these ruffles to give the illusion that they were more than shining hair and good cheekbones.

"Perhaps if I ordered the dress in a larger size." The salesclerk frowned at the bow. Or maybe she was frowning at Shelly's butt. Shelly was tempted to give a belly-dancer shake for the clerk's benefit.

"The size isn't the problem." She reached for the zipper and began to pull it down. "This isn't the sort of dress for my body type." Shelly was a well-endowed size twelve. One hundred percent natural curves. She'd learned long ago to avoid ruffles the way a dieter avoids cheesecake.

"Shelly, please!" Yvonne hurried after her as she headed for the dressing cubicle. "This is my *wedding!*" She said the word as if it was an occasion upon which life and death depended. Who knows? For Yvonne, maybe it was.

Six years ago, on a particularly maudlin evening shortly after her twenty-fifth birthday, a weeping, slightly inebriated Yvonne had vowed to be married by the time she turned thirty. When she'd missed that deadline, she'd plummeted into a months-long funk that had lifted only when she'd won the coveted proposal from Daniel Dunnegan, a commodities broker she'd known all of three months. Still, the man—and the upcoming wedding—made Yvonne happy, so Shelly was determined to keep her that way.

CHAPTER ONE

SHELLY PIPER STUDIED her reflection in the unforgiving glare of fluorescent lighting and mirrors on three sides and didn't know whether to weep or puke. The pale green chiffon bridesmaid's dress stretched across her sturdy frame like a misplaced canopy for Barbie's dream bed. She forced a finger underneath the band of one puffed sleeve, hoping to restore blood flow to her arm. The designer of this thing obviously never met a ruffle, pouf or bow she didn't love, since the yards of billowy fabric were liberally decorated with every frill and fribble imaginable. "I look like a Jell-O mold," she said.

"Oh, now, it's not that bad." Her best friend and bride-to-be, Yvonne Montoya, tried to smooth the full skirt of the dress, which ballooned over Shelly's hips. "I think it's just darling."

"A darling Jell-O mold." She frowned over her shoulder at the bow perched on her backside.

"No, you look beautiful," Yvonne protested.

Only a bride, vision fogged by love and the prospect of her own white satin splendor, would think this. Shelly caught the eye of the salesclerk. The woman's smile was strained. "I'm sure the effect of all the bridesmaids together will be wonderful," she said.

"It's going to be a beautiful wedding." Preparing for her role as maid of honor, Shelly had been practicing saying this repeatedly, a calming mantra for the stressed-out bride.

"But you have to be in it. And you have to wear that dress. It's the perfect dress."

Perfect for what? But she already knew the answer. Since they were kids, Yvonne had harbored dreams of the perfect Cinderella wedding, complete with ruffled dresses, a four-tier cake and a white satin gown with a train five yards long. Having finally won that prized proposal, she had poured twenty years of pent-up longing into creating the absolutely perfect dream wedding.

It was a testament to their friendship that Yvonne hadn't let her less-than-perfect choice of a maid of honor cloud her vision one bit. "I didn't say I wouldn't wear the dress," Shelly said, watching her face in the mirror as she spoke. Same pleasant smile, same calm expression. This is what years of training to be on television will do for you. You could say the most alarming things with a straight face. Fifty homes destroyed by a tornado? Mass flooding in the southern valley? World's worst bridesmaid's dress proudly worn in public? That calm reporter's demeanor never changed. "Of course I'll wear the dress," she continued. "It's going to be a beautiful wedding."

"It is, isn't it?" Yvonne's voice sounded dreamy, as it did too often these days. She drifted away, leaving Shelly to change clothes in peace.

Five minutes later she emerged from the cubicle, herself again in a neat black pantsuit with a beaded top that drew attention to her face and a long jacket that skimmed her hips. After years of dieting, exercise and various desperate measures, she'd celebrated her thirtieth birthday last year by embracing the fact that she was a size-twelve woman in a size-six world. She was healthy, she was strong and she was beautiful, even if not everyone appreciated her beauty. *She* appreciated it, and to hell with the rest of them.

Of course, there were still days when she looked at pictures of size-two models in magazines and wanted to slit her wrists. After all, years of brainwashing couldn't be banished overnight. But she'd come a long way since the times when her mood for the morning was dictated by numbers on the scale. She had a whole new wardrobe of classy, flattering clothes and a new appreciation for her own sexy curves. And she'd discovered there were more than a few men out there who appreciated a woman with a woman's shape.

Now, if she could only convince her bosses at *First for News* to appreciate her as much. After years of slaving away behind the scenes, she'd finally earned a tryout for a weekend on-air reporter's position. But that had been weeks ago. The powers that be were certainly taking their time making up their minds.

"Will that be check or charge?" The salesclerk greeted Shelly at the front register.

Shelly handed over her charge card and tried not to think about how much she was paying for a dress she would wear once and then banish from her closet forever.

"I'm going shopping for stationery this afternoon. Want to come?" Yvonne came to stand beside her. "You can help me pick out thank-you notes."

Oh, joy. Shelly shook her head. "Sorry, but I have to

get back to the station. I'm hoping to catch Darcy by surprise and make her tell me what the higher-ups have decided about the reporter's job."

"You mean they *still* haven't told you?" Yvonne planted her hands on her hips and looked outraged. Or as outraged as a curly-haired blonde with big brown eyes can look. "No one's worked as hard to get that job as you have. Why can't they just give it to you?"

"This is television." Shelly shrugged into her coat, then draped the dress bag over one arm. "Qualifications don't necessarily have anything to do with whether or not you get a job." But dammit, she *had* worked hard to prove herself. She'd volunteered for every shitty schedule, worked overtime turning in award-winning copy, and had taken hours of classes to hone her skills in front of the camera. Going by seniority alone, she was next in line for a promotion. There was no good reason the job shouldn't be hers.

She kept reminding herself of this on the drive from Cherry Creek to downtown. Though six inches of snow had fallen over the weekend, most of it had already melted away. The streets were clear and the sun shining through the windshield made it feel warmer than the thirty-eight degrees showing on the Republic Bank sign. A typical January in Denver.

As the elevator ticked off the passing floors on its way to *First for News*'s offices at the top of the Republic Plaza Building in downtown Denver, she rehearsed the spiel she'd give her boss, Darcy Long. *It's been three weeks. They told me from the first I was one of the top candidates. When will they make a decision?* Polite, firm, a request for action. The key was to act professional and think positive.

As she stepped off the elevator, she caught a glimpse of a woman in a pink blouse and gray slacks darting down the hall. Darcy. And the hallway led to her office. A feeling of triumph surged through Shelly as she hurried after her boss.

She cornered Darcy in her office at the end of the corridor. Darcy's eyes widened as Shelly swept in after her and closed the door. "I don't have time to talk, Shelly," Darcy said, making a show of shuffling papers on her desk. "I have a meeting with Roger in five minutes." Roger was Roger Murphy, executive producer of *First for News*.

"Then you have five minutes." Shelly settled into the chair across from Darcy's desk. "This won't take even that long, I'm sure."

Darcy's face looked pinched, though a series of Botox injections had made it impossible for her to actually frown. "What do you need?" she asked as she dropped into her chair.

"It's been three weeks since my tryout for the on-air reporter's spot," Shelly said. "Have you heard anything?"

Darcy wrinkled her nose. (The only part of her face she *could* wrinkle, Shelly supposed.) "I really don't have time to discuss this right now. Maybe later..."

"How much time does it take to tell me yes or no?" Shelly struggled to keep a pleasant look on her face. Her stomach was doing the backstroke and she was wishing she hadn't eaten that chicken sandwich at lunch.

"All right then, no." Darcy avoided her eyes.

Shelly swallowed hard. "No, you haven't heard anything, or no I didn't get the job?"

Darcy sighed. "No, you didn't get the job."

"What? Are they crazy?" Shelly sprang to her feet, every calm, professional word she'd rehearsed burned from her brain by red-hot anger. "They told me I was a top candidate. That I did great in my audition. I've worked here ten years. My piece on homeless women won an award last year."

"Tamra Smothers won an award for reporting that piece," Darcy said.

"Yes, but *I* did the work. And everyone here knows it." Shelly paced back and forth, clenching and unclenching her fists, before she turned on Darcy again. "What did they say? Why did they turn me down?"

Darcy shuffled papers again. "Oh, they weren't specific. They apparently feel they've found someone else who will connect with viewers better."

The words set off warning bells in Shelly's brain. "What do you mean 'connect with the viewers better?' Who did they hire?"

"I believe her name is Pamela Parsons. Very good credentials, I'm sure."

"Pamela Parsons!" Known in local circles as Perky Pam, Parsons was a bleached-blond beauty queen whose main claim to fame was posing in a bikini in ads for Honest Cal's Used Cars. The ads were plastered all over town, ensuring that everyone knew who Pam was. "She's not a journalist. She's a model."

"She has a journalism degree from the University of Colorado." Darcy stood. "Look, I really have to go now." She offered a patently fake smile. "Don't worry, I'm sure there'll be another chance for you soon."

Right. Just as soon as I bleach my hair and lose forty pounds. "They thought I was too big, didn't they?"

Darcy stumbled on her way out the door and turned to stare at Shelly, her face blanched white. "I didn't say anything like that."

"You didn't have to." Shelly took a deep breath, holding back the black mood she could almost see at the edge of her vision. "I've heard it before."

"You'll never prove anything if you try to sue."

"Oh, the station would love that, wouldn't it? Did they tell you that? 'Don't let her know the real reason she lost the job. We don't want a lot of publicity about size discrimination.'" Darcy's wild-eyed look told her she'd scored a direct hit.

"You wouldn't try to do that, would you?" Darcy asked. "You'd ruin your career before it even started."

Shelly nodded. The news business was amazingly insular. Get a reputation as a troublemaker and you were history. Besides, she'd have to spend a boatload of money and time she didn't have trying to fight something that would be pretty tough to prove. "I don't know what I'm going to do right now," she said. "But I'll let you know."

She managed to hold a hint of a superior smile on her face until Darcy gave her one last angry look and left the office. Then she sank into a chair by the door and let out the breath she'd been holding. "So what has all this positive thinking done for you lately?" she mumbled under her breath.

"JACK, BEFORE WE START the interviews, I need to run some ideas by you for the promo spots." Executive producer Armstrong Brewster cornered Jack Halloran outside the KPRM conference room after lunch.

"Sure." Jack checked his watch, a classy but modest TAG Heuer his father had given him last Christmas. "I've got about fifteen minutes before the first candidate arrives."

"It won't hurt them to wait a little bit on a star." Armstrong stabbed a stylus at the screen of his Palm Pilot. "Now, what do you think of some footage taken at one of the area ski resorts—maybe Loveland, since it's closest? Put you in a sharp-looking ski suit, surround you with snow bunnies."

Jack made a face. "No one wears ski suits these days. And no one calls women skiers snow bunnies. It's sexist."

"Right. Well, if you don't like that one, how about filming you at the gym? Maybe on one of those rock-climbing walls? Play up the whole physical fitness thing and show off your muscles. The viewers love that kind of thing."

"What does any of that have to do with the news?"

Armstrong heaved a sigh and fixed Jack with a pained look. "It might be the news, but it's still entertainment. You have to catch people's attention. And in this case, *you're* what will capture them and, we hope, make them tune in to look."

The idea grated. Surely the kind of people who tuned in to watch his show would be more intelligent than that. "This is a serious news magazine. About issues."

He started toward the conference room, where the job candidates were waiting. Armstrong fell into step beside him. "You think because this is public television we don't have to compete for viewers? We have to get them any way we can. So if sex appeal sells, then we give 'em sex appeal."

"This kind of thing is exactly why I left the networks." He'd lost count of all the times he'd put in long hours, working on gritty investigative pieces, only to find himself pushed into promo fluff pieces that made the station look good. When he'd learned that his last position as prime-time anchor had come not because of his journalistic chops, but because he scored highest with the target market group of twenty-five-to-thirty-seven-year-old women and men, he'd resigned and vowed to find a place where he could be more than just a pretty face stuck behind a desk.

He glanced at Armstrong, who again was stabbing the stylus at his Palm Pilot like a man trying to spear eels. "There's more to life than looks, you know."

"Tell that to a man with a full head of hair." Armstrong slotted the stylus back in the case and looked at Jack. "Now, which of the promo ideas do you like best?"

"None of them." They reached the conference room and stopped outside the door. "Let's finish this discussion after the interviews."

"Maybe I should get Mr. Palmer to decide on a promo spot."

"May I remind you that my uncle is providing the financing for the show—he doesn't want to be involved in production. That's your job."

Armstrong snapped shut his PDA. "In that case, I say we do the spot at the gym. It'll appeal to women *and* men."

Jack shook his head and opened the door to the conference room. He wasn't done discussing this yet, but right now he had to choose a co-anchor for the show. From the first he'd agreed that having two people to present the news was better than making this a one-man show. Adding a woman provided another perspective on issues, as well as appealing to a different demographic.

He might resent that television was ruled by audience numbers, but he wasn't naive. The trick was balancing reality with the way he wanted things to be.

"Hello, everyone. Sorry to keep you waiting." He took a seat at one end of the conference table while Armstrong sat in a chair against the wall. "I'm Jack Halloran and this is the producer of the show, Armstrong Brewster."

Jack studied the four candidates and mentally matched them with the *curricula vitae* and audition tapes he'd studied earlier. A tall African-American woman with a cascade of braids and a model's high cheekbones smiled at him. Angela Lawson. Early morning anchor at a network affiliate in Tulsa. Only four years out of the University of Oklahoma but rising fast.

To Angela's left was a petite woman with a lion's mane of blond hair. Misty Albertson. Blue eyes and peaches-and-cream perfection. She looked like the cheerleader who'd lived next door. The one who'd been the most popular girl in every high school in America. But she wasn't a dumb blonde. She'd graduated with honors from NYU and had been weekend anchor at a large independent in Rochester.

Veronica Sandoval was the third candidate, a native of San Antonio whose black hair was fashionably disheveled—a look he would bet took hours to get so perfect. At thirty-four, she was the most experienced in the group, and the oldest, though she looked at least five years younger than the graduation date on her CV indicated.

He turned to the last candidate, a honey-blonde in a

well-cut blue suit, Shelly Piper. Unlike the others, she wasn't beaming at him with an impossibly wide smile. Instead, she was watching him. Studying him. As if this was all quite serious business to her.

He folded his hands in front of him on the table and addressed the women. "I'd like to start by having each of you talk about why you think you're the best candidate for this position. Ms. Lawson, why don't we start with you."

The African-American woman sat up a little straighter and glanced around the table. "No offense to anyone else here today, but it's obvious I'm most likely to appeal to a young, hip demographic. Public television has a stodgy image. You can pull in viewers by overcoming that."

In the background, Armstrong was nodding his head. He liked the way this woman thought.

"But you have to give people more than fluff."

The woman on his right, Shelly, had spoken. Angela looked annoyed. "Hey, I can deliver serious news." She smiled. "But I can also look good doing it."

Armstrong chuckled. Jack turned to Shelly. He gave her points for speaking up, but she was in the hot seat now. "Ms. Piper, is it?" he asked.

She nodded.

"Why do you think you're best suited for the position?"

"I've got ten years of experience in broadcast journalism. Five of those have focused primarily on investigative reporting. I've lived in Denver for twenty years. I know what's what and who's who in the state and local government. I'm hardworking and tenacious when it comes to tracking down information." She paused and took a deep breath, her eyes still fixed on Jack. "And I care about the stories I do."

He blinked. Her last words were startling. Most reporters he knew went out of their way to affect an attitude of detachment. They prided themselves on being objective and dispassionate. To profess an emotional investment in your work seemed old-fashioned, even unprofessional.

Certainly the other two candidates didn't make that mistake. Veronica stressed her ties to the Hispanic community and her experience as a political reporter. Misty played up her on-air experience and added that she was "a lot of fun."

Not something he'd thought about as a requirement for a reporter of serious news, but Armstrong nodded in approval. Jack wrote *fun* next to Misty's name on his list.

He consulted his notes once more. "Now I have a sample scenario for you to consider. Suppose a state representative has a key vote on a pressing issue to be decided soon in the legislature. He's refusing all requests for interviews through normal channels. How would you go about learning his views on the issue?"

The women looked serious, brows furrowed, lips pursed in thought. Misty was the first to speak. "I'd make friends with his secretary or administrative assistant. They know everything and she could give me the inside track to her boss."

He nodded. Not a bad tactic. "Veronica?"

"I believe persistence pays off," she said. "I'd call and visit his office daily until he agreed to talk to me."

Nagging could sometimes be effective, he would admit. He turned to Shelly. "What would you do?" he asked.

"I'm assuming this is a representative from this district," she said. "Both Tom Murphy and Pete Rodriguez are big skiers. If the session is really tense, with a big issue up for debate, by the weekend they're going to want to take a break on the slopes, so I'd follow them there and maneuver myself to ride the chairlift up with them. Then I'd strike up a conversation. You can learn a lot riding the lifts."

He nodded. "Very creative."

"You ski?" Misty's tone was scornful.

Shelly's expression tightened. "Yes, I ski. As I said before, I've lived here for twenty years."

"You certainly don't look like a skier." Misty looked down her nose. "I mean, you don't look very athletic."

"You mean I'm not skinny."

This remark was met with chilling silence. The women avoided looking at Shelly, though they exchanged conspiratorial glances with one another. Shelly held her head up and turned to address Jack. "Something else I should have mentioned earlier. The average woman in this country is a size twelve. I know how important demographics are in these decisions, so you might think about that."

The atmosphere was a trifle tense after that, and Jack cut the interview short after only a few more questions. "You'll be hearing from us in the next few days," he told the candidates as they filed out. "Thank you for coming."

When he and Armstrong were alone, he turned to the producer. "Well?"

"I liked that Angela woman the best. Though Misty's a close second. They're both young, smart and gorgeous. The viewers would love them, and the two of you together would be dynamite."

It was what he'd expected Armstrong to say, but he was still disappointed. "I liked Shelly Piper the best," he said.

Armstrong frowned. "She was okay."

"She was more than okay. Didn't you hear her answer to my question about landing an interview with the legislator? She's obviously a creative thinker, and her knowledge of the city could prove really valuable and would balance out the fact that I'm so new here."

"Yeah, but she's a little…chunky."

"Chunky?" He frowned. "She wasn't skinny, but she looked okay to me."

"Well, yeah, she looked okay for a woman on the street, but the camera adds ten pounds. You saw that in her demo tape."

"What does that have to do with anything? She sounds like a good reporter."

"I'm just telling you what people are going to say. People expect women on TV to be skinny. You put her on and you're going to get calls. Besides, if we went with Angela or Misty we could do promo spots with you two beautiful people and we'd have viewers tuning in just to look at you."

Which was exactly what he *didn't* want. "That's not the audience I'm going for."

"Then hire Veronica. At least she'd get us the Hispanic viewers. And she's nice-looking, too."

Jack shook his head. His mind was made up on this one. He wanted someone he could work well with. Someone who would get what he was trying to do here, covering solid news stories with a depth the networks couldn't manage. "We're going to hire Shelly," he said.

Armstrong shook his head. "You're making a big mistake."

"No, I think I'm doing exactly the right thing." He rubbed his hands together. He and Shelly Piper were going to be good together, he knew it.

CHAPTER TWO

SHELLY LEFT THE INTERVIEW knowing she was screwed. Her competition had been smart, savvy, gorgeous and, in two cases, ethnic. No way was an ordinary white girl going to win out over that. Hell, even *she* probably would have picked one of the other women. After all, television wasn't interested in average people. The ordinary viewers who tuned in wanted to see people who were more beautiful, more exciting or, as proven by the popularity of daytime talk shows, more screwed up than the viewers themselves were.

She turned into the parking garage for the Adam's Mark hotel and raced up the ramp as if she were competing in time trials for the Grand Prix. She had three minutes to meet Yvonne in the Italian restaurant on the main floor. She'd promised to help evaluate the place as a possibility for the wedding rehearsal dinner.

She walked up to the entrance of the restaurant at exactly 6:30 p.m. Yvonne was waiting. She looked like the Secretary Barbie Shelly had wanted for her eighth birthday, the one with the pink suit and matching pink pumps.

"Thanks for helping me with this." Yvonne stood on tiptoe to give her a hug. "It's so much easier not having to make all these decisions by myself."

"A free Italian dinner? What's not to like?" She made her smile more cheerful than she felt.

Yvonne's mother, a litigation attorney, lived in Connecticut and had no desire to help plan a wedding. "Send us the bills and we'll pay," she'd said. "But I don't have time to look at fabric swatches and interview caterers. Besides, don't you think that's a lot of fuss for someone who's over thirty? You ought to elope and save your money." As if Yvonne needed another reminder that she was past the deadline she'd set to get married.

"When I talked to the events coordinator, she said if we held the rehearsal dinner here, they'd give us a preferential room rate for out-of-town guests who stay at the hotel," Yvonne said as they followed the hostess to a table next to the windows overlooking Denver's Sixteenth Street pedestrian mall. "That's good, don't you think?"

"It's great." Shelly settled into her chair and opened the oversize leather-bound menu. "A lot of your family is coming in from the East Coast, right? Does Daniel have many out-of-town people on the guest list?"

"I think so. Yes."

"Speaking of your intended, why isn't he helping you choose the restaurant for the rehearsal dinner?" She glanced at Yvonne over the top of the menu. "Isn't that one of the things the groom and his family are in charge of?"

"Yes, but Daniel's like me." She smoothed her napkin in her lap, avoiding Shelly's gaze. "None of his family live in Denver. And he's a typical man. He doesn't care about any of the details. If I left this up to him, we'd be gathering in a sports bar after the rehearsal."

A waiter took their order and shortly afterward brought their drinks. Shelly drained half her cosmopolitan in one slurp. The impact of that disaster of an interview this afternoon was beginning to hit her. Two weeks ago, after Perky Pam had won the coveted weekend on-air job, Shelly had seen the advertisement for the anchor position for a PBS news show and had immediately sent in an audition tape. She'd dreamed of stunning Darcy with her resignation, and the announcement that she was leaving to co-star in her own prime-time news magazine.

Why had she thought public television would be any different from the image-conscious networks? The name of the game was ratings everywhere these days, and that apparently required beautiful people.

"I almost forgot! You had a job interview this afternoon, didn't you?" Yvonne said. "How did it go?"

Shelly made a face. "Let's just say Dr. Ruth has a better chance of playing for the NBA than I do of getting that job."

"What happened? Did you say something you shouldn't have? Spill something on the interviewer? Curse on camera?"

Shelly laughed. She had once told Yvonne that cursing on camera was considered one of the seven deadly sins of broadcasting. "No, there wasn't any kind of audition. This was just a group interview with the male anchor and the producer."

"Then how can you say you won't get the job? Wasn't he impressed?"

She shrugged. "Hard to tell. He asked good questions, but he played his cards close to his vest." Jack Halloran had seemed interested enough in her answers, but then again, her brain had been fogged by the sheer force of his good looks. Talk about a face a camera could love.

"What was he like—the anchor? What's his name?"

"His name's Jack Halloran. And he's the most gorgeous man I've ever seen."

Yvonne giggled. "How gorgeous?"

"Brad Pitt, Hugh Jackman and a young Cary Grant gorgeous."

"That good, huh?"

"I promise you, the man stops conversation when he enters the room. He's got it all—blue eyes, great hair, great *butt*. And every time he smiled at me, I lost my train of thought. It was embarrassing."

Yvonne's eyes widened. "My God, he really got to you, didn't he? The two of you must have clicked."

She drained the rest of her drink. "There was no clicking. Any woman would respond to this man."

"Look at you. You're actually blushing. You never blush."

"It's from the drink. I downed it too fast." The rush of heat she felt for Jack Halloran had nothing to do with any connection the two of them had made. Her response merely proved she was a healthy, breathing, heterosexual female. Any woman would feel the same.

The waiter delivered their food. Shelly studied her mussels and falafel and considered ordering another drink. But then she wouldn't be able to drive home. Better stick to water. She sighed and dug in.

"What were the other candidates like? How many were there?"

"Three. All smart, experienced and beautiful."

"You're beautiful."

If she'd been within arm's reach, Shelly would have hugged her. "Next to Jack Gorgeous, any woman would look like a farmhand. Put me on camera and I'd look like a fat farmhand."

"You're not fat."

"Thank you for saying that, but in TV land, I'm livin' large in a bad way. The camera really does add ten pounds."

Yvonne pushed away her plate of lobster ravioli. "Speaking of weight, I should have ordered a salad. I need to lose a few pounds before the wedding."

"Are you kidding?" Shelly paused with the forkful of falafel halfway to her lips. "You look great."

She shifted in her chair. "Yeah, but we're going to St. Thomas and we'll be in swimsuits most of the time." She flushed. "Daniel told me he thought it would be cool if I got one of those thong bikinis."

Shelly snorted. "Nobody looks good in those. The least hint of cellulite shows." She shuddered to think of her own cottage cheese butt in a thong.

"Really thin people don't have cellulite, so I thought if I lost a few pounds…"

Shelly shoved the plate back toward her friend. "Eat up. You're the perfect size. And once Danny boy gets a load of you in a regular bikini, all thoughts of butt floss will vanish."

"You really think so?" Yvonne looked doubtful.

"He loves you, doesn't he? He'll love how you look in anything." At least, that was how it should be. Then again, in a perfect world, Shelly would be delivering the weekend news broadcast instead of Perky Pam.

When Yvonne didn't say anything, Shelly looked at her more closely. "Daniel *does* love you, doesn't he?"

"Of course he does!" Was it Shelly's imagination, or was Yvonne's smile a tad *too* bright? "He's just very visually oriented. He told me so." She took a long drink. "It makes sense, really. Studies show that men are turned on by what they see, while women can be aroused by words and thoughts."

Which explained all the homely men dating fashion models. Of course, so many of those men were *rich,* so maybe money was the real turn-on for the women in those cases. "I just want to be sure you're getting a man who'll give you everything you deserve," she said.

Yvonne's smile seemed more genuine this time. "You're so sweet to worry about me," she said. "But everything's fine. I know I'm going to be really happy with Daniel. This is what I've always wanted." She reached across the table and squeezed Shelly's hand. "I hope you find someone soon who'll make you happy, too."

She shrugged. "I don't mind being single."

Yvonne shook her head. "You don't have to be all brave with me. But don't worry. I know there's someone out there for you."

"Right." She stabbed at a piece of falafel. Good thing she wasn't holding her breath waiting on Mr. Right. She had too many other things to do.

Like finding a new job. One where size really *wouldn't* matter.

THE NEXT EVENING, DANIEL was supposed to come to Yvonne's apartment for dinner. At 6:45, she turned down the temperature on the oven and slumped into a kitchen chair, trying to remain cheerful. Daniel was late, as usual. Her mother always said chronic tardiness was a sign of disrespect for others, but Yvonne knew Daniel was simply too busy to be on time. He was always reminding her what a demanding job he had.

Not that her job at the mayor's office was a day at the beach. Politics was, by its nature, a stressful business, but apparently nothing like the pressures endured by a commodities broker. Or maybe Daniel was one of those people who was more affected by stress.

In any case, he'd be able to relax with her over dinner. She'd prepared his favorite meal: lasagna, crisp green salad and the sourdough bread from *Panera* he liked so much. That and some wine would put him in a good mood in no time.

The doorbell rang and she jumped up to answer it. "Hi, sweetie," she said, greeting him with a kiss.

"Hey, baby. Sorry I'm late." Grinning, he produced a bouquet of roses from behind his back. "I got these for you."

"Oh, sweetie. They're gorgeous." Yvonne buried her nose in the flowers. He was so thoughtful. No wonder she'd fallen in love with him.

"What's for dinner? I'm starved." He moved past her toward the table.

She put the flowers in water, then poured wine for both of them from the bottle she'd opened to breathe. "I made lasagna. Your favorite."

"That's great. I can't wait."

He sat while she retrieved the food from the kitchen. She hummed to herself, wondering if it was possible to be any happier. It probably seemed silly to some, but this was all she'd ever wanted in life. While other little girls had talked of the careers they'd have and the wonderful places they'd travel, Yvonne had looked around the little apartment she shared with her mother and various stepfathers and dreamed of a man to take care of her and a family to make a home for.

When she'd met Daniel, she'd realized he was everything she was looking for in a husband. He was dependable, a good provider, masculine and strong. He was the kind of man who enjoyed taking care of a woman. After so many years on her own, she was ready to be taken care of.

"This looks delicious." Daniel helped himself to the lasagna as soon as she set it on the table. She took the seat across from him and sipped her wine, watching with satisfaction as he filled his plate.

She was lifting a square of the pasta dish onto her own plate when Daniel stopped her. "Ah, ah, ah. Remember what we talked about? I'd really like to see you in that thong bikini on our honeymoon."

She flushed. She'd been really making an effort to cut back, but she was so damned hungry. And lasagna was her favorite, too. But it was a small sacrifice to make, really. Daniel would be so thrilled to see her in that new bikini. "You're right." She settled for half a square and salad with no dressing.

He smiled. "That's my girl. I'm going to be the envy of every man who sees you in St. Thomas."

The compliment warmed her. How could she not want to please him, when he praised her so?

"How are the wedding plans coming?" he asked.

"My friend Shelly and I had dinner yesterday at that

restaurant I told you about—the one at the Adam's Mark," she said. "They have really great Italian food. You'd love it."

He nodded. "Fine. I told you I don't care where we have the dinner, as long as I don't have to be bothered with setting it up."

She winced at his choice of words, disappointment like a rock in her stomach. Did he really see the preparations for their wedding as a *bother?* Couldn't he be a little more enthusiastic?

She pushed back the thought. Daniel was just being a typical man. She chewed a mouthful of dry lettuce and washed it down with more wine. "I'm going to talk to my cousin Sophie next week about the menu for the reception," she said.

Daniel helped himself to a second serving of lasagna. "Remind me again who Sophie is."

"Sophie's my cousin. The caterer? She's going to cater our reception. You remember, we discussed this a while back."

"Are you sure that's a good idea?" He frowned, looking so stern. "Isn't she rather new at the catering business?"

"Not brand-new. And she worked for another caterer before she started her own business last year." Plus she'd offered them a family discount. But Yvonne didn't remind him of that. Daniel was always accusing her of being cheap.

"Still, we don't want to entrust something as important as our wedding to an amateur." He set down his fork and reached into his jacket pocket and pulled out a folded sheet of paper. "Talk to these people before you make a final decision." He handed her a printed list.

She scanned the names on the page. Some were familiar to her. Her gaze landed on the number at the end of the list. "Daniel, there are fourteen names on here!"

"Yeah, my mom sent it over. They're all caterers who have done friends' weddings, so we know they're experienced."

She strangled another cry of protest. She'd only met Daniel's mother twice, but the woman scared the shit out of her. Disdain emanated from her like expensive perfume, and she never hesitated to offer criticism in the guise of helpful opinion. "Then maybe your *mother* should interview them," Yvonne snapped.

Daniel's eyebrows rose. "There's no reason to get upset with me. You're the one who wanted the big wedding. I was only trying to help."

She forced down the bubble of anger that rose in her chest. Of course Daniel thought he was being helpful. She should be happy he was offering any input at all. She folded the list and laid it beside her plate. "Thank you. I'm sure I'll find the perfect caterer on this list." She'd find some way to break the news to Sophie and maybe she could cut back somewhere else to pay the bill.

After dinner, she cleared the table while Daniel took off his jacket and tie and put on some music. Tonight it was sexy blues. She smiled as she put away the leftovers, some of the tension from the meal easing away. He certainly knew how to set the mood for romance.

She returned to the living room and cuddled up next to him on the sofa while he drank the last of the wine. As Susan Tedeschi sang about needing to be with her man, he draped his arm across Yvonne's shoulder, his fingers idly stroking her neck.

"Did you enjoy dinner?" she asked.

"Yeah, it was great." He set aside the empty wine-glass and turned to her. "Now I'm ready for dessert."

She smiled and tilted her face up for his kiss. Whatever little ways Daniel annoyed her, he was a terrific lover.

They kissed deeply, bodies pressed together, tongues twined. She liked this the best, when they were so close and in tune with each other. No matter how tired she was, he could always turn her on.

He slid his hand under her shirt. She sighed as his fingers cradled her breast. She wasn't wearing a bra, only a silky camisole, and the combination of his warm hand and the cool silk against her flesh was incredibly erotic. She pressed against him. "I love it when you do that," she whispered, nipping his earlobe.

"Mmm." He kissed her neck and began toying with her nipple, sending jolts of sensation through her.

"You make me so hot," she moaned.

His lips curved into a smile against her neck. "You're really sensitive, considering there's not much there."

His words lowered her temperature significantly. She pulled away from him a little. "You don't like my breasts?" She knew she was on the small side, but then, she was a small woman.

"Hey, I didn't say they weren't nice." He cupped both breasts in his hands again. "Just a little small. It kind of surprised me when I was so attracted to you because usually I go for women who are really stacked."

She knew this, of course. She'd have to be blind to miss the way he checked out other women, especially ones with big boobs. But to hear him say as much hurt.

"But you are attracted to me. That's the important thing, right?" She latched onto his last words.

"Of course I am, babe." He smiled. "But you can't blame a man for his natural likes and dislikes, can you?" He took his hand from beneath her shirt and stood. "Let's go into the bedroom and get more comfortable."

She let him take her hand and lead her toward the bedroom, but her earlier enthusiasm had waned. He was right; she couldn't blame him for his natural preferences. She ought to appreciate that he was comfortable enough with her to be honest. Honesty was so important in a marriage.

But it worried her that he didn't think she was perfect. Not absolutely perfect, of course. There was no such thing as absolute perfection. But she wanted him to believe she was the perfect woman for him, just as he was the perfect man for her.

Even if it didn't turn out to be true, two people in love ought to start out thinking they were perfect for each other. If they didn't, how else could they even attempt such a crazy thing as happily-ever-after?

THOUGH JACK'S UNCLE HAD given Jack free rein over *Inside Story,* he'd expressed an interest in being kept "up to speed" on what was going on with his investment. And truthfully, Jack valued Ed Palmer's opinion. The man wasn't a multimillionaire because he was dumb. So the evening after he'd interviewed the candidates for the female anchor position, he stopped by his uncle's office to discuss his options.

Ed flipped through the folder of CVs. "Which one do you think we should hire?" he asked.

Jack sat back on the soft leather sofa in his uncle's office. "They're all well qualified, but my choice is Shelly Piper. She's got the investigative experience I'm looking for and she's practically a native, so she'll have insider knowledge of local politics and things like that. Plus she has a real passion for reporting that I liked." When she'd fixed those big blue eyes on him and told him she really cared about her work, he'd certainly been moved. He was betting the audience would be, too.

"What does Brewster say?"

Jack frowned. "He wants to go with one of the others."

Ed raised one eyebrow. "Did he say why?"

"Angela Lawson's African-American and Veronica Sandoval is Latina, so choosing either one of them would be a plus for minority viewers."

He nodded slowly, lips pursed. "Anything else?"

Jack rested his ankle on his knee, then shifted to put both feet on the floor again. "Angela, Veronica and Misty are all gorgeous. They look like models." They were perfect, in fact. He'd had enough of perfection over the years. Every time he looked in the mirror he was reminded of what people thought of him. Not that he was stupid enough to be ungrateful for his looks and all the advantages they'd given him, but why couldn't people see past that to his abilities, too? He was one of the few people he knew who actually looked forward to the effects of aging. Maybe crow's-feet and a few gray hairs would make people take him more seriously.

"And this Shelly Piper? Is she ugly?"

"Lord, no." The very idea shocked him. The whole time he'd been sitting next to her at the conference table, he'd been aware of her curves. She had what they used to call an hourglass shape. Maybe it wasn't fashionable these days, but those curves sure looked good on her. "She's very nice-looking," he said. "Here, let me show you." He opened his briefcase and took out a videocassette. "This is Shelly's audition tape."

He crossed the room and fed the tape into the VCR next to a flat-screen television, then returned to the sofa and punched the remote.

Shelly, dressed in a rich purple suit, introduced a report on cuts in funding for art and music programs in schools. She interviewed a school administrator and a teacher, then shifted the focus to a group of students, who spoke about what the art and music classes that would no longer be funded meant to them.

"A group of parents is working to raise money to restore at least some of the programs," she said as she sat at a student desk in an empty classroom. She picked up a clay sculpture made by one of the students and considered it. "As one parent told me, not every student is a gifted artist, any more than every student excels at athletics. But every student deserves the chance to discover the creativity inside them." She looked into the camera, blue eyes intense. "I'm Shelly Piper, reporting for *First for News.*"

Jack punched the off button on the remote and turned to his uncle. "See what I mean? She has great empathy for her subject. I think viewers will love that. It's what I've been looking for."

"She's not the typical anchorwoman," Ed said.

Some people had called Ed Palmer relentless. Jack usually thought of his uncle's approach as thorough. Attention to every detail had made him a very rich man over the years. But now Jack wished he wasn't so interested in all the details. "Shelly isn't as thin as the other women," he said. "She's very...curvy."

"But you think she's the best for the job?"

Jack sat up straight and looked his uncle in the eye. "Yes. I don't want some model look-alike to balance out the show. I want someone who's smart and talented, someone who can really add to what we're offering viewers."

Ed nodded and slid the folder of applications back to Jack. "I trust your judgment. Hire Shelly Piper, if that's what you want."

"It's what the show needs." And maybe what he needed, too—someone to keep him grounded and remind him of the things that really counted, like hard work and talent and believing you really could make a difference in someone's life.

SHELLY HAD BARELY EXITED the elevator at work two mornings after her interview with Jack Halloran, when Perky Pam descended on her in a fog of *Angel* perfume. "I'm so glad I caught you." The new on-screen darling of *First for News* flashed a broad smile as she grabbed hold of Shelly's arm. "I wanted to know how the research for my special report on Denver's day-care crisis is coming."

Shelly's smile was equally broad, and just as shallow. "I've run into a few roadblocks, but I'm still digging." She shrugged out of Pam's grip.

"Thanks. I'm really counting on you."

Yeah, better take your shoes off and start counting on your toes, too, sister, Shelly thought as she hurried away from her co-worker. *I've been too busy with other things to do your work for you—things like looking for a better job.*

She spotted Darcy up ahead and hurried to catch up with her. "Darcy! I'm glad I caught you. I was just looking for you."

Darcy glanced over her shoulder and continued down the corridor toward her office. "If you're going to complain about Pam, I don't want to hear it. The network thinks she's a fine choice. Ratings have been very favorable."

"I don't have any problem with Pam." Amazing how easy lying was when you'd had so much practice. But this was a business where you definitely had to know when to pick your battles and Pam wasn't worth the fuss. She followed Darcy into her office. "I only wanted to ask you what you know about Jack Halloran."

Darcy collected a stack of memos from her in-box and flipped through them. "I hear he's in town to start a new PBS news magazine."

"Where's he from?"

Darcy frowned at a lengthy message. "He was the prime-time anchor for an ABC affiliate in Dallas."

She knew it. Anyone that good-looking and well-spoken was a natural for an anchor spot. "Why did he leave the network to come to public TV?"

"It caused quite a bit of talk when he left the network, I can tell you. Now people are saying he's smart like a fox. If this PBS deal is successful, he'll have his choice of positions, up to and including a national posting with CNN."

Shelly nodded, digesting this bit of information. "So he's ambitious."

Darcy made a face. "He's in television."

Of course. Everyone in TV was climbing over one an-other to get to the top. Including Shelly, though she'd been trying to get to the next rung so long she felt like she had permanent heel prints on her forehead. "Is he married?"

Darcy looked up from her stack of memos. "I take it you've seen him? He's gorgeous, isn't he?"

She nodded, numb. Where had that last question come from? Why did she care if handsome Jack Hallo-ran had a wife? It wasn't as if he was going to be ask-ing her for a date.

"He's single, as far as I know," Darcy continued. "Though he has something of a reputation as a player. Of course, he probably has women throwing themselves at his feet all the time." She laughed, a short, sharp bark. "Hell, if I thought I had a chance, I might launch my-self in his direction, too."

A player, huh? Like Darcy said, no surprise there. Shelly sighed. She should have known her impression of Jack as smart, compassionate and sexy as hell had been too good to be true.

"Why all the questions?" Darcy studied her, a news-hound's look of interest in her eyes. "Thinking of mak-ing a play for him yourself?" She laughed, as if this was the most amusing thing she'd heard all day.

The laughter did it. Otherwise Shelly might have dis-missed the question with some lie about having seen the name and wondering where she'd heard it before. In-stead, she mustered her most mysterious smile. "Oh, I ran into him the other afternoon and had the most interest-ing conversation. I was just wondering if you knew him."

Darcy's mouth actually dropped open, and she stared at Shelly as if she'd grown a third head. Still smiling,

Shelly pirouetted and beat a hasty retreat down the hall, choking back laughter and a sense of satisfaction.

SHELLY SUCCESSFULLY AVOIDED both Pam and Darcy for the rest of the day, but the next morning she'd scarcely filled her coffee cup in the break room when she received a page from Darcy. *Meeting in my office 10 a.m.* the text message read. So much for flying under the radar. She could hope for a new assignment, but more likely she'd be called on the carpet for dragging her feet on the research for Pam, or given more scut work as befitting her behind-the-scenes role.

Back in her office, she stared at her phone and debated calling KPRM and asking to speak to Jack Halloran. But what would she say if he actually answered the phone? She could pretend to be calling to thank him for the interview, while subtly highlighting all the reasons he should hire her as his co-anchor. She could take the direct approach and ask if she was still in the running for the job.

What if he said she wasn't? There was always begging, but she wasn't ready to stoop that low—yet. She shook her head and powered up her laptop. There were some things she didn't want to hear.

At ten o'clock, she reported to Darcy's office, the knot in the pit of her stomach expanding to bowling-ball size when she saw Pam sitting in the chair in front of Darcy's desk. "Hi, Pam," she said, already backing toward the door. "I didn't mean to interrupt. I'll wait until you and Darcy are done."

"No, no, come sit down." Pam leaned over and patted the empty chair next to her. "I'm here to see you."

Reluctantly, Shelly inched toward the chair. "If this

is about the day-care research, I promise I'll get right on it this afternoon."

"I'm sure you will." Pam's smile didn't dim one watt. Didn't her jaw muscles ache after a while? "Right now, I can't wait to tell you about the wonderful new project Darcy and I have for you."

Shelly sat and eyed Darcy warily. "What new project?"

Darcy flipped a thick brochure toward her. "One of our advertising partners wants to do an on-air promotion. A year-long weekly spotlight."

"We knew you'd be just perfect for this," Pam gushed.

Shelly picked up the brochure and stared at the two photos on the cover—before-and-after shots of a cute young blonde. The before shot had her dressed in baggy shorts, shoulders slumped, hair hanging lank, a morose look on her face. In the after photo, a smiling, bikini-clad and definitely thinner version of the same woman posed for the camera. Denver Diet Centers Challenges You! the cover line read.

The bowling ball in her stomach was now the size of a beach ball. She dropped the brochure on the desk and frowned at Darcy. "What is the promotion?"

"They're offering a free one-year program to a staff person—diet, exercise, lifestyle coaching, the works. Once a week we'd run an on-air segment tracking your progress and highlighting various aspects of the program."

"Isn't it fantastic?" Pam leaned toward Shelly. "The program usually costs thousands, and you'll be getting it free. And in the end you'll be a brand-new you."

"What's wrong with the current version of me?" She looked Pam in the eye, daring her to answer.

But Perky Pam was too dim—or too ruthless—to

take offense. "There's nothing *wrong* with you, of course. But losing twenty pounds or so and getting in shape would be the best thing that could ever happen to you, and your career."

"It's a great opportunity," Darcy said. "You'd have airtime every week. And let's face it—if the prospect of embarrassing yourself in front of thousands of viewers doesn't motivate you to lose weight, I don't know what will."

Shelly blinked hard, horrified at the tears that threatened. She was a veteran reporter, a tough city girl not given to outbursts of emotion. But she dared anyone to sit in her place right now and not be hurt.

She picked up the brochure again and stared at it. Inside were pictures of people, mostly women, lifting weights and running on treadmills, eating salads and shopping for clothes. They were all smiling, obviously having the time of their lives.

This certainly didn't look like any of the diets and exercise regimes she'd tried before. She'd lost some weight on most of them, but eventually always crept back up to her current size. She'd been within five pounds of her present weight for all but a few months for the past twelve years. Didn't that mean this was the size she was supposed to be?

She turned to the last page of the booklet, to a row of photos of thin, smiling people who had supposedly completed the program. What would it be like to be that thin—so thin her shoulder blades and hip bones stood out? So thin her stomach was concave?

"Just think what this will do for your social life," Pam said. "When the single men in this city see your transformation, they'll be standing in line to date you." She giggled. "Who knows? In a few months, we might have to do a follow-up story on your wedding."

So now she was not only *fat,* she was a hopeless, single loser. She gripped the brochure so hard she wrinkled the pages. Would Darcy call the cops if she shoved the booklet down Pam's throat?

And to think skinny people like Pam had accused her of having no self-control! She took a deep breath and laid the brochure back on the desk. "I think expecting everyone to fit into the same size-six mold sends the wrong message to our viewers," she said calmly.

For once Pam's smile faded. "What are you talking about?" She straightened her shoulders. "Anyway, I wear a size four."

Darcy frowned at her. "Are you saying you don't want the assignment?"

She shook her head. "Why not do a series on how people of varying sizes can lead healthy lifestyles? We could feature senior fitness clubs and water aerobic classes and plus-size athletes."

Pam laughed. "Plus-size athletes? There's no such thing."

Shelly glanced at the brochure again. It was certainly tempting…. "I have a friend who wears a size sixteen and she and her husband take long-distance bike tours. I have another friend who's my size who teaches aerobics and weight training at a senior center."

Pam continued to stare at her as if she was a babbling idiot. Darcy looked annoyed. "This is the program the advertiser wants to do," she said. "If you're not interested, we'll find someone else."

"I'm not interested."

"Fine." Darcy took the brochure and stuffed it in a drawer. "But I have to tell you, I think you're making a mistake. You said you wanted a chance to do on-air reporting, but the first time I give you an opportunity, you turn it down. How do you think that's going to look when it comes time to fill other on-air positions?"

"The only reason you gave me this *opportunity* is because you think I'm fat." The more she thought about it, the more furious she became.

Her anger had no effect on the other two women. "I guess this meeting is over, then," Pam said. "I'm sure we can find someone else who won't want to pass up such a fabulous opportunity."

Translation: some other *fatso* who won't be *stupid* enough to turn down a chance to transform from ugly duckling to swan on the nightly news.

"I'm sure you *will* find someone." Shelly stood and glared at both women. "You can also find someone else to do your day-care research and all your other work for you."

Darcy stared at her. "What are you talking about?"

"I quit." Who knew two words could feel so—empowering? All those years she'd told herself she would do anything to make it in her career and—surprise!—she'd finally found something she wouldn't do.

Darcy and Pam stared at her, rendered speechless for once. Shelly grinned at them, knowing she was walking the tightrope between hysteria and relief. But she'd gone this far; no sense trying to turn back. "Goodbye," she said. "And good riddance."

CHAPTER THREE

SHELLY'S EUPHORIA LASTED long enough for her to clean out her desk and drive to her apartment. Once the front door closed behind her and she set her box of belongings on the coffee table, her bravado deserted her and the realization of what she'd done kicked in.

Ten years on the job and a spotless work record blown away with two words. What had she been thinking?

She sank onto the sofa and stared at the sunlight streaming across the floor from the front window. The apartment was absolutely quiet, a silence she never heard on her rare weekends off, when children's laughter or the blare of neighbors' stereos provided a comfortable background hum for housework or catching up on work at home.

In the end, all those extra hours she'd put in hadn't counted for much, had they?

She jumped up, despair breathing down her neck. "The thing to do is to keep busy," she said aloud, unable to bear the ringing silence of the apartment anymore. "This could be a great thing for me. I'll print out my résumé, make some calls. Why did I waste ten years stuck in that place, anyway? They never appreciated me."

She headed for the bedroom. First order of business was to change clothes. Then she'd go online and look at some job boards. There were probably tons of positions she was qualified for.

She pulled jeans and a short-sleeved sweater from her closet, then kicked out of her heels and took off the dark purple suit. The lightweight-wool fitted jacket and knee-length skirt had been a bargain score at the Neiman Marcus outlet. A designer name, in her size! That had been a lucky day.

And she'd have plenty of more lucky days ahead, she was sure. She hung the suit in the closet and turned away, freezing as she caught sight of herself in the mirror.

She could feel a black mood bearing down on her again as she stared at the little roll of flesh at the waistband of her underwear, and at her naked thighs, which suddenly looked enormous. She stood up straighter and sucked in her stomach. Better. But there was no sucking in those thighs. And her knees! When had she developed such pudgy knees?

Her shoulders slumped and she swallowed hard. Maybe Darcy and Pam were right. Maybe she *was* fat. Maybe if she tried harder, she, too, could be skinny, and happier for it. Maybe all she lacked was willpower and discipline and self-control and all those other things articles in women's magazines were always touting as the keys to physical perfection.

She stared harder in the mirror, scrutinizing the image she'd faced a million times before. Though she might not love everything about what she saw, she wouldn't give in to self-loathing, either. As she forced herself to study the roundness of her arms and the curve of her hips, the old resentment rose within her—resentment that some mythical "they" had deemed her shape imperfect and therefore unworthy.

Since when did happiness depend on what someone looked like? She knew plenty of wretched beautiful people. Why would she want to be one of them? Better to make the best of what she had and look for happiness somewhere inside herself. She might not have the willpower to deny herself desserts or the discipline to exercise an hour every morning, but she was smart enough to know that trying to fit into someone else's mold was a recipe for misery.

She turned her back on the mirror and went to get dressed. Maybe she should switch to a career in print journalism. Nobody cared what newspaper and magazine reporters looked like, did they?

The phone rang, startling her. She stared at it, heart pounding. Who would call her this time of day? Everyone she knew would expect her to be at work. She started to let the machine get it. She wasn't ready to explain why she was sitting at home in the middle of a weekday afternoon.

By the fourth ring, she told herself she was being silly. She grabbed up the phone just as the answering machine kicked in. *Hello, you've reached 555-9753. I—* "Hello? Hello, I'm sorry. Just a minute…" She punched wildly at the buttons on the answering machine, trying to silence the message. At last it clicked off. "Hello?" she tried again. "Sorry about that."

"Shelly? Is this Shelly Piper?"

Jack Halloran's voice was relaxed and friendly.

"Y-yes," she stammered. She took a deep breath and fixed a smile on her face, long habit from the college journalism course where the professor had instructed that telephone interviewees would "hear" the smile in her voice. "Jack, how nice to hear from you again."

"I called the station, but the receptionist said you weren't in. I hope it's all right that I called you at home."

Apparently, word hadn't made it to the switchboard that she was no longer a *First for News* employee. Thank God for small favors. "Oh, it's perfectly all right. I, uh, had some things to do, so I took off a little early." Not exactly a lie, though stretching the truth a tad.

"I'm glad I caught you, then. We've carefully considered all the applicants for the co-anchor position and we've reached a decision."

She sat on the edge of the bed and curled her right hand into a fist. Here it comes. A fitting end to what had so far been a really shitty day.

"We'd like to offer you the job."

"I really appreciate your consideration— What?" She stopped, the gracious speech she'd had planned dying on her lips. "Did you say you're offering me the job?"

"Yes. I was very impressed with your credentials, and I think someone with your local connections will be a real asset to the show."

"Yes." She cleared her throat. "I mean, thank you. And yes, I'm happy to accept your offer."

"That's terrific. We'd like you to start as soon as possible, but I understand you'll need to give your current employer two weeks' notice."

"Um, that won't be necessary."

"But I'm sure they must depend on you. In fact, I wouldn't be surprised if they didn't make you a counteroffer, though I hope you won't accept."

Oh, the man was priceless. If he was here, she'd kiss him. She smiled, imagining her lips on Handsome Jack Halloran's. She sat up straighter and banished the smile. She'd definitely have to curb the fantasizing if she was going to be working with him. "Actually, I resigned my position at *First for News* today." That sounded positively sophisticated, didn't it? As if she simply couldn't be bothered with that petty little station anymore.

"You did?" Half a beat of silence. "May I ask why?"

How much could she risk telling him? Oh, hell, she might as well start off being honest. If the truth upset him, she'd have a read on his true colors right away. "Part of the answer is that I'd been there ten years and had advanced as far as I felt I could."

"And the other part of the answer?"

Here goes nothing. "They wanted me to enroll in a weight-loss program and document my progress on air."

"Ouch."

"Thank you." She pumped her fist in the air. Score one for Handsome Jack.

"You don't have to worry about that happening here," he said. "*Inside Story* wants to focus on news that doesn't get in-depth coverage in other local media outlets."

"I can't wait to get started."

"Could you meet me tomorrow afternoon? We can

discuss some stories I have in mind and look at any ideas you might have."

"That would be terrific. What time should we meet?"

"Four o'clock?"

"I'll see you then." She replaced the phone in the cradle and stared at it, then jumped up and danced around the room. Was she living right, or what? *Finally* her dream job had come her way.

And she'd be working with a man who was nice *and* nice-looking. Yeah, he had a rep as a player, but she didn't care about his personal life. He'd offered her the perfect job. She grinned at her reflection in the mirror. As far as she was concerned, the woman who smiled back at her was absolutely beautiful.

JACK HAD A REALLY GOOD feeling about this one. The minute he and Shelly Piper sat down Friday afternoon to talk about the show, something clicked. She immediately grasped the direction he wanted to take the program and she'd added some great ideas of her own.

He watched her now as she shuffled through the various newspapers, magazines and press releases spread out between them on the conference table in his office at KPRM. They'd been talking, what, two hours? The time had flown by.

She pulled a newspaper clipping from the jumble of papers. "Here's something I found in the *Post* yesterday that I thought might be worth looking into further," she said. "It's a couple of paragraphs about publicly funded hospitals turning away uninsured patients."

He nodded. "Health care is always a hot topic. What do you see as the angle?"

She tapped her index finger against the article. "I'm not sure. If tax-supported institutions don't treat these people, what happens to them? Do they become a bigger burden on the system if they go untreated and get sicker? Or look at the flip side—what happens to the cost of health care for everyone if these hospitals treat any- and everyone regardless of their ability to pay?"

"We need to look at both those things." He nodded. "I say go for it. See what you can come up with."

She slipped the article into her notebook and glanced at her notes. "You're developing the piece on home-financing scams, and the historical perspective on forest management and industrial interests?"

"Right. Also the interview with Senator Campbell." He sat forward and flipped through his notes. "What do you think about a story on problems with programs for juvenile offenders?"

She considered the idea a moment, then shook her head. "We need a better balance of stories, I think. Something informative, but upbeat."

He nodded. "You're right. What can we do that's feel-good, but not fluff?"

She tilted her head, lips pursed. She had plump lips outlined in a shade of deep rose lipstick. They looked very soft.

He jerked his gaze away and focused on the notebook in front of him. This wasn't the first time this afternoon he'd found himself riveted on some physical feature of his new co-worker. At various times her long fingers, shiny hair and full breasts had commanded his attention. He usually didn't have any trouble keeping his mind on business with the women he worked with, but for some reason this afternoon his attention kept wandering. Maybe it was because he'd been so busy with the move and developing the new show that he hadn't had time to date. He'd probably spent more time with Shelly than he had with any woman lately, so it was understandable he'd be more aware of her.

"What about a look at successful programs for juvenile offenders?" Her words forced him to focus on business once more. "We could show people what's working to turn these kids' lives around," she said.

He laughed. "You're a genius. I love it."

She made a show of buffing her nails against the lapels of her suit jacket. "So nice of you to notice."

Their eyes met and they both laughed. Jack felt an extra zing of awareness arc between them. Now, where had that come from?

He slid his gaze away from her and began straightening the papers scattered across the table. "I feel really good about everything we've accomplished this afternoon," he said.

"Me, too." She helped him collect the papers, avoiding looking at him. Just as well. If their eyes met, his gaze might linger too long, letting her know the effect she was having on him. "I want to thank you again for choosing me as your co-anchor," she said. "It's the kind of opportunity I've dreamed about."

"You're exactly what I've been looking for." He stepped back and watched as she swept the rest of the papers into a neat pile. Why did he suddenly feel so awkward around her? It was definitely her and not his own long abstinence, he had to admit. Something about Shelly sparked a response in him.

A response he was going to do his damnedest to keep under wraps. Though there was no way of completely avoiding the whole man-woman thing when working with the opposite sex, he prided himself on his professionalism. And though he'd had his share of offers from attractive co-workers, he always kept his business life and his personal life separate. The one time he'd made an exception to that policy had ended badly.

"I didn't realize it was so late." She stacked the papers on the corner of the table and smiled at him. "Would you like to get a drink, or something to eat?"

"Uh, no thanks. Better not." Better not mix alcohol, or any kind of social setting, with Shelly until he had a better handle on the feelings she'd stirred. "Maybe some other time."

She flushed. "Sure. I wasn't thinking. You probably have plans." She slung her leather messenger bag over one shoulder and started toward the door. "I'll see you Monday, then."

He opened the door for her. "Right. See you Monday."

When she was gone he shut the door behind her and sagged against it. He had plans, all right. Plans that didn't include getting involved with his new co-anchor.

He gathered up his briefcase and surveyed his office. This was his dream. He wasn't going to let anyone distract him from it. Once the show was a success he'd have more time for personal relationships, but even then, he wouldn't get involved with a co-worker.

For now, he'd stop by the gym on his way home and work off some of the tension. By Monday morning, he'd be ready to start off with the proper attitude toward Shelly. They were co-workers. Partners in the show.

As long as he remembered to keep things strictly business between them, he'd be fine.

"STUPID, STUPID, STUPID!" Shelly berated herself all the way to her car. What had she been thinking, inviting Jack out like that? He was her co-worker, and her boss to boot. He wasn't anyone she was free to date.

He'd recovered well, but she hadn't missed the flash of panic in his eyes when she'd first issued her invitation. Right then she'd wanted fire alarms to go off or the lights to go out—anything to provide a distraction so she could slink away, unnoticed. He probably thought she was coming on to him. So much for making a good first impression.

She was scarcely in the door of her apartment when her phone rang. "How did it go?" Yvonne's voice was breathless. "I want to hear all about it."

"It went…good, I think." It had been good until that last faux pas. With luck she could make up for that. She'd show Jack she was a true professional, not interested in him as anything but a fellow reporter. "We brainstormed some really good ideas, and I have a couple of stories to work on."

"A girl at work used to live in Dallas and she says he's absolutely gorgeous," Yvonne said.

Shelly grabbed a Diet Coke from the fridge and popped it open. "I told you, didn't I?" she said. "It's a little unnerving, really." Several times this afternoon she'd found herself staring at him, every intelligent thought in her head replaced by admiration for the way the overhead lights picked out the gold tones in his hair, or the way his eyes crinkled at the corners when he laughed. She pressed the soda can to her throat. "Honestly, I thought I was past mooning over handsome guys," she said. "It's even more embarrassing when it's your boss. At least he didn't catch me staring at him." She was pretty sure he hadn't noticed. He had looked at her a tad intently at times, but maybe he merely had been impressed with her ideas.

And why shouldn't he be? She had good ideas. And she was going to do a great job.

"It ought to make going to work that much more fun when you've got a gorgeous guy for a boss," Yvonne said. "I'm almost jealous."

"Don't be. And I'm sure the novelty of it will wear off after a while. Then he'll be just another man." Yeah, and the Rockies were just a bunch of sand dunes. She'd have to be dead to stop noticing Jack's soulful blue eyes and gorgeous profile, but she was woman enough to work around that. This job was too important to screw up by developing a silly crush on her boss.

"I know you're going to do a great job," Yvonne said. "And I hate to bother you when you're so busy, but could you do me one really big favor?"

"Sure. What is it?" She settled onto a bar stool and kicked off her heels.

"Could you help me interview caterers? Daniel gave me a list and I have to talk to them all."

"Wait a minute. I thought your cousin Sophie was going to handle the catering."

"She was…but Daniel thought we should have a professional."

"Daniel thought…I thought he said he didn't care what kind of arrangements you made for the wedding."

"Of course he cares. It's his wedding, too. He just doesn't have time to take care of all the details. He's trusting me to do that."

Shelly rolled her eyes. "What was wrong with Sophie? She's a real caterer, isn't she?"

"Yes, but she's new. Daniel thought we should get someone with more experience."

"Someone he—or better yet, his family—would be impressed with." From what she'd seen, Danny boy put a lot of stock in making an impression.

"You make him sound like such a snob and he's not!" Yvonne all but whined now. "He just pointed out that our wedding day is too important to put in the hands of someone without a track record."

"Right. So he came up with a list for you. He had time to make a list, but he doesn't have time to help with the interviews?"

"I think he got the list from his mother. If you don't want to help me…" Her voice wavered.

"No, I'll help you." Jeez, she could find time to interview a few lousy caterers. She took a long slug of soda, wishing she had some rum to mix with it. "How many are there?"

"Fourteen."

"*Fourteen?* I didn't know there were fourteen major event caterers in Denver."

"Some of these are from Colorado Springs. Oh, and there's one from Aspen."

"I'll bet they charge a pretty penny to come all the way from Aspen."

"Daniel said we shouldn't scrimp on such an important day."

Of course, *he* wasn't footing the bill. Shelly sighed. "Okay. We'll divide the list and each make half the calls. When we narrow it down to the ones we like, we'll talk to them in person."

"Thank you! I knew you'd make this manageable." Poor thing, she sounded utterly frantic.

Shelly shifted the phone to her other ear. "You know, I'm not trying to tell you how to do things, but maybe you should sit down with Daniel and let him know you'd like more help. Planning a wedding is a lot of work. And it's not like you don't have a full-time job, too."

"But Daniel's job is so much more demanding." As usual, Yvonne leaped to her fiancé's defense. "And I'm the one who really wants the big wedding."

"He doesn't want a big wedding?"

"He does *now*. But these things aren't really as important to men. And I have you to help me, too. Daniel and I both appreciate that so much."

Shelly just bet Daniel appreciated it. "You know I don't mind helping you." Yvonne had always been there for her. You couldn't put a price on a friendship like that. So what if Shelly wasn't in love with Daniel? Yvonne was, so nothing else mattered.

"Oh, God, I almost forgot!" The weariness had vanished from Yvonne's voice, replaced by excitement.

"What is it?"

"Daniel gave me my wedding present today."

"Isn't it a little early? The wedding's still six months away."

"He had to give it to me early so I'd have plenty of time to recover before the ceremony."

"You have to *recover* from your gift?" Maybe she hadn't heard Yvonne right.

Yvonne laughed. "That's because he's giving me plastic surgery."

Now she was sure she'd heard wrong. "Plastic surgery?"

"A boob job. Isn't that great?"

Shelly pressed a hand protectively to her chest. "Why is he giving you a boob job? I mean, what's wrong with the breasts you have?"

"There's nothing *wrong* with them. Except they're kind of small. But Daniel set it up with the surgeon and everything. All I have to do is schedule time off and go in to the see the doctor. By the time the wedding rolls around, I'll look fantastic."

Shelly gripped the edge of the bar, fighting a wave of nausea. "Yvonne, you already look fantastic."

"You know what I mean. What's wrong? You sound upset."

"Why aren't *you* upset? The man you're going to marry is supposed to love you the way you are. He's trying to remake you before you've even exchanged vows."

"He's not trying to remake me. He's doing this to make me happy. I've always been self-conscious about being small-chested. You ought to know that."

"The only time you've said anything to *me* about it was when you were drunk and feeling desperate."

Yvonne sniffed. "Maybe I haven't said much about it, but since I've been dating Daniel I've noticed it more. I mean, he really *likes* big boobs."

"Then let *him* have the surgery!" Shelly was shaking, she was so angry. She couldn't believe she was even having this conversation.

"I *want* to do this," Yvonne said. "I should have known you wouldn't understand."

"You're right, I don't understand."

"That's because you've always been a D cup. You don't know what it's like to sit there and watch your boyfriend ogling other women. He even ogles *you*."

Creep. But Shelly didn't say it. She didn't want to hurt Yvonne's feelings any more than they were already wounded. "If he's looking at other women, that's a problem with *him,* not with *you*," she said gently.

"When I've had this surgery, he won't be looking at anybody but me." Her voice softened. "I want Daniel to be happy. I want *us* to be happy."

"Can't you be happy without going under the knife?"

"Oh, I've got another call coming in. It's probably Daniel. I'll talk to you again tomorrow."

"Okay. Just— Think about this some more, okay? Don't rush into anything."

"It'll be okay," Yvonne said. "I promise. After all, marriage is all about compromise, isn't it?"

"And here I thought it was all about love." But Yvonne had already hung up the phone, leaving Shelly to wonder if she was the last hopeless romantic left in the world.

CHAPTER FOUR

SHELLY SPENT MONDAY, her first official day as anchor for *Inside Story,* pinning down sources for the feature on successful juvenile offender programs. Every time she identified herself as "Shelly Piper, with *Inside Story,*" she felt a rush of excitement. She didn't have to fake a smile today. Work hadn't been this much fun since her early days as a reporter.

"Ready to take a break for lunch?"

She looked up from the notes she was making, startled to see Jack standing in the door of her office. "Lunch?" A glance at the clock told her it was almost one. Already? Maybe this light-headed feeling wasn't all related to the thrill of the job. "Yeah, I guess I'd better."

"I thought I'd check out the Thai place down the street. Want to come?"

"Sounds great."

They walked the two blocks to the Thai Bowl, a chilly breeze tempering the heat from the intense sun. Jack was dressed for the January weather in a gray wool suit and black topcoat tailored perfectly to his broad shoulders and slim frame. Shelly noticed more than one woman pause to give him a second look. The thought made her hold her head up a little higher. So what if she wasn't really *with* Jack? They were having lunch together, and even that was good for a girl's ego.

"Have you eaten here before?" Jack asked as they settled into a table by the window.

She shook her head and studied the menu. "I don't think it's been here long. Restaurants tend to have a lot of turnover around here."

"It was the same in Dallas. I'd finally find a place I loved and three months later there'd be a vodka bar or something in its place."

She laughed at his dismayed expression and studied the menu. The shrimp noodle bowl looked delicious. Or maybe the pad thai. Her gaze drifted to the selection of salads. Bold letters declared these were "low in calories and carbs." That's probably what she *should* be eating. What all her thin friends ate. What the women Jack dated probably ate.

This was one of her tests with her dates. If they made any comments about what she was eating or how much she was eating, they failed the test.

Of course, this wasn't a date. She and Jack were merely having lunch. They were two co-workers taking a break. She shouldn't even be thinking of him in any other context.

Her stomach growled, weighing in with its opinion of a lettuce-based meal. "I'll have the shrimp noodle bowl," she told the waitress who appeared at their table.

"Shrimp pad thai." Jack handed his menu to the waitress, then turned to Shelly. "So how's it going?"

"It's going great. I'm excited about this story on successful programs for juvenile offenders. I've got some great interviews set up. I thought this afternoon I'd get with one of the cameramen about coming with me to shoot some footage."

"Have you met Wally and Bess yet?"

She shook her head. "I haven't met anyone. I guess I'll do that this afternoon."

"I apologize. I should have introduced you. We're a small staff. Wally and Bess handle the cameras. Mary Anne Robideaux is our editor, though you and I will handle most of the production duties ourselves. You have experience editing your own stuff, right?"

She nodded. "Some. Though I imagine I have a lot to learn." She squeezed lemon into her water, ignoring the nerves that tightened her stomach at the thought that if she screwed up editing a piece, the whole city would know when it aired.

"How about if I help with your first piece? You'll pick up everything you need to know really quickly, I'm sure."

"That would be great. Thanks." She wiped her hands on a napkin. "What are you working on?"

"I've scheduled the interview with Senator Campbell and started work on the forest piece. And I'm beginning to think more about how the first show is going to shape up."

"I've been wondering about that. If we're going to put on an hour show every week, taking an in-depth look at stories, how are the two of us ever going to produce enough material?"

"I didn't mention you'd be living at the office?" He laughed. "No, you're right. There's no way we could fill an hour every week with only the two of us. Not and keep the quality up. My idea was to have one, maybe two pieces each week produced by us, and fill in the rest of the hour with some regular features. We'll also stock-pile some features we can run whenever there's a hole in the schedule, stuff with a long shelf life. And there will be times we'll have to scramble to fill in with some breaking story." He pointed his fork at her. "I hope you're ready to think on your feet and be flexible."

"I can do that. What about adding an opinion piece about some issue? An editorial?"

"We might do that sometimes. I've asked Wally and Bess to put together some photo-essay-type pieces. They can be light or serious—maybe highlight some environmental issues through video alone, or string together shots of all the baby animals at the zoo for Mother's Day. Things like that."

She laughed. "The viewers will love it."

"They will, won't they?" He grinned. "It's cheap and easy, but effective."

"What else do you have planned?"

"We can mine footage from foreign stations. For example, we can juxtapose a story on how drought is effecting ranchers in southwestern Colorado with a piece from Sydney looking at ways Australian ranchers are coping with their drought. Or look at a foreign dignitary's visit to Denver from the point of view of television reports from his or her home country."

"It's brilliant."

He sat back, clearly pleased with himself. "Brilliance born of desperation, maybe. But I think it'll work. And after a while we can take a few minutes once a month or so to read letters from viewers or that kind of thing. And feel free to jump in with suggestions of your own." He pointed his fork at her. "I'm counting on you to help me put together some of this stuff—editing the foreign-news footage and that sort of thing."

More chances to work closely with Jack? "I think I can be persuaded to help. In fact, you'll have a hard time keeping me from sticking my nose into everything. This kind of reporting is what I've always dreamed of doing."

"Me, too. It's why I left the networks. I knew I'd never get a chance to do things like this with them."

"Why? Because they're too rigid in their thinking?"

"Mainly because I had a hard time getting anyone there to see past this face to my abilities."

"Ouch!" She winced. "I thought women were the only ones who had to deal with that kind of thing."

He shook his head. "I actually had a producer tell me that viewers wouldn't believe a hard-hitting story delivered by a man who looked like the romantic lead in a movie."

Shelly choked on her water. "You're kidding? You're *too* good-looking?"

"He said even if they were inclined to believe me, they'd be too distracted by my appearance to focus on the story."

Okay, she could relate to being distracted. Her heart sped up each time she saw Jack. But there was definitely more to the man than just good looks. He had great ideas and was easy to talk to. "Let's hope public television viewers aren't so shallow," she said.

"I gambled everything, believing they aren't."

The server arrived with their food. Shelly stirred shrimp and noodles together and thought about gambles. She'd spent so many years climbing the television ladder in the traditional way, she hadn't thought much about the benefits of taking risks. It had taken a big blow to her ego to make her see the need for change in her life. It sounded as if Jack might have had a similar experience. "Why did you choose Denver?" she asked.

"That's easy. My uncle is here. He's the one putting up the money for the show." He speared a fat shrimp on his fork. "The weather here is good and the lifestyle suits me. I like spending time out of doors and you can do that here."

"Do you play sports?" He had the athletic build of a jock.

"A little pickup basketball or softball. I ski and am looking forward to doing a lot more of that this winter. I run. What about you?"

"You already know I like to ski. I enjoy walking and hiking, but the only time you'll see me run is if someone's chasing me. And the only sports I enjoy are spectator ones. Can't you tell?"

He smiled, and wisely avoided commenting on her dig at herself. "Denver's a good city for sports, isn't it?"

She nodded. "You name it, we have a professional team—football, baseball, basketball, hockey, soccer, lacrosse, arena football. It's a sports-crazy town."

"That might make a good photo essay sometime—a look at all the different sporting events on any given weekend in Denver."

She laughed. "You do have a one-track mind, don't you?"

"I've been accused of that." His eyes met hers, the light in them like a laser aimed straight at her middle. "I guess you could say that when I want something, I go after it with everything I've got."

She focused on her plate, all the different possible

meanings of that one sentence ricocheting around in her brain. *He's talking about work,* she reminded herself. *Work. That's all* you *should be thinking about where he's concerned.*

It figured. The most interesting man she'd met in ages and he was her boss. Just as well she was more interested in her career than in a relationship right now. Otherwise, she might be in real trouble.

YVONNE CONSULTED HER LIST of potential caterers while she waited for Shelly to meet her at their favorite coffee shop Saturday morning. The list was mercifully short. With only a little more than five months until the wedding, only four of the fourteen caterers on Daniel's list were still available. Of course, he hadn't been too happy when he'd learned that, but there was nothing they could do. She'd assured him that one of those left on their list would be perfect for them.

Cousin Sophie hadn't been happy with the change in plans, either, but she'd cheered up when Yvonne promised she could keep the deposit as recompense for holding the date open for them for so long. That meant the wedding budget was tighter than ever, but she'd find a way to make it work somehow.

She sipped her nonfat latte and frowned at her own reflection in the coffee shop window. If only Shelly could be placated as easily. Though the two friends had avoided saying anything else about Daniel's wedding gift to Yvonne, she knew Shelly was upset about his choice. And she could feel Shelly's disappointment in *her* whenever they were together.

Why did Shelly have to make such a big deal out of

it? Lots of women had plastic surgery every day. It was a personal choice, one that Yvonne had contemplated on her own before. Daniel was being incredibly generous, agreeing to pay for the surgery before they were even married. Couldn't Shelly see that?

"Sorry I'm late." Shelly breezed into the coffee shop, out of breath, face glowing with exertion and excitement. "I had to stop by the station for a few minutes to make some last-minute arrangements with the cameraman for our visit to the juvenile boot camp Monday."

"Boot camp? That doesn't sound like much fun."

"It sounds harsh, but it's supposed to be a really great program for kids who are one wrong step away from prison. I'm hoping to get some great footage for the show."

"Your first broadcast is coming up soon, isn't it?"

"In about three weeks. I can't wait." She fished her wallet from her purse. "Let me grab some coffee and I'll be ready to go."

While Shelly ordered a grande mocha, Yvonne gathered up her purse and the packet of information she'd collected about the various caterers they planned to visit today. She was glad Shelly was in a good mood this morning. Maybe all the excitement over her new job would make her forget all about Yvonne's impending plastic surgery.

Though it hurt, not being able to totally confide in her best friend. Yes, she wanted this surgery, but the prospect of going under the knife was scary, too. She would have liked to have been able to share that with Shelly without being judged.

"Do you have the list?" Shelly was back at her side, coffee in hand.

"Yes." She consulted the notebook where she'd scribbled the names of the caterers she needed to interview. "The first one is Fresh and Festive."

"Great." Shelly led the way out of the coffee shop to her car. "I hope they have good food. I'm hungry."

"Then it'll be great having you along." Yvonne climbed into the passenger seat and buckled her seat belt. "I've been so stressed out lately I haven't been able to eat. And here I was worried losing weight before the wedding would be a problem."

"Yvonne!" Shelly gave her a sharp look. "Why are you stressed out? Is something wrong?"

She shook her head. "I just never realized there were so many *details* to see to."

"I'm sorry I haven't been around to help you more."

"That's all right. I know you have a lot to do, getting a new show off the ground."

"You should ask Daniel for more help, too." She guided the car onto University, headed toward Broadway.

Yvonne tugged at her seat belt. "He has been helping some. Last night he helped me decide on possible menus for the reception." Of course, she'd wanted chicken while he'd insisted on steak. When she'd suggested they offer both he'd accused her again of being cheap.

"I want people to know I want only the best for this occasion," he'd said. "The best bride and the best food."

His attempt to placate her with flattery only annoyed her. "Daniel, steak is expensive. If we're going to have it, I'll need you to help pay for it."

"Fine, then." He'd dismissed her concerns with a shrug. "Just send the bill to my mother."

Her stomach churned as she imagined what Daniel's

mother would have to say about a bride who expected the groom's family to pay part of her reception costs.

"So what did you decide?" Shelly's voice intruded on her worries.

"Decide?"

"The food for the reception. What did you decide?"

"Oh. Steak. Rib eye, or if we can't get that, maybe petite sirloin."

"Sounds good to me. What was the address again?"

Yvonne consulted her list. "It's 508 South Broadway."

"Here we are." Shelly turned into the alley beside the caterer's building and found a parking place beneath a leaning oak tree. A sign directed them to an entrance in the back.

Yvonne felt tension ease from her shoulders the moment she stepped into the pastel-painted showroom of Fresh and Festive. Classical music played softly in the background, while subdued lighting highlighted displays of wedding cakes and table settings.

"Hello, I'm Tamara Smithson. You must be Yvonne." A middle-aged woman dressed in a pale gray pantsuit came forward to greet them.

Yvonne smiled and offered her hand. "Yes. And this is my friend, Shelly Piper."

"It's so nice to meet you. Why don't you come sit over here and you can tell me what you have in mind for your wedding reception." Tamara led them to a round table draped in white linen. She offered them water, then opened a large photo album. "Here are some photos of some other receptions we've done, including close-ups of many of our cakes. If you don't see what you want here, don't hesitate to ask. I enjoy working with my customers to create something especially for them."

"These are all beautiful." Yvonne slowly turned the pages of the album, a fluttery feeling in her chest as she studied the images of flower-trimmed cakes and champagne fountains. How many hours had she spent admiring just such scenes in bridal magazines? And now she was going to have a dream reception of her own.

She paused at a photo of a cake swathed in ribbons of ivory frosting, sugar wedding bells arranged along the sides. It rose in four tiers on ivory pillars, and real satin ribbons spilled from a lacy archway over the figures of a pair of cooing doves on the top tier. "I like this one," she said, tapping her finger against the photo. "Shelly, what do you think?"

"It's gorgeous. And I like the doves. Much more sophisticated than the usual cartoon bride and groom."

She nodded. Sophisticated. Daniel and his mother would like that. "Let's keep this one in mind," she said, sliding the book toward Tamara.

"Wonderful. Now, have you thought about the menu for your reception? You mentioned on the phone that you want a formal dinner."

"My fiancé has his heart set on steak. Rib eye or petite sirloin."

Tamara nodded and made a note on a legal pad. "We can certainly do steak. May I make a suggestion?"

"Certainly."

"As I'm sure you know, steak can be rather pricey. May I suggest instead a beef Wellington?"

Yvonne chewed her lower lip, the feeling of a band

tightening around her chest returning. "Daniel really wanted steak."

"Many men do. But I find they like the beef Wellington just as well." Tamara's smile was warm and encouraging. "It's beef, so the men like that, but you don't have the trouble of trying to get each guest's steak cooked exactly to order. People think it's more expensive than it is, and it makes a nice presentation. Plus we have a very tasty vegetarian version for any of your guests who don't eat meat."

"It sounds perfect." Shelly looked at Yvonne. "If you tell Daniel it's even classier than steak I bet he'll be happy."

"How much is the beef Wellington compared to steak?" Yvonne asked.

"It's roughly half the price."

The band tightened another notch. She nodded. "All right. I think that's the best choice, then."

"Would you like to sample the beef Wellington menu? It will only take a few minutes to prepare. While I'm getting that ready, you can look at some of your table setting options."

"Thank you. That would be wonderful."

"She seems really nice," Shelly said when Tamara left them alone.

"I like her." Yvonne flipped through the pages of table settings. "Do you think it would be better to have several long tables, with a lot of people at each one, or lots of small tables?"

"I like the long tables better. And maybe that way there'd be less fussing over who sits with whom."

She nodded. "I imagine you're right."

"How many guests are you inviting?"

"Two hundred. Maybe two hundred and fifty." She frowned. "Daniel and his mother keep adding names to the list. Most of them are people I don't even know. Business associates of his and wealthy relatives. He says it's important to invite them."

"Mmm-hmm. Maybe he's thinking of gifts."

Yvonne sent her a scolding look. Shelly raised her eyebrows. "Well, people do."

"Tell me about your job." Yvonne closed the book and sat back, ready to change the subject. Anything but continue to listen to Shelly's not-so-subtle digs at Daniel. "What else are you working on?"

"Yesterday I visited a program that pairs troubled teens with dogs from animal shelters. The kids train the dogs so they'll be more adoptable. It's been an amazing success. Some of these children have never been around animals before, and to see them with their dogs, so proud—the audience will love it."

"It sounds great. I would have loved something like that when I was little." She'd always wanted a dog or a cat, but the apartments and trailer courts where they'd lived usually didn't allow pets. And her mother always said she didn't want anything else to look after.

"I'm also working on a couple of things for future shows—one on public hospitals and another piece about local water quality," Shelly continued. "I'm putting in some long hours, but it's not really like work."

"Is it very different from your job at *First for News?*"

"In some ways it's not. In other ways, there's a big difference. For instance, the features I'm doing for *In-*

side Story are much more in-depth and longer. Plus, I'm supposed to do most of my own editing."

"Have you done that before?"

"A little. Jack's promised to help me with the first few pieces, until I get a feel for things."

"How is Jack? Do you enjoy working with him?"

"He's amazing!" She leaned forward, face animated. "He's so smart—he knows exactly what goes into a good news story and has this instinct for finding the right information. And we get along great. We think alike on so many things. Some days we spend as much time talking as we do actually working."

Yvonne couldn't remember when Shelly had spoken so enthusiastically about a man. "He sounds ideal. So, do you think you'll go out with him?"

"Go out with him?" Shelly sat back, clearly stunned by the question. "Yvonne, he's my boss."

"So." She shrugged. "He's single, about your age, and you get along great. And I can tell you're attracted to him."

"What makes you think that?"

"Oh, just the way your eyes light up when you talk about him. And you said he's gorgeous. What woman wouldn't be attracted to a man like that?"

"My eyes do not 'light up' when I talk about Jack." She unfolded her napkin and smoothed it in her lap. "I'm excited about the job, not the man. This is an incredible opportunity for me. What I've always wanted."

"That still doesn't mean you can't date him."

"It's ridiculous to even talk about it. Jack isn't going to ask me out."

"Why not? If you get along as great as you say, he must like you."

"He likes me as a co-worker, not a potential date. I'm not the kind of woman a man like Jack Halloran dates."

"How can you say that?"

Shelly shook her head. "Look, I did some checking before I agreed to take the job—just to make sure Jack was who he said he was, with the kind of background to pull this off. I found out he was, but I also learned he has quite the reputation as a player. Not that that was any surprise. With looks like that, I'm sure he has women throwing themselves at him. But I'm not going to be one of them."

Yvonne was about to argue that Shelly didn't give herself enough credit when Tamara returned with a rolling cart. "Here we are. Beef Wellington with parsleyed new potatoes and baby asparagus and carrots." She set the plates in front of them.

"It looks wonderful," Shelly said.

"Yes, it's beautiful," Yvonne agreed.

"I'll leave you to enjoy your meal, but if you need anything or have any questions, please let me know. And when you're done, I have samples of different cakes for you to try."

For several minutes they were silent, eating. "This one gets my vote," Shelly said. "I've never eaten anything at a wedding reception that was this good."

"It *is* good," Yvonne agreed.

"I think you should go with this place and forget about wasting the rest of the day visiting the other places."

"I told Daniel I'd visit them all."

Shelly shrugged. "He doesn't have to know."

The idea was tempting. She had so many other things

she needed to do today. "We'll need to find another vegetable besides asparagus. Daniel hates asparagus."

"He's not going to be the only one at the reception."

"Yes, but he is the groom, so he ought to be able to eat what he likes."

"What about broccoli? Does he like broccoli?"

She nodded. "Broccoli is good. I'll ask to substitute broccoli for the asparagus." She looked at her plate. Would Daniel be upset that he wasn't having steak? Probably at first. But she'd make him see this was the right choice. "A good marriage is about compromise," she said.

"What was that?" Shelly looked up from her almost-empty plate.

Yvonne rested her knife and fork on the edge of the plate and folded her hands in her lap. "I've been doing a lot of reading lately—everything I can find on how to have a successful marriage. The two big things seem to be communication and compromise."

Shelly scooped up the last bite of potato. "So do you and Daniel communicate and compromise?"

She smiled. "We do. For instance, I'm sure once I explain my reasons for choosing the beef Wellington instead of steak, he'll be willing to compromise, especially since *I* compromised on the question of which caterer we should consider."

Shelly made a face. "I think it's a good thing I've never married. I'm too stubborn to give in all the time."

"You'd do it for a man you truly loved. And you wouldn't do it all the time. Both partners in the relationship have to yield to the other at times, or meet halfway."

Shelly focused on pushing three lone carrot chunks

to the edge of her plate, her earlier exuberance gone. "What is it?" Yvonne leaned toward her friend. "Is something wrong?"

Shelly's eyes met hers. She looked worried, and a little sad. "It's none of my business, I know. It just seems...well it seems to me that *you're* almost always the one who's compromising in your relationship with Danny."

"Don't be silly. Daniel does his part, too. For instance, I'm sure he'll compromise on the reception menu. And he let me choose the colors for the wedding."

"I thought the bride was *supposed* to pick the colors. And besides, you compromised on the honeymoon. You wanted to go to Hawaii, but he insisted on St. Thomas."

"It's still a tropical beach. It's not that important."

"You agreed to wear a thong and that's not your style." Shelly sipped water, her expression growing more agitated. "And what about this boob job? Isn't that a big compromise? Another attempt to placate him?"

"You're blowing this all out of proportion. I want to please my husband. That's not the same as placating a bully. Daniel is not bullying me into doing this."

Shelly looked away, her lips tightened into a thin line. "It would be for me."

"But I'm not you." Yvonne took a deep breath, reining in the anger and hurt that threatened to overwhelm her. "You don't understand. I love Daniel. Doing something to please him isn't a hardship, it's a pleasure. And this surgery isn't just for him. It's for both of us. He's being incredibly generous to give me this gift."

"Maybe so." But Shelly looked unconvinced. She was that way, hiding her insecurities behind prickly bravado. But Yvonne knew that inside she was as vulnerable as any woman.

"One day you'll understand," she said softly. "Someday, when you've found the man you want to spend the rest of your life with, you'll want to do anything so the two of you can be happy."

Shelly looked away, toward the front display window, with its gleaming white cakes. "I think the man I love is going to have to understand there are certain things I *won't* do. If he really loves me, he won't expect them of me."

"I hope you find a man like that." It was a good fantasy—the man who'd worship his wife and give her anything her heart desired. Yvonne herself had believed in it until she'd celebrated her thirtieth birthday without a ring on her finger. Then she'd woken up to the fact that perfect men didn't exist. She'd decided to settle for an imperfect man and do whatever she could to hold on to him.

If that meant eating broccoli instead of asparagus or wearing a different type of bathing suit, or even having surgery to increase the size of her breasts, so be it. It would all be worth it in the end.

CHAPTER FIVE

JACK SCOOTED HIS CHAIR close so that he and Shelly could share the cramped quarters in KPRM's edit bay. "You ready to do this?"

She looked around at the array of buttons, keyboards and screens that filled the space. "I can't wait to learn what all this stuff is for."

"It's easy. You'll catch on quick." He gave her an encouraging smile. She'd certainly hit the ground running with every other aspect of the job. Her enthusiasm gave more energy to everyone involved in putting together *Inside Story.* He toggled the button to start the system. "We use an AVID Newscutter package. Are you familiar with the software?"

"I've heard of it, but I've never worked with it." She flashed a smile, dimples forming on either side of her mouth. "When I was in college, we learned on an old Steenbeck machine."

"Then you'll be amazed at what this baby can do." He accessed the network library. "First thing is to pull up the script for your story."

"Okay." She scrolled to the file labeled juvisuccess.doc and double-clicked. The lines of text appeared on the screen.

"We want to make sure that the film we run synchs with your script. This is going to be about a seven-minute story, so fill in that time down there." She did so, and the script moved to a split screen.

"Now we choose our video. The computer keeps track for us and allows us to add and delete segments of video or of the script with the click of the mouse."

"Amazing."

Their eyes met and, once again, he felt the pull of attraction. He looked away, hoping she hadn't clued in to his feelings. The last thing he wanted was to screw up a good working relationship by complicating it with lust. "Pull up your intro. Then you can add footage from the various facilities you visited and people you interviewed. The alternate-edit button lets you try out two or three different shots to see which looks best, and you can extend or smooth a shot if that makes it synch up better."

"This is great."

He folded his arms and leaned back in his chair, watching as her fingers flew over the keyboard, opening and closing files, inserting film clips, slugs and voice-overs. She'd tucked her hair behind one ear, revealing two tiny diamond studs in her lobe, and the soft curve of her neck. A little V formed between her eyebrows as she concentrated, and the tip of her tongue protruded from her lips. It disturbed him to realize how erotic he found this.

"Damn, no! I didn't want that." She glanced over her shoulder at him. "Help. How do I get rid of that last section?"

"No problem. You just click on this arrow…." He

leaned close and put his hand over hers to manipulate the mouse, his arm pressed against the side of her breast, the floral undertones of her perfume sweeping over him. He caught his breath, heart pounding, every coherent thought wiped out by sharp desire.

"I see now. And then I can insert this." She took over the mouse, sliding it from under his palm, apparently oblivious to his predicament. He sagged back in the chair and swallowed hard, determined to keep a bland expression on his face.

"How's that?" She turned and smiled at him.

He blinked, bringing the screen into focus again. "That looks good. What do you have so far?"

"The intro, and the shots of one of the teenagers I'm focusing on, Eddie Mendoza, playing basketball, then part of the interview with the sociologist who talks about the growing problem of teenage offenders and teenagers at risk."

"Okay, here's something we can do." He leaned forward, forcing his mind onto work again. "We can take those statistics the sociologist is quoting and make them into a color graph or pie chart. Instead of a talking head, the audience can see the graphics while she continues talking."

"Good idea." She glanced at the script on the split screen. "Then we have my visit with Eddie at the Back-country Boot Camp." The screen filled with a shot of the young basketball player, now in hiking pants, boots and climbing gear, dangling from a cliff. "You think this is gonna be a bunch of games out here, then you get here and find out this is really serious shit. I mean, you could die if you screw up out here."

Jack nodded. "Great quote. Okay, what next?"

"Now we segue to my meeting with Sondra Drey-fuss, the teen who's involved in the program that matches juvenile offenders with shelter dogs." She cued up the film, and fast-forwarded to a segment showing Sondra working with a Lab-shepherd mix.

"That's a good dog!" Sondra's voice was high and enthusiastic, in contrast to the sullen mumbling in her earlier interview. "You're just the best dog.

"They depend on you for everything. And they look at you with such trust...trust and love." Sondra's voice rose up over scenes of teens walking, feeding and grooming their dogs. "I never had nobody or nothing love me that way. It makes me feel so happy, and so sad, too, 'cause I know I can't keep her. I got to let her go so she can be adopted by some family that wants a good dog."

Shelly moved in to a close-up of Sondra kneeling be-side her dog, their heads together. "I got to let her go out into the world, and show everybody how good she can be." She sniffed, and wiped the back of her hand against her eyes. "And I got to do the same. I got to go out into the world and show people that I'm good, too. I did some bad things, but I'm good."

Shelly sniffed and reached up for the box of tissue that sat on a shelf above their heads. "Sorry," she said, and blew her nose. "I get choked up every time I see that."

He put his hand on her shoulder, intending to offer a comforting pat, but ended up leaving it there, reluctant to break the contact. "It's a beautiful story," he said. "A great way to start the program."

She nodded and squared her shoulders. "So that's

the quick-and-dirty version. It definitely needs some polishing."

"We'll leave that to Mary Anne. She'll smooth everything out and make sure it flows, plus she'll create some teasers and bumpers and promos for the show." He stretched his arms up over his head and glanced at his watch, amazed to see that it was already past five. They'd been working nonstop for almost two hours. "I'd better get out of here or I'm going to be late."

"Oh?" She quirked one eyebrow, her tone teasing. "Do you have a hot date?"

"I don't know how hot. Just drinks with a woman I met over at City Hall." He'd been telling himself he needed to get out more, and when the clerk in the water-permit office had flirted with him, he'd thought, why not? Maybe seeing another woman would get his mind off of Shelly. "What about you? You have plans?"

Shelly shook her head. "I'll probably go home and watch TV, or work on the hospital piece."

He hadn't pictured a woman like Shelly sitting home alone. At work she was so full of energy and fun. "I didn't hire you to make you a slave to your job," he said.

"It doesn't feel like slavery when I'm enjoying it so much." She stood and pushed in her chair.

He stood also. "Still, I don't want you to burn out. Go out and have some fun."

She tilted her head to one side and tapped her forefinger against her chin. "Fun. I think I remember that. My best friend and I used to go out every Tuesday for drinks and a movie, but since she's gotten engaged, she's too busy planning the wedding of the century."

"I can sympathize." He followed her out of the editing bay toward their offices down the hall. "My sister married recently, and it was as if an alien took over her body. The sweetest woman in the world turned into Bridezilla. It was crazy." He shook his head. "I remember one day she burst into tears when a fabric store called to tell her the wrong color tulle had come in. She was storming around the house, wailing that the wedding was ruined. And my mother went right along with her. It was awful."

Shelly laughed. "Oh, that's hilarious. Not to them, I'm sure, but talk about no perspective."

"Fortunately, my father was there. He looked at both of them and said, 'There are other fabric stores, you know.' And sure enough, when my mother calmed down enough to make a few phone calls, they found whatever it was they needed, and at a cheaper price."

"I supposed it's all about your focus." They stopped outside Shelly's office, and he waited while she retrieved her purse from her desk drawer. "Yvonne's focus is definitely zeroed in on her wedding right now," she said. "I'm praying as soon as that's over with she'll be back to normal."

"In the meantime, don't let your focus narrow in solely on your job," he said when she rejoined him.

"Yes, boss." She executed a smart salute. "Have a good night."

"You, too." Her perfume engulfed him again as she moved past him, and he let his gaze linger on her gently swaying hips as she walked down the hall. He shoved his hands in his pockets, half afraid he might reach out and pull her back. *Focus,* he told himself. *Focus on something besides Shelly.*

SHELLY SAGGED IN THE driver's seat of her car, resisting the urge to fan herself. She checked her reflection in the rearview mirror and was surprised to see her face wasn't flushed. Talk about trial by fire! Keeping her mind on her job while cozied up next to Handsome Jack would try any woman's fortitude.

It was a good thing people couldn't read each other's minds, or her decidedly unbusinesslike thoughts would have ruined her image as a competent professional. Thank God Jack remained oblivious to her feelings. She'd already revealed that she had no social life. Crushing on her boss would make her look even more pathetic.

Seeing her plans for the evening through his eyes had been akin to having an ice cube dropped down her back. Since when was she the type to mope around the house? Sure, she had tons of work to tackle, and she was worried about Yvonne, and she hadn't had a date with anyone but the Energizer Bunny in months, but that didn't make her a lost cause on the social scene.

She started the car and checked her look again in the rearview mirror. Ditch the suit jacket, put on some fresh lipstick and she'd be ready for a night on the town.

She headed toward Lower Downtown Denver, where the restaurants and clubs teemed with freed-from-their-cubicles office workers and sightseeing tourists. After shelling out ten dollars to park, she set out on foot for her favorite martini bar. A sour appletini and some meaningless flirtation with the opposite sex would put her to rights once more.

The Velvet Lounge was packed, the young and not-so-young, buffed and less-than-buffed lined up three deep at the glass-and-chrome bar. Shelly threaded her way through the masses and arrived just as a well-dressed couple was leaving, thereby scoring a bar stool. She'd scarcely ordered her drink when the vacant stool beside her was filled by a broad-shouldered man in a dark blue suit. *Lawyer,* Shelly guessed, catching a glimpse of polished wingtips.

Lawyer who works out, she amended, watching muscles bunch under the suit jacket as he reached across the bar for a bowl of snack mix. "Hi, there," she said, doing her best imitation of a coy smile.

"Hello." Right on cue, he looked her up and down. The move was subtle, but not too practiced. *Recently divorced or split up,* she added to her mental inventory of the man. "This place is a zoo tonight, isn't it?" he said.

"Halfway through the workweek and everyone's ready for a little liquid stress reliever." She saluted him with her martini glass and took a sip. The drink was cold and crisp—and would go right to her head if she didn't watch it.

"I hear you on that." He angled more toward her, committed to the conversation now. "Where do you work?"

"KPRM. Public television. You?"

"I'm an attorney at Gates and Wilco."

Bingo! Could she call them or what? "Civil or criminal?"

"Uh, civil." He tugged at his tie, loosening it. "We do a lot of work for the city. Not very exciting, but it pays the bills."

She waited for him to ask her about her job, but apparently he wasn't schooled in the proper protocol. Instead, he launched into a soliloquy about a recent case he'd handled regarding zoning violations on the city's west side. She sipped her drink and kept a pleasant expression on her face. She'd give him another five minutes. If things didn't get interesting by then, she'd leave and try somewhere else.

A group of laughing people left, creating a momentary thinning of the crowd. Shelly let her gaze wander from her companion, who was recounting an apparently tense exchange with an angry business owner. She spotted a familiar figure entering the bar. Drew Preston, another attorney she'd dated briefly. He worked for the D.A.'s office, an up-and-coming young lawyer who had been good in bed but not very good out of it.

He saw her and waved, then headed toward her. "Hey, Shelly." He turned to her companion. "And, Bernie, great to see you." Said with a false heartiness that telegraphed, to Shelly at least, that he could care less about Bernie, and perhaps didn't even like him much.

Drew looked from one to the other. "I didn't know you two knew each other."

"We just met." She finished her drink and pushed it aside. She couldn't decide if she was glad to see Drew again or not. Their brief relationship had died from mutual indifference. She'd heard shortly afterward that he was dating a secretary from his firm.

"So, Shelly, how are you doing? You're looking great. Very vo-lup-tu-ous." He drew the word out, his gaze focusing on the neckline of her blouse. She could see now that his eyes were slightly glazed, his face flushed. He'd had more than a few drinks.

"If you don't mind, the lady and I were talking." Bernie shifted so that his body was between Shelly and Drew, and glared at the interloper with surprising menace. If testosterone was visible, Shelly was sure the air around them would have shimmered with it.

"S'okay." Drew backed away, hands up. *Look, no weapons.* "Just saying hi to an old friend." He waved to Shelly, then ambled away.

Bernie's smile had more heat now. Of course. Another man had acted interested in her, so she was obviously a prize worth having. "Shelly. That's a beautiful name. Can I buy you another drink?"

For half a second, she was tempted. Bernie the attorney wasn't bad-looking, if a little awkward. He might be fun for a few drinks, or even a casual dinner. But then he'd expect payment for his investment of time and money. Not necessarily sex; most men weren't so crass. They might want it, but they wouldn't *expect* it. But he'd want a few kisses, maybe a little heavy petting. Some physical contact to add to whatever emotional bonding they'd done.

Ordinarily she wasn't opposed to this. If the guy was a good kisser, it could be a very pleasant way to end the day. But not this day. She felt absolutely no spark for the man who sat across from her. In fact, she felt nothing at all for any of the men who'd crossed her path tonight. Not good-in-bed Drew or the surfer-blond young stud by the door or the trio of professional athletes who held court across the room. None of them stirred her. The idea of spending any time at all with them bored her.

She smiled at Bernie, a look of regret. "I'm sorry. Maybe some other time. Suddenly, I'm not feeling very well."

She slid off the bar stool and he rose also. "Is there

anything I can do to help? Maybe if we went somewhere quiet and got you something to eat…?"

She shook her head, already moving toward the door. "Thanks, but I really have to go."

Once outside, she walked briskly to her car, hoping Bernie wouldn't make things awkward by trying to follow her. When she was sure he wasn't behind her, she stopped at an Italian grocery and bought a calzone, which she ate standing up at a counter in the back, washing it down with a bottle of water. The effects of the martini wore off quickly and she thought about what had just happened at the bar.

Had months spent devoting herself to her job numbed her completely to the social scene? She still remembered all the right things to say and do, but the games weren't fun anymore. Why not?

"You need anything else, miss?" The grocer, a stooped, graying man with oversize glasses, paused beside her, dust rag in hand.

She shook her head, wiping her hands on her napkin. "No, I'm fine, thank you."

That was it in a nutshell, wasn't it? She was fine just as she was. She had a nice apartment and a dream job. And even though her physical attraction for her boss was unnerving at times, it did add an extra energy to their interactions.

That's not to say she wouldn't welcome a significant other into her life, but she no longer thought she'd find him bellied up to the bar at the Velvet Lounge or any similar place. Sitting in that crowd tonight, she had felt the anxiety thick in the air—the pressure to hook up, to score, to make a connection before time ran out and you went home alone again.

But going home alone was okay with her. She stood up a little straighter, proud of herself. Sure, when the right man came along she'd welcome him. But in the meantime, she was very good company for herself. How many women did she know who could say that?

SELF-CONFIDENCE WAS SUCH a fleeting thing. Shelly wondered sometimes if the universe waited for her best moments of self-actualization to shoot her down.

Thursday, she and Jack were supposed to shoot some promos for *Inside Story* from the set they'd be using for the live portions of the show. Previously, they'd decided on a fairly traditional approach, with the two of them seated behind a counter on a raised dais. Their nod to innovation was the counter itself, a quarter-moon curve of blond oak, sleek and very modern-looking. A separate set of equally modern chairs and coffee table was available for any live interviews they might do, or for more informal segments, such as reading letters from viewers or introducing the occasional humorous story.

But Thursday morning, she discovered the sleek counter had been replaced by an oversize ebony desk. "What is this?" she asked, frowning at the massive piece of furniture. It looked like something that would have graced a judge's chambers—half a century ago.

"I don't know." Jack joined her beside the desk.

The door to the studio opened and Armstrong Brewster entered. "Good, you're both here. Let's get started."

"What's with the desk?" Jack asked. "What happened to the modern set we chose?"

"Oh, that. It wasn't very *substantial,* you know? It didn't project authority. This is a serious show, right?

We want the viewers to know that from the get-go. Now, Shelly, if you'll just sit behind here…" He steered her behind the desk.

"The stories will project the authority," Jack said. "We don't need a desk to do that for us. Especially not one this ugly."

"It's not ugly. It's imposing. Now, Shelly, have a seat. Let me see how you look."

Reluctantly, she sat. And immediately wished she hadn't. The top of the desk came up to the middle of her chest and her knees were higher than her hips. "Where did you get this chair?" she asked. "It's too low."

Armstrong stepped back from the desk and nodded. "No, you look great. Perfect."

"I feel like a kindergartner in the big kid's desk." She turned to her co-host. "Jack, see what you think."

Still frowning, Jack took the seat next to her. He towered over her by a good eight inches. "My chair seems all right."

She frowned, then looked down. "Now I see the problem. Armstrong, my chair is too low."

"No, it's not. It's perfect."

"It's not perfect! It's at least three inches lower than Jack's. I look ridiculous."

"No, you look great. Now, let's not waste any more time. Let's get going." He turned and signaled to the cameraman.

"Armstrong, what are you doing?" Jack said. "I want our other set back."

"Why?" The producer spread his arms wide. "This is a great set. I really think it's better."

Jack stood and leaned across the desk toward Armstrong. "It's not better. It's ugly. It looks like we raided the Salvation Army. The other set had the cutting-edge look I want."

Armstrong folded his arms, practically pouting. "I think you should go with this one."

"No."

Shelly had had enough. She struggled out of the low chair and joined Jack in scowling at Armstrong. "I know what you're trying to do," she said.

"I told you, I'm trying to give the show an air of authority. A new show has a lot of handicaps against it and I'm—"

Shelly looked at Jack. "He's trying to make me look small."

"He's what?"

She gestured toward the desk. "He's got this big desk and this little chair and he's using them to fool viewers into thinking I'm small. Little. Petite." She glared at the producer. "Not fat."

"No, no, that's not it." Armstrong rushed toward her, his tone placating. "I'm just giving you a more flattering image."

"Get rid of the desk," Jack snapped. "Now."

"Jack, listen to me. This is important. We have to make the right impression with viewers."

Jack's voice was low, scarcely above a whisper, but the menace in it stunned Shelly. "Armstrong, if that desk isn't out of here in five minutes, you're fired."

The producer paled. "Your uncle hired me to help."

Jack looked at his watch. "You're wasting time."

Armstrong looked at them, then turned on his heel and marched out.

Jack walked away, his back to Shelly. His spine was rigid, his shoulders tensed. She rarely had seen anyone so angry. Even Wally, the cameraman, and Mary Anne, the editor, had moved away and avoided looking at him.

But Shelly couldn't tear her gaze away from him. Anger and shame battled in her gut. What was he thinking? Did he agree with Armstrong, that she was too big? Was he second-guessing his choice of her as co-host of the show?

He turned to face her, his jaw tight, the lines around his eyes more pronounced. "I apologize for all this," he said. "It's absolutely uncalled-for."

"Thank you." The shaking in her voice unnerved her further. She took a deep breath and tried again. "It's not your fault."

He shook his head. "You're a professional. You shouldn't be subjected to something like this."

"It's not the first time." She tossed the remark off lightly, trying to break the tension, but it only seemed to upset him more.

"The world is full of idiots," he said, turning away again.

Her throat tightened and her eyes stung. Oh, God, she wasn't going to cry, was she? Please not that. She took another deep breath and dug her nails into her palm. Hard. Nothing like physical pain to distract her from hurt feelings. "I won't argue with you there," she said.

The door to the studio burst open and three men with a furniture dolly rushed in. "This the desk we're supposed to haul off?" one asked.

"Yes, get rid of it." Jack's voice was calmer now. "And bring back the set that was in here before."

"Will do." He directed the others in loading up the desk and chairs. Jack watched them leave, then turned back to Shelly. "So much for trying to get these promos shot quickly."

"I doubt Armstrong will try something like that again." She came to stand beside him. "Where in the world did he find such an *ugly* monstrosity?"

Jack chuckled, and it was as if the temperature in the room rose ten degrees. "It's hideous, isn't it?" He glanced at her. "Sorry I lost my temper just now. I couldn't believe he blindsided me that way."

"I thought for a minute there you were going to hit him."

"For a minute there, I wanted to."

Their eyes met, and she swayed, almost knocked off her feet by the connection between them. "Thanks for standing up for me," she said softly.

He shrugged off her words. "If it makes you feel any better, I once had a producer order the makeup artist to mess up my hair and put in shadows under my eyes."

"What?"

He laughed. "We're a pair, aren't we?"

"Yeah, we are." She felt a little breathless at the idea. If anyone had told her a month ago that she'd have this much in common with a man like Jack, she'd have laughed and asked what they were smoking. Then again, she of all people should know that appearances were deceiving. She was fast learning there was a lot more to Jack Halloran than first met the eye.

CHAPTER SIX

SIMON CARRUTHERS, M.D., Plastic and Reconstructive Surgery, had an office in Denver's tony Capitol Hill neighborhood, in a tasteful stone-and-smoked-glass high-rise with its own parking garage. Dr. Carruthers's suite exuded expensive good taste, from the plush merlot-colored carpet that muffled every step to the original Mondrian oil in the foyer.

"This looks very nice," Daniel said as he followed Yvonne into the doctor's office the second Tuesday in February.

"It's very elegant," Yvonne said. She ran her hand along a carved teak étagère that held a display of African masks. "Very expensive-looking."

"Dr. Carruthers is one of the best in the business. I have it on good authority that some of the most prominent people in the city are his clients."

"It's nice to know he has lots of experience." She swallowed hard, trying to quiet the turmoil in her stomach. She reached for Daniel's hand and squeezed it. "I'm glad you could come with me today."

"Are you kidding? I wouldn't have missed it." He grinned. "I have a vested interest in the outcome, after all."

She tried to laugh, but it came out as more of a

whimper. She could only imagine what Shelly would say to that.

A nurse wearing a pale blue smock came out to meet them. "Hello, my name is Shanna. Welcome to our office. If you'll follow me, I'll show you to the doctor's consulting room."

She led them to a spacious, wood-paneled room with a pink leather sofa and a wall lined with before-and-after pictures. "Dr. Carruthers will be with you in a moment," Shanna said, and left them.

"These must be some of his patients," Daniel said. He stood and studied the photos more closely. "He does nice work." He stopped before one close-up of a woman's breasts. "What do you think of these?"

In the before picture, the woman was fairly small, twin points tented out from her body like the breasts of an adolescent girl's. In the second photo her breasts were very round and full, like melons with nipples. "I'm not that small," Yvonne protested.

"Well, honey, you're not that large, either."

The door opened and a distinguished-looking man wearing a white smock, his thick brown hair graying at the temples, came in. "Hello, I'm Dr. Carruthers." He extended his hand. "So nice to meet you, Ms. Montoya, Mr. Dunnegan."

"Good to meet you, Doctor." The men shook hands.

"Why don't we sit down over here and discuss how I can help you." The doctor led them to the sofa, then took a seat in a tapestry chair across from them. "I understand you're interested in learning more about breast enlargement."

Yvonne winced. She couldn't believe she was sitting

here, about to discuss her breasts with this stranger—
even if he was a doctor.

"Yes. Yvonne and I are going to be married in June
and I wanted to give her this as my wedding gift to her."
He squeezed her hand. "It's something she's always
wanted. Isn't that right, honey?"

She nodded. "Yes." Her voice was barely audible.
She cleared her throat and tried again. "I mean, it's
something I've thought about."

"That's a very generous gift." The doctor consulted
the chart in his hand. "Do you know how much you'd
like to increase your bust size?"

"Well, I thought maybe—"

"I think a D cup would be good."

She stared at Daniel. She'd been about to say a C.
After all, she didn't want to look out of proportion.

"Yes, that's a very popular choice." The doctor nodded.

"If you don't think it's too much…" she said, still
unsure.

Daniel laughed. "There's no such thing as too much,
right, Doc?"

She winced. Daniel was usually never this crass.

Thankfully, the doctor didn't comment. "What I'll do
today is explain the basics of surgery to you," he said,
addressing Yvonne. "Then we'll take some measurements and discuss your options."

He opened a book of medical illustrations and turned
it to face her. "I believe patients are happiest when
they're fully informed, so I like to explain everything
that will happen as completely as possible. The pictures I'm about to show you aren't meant to alarm you,

merely to educate you. If you have any questions along the way, don't hesitate to ask."

She nodded and focused on the first picture, a side view of a woman's breast.

"During the surgery, an incision is made in a place that will be inconspicuous once it is healed. Depending on your anatomy, I may make the incision in the crease under the breast, in the armpit, or around the nipple." He flipped to a picture that showed these various locations.

"Once the incision is made, the breast tissue and skin are lifted and the implant is placed either directly under the breast tissue, or behind the pectoral muscle of the chest wall. I generally prefer to place the implant behind the pectoral muscle, as I believe this causes less complications."

"What kind of complications?" she asked.

"The most common complication is capsular contraction. The scar around the implant contracts, causing the breast to feel hard. This can be usually be corrected with additional surgery."

She nodded. Great. The last thing she wanted to think about was more surgery, when she was working so hard to psych herself up for this go-round.

"Other complications that occur in a small percentage of women are infection, excessive bleeding or unfavorable reactions to anesthesia."

Yvonne sucked in a deep breath, feeling woozy. "What about pain?" She studied the picture before her now, of a post-op breast, stitches like a row of bird tracks along the underside. "It looks painful."

"There is some discomfort and swelling, but it is usually of short duration."

"Besides, you'll have drugs to help," Daniel said.

"Absolutely, we'll prescribe pain medications," the doctor said. "In addition to ice packs for the swelling."

"How long does this, um, discomfort and…and swelling last?" she asked.

"You'll experience the greatest degree of soreness for the first twenty-four hours or so and will have some sensitivity and swelling for three to four weeks. By six to eight weeks, this sensitivity will have faded and the scars will be less prominent."

"That's not long." Daniel squeezed her hand. "And the results will be worth it."

She nodded. That's what she needed to do—focus on the results and not worry about the rest.

"Now, as for your options." Dr. Carruthers leaned back and took a carved wooden box from the credenza behind him and opened it. "There are two types of implants. Both are composed of a silicone shell. This is filled with either saline, or liquid silicone." He opened the box and handed them each a fluid-filled, slightly oval, clear pouch. It was about the size and shape of the beanbags she remembered playing games with in kindergarten, and surprisingly heavy. "The one you're holding, Daniel, is the silicone-filled model, while Yvonne, you have the saline model."

"The silicone feels real," Daniel said, squeezing the pouch in his hand. He traded with Yvonne.

The silicone implant did indeed feel more like a real breast. "Isn't the saline supposed to be safer?" she asked.

"The Food and Drug Administration has ruled only that there is insufficient evidence about the safety of gel-filled implants, and has limited them to women in controlled studies. However, I happen to be one of the doctors participating in a study right now, so if you like, I can offer you the option of the gel implant."

"I like the silicone best," Daniel said. "The other feels more fake."

She was tempted to tell him if he was so concerned with feeling a real breast, he should be content with the real ones she already had. But she held her tongue. "I'll have to think about it."

"Both the gel and the saline implants can rupture if you suffer a hard blow to the breast. If this happens, the saline implant will deflate within a matter of hours or a few days and the saline will be absorbed into the body. In the case of the gel, you may not even notice a leak, especially if scar tissue forms around it quickly. In other cases, the silicone may migrate to other parts of the body, where it can form lumps. There have been reports of women with gel implants suffering from various connective-tissue disorders, but there's no concrete proof at this time of that."

She swallowed hard. Of course she knew there were certain risks, but hearing them listed that way was daunting.

"You're scaring her," Daniel said. He laughed. "The chances of any of those things happening are almost zero, aren't they?"

The doctor nodded. "Complications are rare."

Daniel turned to Yvonne. "You want something that looks and feels natural. You should go for the silicone."

Should she? Was it so important to have breasts that felt more natural, as long as they looked good? It was clear what Daniel wanted. She supposed she had to take him into consideration. After all, he'd be feeling them more than she would. And he was paying for the surgery.

Plus, thousands of women had had breast surgery and you hardly ever heard about anyone having problems. "All right. It does feel much nicer."

The doctor stood. "Let me get my nurse and we'll take some measurements."

When the doctor was gone, she turned to Daniel. "I think you should wait for me outside."

"Why? It's not like I haven't seen you naked."

"Just do it. Please?" The idea of him watching while she was sized up with a tape measure was humiliating.

"All right, but I think you're being silly." He stood and went to the door.

"Thank you."

He left, and while she waited for the doctor and nurse to return she studied the wall of photos. What was it about those pictures that made her so uncomfortable?

She looked at them more closely and realized that none of the women in those photographs had faces. They were all anonymous breasts and stomachs and thighs. This was obviously designed to protect their privacy, but it had the effect of dehumanizing them. They weren't women now, but body parts, individual attributes rendered more significant than the whole.

She told herself she was thinking too much. Having this surgery wasn't just about her breasts. She was doing this to improve her whole appearance and her outlook. This was a positive, empowering thing.

She was just nervous, that's all. She was letting fear, and the negative things Shelly had said, get in the way of all the positive reasons she was here.

Shanna came in, followed by the doctor. "If you'll take off your shirt and bra, please. Thank you. Now, lift your arms."

Yvonne stared at a blank spot on the wall while the nurse measured and the doctor recorded the numbers she called out. While she wasn't as flat as the woman in the picture Daniel had admired, she was not melon-size. She tried to imagine herself with the large, round breasts shown in the picture. How would that feel? Would she feel more womanly? Sexier?

Then she imagined Daniel's reaction when he saw her, and smiled. He wouldn't have any reason to look at larger women then. That thought alone gave her courage.

"When would you like to schedule the surgery?" the doctor asked.

"I'll have to see when I can get time off work. But soon. My wedding's only four months from now and I want to have plenty of time to recover."

"You should be completely healed well before your wedding. But I suggest you schedule as soon as possible. My calendar tends to fill up quickly."

"I'll do that." She was ready to get this over with. Once it was done, she could put all her doubts behind her.

THOUGH THE FIRST EPISODE of *Inside Story* was complete and due to air the third Thursday in February, only two days away, none of the people involved in the production could afford to stop and enjoy the accomplishment. Work had to continue on half a dozen other stories in order to meet the never-ending deadlines of a weekly show.

Friday afternoons were reserved for planning meet-

ings, where Shelly and Jack, and sometimes Armstrong
Brewster, discussed ideas for upcoming shows.

"I'm thinking of a piece on toxic waste generated by
lawn services," Jack said. "I read the other day it's a real
problem in some cities."

"Too alarmist," Armstrong said. "Besides, you're already working on that water-quality piece. This is too
similar."

"No, this is a totally different angle," Jack said.

"I agree with Armstrong," Shelly said. "It's too Death
in the Ice Machine."

"What?" He frowned. Shelly usually sided with him
against Armstrong. Why was she arguing with him now?

"A few years ago, *First for News* did an investigative
series on sanitary conditions in area restaurants. Some
brilliant marketing person tagged the spots 'Death in the
Ice Machine.'" Her voice dropped to a dramatic tone.
"A local comedy show picked it up and did a series of
skits—Death in the Ice Machine, Death at the Salad Bar,
Death in Public Toilets. It took months to live it down."

"This won't be like that at all," Jack said. "I'm not
talking alarmist, I'm talking serious."

"Then you mean boring." Armstrong sat back, hands
folded on his stomach. "This is the reality-TV genera-
tion. You've got to give them something gripping. No
matter how you look at it, lawn care is not gripping."

"He's right, Jack." Shelly gave him an apologetic
look. "You also don't want to do too many environmental stories or the show starts to look one-sided."

He couldn't believe they were ganging up on him this
way. This was supposed to be his show. His ideal. Yes,
he wanted their input, but...

"I know you don't like the word," Armstrong said. "But you've got to entertain them."

"I won't pander to my audience. Yes, stories should be interesting. But they can be informative, too."

"I think you can be entertaining and informative without pandering," Shelly said. "Your piece on forest management showed that. And the water-quality piece has the same potential. What about something political? Politics always interests people."

He opened his mouth to argue further for the lawn-care piece but thought better of it. Though it pained him to admit it, maybe there was something to Shelly and Armstrong's argument. "The mayor's minority-development task force is starting a new initiative focusing on Asian neighborhoods. How is that different from other initiatives in other neighborhoods? What are the cultural differences? What are the prospects for success?"

"That's great," Shelly said. "We could give viewers a better understanding of, say, local Hmong culture, or Denver's thriving Vietnamese community."

Her enthusiasm edged out the resentment he'd felt over her opposition to his idea. And he couldn't fault her commitment to the show. "Or, what about a piece on Vietnamese war veterans?" he said, expanding on the idea. "Soldiers who fought for the Viet Cong, and are now settled here? It could be a totally different Veteran's Day piece."

"Yes!" She leaned toward him, face alight. "You could include some veterans who fought on the U.S. side and show them making peace—or not."

"Great. We'll add it to the list." He sat back, relieved to be past that hurdle. He supposed he shouldn't be surprised that Shelly didn't always agree with him. He'd known she was a woman with strong opinions from that first interview. He'd been spoiled so far by having her always on his side.

"It beats lawn care." Armstrong straightened and checked his notes. "Next?"

"I want to discuss the opening for the show," Shelly said.

"What about the opening?" Jack turned to her, tension knotting his stomach again. "Don't tell me it's boring, too."

"I think we should take turns introducing each show," she said. "So far, you've scripted all the intros for you."

"But it's my show." Did he sound whiny?

"Yes, but I'm the co-anchor. That means we should share equally in the airtime."

Jack looked to Armstrong, who shrugged. He turned back to Shelly. "You think you don't get enough airtime?"

"The point isn't really how much airtime, it's a matter of perception."

He scratched his head. "I'm not following you." It was bad enough her smile and her perfume could get him off balance. Now her words were unsettling him. Where would it end?

"I know that this show is your baby, but you hired me to be the co-anchor. You have to treat me as an equal on the air or the audience won't see me that way. They'll just see Jack Halloran and his chick sidekick."

He winced. "I certainly don't see you as a mere sidekick."

"Great. Then we'll split the introductions."

"All right." He didn't really want to give up introducing the show each week, but Shelly had a valid argument.

"Great." She rewarded him with a smile, which went a long way toward lightening his mood. So maybe he'd grown a tad territorial when it came to his dream show. He had a lot at stake here, and didn't intend to fail. Obviously, Shelly was just as determined to succeed on her own terms. How could he have forgotten how alluring a self-confident woman could be?

SHELLY WONDERED IF ANYONE noticed her walking with an extra spring in her step, or holding her head up higher in the days after Jack agreed to share equal time with her on the show. She congratulated herself on facing up to him, even though she'd been afraid he'd shoot her down. *Inside Story* was his baby, and though he'd probably never admit it, Jack Halloran was a bit of a control freak. From the exact placement of the lights to the props on the news desk, he oversaw every aspect of production. Her minor rebellion had obviously surprised him, but he'd been man enough to give in.

One more thing to love about him.

In a purely platonic sense, of course.

But she couldn't stop to crow over her victory. In-depth features required hours and hours of footwork and interviews. Her feature on public hospitals required most of her time and attention these days.

She had begun researching the feature by talking to the hospitals themselves. Predictably, the interviews arranged by the facilities' public relations people were bland and noncontroversial. But as she was leaving the administrative offices after the third such interview, she passed a door marked Medical Personnel Only.

The room behind the door proved to be a lounge for on-duty doctors and nurses, with sleeping cubicles, coffee and soda machines, cubicles for dictating patient notes and a few sofas and chairs.

"May I help you?" a tired-looking man in green scrubs asked as she looked in the door.

Mind racing, she glanced at the bulletin board across from her and saw a note addressed to Dr. Peterson.

"I'm looking for Dr. Peterson." She smiled warmly at her questioner. "They told me he might be here."

"I don't know who told you that. He's not on duty until Saturday."

"I guess they were confused." She hesitated. "Maybe you can help me, or you know someone who can."

He shrugged. "I can try."

She came into the room, letting the door fall shut behind her. "I'm researching the plight of publicly funded hospitals and wanted to talk to a doctor about the problem of having to turn patients away." It was all a matter of how you phrased the question.

The man's eye's narrowed. "You a reporter?"

"I'm with a new public television news program, *Inside Story*. What department do you work in Dr.—" she glanced at the name tag on his scrubs "—Sabaya?"

"I'm an E.R. physician."

She recalled now that they were very near the hospital's busy emergency room. Perfect. "Then you probably treat a lot of patients who come in without insurance."

"The triage nurses screen everyone who comes in. If they decide it's a matter of life or death, I treat them."

"And if the triage nurse decides their case isn't critical?"

"They have to wait and go to the public clinic when they can get in."

"Do you know how long that usually takes?"

He sighed. "It can take a while from what I understand. State budget cuts have forced the clinic to cut its hours."

"How do you feel about that?"

He hesitated, then looked around. "Can I say something anonymously? Off the record?"

She nodded. If it was something useful, she could always try to persuade him later to let her attach his name to it.

"The policy stinks. People come in here all the time, and if it was up to me, I would treat them. But the hospital board says we can't afford to do it."

She felt the familiar thrill that came with knowing she was on the right track to a good story. "Can you give me an example of a case?"

He thought a minute. "I don't want to say too much. For one thing, there's the matter of patient confidentiality. But there's a guy I can think of who you really ought to talk to. A patient who came in here and was turned away."

"Yes. I'd like to talk to him."

"You got a piece of paper?"

She tore a sheet from her notebook and handed it to him. He scribbled something and handed the paper back to her. "That's him. The second name is his social worker. She works out of the Denver Mission. She ought to be able to tell you how to find him."

She read the two names. "Del Gardner and Sally Truman. Thanks. Thanks a lot, Doctor."

"Yeah, well, maybe your story will help him. As for the rest—" He shrugged. "It's a big problem. I don't know if there's a right answer."

His pager went off. "I better go now. If you come back Saturday, Dr. Peterson should be here."

"Thanks." She doubted if she'd ever talk to Dr. Peterson. But she couldn't wait to interview Del Gardner.

THE FIRST EPISODE OF *Inside Story* aired on Thursday evening at eight o'clock mountain time. At 7:55 Shelly and Jack took their places behind the kidney-shaped counter and Armstrong ran through the last-minute lighting and camera checks.

"Are you ready for this?" Jack asked.

She nodded. "I'm ready." She'd spent the past ten years working toward this moment. Boy, was she ever ready.

"You look nice," he said.

She smoothed the jacket of the bright red suit she'd chosen for her television debut. The nipped-in waist of the jacket and close-cut lines of the skirt showed off her hourglass figure, and the bright color proclaimed she wasn't interested in hiding anything. "Thanks. So do you." He'd chosen a classic dark blue suit with a purple-and-blue tie and a crisp white shirt. Then again, Jack would have looked terrific in anything.

"Ready in ten, nine, eight…" Armstrong's voice was clear in her earpiece. "Three, two, one. Go!"

The red light on the camera came on and Jack addressed the invisible viewers who'd tuned in (they hoped). "Good evening, Denver. I'm Jack Halloran. Welcome to this first edition of *Inside Story.*"

The camera shifted to Shelly, and she lifted her chin

and smiled, though in truth she hadn't stopped smiling since that light first came on. "Hello, I'm Shelly Piper. Tonight we'll be sharing with you an in-depth look at some important stories you're unlikely to see on your usual nightly newscasts. We'll bring you some good news and some not-so-good news, and explore political, environmental, economic and social issues. We'll share some laughs and we hope to make you think."

"So sit back and let's get started," Jack said, the cue for the first segment, Jack's piece on forest management. He made it interesting despite the dry subject matter, choosing to contrast what the average camper and hiker saw with the behind-the-scenes aspects of juggling resources on the state's large sections of federal and state land.

The rest of the hour passed in what felt like only minutes. Jack had a live interview with retiring Colorado Senator Ben Nighthorse Campbell, then Shelly introduced a video about public art in Denver. They wrapped up the night with Shelly's piece on programs for juvenile delinquents.

"We hear a lot about kids in trouble with the law—juvenile offenders who have the potential to grow up to become adult criminals," Shelly said, introducing the story. "Recently, I had the chance to visit two very different programs that are successfully fighting back against this kiddie crime wave."

This was the cue for the prerecorded segment on juvenile detention centers to roll. As the tape started, she sat back and let out the breath she hadn't even realized she'd been holding.

Jack grinned at her. "You did great."

"Thanks. I'll never get tired of hearing you say that." Maybe because she knew Jack wasn't just blowing smoke. His praise meant something.

When the credits rolled and the red light on the camera went out, a cheer went up from the crew. Shelly found herself hugging Jack, then being hugged by Mary Anne. Someone brought out bottles of champagne and plastic glasses. Someone else called for a speech and Jack stood, his glass held high. "You all did a great job tonight," he said. "Here's to many more great jobs."

More cheering and toasting. Shelly sipped champagne and let the fizzy, happy feeling of this moment wash over her. She contrasted this with the misery she'd felt the afternoon she quit her job at *First for News*. She hoped Darcy and Pam were watching her tonight. She hoped they saw what a great job she did with her reports, but she wasn't ashamed to admit that she also hoped they were pea-soup green at seeing how great she looked, sitting up here next to handsome Jack Halloran.

"Ed Palmer, whom many of you know is the underwriter of this show, is hosting a party tonight to celebrate our debut," Jack said. "You're all invited." He held his glass up again. "So drink up and let's go celebrate!"

Shelly stood and prepared to make her way over to Jack's uncle's place. "Why don't we share a cab?" he said.

She agreed, and five minutes later they were sitting in the back seat of a Yellow Cab headed toward Ed's penthouse. "It went great tonight, didn't it?" Jack said.

"It did." She glanced at him. "When will we have an idea of our ratings?"

"Maybe as soon as tomorrow morning. There should be some reviews in the local press, as well."

"I hope they're good."

"How could they not be good? The show came together exactly how I imagined it."

She laughed at his enthusiasm. "I'm looking forward to doing more."

"We will. I know we will. I've got a really good feeling about this."

The cab dropped them off and they took the elevator up. "I'm a little nervous about meeting your uncle," she said as they stood in the otherwise empty elevator, watching the digital display above the doors tick off the floor numbers. "He's a pretty powerful man around here."

"He is. But he's a great guy." His eyes met hers in their reflection in the polished steel doors. "And I know he's going to like you."

"How do you know that?"

"How could he not? Besides, he has a reputation for having excellent taste."

She was still glowing from this compliment when she followed Jack into a surprisingly understated, but most likely very expensive, apartment. The furniture was traditional mahogany and walnut, substantial and not overly ornamented. There were bookshelves lining one wall and a massive home-entertainment system on the other. No art graced the walls and the lighting was subdued. The focal point of the room was the wall of windows opposite the entrance. There, the whole of Denver and the mountains beyond were spread out in an ever-changing panorama of light and movement.

Jack led her to a slight, balding man she recognized from countless news stories. "Uncle Ed, this is Shelly Piper."

"Pleased to meet you." He shook hands, his gaze flicking over her, assessing her.

She stood up straight and looked him in the eye. "It's a pleasure to meet you, Mr. Palmer."

"What did you think of tonight's show?" Jack asked. He rocked back and forth on his heels, like a kid too full of nervous energy to stay still.

"Impressive." Palmer nodded and the two men exchanged grins.

The door opened behind them and more guests arrived. "There's food and plenty to drink." Palmer motioned to the buffet set up in front of the bookshelves. "Help yourselves while I greet my other guests."

Jack headed for the buffet table, but for once, Shelly wasn't hungry. Instead, she accepted a glass of sparkling water from the bartender and went to stand by the window. She'd lived in Denver for more than twenty years, yet she'd never seen the city from this perspective. Snow had begun to fall, the lacy flakes visible in the light from the window, then slipping into darkness again, while the city lights glowed below in shades of green, red and amber.

"I never get tired of this view." Ed spoke from directly behind her.

"It's beautiful." She looked over her shoulder at him, then back to the view. "Mesmerizing."

He came to stand beside her. "That's a very striking suit," he said after a moment. "May I ask why you selected it for tonight's show?"

Did he not like it? She fingered the bright crepe fabric. "Red's one of my favorite colors. It translates well on camera. It's a color that sends a message of power and energy. I think the cut is flattering." She shrugged. "I like it and it makes me feel more confident."

He nodded. "I agree, it's quite flattering. But it's not a color many women can pull off. I would have expected something darker. Perhaps black." He sipped his drink.

"Something more slimming?" She quirked one eyebrow, taking a chance at challenging him.

He laughed. "Maybe." He looked her up and down once more. "I have to tell you, you wouldn't have been my first choice for the show."

"Because of my weight?" She swallowed past the sudden tightness in her throat.

"Partly that. You have to admit, you're not what people are used to seeing when they turn on the news."

"Only because no one's given them a choice."

He nodded. "I was also concerned about your lack of experience in front of the camera. But Jack wanted you and he convinced me you were the right person for the job."

"And what do you think after tonight?"

"I think my nephew's a very smart man. And the two of you together will do very well."

He smiled, a knowing glint in his eyes, but before she could ask him to explain himself, he left to greet another newcomer to the party.

She turned back to the view, the lights below blurring into glowing ribbons as she pondered Palmer's last comment. Of course he meant she and Jack worked well together as a news team. It was only her imagination, and wishful thinking, that wondered at the possibilities they might have on a more personal level.

It was an enjoyable fantasy, imagining she and Jack

as more than co-workers, but she was smart enough to keep it to the level of a pleasant daydream. Some things clearly weren't meant to be.

Of course, that's what people had told her before about the idea of a bigger woman in front of the camera. Tonight had shot that taboo out of the water.

She turned to look around the party and Jack caught her eye. He raised his glass in a salute, and she fought hard not to blush and make some flirtatious gesture in return. Tonight one of her dreams had come true. Still floating from that triumph, she found it harder to rein in other fantasies, even impossible ones involving Jack Halloran.

Or maybe especially those involving Jack.

CHAPTER SEVEN

SHELLY AND WALLY, the cameraman, met Del Gardner in a park off the Sixteenth Street mall, where he panhandled for change. The morning was cold but sunny, and Gardner had refused their offer to meet inside, saying he preferred being out of doors. She brought coffee and a breakfast sandwich, and waited on the bench beside him while he ate. Wally set up the camera a short distance away.

She watched the homeless man beside her out of the corner of her eye. Careful not to stare, her gaze was nonetheless drawn to the puckered scar that stood out bright white against the weathered skin of his jaw. Gray beard stubble grew in ragged patches around the scar, and his hair, gray also, curled in sparse tendrils around his blackened jacket collar.

"It's okay if you look," he said, brushing crumbs from his mouth with a paper napkin, then drinking the last of the coffee. "I've gotten used to people staring."

"Can you tell me what happened?" she asked.

"Sally said you're a reporter?" His eyebrows, like twin strips of cotton batting, formed a V above his eyes as he frowned at her.

She nodded. "I'm co-host of a television news magazine called *Inside Story,* on public television. I'm doing a story on publicly funded hospitals who are turning away uninsured patients."

"That's me. An uninsured patient." He glanced toward Wally. "All right. You can turn that thing on and I'll tell you what I know." He turned his attention back to Shelly. "Sally said you wanted to talk to me about my face." He indicated the scar along his jaw.

"I understand you had some trouble when you went to the hospital. What happened?"

"I got shot and I went to the hospital to get them to take the bullet out and they sent me away."

She blinked, unsure she'd heard him right. "You were shot in the face and they turned you away?"

"Right in the jaw here." He pointed to the scar again. "The bullet kinda stuck in there. They said it wasn't life-threatening, and since I didn't have any insurance, I'd have to go to the public clinic and get them to find a doctor to treat me."

"How did you get shot?"

His gaze slid away from her, and he twisted the napkin in his hand. "I got in a fight with this man."

"What were you fighting about?"

He shrugged. "I don't rightly remember. We'd both been drinking."

"So what happened when you went to the hospital?"

"Like I told you, they looked at me and said since the bleeding had already stopped and the bullet wasn't moving, I'd have to go to the clinic. They said they only had enough money to take care of people who were gonna die if they weren't seen by a doctor right away."

"And did you go to the clinic?"

"Yeah, but they said the same thing. I was stable, and they couldn't find nobody to do surgery if I couldn't pay."

"So you walked around with a bullet in your jaw?" She suppressed a shudder at the thought.

He nodded. "They give me some pain pills, but those ran out pretty quick. I was in awful pain. The bullet broke my teeth and I couldn't hardly eat." He moved his head from side to side, stretching his neck. "And I got horrible headaches. I hurt so bad I couldn't see. I couldn't do nothing but lay down and moan."

She leaned toward him, her voice soft. "What did you do?"

"Every day I'd get up and try a new doctor or hospital. Some of them wouldn't hardly let me in the door. They find out I can't pay, they say I can't come in."

"How long did this go on?"

"About a month. I lost a lot of weight and felt real bad."

"How did you finally get treatment?"

"I walked into this doctor's office one day. The sign on the door said he was a surgeon, so I went in and told the receptionist my story. She at least listened all the way through, then she told me to have a seat and she went and got the doctor. When he looked me over, he got real mad. Not at me, but at those other doctors who turned me away. Then he did the surgery for free. But it was too late to save my teeth, and he had to remake part of my jawbone with a metal plate."

"How long were you in the hospital?"

"Only a couple days. Then I went to his office every Thursday for a few weeks. He apologized for this here scar, but I told him I hadn't been that good-looking to start with."

He laughed, and she wondered at the resilience of a person who could laugh after an ordeal like that. "I'm sorry."

"Me, too." His expression sobered. "I don't understand why they couldn't just treat me that night. It probably would have saved everybody a lot of trouble in the long run."

"Do you think this kind of thing happens a lot? I mean, do you hear stories on the street?"

"What I think is that if I'd been some pretty girl or maybe a kid, or even some deadbeat who looked like he had money, they might not have sent me away. But they see this dirty old man who maybe don't smell good, who drinks too much, and they don't see the human being behind the dirt and smell. That doctor who treated me, he looked closer."

"What was the doctor's name? I'd like to talk to him."

He looked at her a long moment, then nodded. "You do that. But maybe you better not use his name on your show. The man could go broke trying to help all the sick people in this town who can't pay. But maybe if a few more like him got together to donate their services every once in a while, it would help." He shook his head. "Problem is, I don't know if there's many out there like him, who can see past the outside stuff to the human being within."

She waited a few seconds, to see if he had anything else to add, then nodded to Wally to turn off the camera. "Thank you, Mr. Gardner." She'd folded a twenty into her hand and now she offered it to him, not as payment for the interview, but because she knew he needed it.

He accepted the money with grace, slipping it into

his pocket and nodding to her. "Thank you very much, miss. I hope your story does some good. I don't have a lot of confidence it will, but it might."

She met Wally at the entrance to the park. "What do you think?" she asked.

"I think if I had a bullet in my jaw I'd be demanding a doctor see me or I wouldn't leave." He shifted the video camera to his other shoulder. "Then again, I never had to worry about whether people saw me as a human being or not."

She nodded. "That part struck me, too. We have a hard time separating people from their appearances, don't we?"

"It's the way we're wired." He turned his head, his gaze tracking a young woman in tight jeans as she passed.

He looked back at Shelly, grinning. "Our first impressions of people are how they look. It's not always a bad thing."

"It is if we make judgments about them, based on their looks, that simply aren't true."

"Maybe it goes back to our ancestors. Cavemen and women probably had to size up a stranger pretty quick, decide if he was friend or foe before they got hit over the head with a rock or something."

"This is the twenty-first century. We ought to be beyond all that."

"We ought to stop smoking, exercise more and spend more money finding a cure for cancer than we do on professional sports, too." He shrugged. "Nobody's perfect."

"Right." She headed toward her car, Wally trailing behind. But that didn't stop people from trying for the appearance of perfection—whatever the definition was this week. She was glad she'd stepped off that merry-go-round when she turned thirty, but she was smart enough to realize the temptation of getting back on. Better-looking people seemed to have an easier time of it in life, and who didn't want that, even if it was only an illusion?

"GOT THE INITIAL RATINGS feedback for the first edition of *Inside Story.*" Armstrong breezed into Jack's office, waving a computer printout.

"What does it say?" Not waiting for an answer, he snatched the paper out of the producer's hand and scanned it.

"It says we drew a ten share," Armstrong said. "Very respectable for public television."

"It's a good share for any kind of television these days." Jack grinned.

"Don't start celebrating just yet." He pulled a folded newspaper from under his arm and opened it to the front page of the Entertainment section. "Take a look at this."

Jack picked up the paper and zeroed in on the article headed News Heartthrob Takes to Local Airwaves. He groaned but kept reading. "Jack Halloran, who might possibly be the hunkiest reporter to deliver the news since 'Scud Stud' Arthur Kent, debuted his new show, *Inside Story,* last night to mostly positive response. The magazine-style show gives a local slant to in-depth news stories, with a nice mix of serious and light in this initial offering. Halloran has a pleasing delivery and a killer smile that will have women all over the city tuning in. Co-anchor Shelly Piper, a newcomer to the broadcast scene, had the best story of the night, a piece on successful programs for troubled teens. But this pairing of Handsome Jack with a plus-size partner may have male viewers demanding equal eye candy."

He flung the paper down on the desk. "What is this—a media review or a gossip column? Besides, Shelly isn't plus-size."

Armstrong unfolded another paper. "This one calls her *substantial*."

"That doesn't sound as bad."

Armstrong frowned. "Except they both mean fat."

"Shelly is not fat! She's just an ordinary-size woman."

"People aren't used to seeing that on TV. Not on the news." He sat on the edge of the desk. "Look, you're a good-looking guy. People expect you to be paired with a gorgeous woman."

"Shelly's very attractive."

"But she's not gorgeous. She doesn't look like the viewers expect a female newscaster to look."

"Give me that." Jack grabbed the section from Denver's other morning paper and read it. Though not as bad as the first article, this one, too, focused more on his and Shelly's appearance and audience appeal than the substance of the show. "Can't they say something about the concept, or the quality of the reporting?" He looked at Armstrong. "Has Shelly seen these yet?"

The producer shook his head. "She and Wally are out shooting some footage for the public-hospital story."

"Do me a favor. Don't go out of your way to show these to her. These articles will only upset her."

"Whatever. She's bound to see them sooner or later.

If she's going to be in this business, she might as well develop a thick hide."

"She's been a reporter for ten years. I'm sure she's not a wimp. But I'd like to talk to her before she sees these, make sure she understands these digs don't matter."

Armstrong rubbed his thumb along his jaw and studied Jack. "There're not some personal feelings involved in this, are there?" Armstrong asked.

Jack looked up from rereading the article. Not that most of it wasn't already burned into his brain. "What do you mean, 'personal feelings'?"

Armstrong shrugged. "You seem awfully defensive on Shelly's behalf."

"Of course I'm defensive. She was my choice for the position. Not to mention I know what it's like to have my professional abilities questioned because of my appearance." He tossed the paper onto the desk with the other one. "Hell, it's still happening."

"You should have at least tried the big desk. Or we could ask her to wear a black suit. Black is supposed to be slimming."

"Armstrong…"

The producer held up his hands. "I'm just trying to help."

"And what am I supposed to do? Mess up my hair and slouch in an attempt to look less attractive?" He turned away. "If I thought it would work, I might even try it."

"Excuse me if an ordinary Joe like me isn't sympathetic."

"Yeah, yeah. I don't have any right to complain." He picked up the papers and tossed them into the trash can beside the desk. "At least the ratings are good. That's all we need to worry about."

Armstrong stood. "If anything, maybe these articles will get people curious and they'll tune into the show."

"Yeah. And maybe they'll even pay attention to the actual reporting. Can you imagine?"

"It could happen. Okay, I'll leave you to get back to work."

"Tell the front desk to let me know when Shelly arrives," he said.

"Will do."

When Armstrong was gone, Jack sat behind the desk and stared at the newspapers in the trash can. Truth be told, he could care less what the print media had to say about him; he'd heard it all before. But Shelly was new to this side of broadcasting, plus she was a woman. In his experience women took this kind of thing more personally. He hoped this didn't dampen her enthusiasm for the job.

One of the unexpected bonuses of starting *Inside Story* was working with Shelly. She was smart and funny and so interested in everything. And she absolutely got what he was trying to do here.

Not to mention that one smile from her could turn his whole day around.

So yeah, maybe there were some *personal* feelings influencing his defense of her. That didn't mean he'd ever let *her* know about them.

"Jack? Armstrong said you wanted to see me."

As if summoned by his thoughts, Shelly stood in his doorway. He sat up straighter and greeted her with a smile. "Yes, come in. How'd the shooting go this morning?"

She sat in the chair across from his desk. "It went well. Pretty intense. I think this is one of those pieces where the more I dig, the more I find." She reached up and tucked a lock of hair behind her ear. "This is one of those emotional stories that has the potential to stir things up—to really get people talking. I mean, we all know there are people out there without insurance who get sick and can't afford the care they need, but to actually see their suffering and hear their stories…" She shook her head.

He came out from behind the desk and leaned on it, facing her. "This is where I'm probably supposed to warn you against getting too emotionally involved in a story, but frankly, that's one of the things I like about your work. I think you communicate to the viewers how much you care about the pieces you put together."

"Thanks. I think. That is a good thing, isn't it?"

He nodded. "I've already heard great comments about your segment on the juvenile detention centers."

"Any ratings yet?"

"As a matter of fact…" He reached back and picked up the computer printout Armstrong had delivered earlier. "Take a look at these."

She accepted the paper and scanned it, then a smile lit her face. "That's terrific. Better than I expected, to tell you the truth."

He nodded. "Let's hope the trend continues."

She tossed the paper onto his desk and sat back, still smiling. "That feels great. At least we know we aren't putting all this work into stories only our friends and relatives tune into."

"I think our audience will only grow as word gets out

about what we're doing here. Pieces like the public hospital story you're putting together will help make our reputation."

"I hope so. Any comments on the show in the local press? I meant to grab copies of the *Post* and the *News* this morning but I never had the chance."

He picked up a chunk of river rock he used as a paperweight and passed it from hand to hand. "There were a couple of short pieces."

"You don't sound too pleased. What did they say?"

He set the rock down again and met her gaze. "They spent more time critiquing our appearances than they did writing about the content of the show."

Her expression didn't change, though her shoulders stiffened. "Your appearance, or mine?"

"Both. I am apparently 'the hunkiest reporter to deliver the news since 'Scud Stud' Arthur Kent.'"

She put her hand over her mouth but was unable to hold back the laughter. "Oh, my! Since the 'Scud Stud,' huh?"

He nodded. "I'm afraid so."

"And what did they say about me? Or do I have to ask? They said I was fat."

He shook his head. "Not exactly."

"You're right. Everyone's afraid of the *F* word. What lovely euphemism did they use?"

He made a face. "I don't want to dignify them by quoting."

"Zaftig? Plus-size?" She leaned toward him. "God, please tell me they didn't say I was 'portly.'" She rolled her eyes in exaggerated disgust.

His laughter surprised him. "I believe one of the articles referred to you as 'substantial.'"

"Oh, now that sounds good, doesn't it? I may have a *substantial* glass of wine when I get home this evening to toast the clever person who came up with that one."

"Seriously, they *did* compliment you on the juvenile piece. One reporter even said it was the best thing about the show."

"They must have been out buying a thesaurus when your segment on forest management was running."

He couldn't believe this conversation, which he'd dreaded, was ending in laughter. Almost any other woman—make that almost any other *person*—would have been either raging, or moaning. In fact, hadn't he come closer to those responses? Shelly was showing him what he should have done all along—refused to give the reports any credit. "I like your attitude," he said.

"My attitude is great." She raised her chin, a gesture of defiance. "What does Armstrong say about the articles?"

"You know Armstrong." He shrugged.

She nodded. "He agrees with them. He thinks I'm fat."

He winced. "I'm beginning to hate that word. Besides, even he doesn't believe you're fat."

"Oh? What euphemism does he prefer?"

"He says you're 'not what viewers expect.'"

"Not what viewers expect." She nodded and shifted to meet his gaze once more. "I like it. In fact, I'll take it as a compliment. We should use it as our motto for the show. 'Not what you'd expect from a news show.'"

His heart beat faster, the way it did when he knew he'd uncovered a bit of breaking news. "I love it. We should definitely use it."

"You're serious?" She smiled. "I was just mouthing off."

"One of the things that makes me glad I hired you."

"Not as glad as I am that I came to work for you." Their eyes locked again, and for an instant he felt his strictly business facade crumbling at the edges to reveal his growing attraction to the woman who sat before him.

He looked away and sucked in a deep breath, pulling himself together again. "Speaking of the show…" He leaned back once more to sort through the papers and pulled out a manila folder. "I want you to do a live interview on our next show with this guy."

She took the folder and flipped through the contents. "Prince Amir Ben Fatin? Should I know him?"

"Probably not. Most of our viewers probably don't know him, either, but he's a very interesting guy, part of the Saudi royal family."

She arched one eyebrow. "Wealthy?"

"Very, and politically well connected, *and* involved in a number of business ventures in and around Denver."

"And he's agreed to be interviewed on our show? Why?"

"Good question. We finagled an exclusive if we agreed to talk about the children's charity he's overseeing, but I also want you to look into his local business connections. He sits on the board of a development group and owns a lot of property in the city. See what you can find there."

"So dig for dirt, but be sneaky about it?" She grinned. "That's my kind of job."

"I'm counting on him being so blown over by your beauty and charm that he doesn't see the tough questions coming."

She laughed again, a sound that did strange things to his stomach.

She stood. "I'd better get to the editing room and take a look at the film we shot this morning," she said. "Then I'll make a few calls about this prince. Anything else?"

Would you have dinner with me? But he didn't say the words out loud, even though he couldn't think of a better way to spend the evening than talking with her, and watching the way her eyes shone when she laughed. He turned away. "No, that's all right now. Keep me posted on how the hospital story is going."

"I will. Talk to you later."

He waited until the sound of her high heels striking the floor had receded down the hall before he sank into his desk chair. Shelly was certainly not what *he'd* expected when he'd hired a female co-host. And his reaction to her was also totally unexpected.

The women he'd been involved with before had been, without exception, strikingly beautiful. As if he'd purposely sought out women who could draw attention away from his own looks.

Not that Shelly wasn't beautiful, but her beauty was more subtle. He found himself mesmerized by the way she tilted her head when she thought, or the sound of her laughter. He could have talked to her for hours and never tired of hearing what she had to say. She excited his mind as well as his body. She made him think, and the give-and-take between them acted like an aphrodisiac. Was it the novelty of their relationship that aroused him, or was there more? Something deeper?

Something he couldn't afford to examine too closely. The show was on its way to being a success, partly because of Shelly. He didn't want to jeopardize that by taking their relationship into more intimate territory. Better to keep hold of the success they had than risk losing it all.

CHAPTER EIGHT

SHELLY HAD INTERVIEWED hundreds of people in her reporting career, but none live in front of a television audience. In the days leading up to her on-air chat with Prince Amir Ben Fatin, she had become a serious chocolate addict, inhaling dark chocolate Dove squares at the rate some chain-smokers consume cigarettes.

Unfortunately, chocolate was only a temporary fix for stressed nerves, and the biggest result from her binge was that she could scarcely button the waistband of her favorite purple suit.

"Thank God for control-top panty hose," she muttered as she surveyed her reflection in her dressing-room mirror the night of the show. Though honestly, she didn't know why she bothered looking in the mirror, given her current state of mind. Though she'd laughed off the print media's comments in Jack's office the other afternoon, ever since then she'd felt like a huge, bloated version of herself. Every bulge seemed magnified to twice its normal size and she had nightmares of strangers fleeing in horror at the sight of her grotesque self.

"Shelly? You almost ready to go?"

She turned away from the mirror. "Ready as I'll ever be."

The dressing-room door opened and the editor, Mary Anne Robideaux, stepped inside. "That purple looks gorgeous on you," she said. "Prince Charming won't know what hit him."

"Have you met him yet? Is he really charming?"

"Yes and yes." Mary Anne cradled a clipboard in her arms. "Of course, you're talking to a woman who's always had a thing for any man who's tall, dark, rich and royal."

Shelly laughed. "Met a lot of those, have you?"

"Only in my wildest fantasies." She held the door open wider. "Come on. I'll take you down to the green room and introduce you."

The green room wasn't really green, and it wasn't even a specific room, merely an empty office where the occasional live guests could wait for their turn on air. When Mary Anne and Shelly entered, Prince Amir Ben Fatin was standing with his back to them, gazing out the window at the distant mountains. At the sound of the door opening, he turned to greet them.

"Prince Amir Ben Fatin, I'd like to introduce you to Shelly Piper. Shelly will be interviewing you on the program this evening."

"Hello, Your Highness. I'm pleased to meet you." Shelly offered her hand, amazed at how calm her voice sounded, considering her heart hammered away like a dot matrix printer.

"The pleasure is most assuredly mine." The prince took her hand and held it, his black eyes knifing into her like twin lasers, the corners of his full lips tipped up in a smile that would have done Rudolph Valentino proud.

Shelly pulled her hand away and took a step back.

On second glance, the prince was more imposing than handsome. He was about six foot three, with a linebacker's shoulders and a slightly thickening waist disguised by a well-cut gray suit. He had thick black brows, a neatly trimmed black beard and deep-set black eyes with long lashes she immediately envied.

"They did not tell me I would be interviewed by a woman of such great beauty." His gaze swept over her again and his eyes sparked with unmistakable interest.

She fought back a blush. She didn't believe for a minute his words were more than hollow flattery, but they were still gratifying to hear. A great beauty, indeed!

"I believe our interview is the first segment after the introduction," she said. "So we won't keep you too much longer."

"I will look forward to it."

How was it an otherwise dignified man could send such suggestive messages with his eyes? She decided nerves were making her delusional. She did her best to look composed and said, "I have to go now. I'll see you on the set shortly."

Mary Anne followed her from the room. "My, you certainly made an impression on him," she said.

"Was I that bad?"

"What do you mean, bad? You were fabulous! He couldn't take his eyes off of you."

She blushed. "Don't be ridiculous. He's just one of those men who flirts with every female."

"He certainly didn't look at *me* that way and, last time I checked, I believe I qualify as female."

Shelly shook her head. "He was probably trying to soften me up for the interview."

"You don't give yourself enough credit. I think our handsome prince was quite taken with you."

She didn't have time to argue the point further, as the show was about to air. She joined Jack behind their counter and clipped her mike to her jacket. "You look great," he said. "Royal purple to go head-to-head with our guest royalty."

"I guess so." She tucked in her earpiece and arranged her hair to hide it. "Let's get this show on the road." The sooner this was done, the sooner she could get out of this too-tight skirt and eat more chocolate.

Armstrong's voice was clear in her ear. "Okay, folks. Five. Four. Three. Two. One."

Shelly smiled at the camera. "Good evening and welcome to *Inside Story*. I'm Shelly Piper."

"And I'm Jack Halloran. Tonight's show has an international flavor, as we look at Asian gangs in Denver, visit a detention center for foreign nationals, and take you on a tour of Denver's sister cities around the world. But first up, Shelly has a live interview with Saudi Arabian Prince Amir Ben Fatin Abu Nadir, who may well be one of the most influential men in our city, even though most people have never heard of him."

While Jack gave the introduction, Shelly hurried from behind the counter and circled the cameras to meet Prince Amir as he settled into one of the tapestry armchairs in the set's "living room." She had to sprint to make it in time and arrived out of breath, silently cursing the waistband of the skirt that dug into her.

"How nice that you are so eager to talk with me." The prince's tone was teasing, his eyes full of laughter.

"But of course." Hey, if the guy was going to flirt

with her, she'd flirt right back. But she wouldn't be any easier on him when it came to asking questions. Right on cue, she turned to the camera and began the interview.

"Your Highness, I understand you're currently in the United States on behalf of the Caroli Disease Foundation."

"Yes. I established this fund in 1998 to collect money for research into the causes and cures of Caroli disease, a congenital disease that affects the liver, and to promote awareness of the disease."

"What led you to establish the fund?"

"My firstborn son was diagnosed with this disease when he was seventeen years old. At the time, I had never heard of it. I set out to educate myself, then determined to educate others."

"And were you able to help your son?"

"No, I was not. This illness killed him before his twenty-fifth birthday. But I continue this work in his honor."

"This isn't your first visit to Denver, is it, Your Highness?"

"No. I have visited your city many times. It is a city of great beauty." His gaze lingered on her.

Mary Anne was right. He was definitely Prince Charming. She forged on. "In fact, you own quite a bit of property in the city, don't you?"

A shrug of his shoulders. "Real estate is always a good investment."

"Particularly if it's in prime redevelopment areas, bought cheaply and sold at a fat profit to various government agencies."

His suave expression never wavered. "I believe that

is a better way to do business than to buy at a high price and sell cheaply."

"Yes, but you seem to have an uncanny knack for finding properties that in a few months' time will be in high demand." She consulted the notes she'd made on a stack of file cards. "Five years ago you bought an acre of vacant land on Quebec Street and sold it nine months later to the United States Postal Service for a new mail-sorting facility, realizing a profit of $790,000. In 1999, you sold twenty acres to Centennial Airport for a runway expansion, property you'd owned only four months, having acquired it from the original owner for roughly five thousand an acre. The airport paid you fifteen thousand dollars an acre. You also bought a condemned warehouse in 2001 that is now the site of the city's new convention facility." This was the signal for a graphic showing half a dozen of the prince's most suspicious real estate transactions to appear on the screen alongside the man himself.

"I was considering using the warehouse for a shipping facility for an organic-foods business I had an interest in, but it could not be brought up to health department standards. I considered razing it and building apartments, then I heard the city was trying to acquire property to build a hotel. The deal we made solved problems for both sides."

She fixed him with her best hardened reporter's stare. "How could one man be involved in so many immensely profitable real estate transactions if someone didn't tip you off beforehand as to the properties' probable future uses?"

"I have the ability to see potential where others do not." He shrugged again. "It is a gift."

He was gifted, all right, with a smoothness that had probably helped him skate through many a suspect situation. "You also apparently have a gift for making friends in high places." She consulted a second note card. "This list of donors to the Caroli Disease Foundation reads like a Denver who's who—the mayor, several city council members, as well as members of the various boards and planning commissions who've been involved in purchasing property from you."

He nodded. "When I make business contacts, they automatically are added to the mailing lists for the foundation. Many of them have been generous enough to respond to our pleas for assistance. They, of course, recognize that this is a very worthy cause." He smiled, teeth gleaming white against his black beard. "I believe, in the American business world, this is called networking."

"So these high-profile people who've made donations to your foundation haven't done you any other favors, such as alerting you ahead of time when their organization is considering purchase of a particular piece of property."

"Such a thing would be illegal, would it not?" He shook his head. "I would not be a part of such a thing. Why should I? My family has more money than I would ever need to spend."

"You've certainly done your part to add to the family coffers," she said.

He waved away her words. "Business for me is a fascinating hobby, one that allows me to use my natural talents."

His smoothness amazed her. He never flinched or raised his voice. If not for all the suggestions of shady dealings she'd accumulated, she might think he was completely innocent.

Armstrong signaled that it was time to wrap up the discussion. "I'm afraid that's all we have time for now," Shelly said. "Thank you for joining us this evening, Your Highness."

He nodded. "You are quite welcome."

Jack began the segue into his story on Asian gangs. She stood and prepared to hurry back to the anchor desk.

The prince took hold of her hand, stopping her. "Please say you will have dinner with me after the show," he said. "We will continue our conversation."

She stared at him. "I just accused you on air of shady business practices. Why would you want to have dinner with me?"

He released her hand, though his eyes remained locked to hers. "I am always intrigued by the American woman's forthrightness. In my country such behavior would be considered rude."

She squared her shoulders. "I'm a reporter. If I'm to do my job, I can't always be concerned with subtleties."

"Of course. But in many ways, you are not like the typical businesswomen I have had the occasion to interact with."

She frowned. "How is that?"

His smiled was sudden and devastating. "I find you much more captivating than most of the women I have met in this country."

She stared at him, not even pretending to be unmoved. "What are you talking about?"

"You have a certain—what is the word? *Lushness* most women I meet lack. They are all too thin and hard." He shook his head. "A woman should be soft, with an abundance of flesh that indicates a generousness of spirit and an appreciation for the physical joys in life."

She let his words wash over her, his velvet voice rounding the syllables and drawing them out until they made her feel every bit as sensuous as he described. Was he saying he was attracted to her because she was *fat?*

Okay, not fat. But not thin. Whereas too many people apparently saw this as a sign of a character defect, he obviously saw this as a plus.

"Are you serious?" she asked. "Or is this some kind of line? Though if it is, you get marks for originality."

He chuckled, a deep rumble that sent heat curling through her middle. "It is no line. I want to have dinner with you."

"Shelly! You've got ten seconds until the intro for your next segment," Armstrong hissed into her earpiece. "Move it!"

"I have to go." She whirled and headed for the anchor desk. Three steps away she froze and turned to face him once more. "I'll have dinner with you," she said. She'd be a fool to pass up the chance to dig deeper into his business *networking,* not to mention that an evening with a sexy guy who thought she was hot would do wonders for her ego.

For the rest of the broadcast, whenever Shelly looked

to her right, she could see the prince waiting behind the cameraman.

"What is he doing?" Jack leaned over and whispered to her while the footage they'd assembled from Denver's sister cities aired.

"I think he's waiting for me." She tried, but failed to hold back a smile.

Jack frowned at her, but before he could continue the conversation it was time to wrap up the show.

When the credits rolled, Shelly stood and collected her notes. "Good night, Jack. I'll see you tomorrow."

"Wait a minute. Where are you going?" He glanced toward the prince. "You're not going out with him, are you?"

The sharp tone of Jack's voice startled her. "He's asked me to dinner."

"Are you sure that's a good idea? You practically accused him of swindling the state, county and federal governments."

"I know." She risked a glance at Jack. He was scowling, his mouth tightened to a thin line. "I thought this would be a good opportunity to try to learn more."

Jack shifted his gaze from Prince Amir to Shelly. "Are you sure that's safe?"

"Why wouldn't it be safe?" She started to laugh, but the real worry in Jack's expression silenced her.

"I don't trust the guy," he said. "I don't like the way he's been staring at you all night. He's up to something."

His concern touched her. She put her hand on his arm. "He's not up to anything. It's just dinner."

He glanced toward the interview chairs. "What did

he say to you over there, after the interview was over? I saw the two of you talking."

"He invited me to have dinner with him."

"Is that all?"

Really, this interrogation was too much. "He said he thought I was very sexy." Maybe it wasn't the most professional thing to say, but it felt so good to repeat the words.

A scarlet flush swept up Jack's neck. "Now I really don't think you should go out with him."

"Why not?" she snapped. Did Jack think it was so far-fetched that another man would find her sexy?

He leaned closer to her. "He's trying to seduce you."

"*Seduce* me?" She struggled to keep her voice low. "Jack, that's ridiculous."

"It is not." He leaned closer still, his gaze intense, searching. "He thinks he can turn on that exotic charm and you'll forget all about his shady dealings. But you're smarter than that."

"Of course I am." But Jack's words had planted the seeds of doubt. Was the prince's flattery merely a smoke screen to distract her? Was she a fool for wanting to believe his praise was heartfelt?

"Are you ready to go?" The velvet voice at her side interrupted the conversation.

She turned to greet Amir. "Yes, I'm ready." She glanced at her coanchor. "Good night, Jack."

"Good night." The words were more of a growl. His irritation might have amused her if she hadn't been so annoyed with him for interfering with what was, after all, her private time. Why shouldn't she accept an invitation from a handsome, charming man? So what if that man might also be a crook? It wasn't as if she was going to start anything serious with him.

A black stretch limousine waited at the curb to whisk them to the side entrance of Tante Louise, Denver's premier French restaurant. They were shown to a private table at the back, where a bottle of wine was immediately presented for the prince's approval. When he nodded, the waiter poured two glasses, then faded into the background while they perused the menus.

"What did your co-worker say to you before we left?" Amir asked after they'd ordered their meals. "He seemed upset about something."

"He wasn't sure it was wise for me to go out with you."

"Oh?" He smiled and spread his napkin in his lap.

"What does that mean—'Oh'?"

He picked up his wineglass. "I think perhaps he is jealous."

She choked back laughter, and had to take several sips of water to regain her composure. "No, I don't think that's it." Jack, who had women all over town waiting in line simply for the chance to talk to him, would not be jealous of a guy showing interest in her.

Amir looked unconvinced. "Then what reason did he give?"

She tried to think of a diplomatic answer. In the end, she settled for the truth. "He accused you of intending to seduce me, in order to distract me from looking further into your business practices."

"And is it possible I could do this?"

She looked at him over the top of her glass, and the

tingle of barely suppressed desire warmed her. "Seduce me, or distract me?"

Perfect white teeth flashed. "Both."

She raised her chin. "I take a great deal of pride in my work. You couldn't distract me."

He leaned toward her, his voice low. "That leaves seduction."

Even if a woman is not particularly interested in her pursuer, there's something to be said for being the object of a well-mannered pursuit, Shelly decided. Having declared his intentions, as it were, Amir devoted his energies to charming her. He flirted and cajoled, complimenting her beauty and her intelligence, and laughing at her jokes. He fed her the strawberries that garnished his dessert, and though she had no intention of going to bed with him, she enjoyed speculating on what sex with him would be like.

Mostly, she basked in the attention, letting the heat of his gaze warm her like a fire. "You are enjoying the evening?" he asked as they lingered over coffee.

"Yes." She added cream to her cup and stirred. "Despite my reservations about your business ethics, you've been very good company."

He arched one eyebrow. "Merely good company? What is the saying you have—damned by faint praise?"

She smiled. "I've enjoyed our dinner and conversation, but I don't see us taking things any further, do you?"

He studied her a long moment, then sighed theatrically. "Then I have failed in my quest to seduce you."

"I'm afraid so."

"Is it that someone else has your affections?"

She shook her head. "I find it better not to mix business with pleasure."

"Ah. You Americans so love to put everything into neat compartments. This way of doing business is good. This other way is bad. Work is for this time with these people, while pleasure is in another box over here." He shook his head. "You try to make life neat and orderly, but of course, it is rarely so."

"Maybe not, but we're used to dealing with things this way."

"And I cannot persuade you to make an exception?" His tone was teasing now, no longer seductive.

She shook her head. "Not tonight."

The limo took them back to the station, where the prince got out and escorted her to her car. "Good night," he said, and kissed her hand. "I am jealous of the man who will win the affections of such a beautiful woman."

"I'll never get tired of hearing you say that."

"I promise I am quite serious. And I am not the only one who thinks so." He looked up, to a single lighted office on the seventh floor. "That is your television station's office, is it not?"

"Yes. That's Jack's office, I think." What was he doing working so late?

Amir nodded. "I think he is waiting up for you. To make sure I have not succeeded in my efforts to seduce you."

She flushed. "It's really none of his concern."

"That never stopped a man who wants a woman, I promise you."

He nodded and left her then. She sat in her car for a

long time after the limo drove away, looking up at the light. Was Jack really waiting on her?

She debated going to see him but resisted the idea. Better to go home with the fantasy that he was concerned about her—that he *wanted* her, as the prince had suggested—than to find out he was merely catching up on paperwork while the office was quiet.

At least this way she could imagine what might be, instead of confirming what would most likely never happen. As far as she could determine, the attraction she felt for Jack was unreturned. He was a devastatingly handsome man, known for dating fabulously beautiful women. Women at least four sizes smaller than her. And even without the added weight, she doubted she was in Jack Halloran's league.

CHAPTER NINE

"TELL ME AGAIN WHY YOU wanted to shop at *this* particular store?" Shelly asked Yvonne as the two women studied a window display featuring a mannequin dressed in a feather-trimmed white satin bustier and sequined thong.

"I thought it might give me a little inspiration," Yvonne said, leading the way into the boutique, which was appropriately named Seductions.

Certainly Shelly was seduced by the display of chiffon gowns on a rack near the door. The lighter-than-air gowns, in sherbet colors, were the kind of thing to make any woman feel more feminine.

"What about this?"

She turned to see Yvonne holding up a fire-engine-red merry widow with ribbon-trimmed garters. "Depends on what you want to be inspired to do."

Yvonne stuck out her tongue and replaced the lingerie on the rack. "Daniel would love it, but I'd feel ridiculous wearing it."

"I doubt if you'd be wearing it for long." Shelly joined her friend in the bra section. "What do you need inspiration for?"

Yvonne glanced at her, then her gaze slid away. "I saw the plastic surgeon last week."

Shelly's stomach constricted. "I didn't know."

"I didn't tell you because I knew you'd be upset." Yvonne's eyes met hers again. "But then I thought, you're my best friend and I ought to be able to tell you anything, right?"

Shelly nodded. "Sure." She wanted to hear about this thing that was so important to her friend—and yet she didn't. "So, how'd it go?"

"It went okay." She reached up to finger a net-and-silk underwire bra. "The doctor was really nice. He explained everything that's involved in the surgery."

"And you were okay with that?"

Yvonne made a face. "The pictures made me kind of queasy. I mean, I know it's safe, and this doctor has done hundreds of these procedures, but still."

"Still, it's hard to be completely calm when it's you going under the knife." Shelly squeezed Yvonne's arm. "You don't have to do this, you know."

Yvonne nodded. "I know. But Daniel's put down the deposit." She replaced the bra on the rack and chose another. "Besides, I really do want to do this. I'm just nervous about the surgery itself. So I thought if I bought something nice in my new size, it would inspire me. You know, give me something to look forward to."

"Maybe." Shelly couldn't hide her doubt.

"It's like when a woman is dieting and she buys a dress in the size she wants to be and hangs it where she'll see it all the time."

"That never worked for me," Shelly said. "It just made me feel worse when I could never fit into the dress."

"But I know I'll be able to fit into my new outfit, after

the surgery." Yvonne held up a peach lace demi-bra. "What do you think of this?"

"It's gorgeous. You'd look gorgeous in it." Shelly turned away, determined not to let her own reservations about this whole thing upset Yvonne. If her friend was determined to do this, then all Shelly could do was support her in her decision, difficult as that might be.

"It's a definite possibility. What about you? Do you see anything you like?"

"I don't know." She turned and came face-to-face with a mannequin who wore a royal-blue camisole and tap pants with lace inserts.

"That would look gorgeous on you," Yvonne said. "You should try it on."

"I don't know. I don't really need any lingerie." Shelly didn't own anything this fancy—or this revealing. She favored clothes that covered up more, but maybe she *should* show off more. After all, she was a beautiful woman. Prince Amir certainly thought so.

"One doesn't buy an outfit like this because one needs it in a practical sense." An older woman in a chic black pantsuit and a name tag that identified her as Rochelle, approached. "One buys something like this in order to pamper one's inner woman. Or to impress a special man." She gave them a knowing look.

Why did Shelly immediately think of Jack? She pushed the image away. Her *boss* was never going to see her in anything like this. Yes, their relationship was more that of equals than employee and employer, but technically, he was the one who had hired her and she couldn't afford to forget that.

Besides, in the week since Prince Amir had speculated on the reasons for Jack's waiting up for her, Jack had been nothing but businesslike.

"Go on, try it on," Yvonne urged.

"This outfit was made for a woman with curves like yours," the salesclerk said. She visually sized up Shelly, then selected an outfit from the rack. "You should try it."

"All right, I will." In the dressing room, she stripped and slipped into the new outfit. The satin was cool against her skin, draping softly. Nerves humming with excitement, she turned to look at her reflection.

The salesclerk was right. The cut of the outfit accented all her pluses and camouflaged the minuses.

Or maybe that was the lingering aftereffects of her evening with Prince Amir. The man's raving about her *lush* beauty had definitely done wonders for her self-image.

Someone knocked on the dressing room door. "Let me see," Yvonne said.

Shelly opened the door. "What do you think?"

"I think it's gorgeous. Are you going to get it?"

She nodded. Why not? She never knew when she might meet another man who'd appreciate her curves.

"What are you smiling about?" Yvonne asked when Shelly emerged from the dressing room a few minutes later.

"I like the outfit. Why wouldn't I smile?"

"Yeah, but this isn't an I-like-the-outfit smile. This is more...I don't know...smug. Like you have a secret."

She laughed. "No secret. I was just thinking about a man I went out with the other night."

"A new man?" Yvonne squealed. "You've been holding out on me, girlfriend."

"I haven't really talked to you much since then. Besides, it wasn't a date, really."

"Then what was it? Who was he?" She grabbed Shelly's arm. "I want details if he makes you smile like that."

"I had dinner after the show with that Saudi Arabian prince I interviewed."

"Get out! Dinner with a prince? I only caught part of the interview, but I seem to remember he was pretty good-looking."

"He was." She shrugged. "But not my type."

"Still, dinner with royalty must have been a kick."

"It was. He was very charming." She followed Yvonne to the front counter, where she paid for the blue outfit while Yvonne purchased two bras and matching panties.

"Where did the prince take you for dinner?" Yvonne asked as she and Shelly left the store.

"Tante Louise. In a limo."

"Wow—I've only been there once. Very chichi. And a limo." She elbowed Shelly in the side. "Are you sure he's not your type? A woman could get used to treatment like that."

Shelly shook her head. "He's really not my type. But he was good for my ego. He was very complimentary."

"I'm glad. Do you think you'll see him again?"

"I doubt it. Last I heard, he was on his way back to Saudi Arabia. Now that I've raised the red flag over some of his real estate deals I imagine he'll stay there awhile."

"Talk about your job ruining your love life."

"Yeah, I guess so." She spotted a coffee shop up ahead. "I could go for a latte about now."

"You're reading my mind."

The women stopped and ordered lattes, then took them to a table looking out onto the mall. "Speaking of work, how's the news-magazine biz going?" Yvonne asked.

"Great. The response seems to be good so far. It's tons of work, but I'm loving all of it. Even the drudge stuff." She stirred a packet of sugar into her coffee. "Right now I'm working on a really interesting story, about health care for people with no insurance."

"That's why you're the reporter and I'm not. I wouldn't know where to begin working on a story like that."

"So how are things down at the mayor's office?"

"Okay. I'm trying to figure out how to break it to my supervisor that I need to take time off for this surgery— and then another two weeks for the wedding and honeymoon. She's not going to be happy."

"How long will you have to take off for the surgery?"

"I'm hoping to get by with a long weekend. It just depends on how things go. And I don't want to tell her why I want the time off, so I'm going to tell her I have some family business to see to."

"Yvonne! Don't you think people will notice your, uh, transformation when you return?"

"Well, yeah. To tell you the truth, I'll probably be disappointed if they *don't* notice. I just don't want them talking about me while I'm out for the surgery."

"Okay. I guess I can see that." God knows she'd suffered enough snide remarks of her own from office gossips at *First for News*. Why had it taken her so long to leave that place?

"Is Jack as nice as he seems on the air?"

"Yeah." She smiled, thinking of her co-anchor. "I feel so lucky working with him."

"Nice and handsome. I still think you ought to go after him."

She shook her head. "I can't date somebody I work with."

"Why not?"

"What happens if it doesn't work out? This is Jack's show. Who do you think is going to be out the door?"

"Yeah, there is that. But what if it does work out? What if he's *the one?*"

"Yvonne, I'm thirty-one years old. I don't believe that, with all the men in the world, there is one out there with my name on him. I mean, come on."

"Then what do you believe? If some people aren't destined for each other, how do you explain true love?"

"I don't think it's destiny, if that's what you're asking. I think it's more a matter of two people being attracted to each other, finding out they're compatible, their feelings for each other growing until they decide to make a go of it. Some of them are successful, some of them aren't."

"So you don't think you and Jack could be successful as a couple?"

"Maybe we could. But I don't think it's worth risking my dream job to try. I'm not at the point in my life right now where the relationship stuff is so important, anyway."

"I don't know what you're waiting on."

Shelly sent Yvonne a warning look.

"Okay, okay." Yvonne tossed her coffee cup toward the trash can. "I know you're very happy being single. But you shouldn't rule out the possibility that you *could* find a man you'd be even happier with. And it's not unreasonable that that man would be someone you work with."

"Not Jack. He and I are just friends."

"You said yourself, that's how it starts."

"What is this? When you got that diamond on your finger did it automatically send you into matchmaking mode?"

"All right. I'll shut up. But I'd like to see you find somebody to wear that gorgeous lingerie for."

"I'll wear it for myself." But even as Shelly said the words she felt a little hollow inside. She hadn't lied to Yvonne. Most of the time she was content to be single and focused on her job.

But sometimes, she had to admit, it would be nice to have someone to share her life with. She wasn't desperate, but maybe Yvonne was right. Maybe Shelly ought to be more open to letting a man into her life.

Not Jack. He was still off-limits. But maybe there was another man out there like him—smart and funny and genuinely nice.

It wouldn't hurt if he looked like Jack, either, but that was probably asking too much. A man like that didn't come along every day.

"Now that people are starting to talk about the show, we need to do a promotions push to really fix it in the public's mind." Armstrong sat across from Jack's desk and pulled out his PDA. "I'm talking billboards and print ads, as well as PBS promo spots."

"Sounds great." Jack sat back and steepled his fingers together. "What do you have in mind?"

"Exactly what I've had in mind from the beginning. We need to feature you as someone our viewers can relate to. I figure we can do a whole series of spots, with you hiking, biking, skiing, maybe climbing up the side of a cliff—you know, show you as an active, on-top-of-things guy."

"No." Jack sat forward, palms flat on the desk. It was either that, or attempt to slap some sense into his producer, who obviously hadn't paid attention to a thing Jack had said the half-dozen other times they'd discussed this issue. "That's not the approach I want to take."

"I know it's not, but that doesn't change my opinion that it's the one we should take. You hired me to do the best job I know how to do with this show, not to go along with everything you say."

Jack inhaled a deep breath. "You're right. But we're never going to agree on this one. And I fail to see how this kind of advertising will do our reputation any good in the long run."

"That's because you don't pay attention to public opinion the way I do. I've read everything anybody has written about *Inside Story,* including postings on Internet news groups and comments from callers to radio talk shows. And the one thing everyone mentions, sooner or later—the thing people talk about the most—is you. Your personality. Your looks. Your sense of humor." He consulted his PDA. "You even have a fan club online. FansofJackHalloran.com."

Jack groaned. The fan club wasn't new—it had sprung up while he was in Dallas. But he'd hoped his move to more *serious* work would silence the groupies. "Don't these people have lives? What normal person obsesses over a *stranger* like this?"

"You're not a stranger to these people. You're in their living rooms every week. They feel as if they know you, even if they don't. Which brings me back to my point. If you're what's drawing people to the show, then we should play to that. We should give people what they want."

He shook his head. "*Inside Story* is not about me. It's about the news we report. The stories we focus on. And what about Shelly?"

Armstrong checked his notes again. "She has her fans, too, though not all of the comments about her are complimentary. A lot of people think she should lose weight."

"Oh, they do?" Jack clenched his fingers into fists. "Tell me, do any of these people say anything about the content of the show—the news we report?"

"Oh, yeah. People are interested in that, too. And a lot of people are paying attention. After Shelly's interview with Prince Amir, the governor appointed a special commission to take a closer look at all the state's dealings with Amir."

"That's what we should focus on—the fact that we report on stories that make a difference." He leaned toward Armstrong. "Shelly and I were talking a while back and she said something I think should be our slogan—something we should use in all our promos."

"What is that?" Armstrong looked skeptical.

"'Not what you'd expect.' *Inside Story* is not what you'd expect from a news show. We're different and that's what we should be selling people. Not beefcake photos of me."

Armstrong frowned. "I'm not saying I don't like it, but it's not something people are going to remember.

Not without your picture in the ads, too. Like it or not, people do judge by appearances. They like how you look and they've already linked you with the show. If we ignore that, we're wasting our advertising efforts."

"Then maybe we shouldn't advertise at all. Not if we want to avoid sending the wrong message."

"You know what your problem is?"

"No, but I have a feeling you're about to tell me."

"Your problem is that you can't embrace the gift you have and use it to your advantage. Instead of accepting that you lucked out in the looks department you act like it's some horrible curse." Armstrong shook his finger at Jack. "You could be using your popularity to get people's attention, after which you could send any message you want. Instead, you'd rather ignore your best asset."

"I think my best asset is being smart enough not to rely on my looks for everything."

"You might add stubbornness to the list, too." Armstrong stood. "I'll work up something with the 'not what you expect' slogan, but I think you should reconsider doing at least some spots with a little more personality. People relate to other people, and the evidence clearly shows our viewers relate to you."

"I'm not the only stubborn person in this office, am I?"

Armstrong smiled. "I have to be to keep up with you. Between you and Shelly, I get no peace."

"And that's the way we like it."

Armstrong left, and Jack turned his attention once more to his computer. He was supposed to be working on the script for a segment on steroid use among high school athletes, but Armstrong's mention of Shelly had distracted him.

He hadn't worked up the nerve to ask her about her date with the prince, but he couldn't help noticing what a good mood she'd been in ever since. She'd practically strutted into work the next day, and he'd heard her humming to herself several times when he passed her office.

If a male co-worker had been acting this way, he would have assumed he'd gotten laid. And maybe that was the case with Shelly, though he shied away from the thought. The humming worried him. Had she actually fallen for the smooth sheikh? He'd believed she was too smart to be taken in by bedroom eyes and foreign charm, but how well did he know her, anyway?

He knew she was smart and hardworking, with a good sense of humor. That she was ambitious. Unattached. (At least she'd never mentioned a steady boyfriend, and there were no pictures on her desk.) She normally had a cheerful disposition, but people could fake that, especially on the job where things moved at a hectic pace.

So what was Shelly Piper *really* like? He was tempted to put his investigative skills to use finding out, but rejected the notion. Shelly's personal life was really none of his concern and he had no business trying to change that.

OVER DINNER AT YVONNE'S apartment a few days after her lingerie-buying expedition, Daniel asked the question she'd been dreading. "Did you call the doctor and schedule your surgery yet?"

"Not yet." She pushed the last dressing-soaked bits of lettuce around her salad plate and avoided looking at him. "I have to figure out the best time to take off work.

My supervisor isn't going to be happy about it, with all the time I've already taken for wedding preparations, plus the vacation I've scheduled for the honeymoon."

"Who cares what she thinks? You've got plenty of comp time saved up, don't you?"

"Yes."

"Then what's the problem?" He pointed his fork at her. "You're not going to back out of this, are you?"

Anger tightened her throat in response to the sharpness of his words. She reached for her wineglass and took a big drink, trying to calm herself before she spoke. "What if I did? What if I decided I couldn't go through with it?"

His knife and fork clattered against his plate as he laid them aside. She looked up and found him watching her—studying her, really, as if trying to decide which answer would be most effective. "I'd be disappointed," he said at last.

"Disappointed that I didn't have big boobs?" She pushed the words past the constriction in her throat.

"Disappointed that you didn't love me enough to do this for me. To do this for *us*."

The words were a well-aimed dart, deflating her attempt at defiance. "Of course I love you," she protested. "And I want to do this. I'm going to do it." She looked down at her plate, fiddling with her silverware. "It's just scary, you know?"

His chair scraped against the floor, and the next thing she knew, he was standing over her, his hand on her shoulder. "I know. But I'll be right there with you. You'll do great."

He bent and kissed her, then took her by the shoulders and pulled her out of the chair, into his arms. The kiss quickly turned from gentle to ardent, tongue probing, hands squeezing. "I swear, I get so turned on just *thinking* about how you'll look after the surgery." He pressed against her, letting her feel how turned on he was. He slid his hand down her back to cup her bottom. "You're a gorgeous woman, you know that?" he whispered. "And you're going to be even more gorgeous."

His eagerness was contagious. Within seconds she was on fire for him, arching her back, her breasts pressed tightly against his chest.

"You're a wild woman, aren't you?" He nipped at her earlobe as he hiked her skirt above her hips. "You just can't get enough of me, can you, baby?"

"No, I can't. I want you." She clawed at his shirt buttons. "I want you now."

The sound of dishes crashing to the floor startled her. She turned to look, but he forced her mouth back to his. "Don't worry about it," he said. "I'll buy you new ones." Then he picked her up and laid her on the table, where they'd been eating dinner only moments before. He pushed her skirt up farther and tore off her panties, while she finally succeeded in ripping open his shirt.

"That's it, show me how much you want it." He shoved down his pants and grabbed her knees, pushing her legs apart. "Tell me you're ready for your dessert."

"I'm ready, baby, I'm ready for you." She was panting, half wild with desire.

He drove into her hard, and she wrapped her legs around his hips, urging him deeper and faster. He caressed her breasts, and pinched at her nipples, making love to her with words as well as his body. "That's it, baby. I'm the only one for you. The only man who can make you feel this way. You like it hard, don't you? You like it a little rough, sometimes. Hard and deep and quick, isn't that right?"

"That's right, baby," she gasped. "You know just how I like it." Some part of her was aware that the table was cold and hard against her back, and that the inside of her thighs ached from being stretched around him. But that was all in the background, underneath the need that drove her past the discomfort, reaching toward the incredible release that was almost there.

He came first, with a groan that she matched, though hers was more one of disappointment. She was half afraid that now that he was satisfied, he wouldn't go on long enough for her to join him. "Don't stop!" she panted. "Please don't stop."

He raised his head and grinned at her. "I won't stop. You're almost there, aren't you?" Without waiting for an answer, he reached down and ran his thumb over her clit, pressing down hard, then dragging back up to repeat the move.

She thrust hard against him, a keening cry accompanying the climax that shuddered through her. She was dimly aware of him laughing. "I knew I could do it for you," he said. "I knew it."

He pulled away and helped her off the table, then she tottered to the bathroom to clean up. It had been a long time since their lovemaking had been that intense. Did she have her upcoming surgery to thank for that? She smiled to herself as she dried her hands, then went to find a broom to sweep up the broken dishes. Monday morning, she'd schedule time off with her supervisor.

Then she'd call the doctor. After all, what were a few moments of pain compared to a lifetime with a husband who would love her the way she'd just been loved?

CHAPTER TEN

SHELLY WAS USED TO DEALING with interview subjects who were nervous in front of the camera. In her time as a reporter she'd also dealt with her share of angry people. A few times she'd even been in the unenviable position of questioning people while they were in the throes of grief.

But the woman across from her now was harder to read. Michelle Dickson sat on the worn-out sofa in her apartment with her arms folded across her chest, lips pinched in a tight line. Combined with her shaved head and the multiple tattoos on her bare arms and legs, the posture gave her a fearsome look.

Except that her right foot jittered constantly against the floor, next to the toddler who played with a pile of plastic blocks, oblivious to his mother's distress. When Michelle reached for another cigarette her fingers shook so hard she could barely get the cig out of the pack. And her eyes—expressive brown eyes heavily lined in kohl—shimmered with unshed tears when she finally looked at Shelly. "I don't know if I can do this," she said.

"You can do it. Take all the time you need. If you want to stop and take a break at any time, we can do that, too." Shelly tried to make her voice as calming as possible. Her source at the hospital had told her Michelle might be a difficult subject, but once she'd heard a little of the woman's story, Shelly knew she had to have it for the segment on public hospitals.

Michelle worried her lower lip between her teeth. "How do I know you won't make me look stupid?"

Shelly paused, considering her answer. A simple denial probably wouldn't work with someone like Michelle. "You don't look stupid to me," she said at last.

"Yeah, but I know people can do anything with cameras and computers. You can take the stuff I say and twist it around to mean what you want."

Shelly nodded. "That's not what this story is about. You're just going to have to trust me on this."

Michelle's eyes narrowed. "Why should I trust you? I don't even know you."

"That's true." She glanced down at the little boy, Trevor, on the floor. "But sometimes you just have to do something because it's important to let others know what happened." She met Michelle's cold gaze again. "I can't promise this will make any difference to you or anyone else. But it might."

Michelle took her time digesting this information, her expression unchanging as she sucked hard on the cigarette, the end glowing like the red light on the camera opposite. Finally she flicked ashes into the cracked saucer that served as her ashtray and nodded. "Okay. I'll do it."

Shelly let out a deep breath and felt the tension ease out of her spine. She glanced at the cameraperson, Bess, and nodded, the signal to begin filming. She looked toward Michelle. "Tell me, in your own words, what happened at the hospital, and afterward."

Michelle sat up straight and looked right at the camera, unblinking. "First thing, you see how my head is shaved. And back here is this big scar." She tipped her head forward so the camera could catch the jagged half moon across the back of her head. "That's because I had this tumor, and they had to do surgery to cut it out." She straightened. "That's really the end of the story, but I wanted to say it first so you won't think I'm some kind of freak, walking around with a shaved head."

She glanced at Shelly, who nodded encouragingly.

"I used to have really pretty hair." Michelle reached up and touched her scalp, where a thin shadow of bristles was starting to appear. "It was long—almost to my waist. People used to always compliment me on my hair."

She looked away from the camera and reached for another cigarette, hands shaking as she struggled to get it lit. She inhaled deeply and blew the smoke in twin streams out her nose. Shelly waited, praying she wouldn't stop talking now.

"Okay, so here's the thing." Michelle's voice was stronger now. "About three months ago, I started having these headaches. Really bad headaches, like somebody was driving an ice pick right into my brain. I tried aspirin and everything like that, but nothing would get rid of the pain, and it got worse.

"So one Friday night, I couldn't stand it anymore. It got so bad I was scared. I mean, your head isn't supposed to hurt that bad, is it?" She addressed her question to the camera, then her gaze shifted to the child at her feet. "I didn't have anybody to watch Trevor, so I took him with me to the emergency room over at Mercy Medical. When I got there, I told them what was wrong, that I was hurting really bad. The nurse looked me up and down and told me to have a seat, I'd have to wait."

She paused and took a shuddering breath, clenching and unclenching her left hand. "I waited a long time. Like three hours. Trevor was cranky 'cause it was way past his bedtime and other people in there were giving me dirty looks, like I was some kind of child abuser or something. I finally went up to the woman at the desk and got in her face. I told her I had to see a doctor right then, that I was hurting really bad and I knew something was really wrong.

"She got all huffy and told me to take a seat, but in a few minutes another nurse came and got me and a few minutes after that, this doctor came in. I started to tell him what was wrong, but he told me to be quiet while he examined me. He looked in my eyes and listened to my heart and stuff and then he told me he didn't see anything wrong, that 'in his opinion' I was only there looking for drugs and he wasn't going to prescribe me anything."

Her voice broke and she pressed the heels of her hands over her eyes. "I'm sorry," she whispered.

"It's okay." Shelly got up to look for tissues. Finding none, she went into the bathroom and tore off a long strip of toilet paper and passed it to Michelle, who scrubbed at her eyes and nose with it, then looked at the camera again. "It's just hard to remember that part. That doctor looked at me like…like I was something he'd scrape off his shoe. Like I wasn't *human*."

She held her hands out to her side. "I guess he saw this fat white girl with all these tattoos, and a half-black baby, and he thinks that means I'm a drug addict. That

I couldn't really be sick and hurting like I said." She looked away. "I cried. I begged him to help me and he told me I had to leave." She swallowed hard. "I think if it hadn't been for Trevor, I could have laid down right there and died."

For the next minute, the only sounds in the room were Michelle's sniffling, the soft whir of the camera and Trevor's babbling as he played with his blocks. When Michelle looked more composed, Shelly asked, "What happened next?"

Michelle shook her head. "That night was bad. I couldn't sleep, the pain was so bad. I paced all night. I was worried I was going to die and Trevor would be there all by himself, so I called his father, who was supposed to come see him the next day, anyway, and asked if he could come over early, that I was sick.

"I don't remember much after I hung up the phone. Darnel says when he got there, he had to get Trevor to open the door. My baby was crying and carrying on. When Darnel got inside, he found me in the bathroom, passed out. He thought at first I was dead, but when he felt I was breathing, he called an ambulance. They took me back to the hospital, where they found out I had this tumor, and did emergency surgery to take it out.

"The doctor who saw me—not the one I'd talked to the night before—told me I was lucky to be alive. He said that tumor could have killed me, and why didn't I get to the doctor sooner. When I told him what happened at the emergency room, he didn't say anything else."

"Do you think if you had looked different, the doctor would have treated you differently?" Shelly asked.

"Yeah. I think if I'd looked more, I don't know, *re-*

spectable, or if I'd had money to pay or insurance, then he might have spent more time trying to find out what was going on."

Her face crumpled again. "I could have *died*. My baby wouldn't have had a mother anymore." She shook her head, tears spilling down her face. "All because that doctor took one look at me and made up his mind about who I was and why I was there."

Shelly struggled to retain her own composure. "I'm so sorry you had to go through this," she said. "But maybe when others hear about this, things can change."

Michelle shrugged. "I don't know. I guess I don't have much faith in that." She bent and picked up Trevor and held him in her lap, cuddling him to her. "The worst thing isn't even having to shave off my hair and have the surgery and all that pain. The worst thing is the way that doctor made me feel. That's a scar inside of me that won't heal for a long time, I think. Maybe never."

Shelly and Bess left soon after, down three flights of dimly lit stairs to the narrow side street below. Neither woman said anything on the walk back to the news van. At the van, Bess blew out a breath as she loaded the camera in the back. "That was pretty intense," she said.

Shelly nodded. "Yeah. Can you imagine going through something like that?"

Bess shook her head. "You know what the worst part is?"

"What?"

Bess looked away, tight lines fanning out from her mouth. "When we first walked into that apartment and I saw her sitting there, *I* started judging her, too. I mean, the tattoos, the shaved head, the public housing, the baby with no father around—every stereotype I'd ever heard was running through my head." She heaved herself into the driver's seat of the van. "Doesn't make me very proud of myself, I tell you."

Shelly nodded. "I know. We all do it, though. I just hope I never do it to the extent that doctor did."

"You wouldn't. You have too much compassion for that." She started the van. "Just don't let that soft heart of yours get you into trouble. You can't solve the world's problems, you know."

"Maybe not. But is it so bad to want to solve a few?"

Back at the station, the women went their separate ways. Shelly retreated to her office, intending to write the script for this portion of the story while the interview was still fresh in her mind. She was scarcely in the door when her phone rang. "Hello?"

"Shelly, this is Yvonne. I wanted you to be the first to know."

"The first to know what?"

"I've scheduled my surgery. It's going to be March 14. I'll go in Friday morning and come home Sunday."

Shelly squeezed her eyes shut and pinched at the bridge of her nose, fighting tears. Why was Yvonne doing this?

"Shelly, are you still there?"

"Yeah…yeah, I'm still here. I—I don't know what to say."

"I know you're worried, but it's going to be all right. I'm looking forward to this."

She nodded, even though Yvonne couldn't see her. Right. Yvonne was the one having the surgery, so her opinion was the only one that mattered. "Good luck. I hope everything goes smoothly for you and things turn out just like you want."

"Thanks. I have to go now and call Daniel. Can you believe I haven't even told him yet? He's going to be so excited."

"Yeah." But Yvonne had already hung up the phone.

Shelly laid the receiver on the cradle and stared at her blank computer screen, sadness dragging at her like an anchor. She'd spent the afternoon with a woman who had almost died because she couldn't convince a doctor there was something really wrong with her. And now her best friend was having a completely unnecessary surgery—mutilating herself, even—for the sake of vanity, or to please some man who didn't appreciate how special she was just the way she was.

Michelle hadn't been good enough for the doctors to listen to. Yvonne wasn't good enough for Danny or, apparently, for herself. Did that mean Shelly was fooling herself, thinking she was good enough, despite her own imperfections?

It hurt too much to think about. All she knew to do was to lay her head down on her desk and sob.

JACK HAD SPENT ALL DAY following leads for a planned segment on industrial polluters. He'd been up since 5:00 a.m., having agreed to meet an anonymous whistle-blower at a Waffle House off Interstate 25, and had spent the rest of the day hiking along creek banks and slogging through wetland bogs, getting footage of illegal discharges and environmental damage. There'd been no time for lunch other than a petrified PowerBar from an emergency stash he kept in the glove compartment of his Jeep. He'd ripped his shirtsleeve on a barbed-wire fence and wrenched his ankle climbing down a river embankment. By six o'clock that evening the adrenaline rush of following a big story was beginning to fade, replaced by bone-deep weariness.

When he stopped by the office to check his messages, his focus was on clearing out of there as soon as possible. A hot shower, a stiff drink and a substantial meal beckoned. But on his way out, he heard a muffled noise that stopped him in his tracks. He froze and listened more closely. Was that someone moaning? Someone hurt?

Heart in his throat, he followed the noise to Shelly's office. The door was half-open, but he couldn't see her from here. He hesitated, then knocked on the wall beside the door. "Shelly? Everything okay?"

More scuffling, then her voice, higher-pitched than normal. "I'm fine. Just finishing up some things."

Something in her voice bothered him. He knew he wouldn't be comfortable until he saw that she was all right. He pushed the door open and stepped inside.

She looked up at him, startled. Her makeup was smeared and her eyes red. She clutched a soggy tissue in her hand. He caught his breath and stepped back, uncertain what to do. He didn't know for sure, but he'd always had the sense that Shelly wasn't a crier. She wasn't one of those women whose major emotional response was tears.

So to find her so obviously upset unnerved him. His first instinct was to run as fast and as far from the sound as his aching legs would take him.

But as soon as the thought formed, another part of his brain screamed, "Coward!" Shelly was distraught over something. As her boss and co-worker he should stay and find out what that something was.

"Wh-what's wrong?" he stammered.

"Nothing." She swiveled her chair away from him and scrubbed furiously at her eyes with the mangled scrap of tissue.

He walked over to her desk. "Here, use this." He offered his handkerchief.

She hesitated, then took it. "Thanks," she whispered.

He put his hands behind his back and looked up toward the ceiling, anywhere but at her. "Want to talk about whatever has you so upset?"

She shook her head. "I didn't mean for you to hear. I can't believe...I thought I was alone." She repeatedly wiped her eyes, smearing black mascara across the white linen.

He sat on the corner of the desk, striking a casual pose, though what he really wanted was to gather her into his arms and comfort her. Better not go there. He was too aware of the fact that once he held her, he might not want to let go. "What happened?"

"Nothing."

"You don't have to tell you if you don't want to, but I don't believe you're the type to cry over nothing."

"It's stupid." She sniffed. "I mean, I know I shouldn't get so caught up in the stories I'm working on."

He searched his mind. What had she been working on this afternoon? "You had an interview this afternoon for your hospital piece, didn't you?"

She nodded. "Michelle Dickson. A young mother who almost died from a brain tumor because when she went to the emergency room the doctor assumed she was trying to scam pain pills." She sniffed again and gave him a weak smile. "Honestly, I don't know why her story upset me so much. It had a good ending. She got the surgery she needed and she's going to be all right."

"Obviously you felt a lot of empathy for her." It was one of the things that touched him about Shelly—her ability to feel what the people she wrote about felt. That came out in her stories.

She nodded. "I guess I did. She said…she said the doctor made her feel like she wasn't human. That if she'd been someone different, someone prettier or more conventional, things would have turned out differently. I guess…" She looked away, biting her lip.

"You guess what?" He leaned toward her, curious as to what she would say.

"I guess— It's just that I've felt that way, too. On a smaller scale. I know that feeling that if I'd just been someone different, someone thinner or more willing to do what it takes to get there, then I'd have gone further in my career. That I'd have gotten more respect." Her gaze shifted to him again and the stricken look returned to her eyes. "Oh, God, I can't believe I just said that. To you of all people."

"Why not to me?" It wounded him to think she felt she couldn't confide in him. As if she didn't trust him.

"This is my office. I'm supposed to be a professional." Her gaze shifted around the room, as if she hoped for some escape.

"I don't recall any requirement that you leave your humanity at the front door."

"Still, I don't like looking such a mess in front of my boss."

His heart twisted again at the words. Was that all he was to her? An authority figure who would judge her by how well she maintained a "professional" demeanor? He dropped his chin to his chest, thinking. "I am your boss," he said. "But I hope I'm also your friend."

She looked at him, eyes ringed with smudged mascara, lashes wet with tears, cheeks flushed; she was indeed a mess, but her very vulnerability touched him.

"All right," she said. "Do you want to know what's really bothering me?"

"I do."

She cradled the knuckles of one hand in the palm of the other and contemplated them for a moment, then said, "My best friend in the whole world is marrying a man I don't think is good enough for her. But I told myself if he made her happy, that's all that mattered, so I didn't say anything."

"That's wise."

"Well, to be honest, I *have* said a few things. Nothing *too* harsh. But now this man has decided she isn't good enough the way she is—that she'd be better off with bigger breasts. So he's paying for a boob job and she's going along with it—as if major surgery is just another part of the wedding preparations, like picking out a caterer or going for a fitting for her wedding gown."

"Ouch."

Her eyes met his, the hurt reflected there painful to him. He told himself he'd feel the same for any friend who was suffering, but would he feel it to this degree?

"Maybe I'm making too much of this, but it tears me

up inside to know that this sweet, wonderful woman thinks she has to remake herself in order to hang on to this man—as if she isn't good enough without him to validate her." She swallowed convulsively, her voice growing wavery. "What does that say about the rest of us imperfect slobs?"

She shook her head and squinted up her eyes, as if trying to squeeze back a flood. But tears leaked around her clenched eyelids and glittered on her lashes before sliding down her ravaged face. She was absolutely still, and mute.

Those silent tears were his undoing. He moved around the desk and gathered her into his arms, cradling her head on his shoulder, smoothing her hair. He wanted to tell her imperfections didn't matter, that they were what made people interesting. He wanted to tell her how working with her, seeing her almost every day, had become the high point of his life.

But he didn't tell her any of this. He merely held her, his arms tightly around her, relishing her warmth and the feel of her soft curves pressed against his body, only a twinge of guilt mitigating the pleasure.

"I promise I'm not usually like this." She sniffed and inhaled a shuddering breath. "I'm not one of those women who cries at the drop of a hat."

"Maybe you just needed to let go. Everyone needs a release sometimes."

She blotted her eyes with the now-sodden handkerchief and glanced at him. "So what's your release?"

He furrowed his brow, trying to think. "I play racquetball."

"Racquetball?"

He nodded. "There's nothing like whacking the hell out of the ball for an hour or so to get rid of a lot of negative emotion."

"It figures a guy would go for sports." She sighed. "Women cry, or eat. Or both." Her eyes met his again. "I never met a problem fudge brownies couldn't make a little easier to handle."

He smiled and reached up to wipe a smudge of mascara from her cheek. She had the softest skin. When she returned the smile, his attention shifted to her mouth. Her lips looked soft, too. Full and slightly moist and oh, so tempting.

Her lashes fluttered closed and she leaned toward him in silent invitation. His response was as natural as breathing, instinct and need overruling reason as he bent to kiss her.

She was as soft and yielding as he'd imagined, as responsive as he'd hoped, tilting her head to press her lips more firmly to his, her body arching toward him. With a sigh that was half moan, he gathered her closer and coaxed her lips apart. Her tongue swept across his teeth, sweet and enticing. The desire he'd been holding back for weeks now hit him like a wave breaking over a dam, almost overwhelming in its intensity. He smoothed his hand down her back, then her side, tracing the curve of her breast as she pressed against his hand, all the while keeping his lips locked to hers, making love to her mouth the way he wanted to make love to the rest of her. All the fantasies he'd allowed himself in private moments rushed through his mind as possibilities for later tonight.

But for now, there was this kiss, this incredible, dizzying meeting of mouths, a communication beyond words that touched him at the core. It might be all wrong, but he was too far gone to care.

The ringing of the phone in the office next door was like an alarm bell, breaking the spell and sending them both reeling back. They stared at each other, like two strangers who've awakened in bed together, awkward and unsure.

She was the first to pull away, and he reluctantly released her. "Oh, my." She covered her mouth with her hand and turned her head.

"Yeah." He looked down at his hands, unnerved to find them shaking. He leaned back against the desk and shoved them into his pockets. Did she think he was a real jerk now, taking advantage of her when she was vulnerable? "Look, I didn't mean—"

"I know." She nodded. "It's okay." She managed a shaky smile. "You certainly know how to take a woman's mind off her problems."

Was that what she thought? That he'd kissed her merely as a way of distracting her? "Shelly, I—"

"It's okay. I'm fine now." She jumped up, the chair rolling back until it came to rest against the credenza behind her. "I'd better go."

"Are you sure you're okay?" He straightened. "Let me walk you to your car."

"No, I'm fine. Thank you. Really." Both words and movements were jerky as she took her purse from the desk drawer and slung it over her shoulder. "I'm sorry. I really have to go."

"All right. Be careful." Why was she apologizing? He was the one who ought to say something, to explain what had just happened.

But he couldn't find words that made sense. He could only nod dumbly and watch her leave, her heels thumping hard on the carpet as she hurried toward the elevators.

When he heard the elevator doors open and shut again, he sank into the chair she'd vacated, conscious of her warmth still lingering there, the way the taste of her remained on his tongue, the feel of her imprinted on his fingertips. He was shaky and sick to his stomach, like someone coming down from an adrenaline rush. God, what had he been thinking? She'd confided in him as a friend and he'd turned it into a blatantly sexual encounter.

Never mind that she'd responded, too. She'd been vulnerable and he'd taken advantage of it. He was her *boss,* dammit! He was supposed to know better.

Tomorrow, he'd apologize. And he'd keep his distance to allow his feelings for her to cool off a little. Although judging by the intensity of their kiss, that might take a while.

A long while.

CHAPTER ELEVEN

SHELLY DIDN'T KNOW whether to shout for joy or moan with embarrassment. Yes, her dream man had kissed her, and that was great. But it had happened in her office, after she'd sobbed all over his shirt and bared her soul and proved without a doubt that she was capable of amazingly unprofessional behavior.

And then she'd made matters worse by making that crack about him knowing how to distract her. As if the whole episode were nothing more than a joke.

If the scene had taken place in a bar or an apartment, or even a parked car, the outcome might have been different, but because it happened at work—at her *desk,* no less—she saw it in a different light. Jack was her boss. What had she been thinking?

And what had *he* been thinking? That had been some kiss, after all—a toe-tingling, mind-blowing, lay-me-across-the-desk-and-take-me-now kiss. Was it a sympathy peck on the lips that had gotten out of hand, or a case of hormones taking over? Testosterone meets estrogen and tells the brain cells to take a hike.

Or had they both been acting on something that was already there between them? Could it be that Jack felt this…this *tension* between them, too?

And now that they'd finally acted on those feelings, she'd been a big coward and run away.

Okay, maybe she was taking things too far. Driving home, she tried to look at the moment objectively, to remember *exactly* what had happened. One minute she'd been wiping her nose with Jack's monogrammed hankie and the next minute they'd been going at it like two teenagers in the backseat of a Chevy. It was the stuff in between that was fuzzy, wiped out by the memory of Jack's lips on hers, his hand pressed to her breast, the scrape of his five o'clock shadow against her jaw.

As a result, she didn't remember driving home, either. She had the sensation of floating up the walk to her apartment and into the kitchen.

When she finally snapped out of her daze, she was standing in front of the freezer, eating cookie-dough ice cream right out of the carton with a large spoon.

"Why aren't carrot sticks a comfort food?" she groused as she snapped the lid on the ice cream and shoved it in the freezer.

She stared at the phone, wishing she could call Yvonne and vent to her. But Yvonne was probably with Daniel, celebrating her upcoming transformation. Yvonne was gaining a husband and two new breasts, while Shelly felt as though her best friend was slipping away from her.

"Gee, why don't you just talk yourself into a full-blown depression?" she said out loud. "Then you can really wallow." Her voice boomed in the overly silent rooms. She covered her face with her hands. It was probably a bad sign when you started talking to yourself—and listening for an answer back.

She sighed and lowered her hands. Unfortunately, she was facing a mirror, and the woman who stared back at her looked like a refugee from a Kiss concert. With the kind of horrid fascination usually reserved for grisly automobile accidents, she studied the mascara smudged under her eyes and streaked down her cheeks, and the wild mane that had once been a respectable hairdo. How could Jack have kissed this? Was the man crazy?

Shuddering, she turned away from the mirror and went into her bedroom. Any more of this wallowing in misery and she'd be drinking wine right out of the bottle and crying over old B movies.

She stripped off her clothes, intending to hit the shower. Maybe a good dousing with hot water would snap her out of this black mood.

So Jack had kissed her. So what? It had been a damn good kiss and she'd enjoyed it while it was happening. But it wasn't as if it would lead to anything.

Maybe he *had* felt some physical attraction for her. That didn't negate the fact that they had to work together, and that work was a priority for both of them. They wouldn't risk their jobs for physical gratification. They were both too smart—too driven—to make that mistake.

So the kiss had happened and it wouldn't happen again and she might as well live with it.

If the shower and the pep talk didn't work, there was always the rest of that ice cream….

ON HER WAY TO WORK the next morning, Shelly rehearsed a speech to Jack. "Jack, I'm really sorry about yesterday evening. I don't know what came over me. I didn't mean to dump on you like that. And as for that kiss. Well, we both know that didn't mean anything, right? You don't have to worry about anything like that happening again, I promise."

Should she be so insistent? What if Jack *wanted* it to happen again? She shook her head and flicked on her blinker for the turn into the station lot. Jack had never shown the slightest romantic interest in her before last night. Thinking that kiss had been anything but a fluke was dangerous. Better to keep things as they'd been before—friendly, but businesslike.

She checked her hair and makeup in the visor mirror. No more shock-rock queen. She was back in mild-mannered television journalist mode. Professional. Secure.

Absolutely not about to blow her breakfast right there in the elevator.

As she entered the KPRM suite, Jack emerged from his office midway down the main hallway. Shelly froze, her right foot tapping, fighting the urge to make a dash for it. Was the rubber tree over there in the corner large enough to hide behind?

"Shelly!"

Too late. He'd spotted her and was headed this way.

"Good morning, Jack." Her face was so rigid with terror that smiling hurt, but she forced herself. Better to get this over with right away. What was that old saying—something about eating a live toad for breakfast every morning meant the rest of the day could only get better? "I need to talk to you."

"I need to talk to you, too. Come into my office."

She followed him into his office, which was equally

as cramped as hers, though considerably neater. He deposited a stack of file folders on the desk, then turned to face her.

They both spoke at once. "About yesterday—"

They stopped and tried again. "I never meant—"

"You first." He motioned for her to begin.

She shook her head. "No, you. Please." Anything to keep from having to make that speech she'd rehearsed in the car.

He shoved his hands in his pockets and looked at the floor, then cleared his throat and raised his gaze to meet hers. "First up, I want to apologize for my behavior in your office yesterday afternoon. You were upset and I was completely out of line to take advantage of you that way." He swallowed, his Adam's apple bobbing. "I don't have an excuse for why I did what I did, except that you're an attractive woman and I haven't been in a relationship for a while." He looked away. "That sounds incredibly lame, even to me, but it's the only explanation I could come up with. I hope you'll forgive me, and I promise nothing like this will happen again."

He looked so dejected it was all she could do not to put her arms around him and comfort him.

But of course, that was how this whole mess had started. Better not go there. "It's all right, Jack. Really. And you have nothing to apologize for. If anything, I should apologize for dumping my problems all over you."

"No, I'm flattered you trusted me enough to confide in me. But it never should have ended the way it did."

He was carefully avoiding any mention of the actual kiss. Now, why was that? Was it too painful to remember? Or was he trying to protect her delicate sensibilities? At this thought it was all she could do not to roll her eyes.

"What did you want to talk to me about?" he asked.

"Oh. That." Her cheeks felt hot. *Keep it together.* She drew herself up straighter. "I wanted to clear the air about last night, too." *Right. Except that things felt muddier than ever.* "You're right—it shouldn't have happened and I'm sure it won't happen again."

He studied her, eyes searching. For what? Guilt? Innocence? Was he remembering how horrible she'd looked yesterday—or how fantastic that kiss had been? *Don't go there.*

"Right." He nodded and stepped away. "I'm glad we've straightened that out." He moved behind the desk and began shuffling through the folders he'd deposited there moments before. "So what are you working on today?"

Back to work, then, as if nothing had happened. It was what she'd wanted, but what she hated, also. If Jack wasn't her boss she could have thrown herself at him with abandon and never worried about repercussions. But she couldn't jeopardize the career she'd worked so hard for over an attraction that had no guarantee of lasting or of ever growing into something more.

"I'm tracking down one last source for the hospital piece and editing the segment on arson investigators for next week's show."

He nodded, not looking up. "That's great. I can't wait to see it."

She waited for him to say something else, but he didn't, so she edged toward the door. "See you later, then."

He grunted, which she guessed was all the answer she'd get, so she turned and hurried away.

At the end of the hallway, she almost collided with a tall blonde. "Oh, excuse me." Stepping back, Shelly looked up into a strikingly beautiful face that was also vaguely familiar.

"Quite all right." The blonde scarcely glanced at her. "Can you tell me where I can find Jack Halloran's office?"

"Yes, it's just down the hall there, on the—"

"Never mind, I see him."

Shelly turned to see that Jack had indeed emerged from his office. "Jessica? What are you doing here?"

"I came to see you, of course." The two embraced, and the next thing Shelly knew, they were kissing. And not just a friendly buss—the blonde had her arms wrapped around Jack and her lips pressed firmly to his.

Feeling sick to her stomach, Shelly turned her back on the couple and hurried to her office, where she sank into her chair and took great gulps of air, trying to stay calm. So much for thinking the memory of the kiss they'd shared would haunt Jack forever. His lips were scarcely cold before he'd latched onto someone else.

Someone tall, gorgeous and *thin*.

Shelly yanked open the bottom drawer of her desk and deposited her purse, then slammed the drawer shut. Darcy had told her Jack was a player, hadn't she? Not surprising news, really. Shelly had seen the way women followed him and flirted with him.

Oh, God, what did it say about *her* that she was reacting this way? One kiss and she was the jealous, possessive girlfriend.

All the more reason to keep her distance from him. The man messed with her head too much. So much for telling herself she could handle the attraction. That she could keep things under control. If one kiss threw her this much off balance, how was she ever going to do her job if she allowed things to go any further?

"JACK, IT'S SO GOOD TO see you. How long has it been?" Jessica Peabody moved out of Jack's arms and patted her hair, as if checking to see if a single golden strand was out of place.

"It's been a while." Jack frowned at Jessica, aka the former Mrs. Jack Halloran.

Though till death do us part had turned out to be scarcely fifteen months, the pain of that failure still stung. Jessica, of course, had accepted the divorce philosophically. "We made a lousy husband and wife," she said at the time of the split. "But I like to think we'll always be friends."

Was today's visit another attempt to keep the tenuous friendship alive, or did Jessica have something else in mind? "Why did you come to see me?" he asked. With Jessica, the direct approach was best. Otherwise he could spend the next hour wading through the small talk and newsroom gossip she loved, waiting for her to get to the point.

"I was in town and wanted to say hello. Plus I heard through the grapevine your new show is doing very well. Congratulations."

Since when was the woman once dubbed by coworkers "Jugular Jessica," the most ambitious woman he knew, interested in local PBS news shows? "I didn't know you kept up with local broadcasting," he said mildly.

"I don't. But I make it my business to keep up with

you." She tapped his chest with one perfectly manicured finger. "I must say, I was shocked when I heard you were leaving the network. I thought you were their golden boy."

He made a face. "I don't care to be anyone's *boy,* golden or otherwise. I wanted to be my own boss for a while, try doing the kind of reporting I've always wanted to do."

"Investigative work. See, I remember." She nodded. "You were never happy behind the anchor desk."

"But you were. I assume you still are."

"Not exactly." She attempted a coy look, but she was too perfectly put together to play the ingenue.

"Then what, exactly?" She wanted him to play her game, to tease the news from her, clue by clue. But he didn't have the time or patience for that anymore.

She formed her plump, perfectly bow-shaped, collagen-enhanced lips into a pout. "You certainly know how to spoil a girl's surprise."

"You're not a girl, and it's not very flattering for you to act like one."

Her expression clouded, and he could see she was debating how she should react to the gibe. She chose to ignore it. Maybe she was growing up, after all.

"I've landed a reporter's position at CNN's Denver bureau," she said, her attempt at a modest smile finally giving way to a full-blown look of triumph. "I've been sending audition tapes for months now and they finally called me in for an interview. Once they met me in person, the job was mine."

"Congratulations." He had no trouble believing Jessica had wowed the CNN brass at her interview. She was smart, talented and frankly gorgeous—everything television executives and television audiences wanted in a news reporter. "When do you start?"

"I started last week. So far I've already had my first piece broadcast nationally. I expect I'll be doing a lot more."

He looked at her warily. "Why Denver? I didn't think you liked the city." At least she'd told him as much when he'd relocated here.

She smoothed back her hair. "It was too good an opportunity to pass up." Her smile was warm, flirtatious even. "There are rumors circulating that there could be another reporter slot opening up here soon. I could pull some strings and get you on the short list for the job."

A job at CNN? There had been a time when he'd have sold his left kidney for a position like that. But now that he had his own show, doing things his own way, the network job—even for an all-news network—didn't seem so perfect. "Thanks, but I intend to stay with *Inside Story* for a while longer."

"I understand this is your baby, but Jack—think about this. Your local news magazine will never be anything but a local show. And we're talking CNN here. Once you've got your foot in the door there, you can pretty much write your own ticket."

He nodded. "*Inside Story* is a local show for now. But I think this format has the potential to go national."

She pursed her lips in disapproval, an expression that was all too familiar to him. "Lofty ambitions are nice, Jack, but you know as well as I do that this kind of opportunity simply doesn't come around. Besides, I'm working weekends at CNN now. This would be a chance for the two of us to work together again." She laid her hand on his chest, her palm centered over his heart, and looked into his eyes, her voice lowered to a sultry purr. "Just think—it could be like old times."

In his younger years he'd been flattered by such attention, but now he knew the set of gestures for what they were—one more part of Jessica's carefully rehearsed act. She wanted something and she was very practiced in getting her way. But what did she want? "The old times didn't turn out so great, did they?" he said.

"We're older now, Jack. We wouldn't make the same mistakes this time." She took her hand away and stepped back. "Besides, I'm not talking a personal partnership, merely a business one."

"A business partnership?"

"You and I had great chemistry on the air. When the network began selling us as a couple it helped both our careers. It could do the same at CNN."

What Jessica called chemistry, he'd once thought of as love. When the network had discovered they were seriously dating, management had launched a series of promos with all the subtlety of soap-opera teasers. Ratings had skyrocketed, and for a couple of years Jack and Jessica had been local A-list celebrities. Jessica had thrived in the spotlight, never missing a chance to preen for the cameras and cater to her "public." Jack, however, had loathed the whole publicity circus.

This difference of opinion had contributed to their drifting apart and eventual divorce, which was also played out in the public eye, adding to the pain Jack felt. Jessica, of course, played the star card to the end, leveraging her new single status into a posting to the network's Washington bureau, leaving Jack to nurse his wounds and rebuild his reputation in Dallas alone.

He shook his head. "No way would I go through that whole media fiasco again," he said. "Besides, you don't need me to help you climb the ladder at CNN. You're good enough to get to the top on your own."

"Eventually, yes." She dismissed the obvious with a wave of her hand. "But competition is really tough over there. Teaming with you again could launch us both up the ladder a lot faster than if I wait around to be noticed on my own."

"Sorry. You'll have to find yourself another partner for this one. I'm not interested."

She huffed out a sigh, though her expression remained passive. Jessica never frowned; she'd read once that it caused wrinkles and had trained herself to respond to every situation with studied blandness. "I can't believe you're determined to stick with this newsmagazine idea. Honestly, Jack, local public TV? Where do you think that's going to get you?"

"I thought you said you'd heard good things about the show."

"Well, yes. Here in Denver. But this is still a cow town to the rest of the world—the part that really counts."

He wanted to deny this, but he'd been in the business long enough to know there was some truth in what she said. He'd known going into this he was taking a gamble—risking his uncle's money and maybe even his own career. But now that he had a few shows under his belt, had seen what he could do on his own and the difference he could make, he couldn't see going back. Not yet. "I fully intend to move on to bigger things," he said. "But on my own terms."

"What? You're not making sense."

He shrugged. "I like calling the shots here at *Inside Story*. I'm through with letting other people decide the direction my career should take."

She stared at him a long moment, then took a step back. "I guess the divorce had a bigger effect on you than I thought." She shook her head. "I'm sorry, Jack. I had no idea our splitting would make you stop caring about everything you'd spent years working for."

"You don't get it, do you? I do care. More than ever. And I've learned that for me, the best way to make things happen is to do them myself."

"Of course." She made a show of checking her watch. "I have to go now. It was wonderful seeing you." She leaned forward, lips puckered for a goodbye kiss.

He gave her a peck on the cheek, then stepped back. "Good luck at CNN. I know you'll do great."

"We could have been great together, if you weren't so stubborn."

He laughed. "You're right. I'm stubborn. Almost as stubborn as you are. That's probably one reason things never worked out for us."

"I'm stubborn when it will get me closer to a goal or help me get ahead," she said. "I sometimes think you're obstinate simply because you can be." She didn't wait for an answer, merely nodded goodbye, then turned on her heel and left, hips swaying provocatively. Except now, watching her exit his office, he only felt the old annoyance resurfacing, that he'd ever let himself be sacrificed on the altar of her ambition. Of course, early on, it had been his ambition, too, before he'd accepted that his whole career path—hell, way too much of his life— was built on appearances. How he looked himself. How he and Jessica looked together as a couple. He'd begun to wonder if he was anything more than another pretty face—if he really had in him what it took to succeed on his own terms.

Inside Story was his chance to find that out, once and for all. Whether he succeeded or failed with this, at least he'd know the responsibility was his alone, and not because of how he looked or with whom he associated.

It was a big weight to carry, but so far it didn't feel too heavy. In fact, it felt absolutely right, as if after picking up and setting down a lot of different burdens, he'd finally found the one custom made for him alone.

CHAPTER TWELVE

SHELLY WENT THROUGH the motions of working: she telephoned a few sources and left messages. She sorted her mail. She opened a computer file and stared at it, the words blurred by the image of Jack and the mysterious blonde kissing. As much as she tried to believe she didn't care, the very fact that she couldn't let go of that image proved her a liar.

Feeling foolish but unable to stop herself, like a woman on a diet who can't stay away from an open bag of cookies, she picked up the phone and punched in the extension of the receptionist in the lobby. "Judy? This is Shelly Piper up at KPRM. A blond woman just came up to our floor and I don't know what's wrong with me this morning, but I've already forgotten her name. Can you keep me from looking like a complete idiot?"

"Jessica Peabody?" She jotted the name on a sticky note. "Thanks, Judy. You're a lifesaver."

She hung up the phone and stared at the name. Jessica Peabody. It was vaguely familiar, but why?

She glanced over her shoulder to make sure no one could see, then closed her word-processing program and logged on to the Internet. She brought up Google and typed in Jessica Peabody.

She gaped at the listings that came up. There were over *nine thousand* references to Jessica Peabody! She clicked on the first and found herself reading the bio for CNN's newest Denver bureau reporter.

That explained why the name was familiar. But what was she doing visiting Jack? Everyone said Jack was destined for CNN. Had Jessica come here to recruit him for a position there? Shelly shook her head. She hadn't met a corporate recruiter yet who greeted potential recruits with a kiss like the one she'd witnessed in the hall.

She read a second listing, and a third, a mixture of admiration and envy churning her gut. Jessica Peabody, former Miss Dallas County, graduate of the University of Texas's television-and-film program, internship at KSAT in San Antonio, production work at KZTV, Corpus Christi.

She had had the career Shelly had always wanted. The one she'd worked so hard for.

The one she'd probably have had if she looked like the five-foot-ten-inch, one-hundred-and-eleven-pound Jessica Peabody.

Her gaze fixed on the last line of the bio. *Before joining the CNN team, Jessica worked as evening news anchor at KXAS in Dallas, Texas.*

The same station where Jack had worked.

Past guilt and well into compulsion now, Shelly googled Jack Halloran *and* Jessica Peabody. Even as she typed, she felt ridiculous. Honestly, someone over thirty ought to be past this kind of thing. She was as bad as some high schooler crushing on the star quarterback. But shame wasn't enough to stop her.

The first site brought up a newspaper article about the

gorgeous duo. *Newlyweds Jack Halloran and Jessica Peabody have added a touch of society glamour to the evening news these days. Following a honeymoon in the Caribbean, the couple have moved into a townhome in fashionable Highland Park.*

Shelly read the sentence three times, trying to absorb the information. Jack and Jessica—married?

She read the words again, but they still added up to the same news. She sat back and gave herself a mental shake. Why was she so surprised? They were both young and intelligent. They worked together. They were both from Texas. And they were both attractive people.

Gorgeous people.

Who was she kidding? The combination of the two of them probably stopped traffic. No doubt people had tuned in to the evening news simply to admire them. Jessica was exactly the kind of woman meant for a man like Jack.

And obviously a man like Jack would prefer a former beauty queen to a queen-size beauty.

Feeling sick to her stomach, Shelly scanned half a dozen other articles, until she came to a notice about the couple's divorce. The measure of relief that surged through her made her feel small and ugly.

But if they were divorced, what was Jessica doing here now? And why were she and Jack kissing?

The buzz of the phone startled her out of her reverie. She hastily logged off the Internet and answered it. "Shelly Piper, *Inside Story.*"

"Ms. Piper, this is Alexander Lang. I had a message you wished to speak to me?"

"Professor Lang, thank you for returning my call." She shuffled through her files, trying to focus on work once more. "I'm working on a piece right now on health-care services for the poor at Denver's publicly funded hospitals." She relaxed as she found the page of notes she was looking for. "I understand you've done a great deal of research on how a person's appearance influences how they're perceived by others. Is it possible that the way someone looks would affect the type of medical care they receive?"

"It would depend on the person and the circumstances, of course, but it is possible." Professor Lang had a deep, rumbling drawl that had no doubt lulled many a student into a stupor during class lectures. "The studies we did involved measuring people's perceptions of how suitable others were for jobs, as well as assessing opinions of another's intelligence, friendliness and capabilities, based on pictures we showed of them. In almost every case, more attractive people were judged to be smarter, friendlier and more capable than less attractive people and were seen as the best candidates for jobs."

"But how do you define *attractive?*"

Professor Lang cleared his throat. "In general, tall, slender people with regular features and a neat appearance were more likely to be hired than heavier, shorter people with irregular features."

Thank God she had "regular" features. "Can other factors overcome this prejudice?"

"In certain cases, identifying the subject as wealthy can counteract the impact of their appearance. Also, personality can often outweigh appearance, if someone has the time and opportunity to get to know another person better. But we're talking first impressions here."

"So if someone comes into, say, an emergency room, and that person is both unattractive and poor, he or she is screwed?"

"Again, it would depend on the circumstances. When people are made aware of this tendency, they can deliberately overcome it, to some extent. Also, I would think that most people who come into emergency rooms seeking treatment are not going to look their best."

Still, she'd bet if Jessica Peabody showed up complaining of a headache, no one would accuse her of trying to score drugs.

"Thank you, Professor, you've been very helpful. Is there anything else you can tell me?"

"I'd like to go back and correct one misstatement you made earlier. I wouldn't term this tendency prejudice so much as genetic programming."

She rubbed the bridge of her nose, trying to massage away the headache that was rapidly forming behind her eyes. "Genetic programming?"

"It is my belief, and numerous experiments with animals as well as humans have borne this out, that humans are genetically predisposed to respond more favorably to the most beautiful of the species."

"Right." She didn't have the strength to pursue this further. "I may have more questions for you later, but for now, you've given me a lot to think about. Do you know where I can locate copies of these studies of yours?"

"I'll be happy to send you copies."

"Great." She rattled off her address, thanked the professor once more and hung up the phone, only to find herself staring at her own reflection in the darkened computer monitor.

Puffy eyes, sagging skin…oh, God, was that a zit on her chin? She resolutely turned her back on the image. A sleepless night and her own sour mood weren't doing her perceptions or her actual appearance any favors.

At the sound of approaching footsteps, she sat up straighter and shuffled papers on her credenza, trying to give the appearance she was engrossed in her work. Jack stopped in the doorway. "Shelly, I'm going out for a while. Call me if you need anything."

She looked up, smile firmly in place. "Sure, Jack. See you later."

She held the smile and the upright posture until she heard the elevator door close, then she sagged against the chair. Talk about screwed! She'd gone and done the most stupid thing she could think of—she'd fallen hard for the one man in her life who was most out of her reach.

Not only was Jack off-limits because he was her boss and co-worker, but if his marriage to Jessica Peabody was any indication, he had a definite preference for beautiful babes. She'd never considered herself ugly, but she knew she didn't qualify as a babe.

Jack was out of her league, and it wasn't even his fault. He was "the most beautiful of the species," so naturally he'd gravitate toward other beautiful people. Shelly didn't stand a chance. According to Professor Lang, even evolution was against her.

"I'M SORRY I'M LATE," Yvonne said as she rushed to take a seat across from Shelly at the Cheesecake Factory two nights later.

"I haven't been here long." Shelly looked out at the

crowd just beyond the iron railing separating the popular restaurant's patio from the Sixteenth Street Mall. "The traffic was horrible getting here. Did it hold you up, too?"

"No, I had to wait for Daniel to pick me up. He was using my car today." She tucked her purse beneath her chair. "His was in the shop so I dropped him off there before coming here."

"Oh? What happened to it?"

"Nothing. He was having it detailed." As soon as she saw the look of disapproval on Shelly's face, Yvonne wished she'd lied and said the traffic had made her late, not Daniel.

A waitress arrived to take their drink orders. Yvonne hesitated, torn between the no-cal diet soda she probably *should* order, and her need for something a little stronger. "I'll have an appletini," she said finally.

"Make that two," Shelly said.

Yvonne had hoped the interruption would distract Shelly from more talk about Daniel and his car, but she was out of luck.

"Couldn't Daniel have had his car detailed some other time?" Shelly asked. "I mean, he knew we were going out tonight, right?"

"I told him." Yvonne spread her napkin in her lap. "But he never remembers things like that." She shrugged. "You know how guys are."

Frown lines furrowed Shelly's forehead. "You should have told him he needed to find another ride."

"I said I was sorry, okay?" She smoothed the napkin across her thighs, running her hand over and over the starched linen, as if that would somehow soothe her jittery nerves. She was always apologizing lately—to her boss for being distracted, to Daniel for forgetting to pick up his dry cleaning, to Shelly for being late for their dinner date. Why was everything her fault all of a sudden?

"You're right. Let's forget it." Shelly opened the menu. "I'm starving. What are you going to have?"

"I always get the Chinese chicken salad, but maybe I should have the grilled fish instead."

"Still dieting?" Shelly asked.

Yvonne shook her head. "Not tonight, anyway. After all, this is the Cheesecake Factory."

Shelly laughed. "Yeah. This isn't exactly the place to come if you're counting calories."

Yvonne laid aside her menu. "Besides, I figure I'll lose a few pounds while I'm in the hospital. Well, at least where it counts. Otherwise, I'll probably gain a few pounds up top."

"Let's not talk about it." Shelly pressed her hand against her chest. "It makes me hurt thinking about it."

"All right." Truthfully, Yvonne would have liked nothing better than to tell Shelly about her visit to the doctor to finalize the details for her surgery, about the models of breasts she'd viewed, and the ones she'd finally selected as her ideal, and about the dizzying array of release forms she'd signed, with their grisly list of possible consequences of undergoing surgery. Her hand had shaken as she signed them, though the nurse had assured her the horrors detailed were very rare.

The waitress arrived with their drinks and took their orders. Shelly asked for a cheeseburger, while Yvonne went for her long-time favorite, the Chinese chicken salad. When they were alone again, she made another attempt to get the conversation onto a more pleasant track. "How's your job going?" she asked.

"Good." Shelly nodded. "I've been really busy."

Was it Yvonne's imagination, or did Shelly seem distracted? "Do you still enjoy working with Jack Halloran?" she asked.

"Jack? Oh, yeah. He's great." But there was no enthusiasm in her voice.

Yvonne sipped her drink. Since she'd skipped lunch, she could already feel a warm buzz surging through her. She wanted this evening to be like old times—her and Shelly drinking, eating and dishing, the tension that had been growing between them in recent weeks forgotten. She adopted a teasing tone. "Have you heard anything more from the handsome prince?"

"I've been too busy to date."

"That sounds like an excuse to me."

Shelly shrugged. "Maybe. I never really liked dating, anyway."

"Well, duh!" She set down her glass with a *thunk!* "Nobody actually likes the dating part. Not the meeting-someone-new-trying-to-make-conversation-and-figure-out-if-he's-a-jerk-or-not part. But being in a relationship—caring about someone and knowing they care about you—that's worth going through a little discomfort for."

Shelly moved her fork a half inch to the right, picked up her knife and set it down again. "I don't know if it is to me. Maybe I'm one of those people who's better off single."

"Alone?" Yvonne shook her head. "Maybe there are people who are meant to spend their lives alone—who

are happy that way, even. But you're not one of them."
She studied her friend closer, assessing the slumped
shoulders, the chipped polish on three fingers, the layer
of concealer beneath Shelly's eyes that didn't succeed
in hiding the dark half moons. No, Shelly definitely
didn't look happy. In fact...

Yvonne leaned closer. "If I didn't know better, I'd
swear there *is* a man in your life. And something's happened with him to make you very unhappy."

Shelly sipped her drink. "Don't be ridiculous. What
would make you think something like that?" But she
avoided raising her eyes, so Yvonne knew she was on
to something.

"I know you. I've known you most of your life. I remember when you were dying for Roger Mosely to ask
you to the homecoming dance and you found out he'd
asked Mina Carruthers instead. Back then you looked
exactly the way you do now—except you chewed all
your fingernails instead of just chipping your polish."

Shelly stretched out her fingers, studying the nails.
"These acrylics are too hard to chew."

With impeccable timing, the waitress arrived with
their food. As Yvonne stared at the enormous salad in
front of her, she wondered if the waitstaff were trained
to interrupt all conversations at crucial moments.

When they were alone again, she stabbed a fork into
her salad and asked, "So what's going on? You can tell me."

Shelly carefully arranged lettuce and tomato on her
burger. Yvonne watched as she spread mustard, then
salted and peppered her fries, ignoring the question.
"Shelly?" she prompted.

Shelly looked up at last. "It's really silly."

"It's not silly if it's upset you like this. Not to me, anyway." Shelly might think Yvonne had gotten shallow because she was getting a boob job, but that wasn't true. She cared about the people she loved—cared enough to have this surgery to make Daniel happy, and cared enough to listen to whatever her oldest and dearest friend had to say.

Shelly glanced over her shoulder, then leaned in close, her voice scarcely audible above the chatter around them. "I found out a couple of days ago that Jack was married before."

Yvonne almost choked on a mouthful of lettuce. She reached for her water glass and took a big drink. Still, her voice was raspy when she spoke. "Jack, your gorgeous co-anchor Jack?"

Shelly nodded. "I met his wife. Actually, she's his ex-wife, but they were very friendly."

"That says a lot about a man's character, if he's still on good terms with an ex."

"I mean *very* friendly. When they met in the hall, she kissed him. A real kiss, not just a peck on the cheek."

Yvonne winced. "Maybe she's one of those over-the-top kind of people. Or maybe he's a really good kisser and she couldn't resist." She wanted the man Shelly obviously cared about to be a nice guy, not a jerk.

The blush that swept across Shelly's cheeks startled Yvonne. "Shelly!" She leaned closer, until their heads were almost touching across the table. "Do you have some, um, *personal* experience with Jack's kisses?"

Shelly ducked her head and rearranged her French fries with her fork, as if the answer to all her problems was buried somewhere under the ketchup and salt. "Yeah. Once," she finally admitted.

"When? What happened? I can't believe you've been holding out on me." Yvonne couldn't help grinning. Even though Shelly looked miserable, if Jack had actually kissed her, that *had* to be a good sign.

"I wasn't holding out on you. It was nothing, really."

But the dreamy look in her eyes told Yvonne that the kiss was very much *something,* at least to Shelly. "What happened?" she asked, her salad forgotten.

"I'd had a hard day and had just gotten back from a really tough interview and…and other things were bothering me. You know how sometimes you just feel blue, and the only thing to do is cry?"

"Yeah. We all have days like that." Lately just the thought of all Yvonne had to do before the wedding was enough to send her into a crying jag.

"So I was in the office, sobbing, and I guess Jack heard me and came to see what was wrong." Shelly looked wistful. "He was so sweet. So kind. At first he was just patting my back—like anyone would, really. Then the next thing I knew, we were kissing."

"That doesn't sound like nothing to me."

"It was an accident, really. It *didn't* mean anything." She frowned. "Obviously, since the next morning he was kissing his ex-wife, practically in front of me."

"Did he know you were there?"

She hugged her arms across herself. "I'm not sure."

"Besides, was he kissing her, or was she kissing him?"

"What difference does it make?"

"A lot. So tell me more about this kiss he gave you. Did anything else happen? Not that I'm nosy, but, well, I am! Did you have sex?"

Shelly's face turned the color of an eggplant and she

looked in danger of fainting. "No, we did not have sex," she hissed. "I told you, the kiss didn't mean anything. We both agreed to pretend it never happened."

"It must have meant something." Yvonne stabbed at her salad again. It was either that, or reach over and shake Shelly for being so obtuse. "I mean, people don't just kiss other people for the heck of it. Unless…" She paused, remembering some indiscretions from her own past. "Had you been drinking?"

"No." Shelly shook her head. "At least, I hadn't. I don't think he had, either. It didn't taste like it."

"Didn't taste like it?" Yvonne laughed with delight. "Girl, that must have been some kiss!"

Shelly hunched her shoulders and glanced from side to side. "Shh. I don't want anyone to know."

Yvonne sat back and folded her arms across her chest, considering the matter. "Okay, so you both agreed what happened between you two didn't mean any-thing—even though I don't believe that. And then the next morning you see him and his ex-wife kissing in the hallway. I can think of two explanations. One—" she held up a finger "—he's a self-absorbed playboy who's ready to take whatever he can get from any woman who crosses his path. And from what I've seen, he probably doesn't have a problem finding women to go along with that plan. Or two—" a second finger joined the first "—his ex caught him by surprise, and that kiss was the one that didn't mean anything. So which explanation do you vote for?"

Shelly brought her thumb to her mouth, then jerked it away and reached for her drink instead. After a long swallow, she shook her head. "I don't know. I mean,

Jack never struck me as self-absorbed before. He's always seemed really…kind." Her expression softened. "I mean, he actually listens when you talk to him. But he does date a lot."

Yvonne dismissed this information. "He's gorgeous and single. If he didn't date a lot I'd worry. So if one isn't the right explanation, what about two—the kiss with his ex was meaningless?"

"Maybe." Shelly shrugged. "Even if that's true, it doesn't make things any better. Not really."

"Why not? It means he's still unattached. And you're unattached. And he *kissed* you. So why not build on that kiss? Start something and see where it leads."

Shelly laughed, but there was no mirth in the sound. "Fat chance of that. Jack's not going to start anything with me."

"Why not? The two of you get along, right? You have a lot in common."

She shook her head. "Yvonne, I saw his ex. Jessica Peabody. She was gorgeous."

"So? You're gorgeous."

"No, I mean, *gorgeous.* She's a former Miss Dallas County. The two of them together look like a sexy magazine ad. That's the kind of woman Jack is used to having in his life. Not an ordinary chick with big thighs and a roll at her waistband."

Yvonne hadn't heard Shelly talk like this in a long time. What was wrong with her? "You don't give yourself enough credit. And you don't give him enough credit, either. All men aren't so superficial."

"Oh, no? Aren't you marrying a man who's giving you a boob job because *he* likes big-breasted women?"

Yvonne flushed. Okay, she guessed she'd walked right into that one. Maybe Daniel was being a *little* superficial. Everyone had their faults. Part of succeeding in marriage was learning to accept this. "Daniel has a *preference* for women with larger breasts. That didn't stop him from falling in love with me and marrying me. Even if Jack has *in the past* gravitated toward beauty-queen types, that doesn't mean he couldn't fall in love with someone more normal. Someone *real*. Someone like you."

"And then what? He gives me liposuction and a treadmill as a wedding present?"

Yvonne gripped the fork so hard it was in danger of bending. She set it aside and glared at Shelly. "That was a low blow. I know you don't approve of what I'm doing, but you're my friend. I expect you to support me, not say nasty things like that."

"Maybe I'm saying them to try to wake you up to what's going on here."

"What's going on is that I'm doing what I want to do to please my future husband—and to please myself. *Lots* of women would do the same thing if they were in my shoes."

"I wouldn't." Shelly's voice softened and she leaned across the table again. "I'm worried you're doing it for the wrong reasons."

"No, I'm doing this for the right reasons. After the surgery, I'll be more confident, Daniel will be more attentive, and clothes will fit better. Daniel has promised me a great new wardrobe."

"You're doing this for a new wardrobe? Come on, Yvonne. That's not a good reason."

"You haven't been listening to anything I've said, have you?" She wadded up her napkin and threw it down next to her plate. "You made up your mind about this the minute it was mentioned and you haven't even tried to understand my side of this." She stood, blinking back angry tears. "You're supposed to be my *friend*, not my *judge*."

"I don't want you to be hurt."

"Then why can't you see how much your attitude is hurting me?" Dangerously close to meltdown, she fled, pushing blindly past the hostess and a group of arriving diners, through the restaurant and out into the street beyond. She didn't stop until she reached her car, where she slumped in the front seat, her forehead pressed against the steering wheel, shaking with pain and anger. This was supposed to be the happiest time of her life, and Shelly was ruining it.

After all the years they'd known each other, couldn't she understand that, while she might be content to go through the rest of her life alone, Yvonne wasn't? Or was Shelly so wrapped up in her own misery she couldn't see her friend's pain?

She forced herself to straighten and start the car. She couldn't change Shelly's mind about things, so she might as well stop trying. But she wished with all her heart she could make her friend understand there was nothing wrong with wanting a little happiness for yourself—and doing everything you could to get it.

CHAPTER THIRTEEN

"MR. FITZSIMMONS, AS THE chief financial officer of Mercy Medical, how do you answer critics who have charged that it's wrong for a public hospital to turn away patients based on their ability to pay?"

Shelly leaned forward in her chair at the anchor desk, eyes riveted to the video screen, intent on the prerecorded interview that made up the next-to-last segment of her feature on Denver's public hospitals' care of indigents. Should she have phrased that question differently?

"Mercy Medical is indeed a 'public' hospital, meaning that we receive a certain amount of public funds. But those funds are only one part of our budget—and a part that's shrinking every year." Fitzsimmons folded his hands on the desk in front of him, the picture of grandfatherly concern. "Though we are a hospital, we are also a business, and the hard truth is that no business, even a charitable one, will survive long if it does not make a profit. Therefore, we're forced to try to balance the charge to serve the needy with the mandate that we pay our bills. That means limiting charity cases to the most critical cases only."

"Which leaves other seriously ill people with no place to turn."

"That is so." He nodded, his expression grave. "But we are only one hospital. We cannot take care of everyone. If we tried to do so, we would have to close our doors within a year. Would anyone be better off then?"

"So how do you balance the two objectives—the charitable one and the profitable one?"

"We set certain protocols and do our best to follow them. And we try even harder to attract paying patients to fill the gap."

"So the new birthing center is an example of your efforts to attract a more well-heeled clientele?"

"The center has been very well received."

"If an uninsured woman, or one on Medicaid, showed up at your hospital in labor, would she be taken to the birthing center?"

Fitzsimmons looked genuinely puzzled. "Of course not."

"So those facilities are only for those who can pay?"

He nodded. "We're trying to create a certain atmosphere—one of luxury and special attention for those who can afford it."

Cut to a shot of Michelle Dickson, her baby in a sagging diaper on her knee, her scar turned toward the camera, a harsh pink against the paleness of her scalp. "It says 'Mercy' right over the door, but no one there had mercy for me," Michelle said. She turned to look at the camera, eyes burning amid their layers of mascara and liner. "I can't help think that if I looked different—better—then I wouldn't have had to go through any of this. And that's not right, is it?"

Fade to black. Time for a pledge-drive break. Shelly sagged in her chair, as spent as if all the weeks she'd devoted to putting this story together had been compressed into the nine minutes it had taken to air.

To her left, someone started clapping. Startled, she looked over and saw Mary Anne, a big smile on her face. Soon others joined in: Wally and Bess, and even Jack, who smiled at her across the desk. "You did a fabulous job," he said. Did she imagine the warmth in his eyes?

The pledge break ended and it was time to get back to work. Floating on a wave of euphoria, she read the introduction to the final video segment without registering the words. And then before she knew it the show was over and people were gathering around her, congratulating her.

Even Armstrong Brewster patted her back. "Dynamite job. That piece will have everyone in town talking. Great for ratings."

Considering the source, she figured this qualified as a rave. But the biggest surprise came as she was heading for her office to retrieve her purse and was waylaid by Mary Anne. "Here." The editor shoved a phone into her hand. "Mr. Palmer wants to talk to you."

"Hello, Mr. Palmer. This is Shelly."

"I just wanted to congratulate you on a fine piece of television journalism," he said. "One of the finest I've seen. You should be very proud."

"Thank you. I was pleased with how it turned out. I worked very hard on it."

"And it shows. Keep up the good work."

"Thank you."

"I won't keep you. Just wanted you to know what I thought. Good night."

"Good night, sir."

When she clicked off the phone, she turned and found Jack standing at her elbow. He grinned. "What did my uncle have to say?"

"He liked the story." She laid aside the phone and smoothed back her hair. "Actually, he loved it."

"Everyone loved it." His gaze held hers, warm and sexy and way too tempting. He put his hand on her shoulder. She didn't moan, but she thought about it. "Want to grab some dinner, maybe drink a toast to your success?"

And then what? She was feeling far too vulnerable to sit through dinner with him and not let on that she hadn't forgotten the kiss they'd shared. She needed more time before she could slip back into "friendly co-worker" mode. "Thanks, but I can't." She managed a weak smile. "I'm exhausted, so I better go home and get some rest."

His look changed to one of concern. "You have been putting in a lot of hours lately. Go home and take it easy. We don't want you to burn out."

"No danger of that." She wouldn't burn out from work, anyway. Life in general, however, was starting to get to her. The memory of the fight with Yvonne was like a stone lodged in her chest, a persistent ache that kept her awake nights. A thousand times she'd replayed their last conversation in her head, wishing she could take her words back, or phrase them differently. But the right apology escaped her. Nothing she could say would change what Yvonne was going to do, or how Shelly felt about it. So she said nothing and was miserable.

And she said nothing to Jack about the kiss, and the attraction that still shimmered in the air between them like heat off asphalt on an August afternoon. Her awareness of him tempted her to do things she feared she'd regret.

Given time, she was sure she'd find a way to handle her feelings, to control them or shut them off, the way she did self-doubt and self-pity, and a host of other unattractive emotions. But they still escaped sometimes, when she was tired or discouraged or weak. For now, she was doing her best to avoid Jack when she felt herself wavering. She wasn't ready to find out what she might do with him in a moment of weakness, or where that might lead them.

SMALL ARTICLES PRAISING Shelly's public hospital story appeared in the local papers the next day. By that evening, the networks had picked up the story and added their own twists. The following Monday, the governor held a press conference to announce the formation of a commission to investigate whether hospitals such as Mercy Medical were fulfilling their obligation to provide charity care.

Wednesday morning, Jack dropped a copy of *USA Today* on Shelly's desk. "Check out page eleven," he said, grinning.

Puzzled, she turned through the pages of the paper until she came to a story about *her* story. "News Magazine Triggers Investigation," the headline read. "They even mention your name as the reporter responsible." Jack leaned over her shoulder and pointed out the reference to her.

"Wow." She stared at her name, stunned that she'd made a national paper.

"It gets even better. There's talk of your being nominated for an Emmy." His eyes met hers, his expression almost gleeful. "I predict your career is going to take off, in a big way. Just remember us little people when you're rich and famous."

His obvious delight in her success thrilled her as much as his optimistic prediction. "You deserve some of the credit, too. You gave me this chance." She looked away, suddenly shy about expressing her feelings. But it was past time he knew how grateful she was. "Thank you for choosing me for the co-anchor slot. I know I wouldn't have been the obvious choice for a lot of people, especially considering my competition."

"I chose you because I knew you were the right person for the job." He tapped the newspaper with his forefinger. "All this is proving me right. So what next? How do you follow up this story?"

She could think of a few things she'd like to do next—most of them involving Jack and a very big, very comfortable bed. But she pushed those fantasies aside and focused on work. Losing herself in her job would get her over this infatuation with Jack if anything would.

"I saw an article the other day that said children's beauty pageants are a billion-dollar business these days. Who's paying all that money, and what do they get for it? Are these things scams or legitimate avenues to success?"

"And what kind of message does it send to kids to have them compete against one another on the basis of appearance at such a young age?" Jack asked.

The edge to his voice made her curious. "Were *you* ever in a beauty pageant?"

He shook his head. "Thank God, no. But I did do

some modeling in high school. At first, I was flattered when the recruiter approached me, but after a while I felt like some inanimate object. I was just a body to those people, not a person." He shrugged. "My friends thought I was crazy to give up that kind of money, but I guess even then, I wanted more."

More what? But she thought she knew the answer to that question. It was the same thing she wanted, the same thing Michelle and Del Gardner had wanted: for someone to see them for what they were, not what they looked like.

FRIDAY EVENING, JACK HAD a date with Deirdre, a woman who lived in his apartment building. They'd met in the laundry room one Sunday afternoon, and by the time his dryer had stopped she'd invited him to go with her to hear a band at a local club. The casualness of the evening pleased him. Too many women tried to impress him. He wanted someone he could relax with.

Unfortunately, the evening was not turning out to be as relaxing as he'd hoped. Deirdre had a cell phone that played "Reveille," which rang no less than four times while they were eating fish and chips and waiting for the band to start. While those around them sent her dirty looks, she had animated conversations with her sister, a co-worker, someone he thought might be her beautician and the sister again.

"You should shut your phone off before the band begins," he said after the last call, struggling to hide his annoyance.

"I can't do that. My sister is pregnant and I'm her birth coach. If she goes into labor, she has to be able to reach me."

"When is she due?"

"The doctor says in another five weeks, but you should see her. She's huge!" Deirdre spread her hands out in front of her, as if cradling a huge belly. "I think she's going to have the baby early."

"Then maybe you should turn off the ringer and set the phone to vibrate only."

"I should, but I lost the manual and I can't figure out how." She laughed. "Besides, it plays my favorite song. Isn't that a kick?"

Everyone has faults, he reminded himself as he leaned back in his chair and tried to enjoy the concert. But some were easier to take than others.

A flash of brown out of the corner of his eye made him sit up and turn to look. He sank down again, disappointed. The woman he'd glimpsed wasn't Shelly. If it had been, he'd have been tempted to ditch his date and go talk to her.

Unless, of course, Shelly was with a date. The thought made the meal he'd just enjoyed sit less well in his stomach.

Despite his best efforts, he hadn't forgotten the kiss he and Shelly had shared. He knew it was in both their best interests to put it out of his mind. The fiasco with Jessica had taught him everything he needed to know about the hazards of a relationship conducted in front of television cameras. But the memory of that moment wouldn't leave him.

Still, he was determined. With time, and enough other women to keep him occupied, he'd be able to put his feelings for Shelly into proper perspective. She'd always be special to him; best to leave it at that.

He glanced at Deirdre, who was involved in yet another phone call. Maybe her sister *would* go into labor and he'd have an excuse to end the evening early.

If Shelly was on a date tonight, he hoped it was more enjoyable than his.

Dear Ms. Piper,
You would be a very attractive woman if you would only lose a little weight. As someone who has struggled with my own weight in the past, I thought I would share my secret with you.
    Prunes.
    I eat two prunes every four hours. I also have one-quarter cup of apple cider vinegar in a little hot water twice a day. Since I started this regimen, I have lost thirty pounds and kept it off. I'm sure it would do wonders for you, too.

Shelly made a face and laid aside the letter. She'd received half a dozen similar communications in the weeks since *Inside Story* debuted. Invariably the letter writers offered a solution to Shelly's *problem*. One man had offered to hypnotize her, while others, like the prune woman, touted various bizarre eating plans. Her favorite, though, was the woman who wrote that losing weight was "easy. It's a simple matter of eating less and exercising more." Uh-huh. If it was so easy, why didn't more people do it?

Mary Anne stuck her head in the doorway of Shelly's office. "Ready for lunch?"

"Sure." Shelly took her purse from the bottom desk drawer and slung it over her shoulder. "As long as we go somewhere that doesn't serve prunes."

"Prunes?" Mary Anne made a face.

"I'll explain later."

They ended up at a deli two blocks from the office. Shelly chose a Greek salad, then resolutely slid her tray past the dessert selections.

"Oooh, doesn't that ginger-lime cheesecake look to die for?" Mary Anne leaned in for a closer look at the delicacy.

Shelly's mouth watered. She loved cheesecake better than brownies, even. "It looks wonderful."

Mary Anne glanced back at her. "Shall we split a piece?"

Shelly hesitated, then nodded. "Why not? You only live once."

Mary Anne added the cheesecake to her tray. "My motto is 'Life's too short to skip dessert.'"

They unloaded their trays at the table and Shelly let out a sigh as she settled into her seat and picked up her fork. "Everything's been so hectic lately, it's good to sit down and relax a minute."

"That's the price of fame." Mary Anne smiled. "So tell me how the beauty pageant story is coming. I saw lots of cute footage of adorable tots dressed up like fashion dolls."

Shelly nodded. "It's amazing how into this stuff some parents are. And the children *are* precious. And most of them seem to really enjoy competing."

"Yeah, but why do first- and second-graders need to compete in *anything?*" Mary Anne slathered butter on a triangle of garlic toast. "Of course, I didn't even want my son to play soccer until my husband promised to coach the team and make sure every child got to play."

"It's like anything else, I guess. It's okay as long as the parents don't take it too far."

"But so many of them do. At least they did with soccer. I've actually heard grown men boo a nine-year-old who missed a shot." She shuddered. "I was never so relieved in my life as when Kurt said he wanted to take up skateboarding instead. He might break a bone at the skate park, but at least I don't have to worry about some overgrown bully breaking his spirit."

"The focus of my story is about how some pageants promise big payoffs, but the only people who really make money are the promoters who put them on." She pushed aside the empty salad plate and reached for the cheesecake. "Should I wait to divide this?"

"No, I'm ready." Mary Anne licked her fork clean. "Should we do like my mother always did—one person cuts and the other chooses?"

Shelly laughed. "What? You don't trust me?"

"I trust you. Go ahead."

She sliced the cheesecake and moved half onto her plate, then pushed the rest toward Mary Anne. She moaned as the first bite hit her tongue. "That's divine."

"Excuse me, aren't you that woman on that news show—Shelly Peters?" A tiny woman with salt-and-pepper hair and round wire-rimmed glasses magnifying her watery blue eyes stopped beside their table.

"Shelly Piper." Shelly wiped her hand on her napkin and offered it. "What can I do for you?" Lately a few people had asked for her autograph. It was flattering, if a bit disconcerting.

"I just wanted to say how much I've enjoyed the

show." The woman's gaze zeroed in on the cheesecake in front of Shelly and she made a tsking sound. "You know, dear, the camera really does make you look heavier. As we get older, we have to be even more careful about what we eat."

Mary Anne made a choking sound and reached for her glass of water. Shelly froze, smile fixed on her lips. How was one supposed to respond to rudeness disguised as concern? "Um, I suppose that's true."

The woman held her head up. "I haven't had dessert in thirty years. It's how I've kept my figure."

Well, bully for you. Shelly scooped up a large forkful of cheesecake. "I happen to enjoy dessert. Very much." She slid the fork into her mouth. "Mmm."

The woman gasped. "I was only trying to help," she said.

"Thank you, I'm sure."

When she was gone, Mary Anne leaned across the table and spoke in a low voice. "Please tell me this kind of thing doesn't happen often."

"That was a first." She ate the last bite of cheesecake, though truthfully, the woman had spoiled some of her enjoyment in it.

"I can't believe someone would be so rude!"

"You should read some of the letters I get."

"You get letters? From people like her?"

"Oh, yes." She described some of the letters, including the one from the prune eater. "Some of them are quite funny, really."

"I think it's pathetic that people don't have better things to do with their time. Does Jack know about this?"

"No!" The idea alarmed her. "Why should I tell him?"

"It's his show. I think he'd want to know, though I'm sure it would upset him."

"It's just a few letters. And there's nothing he can do about them, anyway."

"Still, I think he should know."

"Mary Anne, no! Please. It's embarrassing enough without Jack knowing about it."

"All right. I won't say anything. But if it gets to be a real problem, you need to do something about it. Maybe have someone screen your letters."

She shook her head. "It's not that big a deal. I'll handle it myself." She'd ignore the letters, and the other criticism, the way she'd ignored all the other snide comments about her weight over the years. The words still hurt, but she'd learned not to let the pain show.

True, being in the spotlight made things harder. Now that she was a celebrity of sorts, she was aware of people watching her. Judging her. The idea hurt, and made her avoid looking into mirrors. She was too afraid she'd see what her critics saw—a fat, unattractive *loser.*

THREE DAYS LATER Armstrong Brewster walked into Jack's office and laid a thin sheaf of letters on his desk. "I wanted you to see some of the mail we've gotten," the producer said.

"That's all the mail we've gotten?" Jack said. "I would have expected more."

"We've got tons of mail, good and bad, but I thought you ought to see these in particular."

Jack picked up the first letter and scanned it. *Why do you have that fat girl on there when there are so many other good-looking women on TV? More people like me would watch if you had a real babe on the show.*

Frowning, he read the second letter. *Shelly Piper is a fine reporter, but she could stand to lose twenty pounds or so. Why don't you make her go on a diet?*

He glared at Armstrong. "People actually wrote these?"

Armstrong nodded. "We also have some from people congratulating us for having the guts to have a 'normal size' woman on the air."

"What difference does it make how much Shelly weighs?" He threw down the letter, anger choking him.

"I told you before—people have certain expectations. When you go against those expectations, you're going to have some folks upset. It's not a big group now, but it could grow."

"So what are you saying we should do? Fire Shelly? That would look really good, wouldn't it? Especially if she gets the Emmy nomination everyone's talking about."

"No, you don't have to fire her." Armstrong looked uncomfortable. "But maybe you could talk to her. Ask her to slim down a little."

"I'm not believing this. Should I suggest she bleach her hair and wear low-cut blouses, too?"

"There's no need to take that kind of attitude." Armstrong gathered up the letters. "I'm only trying to help. It might not be so bad if you weren't so good-looking. People want to see you paired with a woman who looks as great as you do."

A woman like Jessica, no doubt. "So this is my fault? Thanks."

"I'm not responsible for how people think, you know."

"Then maybe we should try to change how they think."

Armstrong frowned. "How are we going to do that?"

Jack leaned back in his chair, torn between his own principles and the need to do something drastic to help Shelly. "So you think part of the problem is that people don't see me and Shelly as a compatible team?"

"Some of them don't think the two of you really go together."

He nodded. "So we'll show them that we do go together. That we are a matched team."

"How are we going to do that?"

He met the producer's puzzled gaze. "Are you still interested in those promo spots you proposed—the ones of me doing athletic things, like skiing and rock climbing?"

"Absolutely."

"Then I'll do them—but only if we feature Shelly doing them with me. I want the emphasis on both of us equally, as a team."

"I don't exactly see Shelly rock climbing."

"Maybe not, but she's a skier. She said so during that first interview. We ought to be able to get some good footage at one of the ski resorts around here. We can take a day to film and run a whole series of print and television ads."

Armstrong looked skeptical. "Will she even go for it?"

"I think she will." He nodded. "I'll ask her to do it as a favor to me."

"I'll see what I can do." He turned to leave.

Jack drummed his fingers on the desk. Should he call Shelly now and tell her what he had planned? No, he'd wait until he had more details. He smiled to himself. It would be good for them both to get away from the office for a day, to kick back and relax on the slopes.

As much as he'd hated the whole idea of this kind of publicity campaign, he had to admit he was looking forward to this chance to get to know Shelly a little better.

Away from the office, from the work that had brought them together, would he feel the same pull of desire for her? Would the doubts that kept them apart still seem like common sense? Or cowardice?

CHAPTER FOURTEEN

"YOU WANTED TO SEE ME about something, Jack?" Shelly stood before Jack's desk, hands twisted together, fighting to look calmer than she felt. Why was it no matter how old she was, being calling into the boss's office left her with the same feelings as when she was a child and had to report to the principal?

"Sit down." He smiled and motioned to the chair beside her. "How are things going?"

"They're going fine. Great." At least as far as work was concerned. She'd shot a great interview this morning with the promoter of the Little Miss Colorado pageant and the story was coming together nicely.

On the personal side, things weren't so rosy. She and Yvonne still hadn't spoken since their fight at the restaurant weeks ago, and she wasn't any closer to resolving her feelings for Jack. "How are things with you?"

"Good." He nodded.

It struck her that this was the most awkward conversation they'd ever had. Always before it had been easy for them to talk. What was wrong this time? "Why did you want to see me today?" she prompted.

He shuffled through a stack of mail in his in-box. "Armstrong's been after us to do some promotion for the show. He thinks we should build on all the great feedback we've been getting lately." He glanced at her, then shifted his gaze back to the mail. "It's not something I particularly enjoy doing. I'd much rather focus on the kind of stories we've developed than the personalities associated with the show, but I've been around long enough to know that people do tend to be drawn to personalities more than issues."

She nodded. "Just look at any presidential race."

"Exactly." He smiled and looked at her directly for the first time since she'd entered the office, his expression warm. "I knew you'd understand."

She shifted in her chair. "Understand what?"

"Why we have to do this photo shoot Armstrong has planned."

"A photo shoot?" She swallowed hard. Though she'd appeared on camera a number of times now, it was always in the context of interviewing someone else, or introducing a story. She wasn't so sure about being the main focus of the lens. "What kind of photo shoot?"

"He wants to film us doing something active and outdoorsy. You know, very Colorado." He slid a brochure toward her. It showed a man and woman skiing down a sunlit slope, snow flying in their wake. "Copper Mountain has agreed to comp us lift tickets and accommodations in exchange for a sponsorship slot. Armstrong's booked us there next weekend, if you don't have any other plans."

She shook her head, stunned. "A whole weekend?" *With you?*

He cleared his throat. "I know it's a lot to ask. You might not have to stay the whole weekend if you have other plans. We can probably get the shots we need the first day. But the resort is comping us the whole weekend, and since you've been working so hard, I thought it would be a nice getaway for you. I know you like to ski."

"It sounds wonderful." Sun, snow and Jack, away from the tensions and pressures of work.

A dangerous combination. But maybe it was time to live a little dangerously. Playing it safe hadn't gotten her anywhere so far. Why not risk exploring Jack's feelings for her a little further? This weekend, away from work, might be her best opportunity to find out if the kiss they'd shared had been a passing fancy, or the spark of a real connection between them.

THE WEEKEND AT COPPER MOUNTAIN might have been a relaxing getaway, if not for the entourage, consisting of a photographer, a videographer, a makeup person and Armstrong Brewster, who followed Shelly and Jack everywhere.

"Wait! Wait! Stop here." Armstrong skidded to a stop beside them as they attempted to make their way to the bottom of a relatively easy ski run that ended at the resort's Center Village. "Let's get some shots with the mountains in the background. Jerry, give me some good stills of Jack. Think billboard quality." He motioned the photographer over.

Shelly started to move out of the way, but Jack stopped her. "We need to get Shelly in here, too," he said, grabbing hold of the sleeve of her parka. "The idea is to showcase us together, as the *Inside Story* team. Isn't that right, Armstrong?" Jack gave the producer a hard look.

"Uh, right. Shelly, move in next to Jack. That's good. Maybe a little closer."

"I feel like I'm posing for one of those tourist-vacation shots resort photographers always take," Shelly said. "All we need is a plastic palm tree or a sign that reads 'Merry Christmas from the Smith family.'"

"That could probably be arranged." Jack put his hand on her shoulder and smiled for the camera. "Think they've got enough footage yet?"

"How much could they need?" At the photographer's direction, Shelly turned sideways and raised her chin, then froze in this pose, her lips barely moving when she spoke. "They've filmed all morning. I swear if I have to stop one more time before reaching the bottom of this run, I'm going to scream."

"I hear you." Jack smiled broadly for the camera. "What say we make a break for it?"

"What?"

The camera whirred, catching Shelly's look of surprise. If Armstrong had any sense, he wouldn't use that one, but you could never tell about the producer.

"That should be enough," Jack said. Before Armstrong could protest, he nodded to Shelly, then took off down the slope.

She was right behind him, darting between wobbly tourists and around family groups, sliding into the lift line right behind him.

"What now?" she asked, slipping her hands out of the pole straps and catching her breath.

"Now we lose them."

She followed his gaze to where Armstrong and the photographer were just now making their way to the lift line. Armstrong was craning his neck, trying to find them in the crowd.

She turned back to Jack, hunching slightly. "Sounds like a plan."

They rode the lift up with two teenagers from Texas who were intent on critiquing each other's terrain park moves. At the top, Jack skied across the slope to another lift that headed farther up the mountain.

Shelly followed, and they watched from the chair as Armstrong and Jerry unloaded from the first lift and searched for their quarry.

Within seconds, Jack's walkie-talkie, designed to keep him in touch with the promo team, buzzed.

"Are you going to answer that?" Shelly asked.

"Nope." Grinning, he reached into his parka and switched it off.

Shelly laughed. "How long do you think it will take them to figure out where we've gone?"

"If we're lucky, they won't figure it out." He shoved his goggles on top of his head and looked at her. "Are you up for a challenge?"

The words, innocent as they were, sent a thrill through her. "That depends. What do you have in mind?"

"We could head over toward the back side of the mountain, to some of the bowls. There should be some good powder there, and from what I've seen, Armstrong's not a good enough skier to tackle those black-diamond runs."

"And you think I am?"

"I'm asking—are you?"

Right now she'd have followed Jack anywhere. Fortunately, she was confident her skiing skills were up to it. "I'm there."

Three chairlift rides later they found themselves in the much less crowded terrain of Copper Bowl. The steep, wide area was soft with fresh powder snow, and they had the entire area almost to themselves.

"Armstrong will never find us here," Shelly said.

"Race you to the bottom." Before she could answer, Jack took off.

She followed, the thrill of sudden freedom, the excitement of breaking the constraints of proper business decorum, and the heady mix of crisp air and bright sunshine helping her fly through the snow. She practically floated over the surface, carving perfect turns, sending up plumes of light-as-air powder in her wake.

She swung around in front of Jack at the bottom of the hill, spraying him with snow and laughing at his mock howl of rage. "You'll pay for that," he said, brushing snow from the sleeves of his parka. But his grin promised the punishment would be every bit as enjoyable as the prank itself.

For the next hour, they took run after run, sometimes racing, sometimes taking it easy. Jack approached skiing the same way he approached a story, with an infectious zest and eagerness. She couldn't remember an afternoon when she'd pushed herself harder—or laughed more.

She felt worlds away from work and everyday life. It was as if she was in some alternate universe, where they weren't employer and employee or co-workers, but simply a man and a woman, two friends enjoying each other's company and the day.

"Let's stop a minute," Jack said halfway down yet another run. "I need to rest." He moved to the side of the run and leaned against a boulder.

Shelly skied over next to him. "I'm starving," she said.

"I can help with that." He unzipped a pocket on his jacket and took out an energy bar. "Here you go."

She stared at the bar. Chocolate. With nuts. Her favorite. "I can't take all your food."

"That's okay. I have more." He opened more compartments, and took out nuts, cheese, dried apricots.

She laughed. "It's a ski bum's feast."

He tore the top off the package of nuts. "It should hold us for a little while, anyway."

She opened the energy bar and gave him half, and accepted a portion of nuts in exchange. "You've been planning this."

He nodded. "Absolutely. As soon as Armstrong told me about his plans for the day, I started plotting my getaway. I didn't come up here to this gorgeous resort to spend the weekend posing for pictures."

"Well, thanks for breaking me out with you."

"I wouldn't have it any other way." He looked around. They were alone on the run, which looked out onto snow-shrouded forest and a jagged mountain range. The voices of other skiers and the squeak of the lift were muffled by the vastness. "I can't remember when I've enjoyed a day more."

She looked away, pretending to study the view, too afraid of what he would see if he looked into her eyes. Today had been the stuff of fantasies, the kind of day depicted in magazine advertisements for exotic perfumes or pricey jewelry. She resisted the urge to pinch herself, to make sure this all wasn't a fevered dream. "It is a gorgeous day," she said. "The snow, the weather— everything's perfect."

He brushed crumbs from his hands. "It is great, but that's not what's made this day so perfect."

"Oh?" She could feel his eyes still on her, but she didn't dare look at him. Instead, she took a deep breath and spoke in an overly bright tone. "We've both been working so hard on the show, a day off is that much more special."

"I could take a day off anytime I want." He slid closer and put his hand on her shoulder.

She leaned into his touch, unable to stop herself. *Snap out of it,* she scolded herself. *Act normal. Smile. Let him think you're the same "gal pal" you've been pretending to be all day.*

She looked back over her shoulder at him, her vision focused somewhere past his ear. If Jack mistook this for normal, he probably believed in UFOs and vampires, too. "What is it, then?" Her voice was unnaturally high-pitched.

"It's you." He squeezed her shoulder, sending a shudder through her. "Getting to spend time with you."

"You and I have spent a lot of time together."

"Not like this. Away from the office. Not working. Just…being. Enjoying each other's company."

She looked away again, unable to speak. Her feelings were too close to the surface, too dangerous.

"What's wrong?" He moved around to where he could see her face. "You look terrified. Of me?"

She shook her head, still mute. *Come on, get it together!* But her emotions were mutinying over common sense today, refusing to obey orders.

He put his hand under her chin, the fabric of his ski glove rough against her chilled skin. "You know I would never do anything to hurt you."

Maybe not on purpose. She nodded, a single dip of her head. "I know."

"Then what is it?"

Silence. She couldn't think. Not with him touching her.

"Are you thinking about that kiss we shared?" He slid closer, his thigh alongside hers.

She let out the breath she hadn't even realized she'd been holding. "Yes." Yes, she'd been thinking about it. Hadn't stopped thinking about it.

"So am I. It's the kind of kiss a man doesn't forget."

"I haven't forgotten." She'd come closer to forgetting her own name.

He slid his hand back to her shoulder. "Lately I've been thinking a lot about repeating that kiss."

Her eyes widened. Not that the same thought hadn't crossed her mind, but she knew better than to risk it. "I'm not sure that would be a good idea."

He looked puzzled. "Because you don't want to?"

"No. Because we work together every day. You're my *boss.*" Hadn't they settled this before?

"Not today. Not now." He pulled her closer. "Right now I'm just a man who's very attracted to you. And you're the only woman I've wanted since we met."

She opened her mouth to protest but was silenced by his lips on hers, his tongue sweeping across her teeth. If she'd been standing, her knees would have buckled; as it was, she started to slide down the rock.

He caught her, his arms wrapped around her, pulling her close as his mouth caressed hers, in turn gentle and insistent. That Jack, a man who was normally the picture of calm and self-control, would kiss her with such ferocity—such *need*—was her undoing. She put her arms around him and slid her gloved fingers into his hair, wishing she could feel more of him. In her imagination, she saw them both naked, and the vision destroyed the last fragment of hesitation. She arched against him and deepened the kiss. Only their many layers of clothing and the awkward skis kept her from abandoning herself to him altogether.

They were both breathless by the time they broke apart. When she opened her eyes she expected to see the snow melted around them, but nothing had changed, except perhaps her own outlook on their situation. She unzipped her parka and fanned herself.

"Yeah, I know what you mean." He sat back and opened his parka, too, then glanced at her. "So I wasn't imagining the chemistry between us."

She shook her head. Chemistry. Attraction. Whatever you called it, it was powerful and almost irresistible. "What are we going to do now?"

He stood and pulled his ski poles out of the snow. "I think we should ski some more."

She stared after him, debating racing after him and tripping him. Just like a man to stir up trouble and run away.

But as she started out after him she changed her mind. Maybe Jack had the right idea after all, putting some distance between them, letting things cool off a little. In the throes of passion was not the place to make decisions about relationships. They needed to think this through with their heads as well as their hormones.

But her hormones definitely voted for another kiss, and she doubted all the ice and snow in Colorado would cool the fire Jack had kindled in her.

JACK SCARCELY NOTICED his surroundings as he raced down the run. Was he crazy? Yes—crazy about Shelly. He'd told himself spending the afternoon with her, involved in some strenuous physical activity outside of the bedroom, would prove the two of them could manage a platonic friendship.

That theory had been shot to hell the first chairlift ride up. He'd been aware of every curve pressed against him, the scent of her perfume taunting him. He'd skied hard, trying to outrun his feelings, but when they'd stopped and shared lunch together, he'd been too tired to fight himself and his desires anymore.

So he'd kissed her. And she'd kissed him. What now? Did he risk everything he'd worked so hard for—having his own show, doing things his own way—for the sake of a fantasy? If things went bad between them, it could mean the end of *Inside Story,* as well.

He stopped at the bottom of the run and looked up at her. She skied with an easy grace, her gaze focused down the slope, seemingly unaware of him. Shelly wasn't like Jessica. She wasn't self-centered and conniving. But he couldn't lie to himself. Shelly was ambitious. If she had to choose between him and her career, what chance did he have?

It was decided, then. They couldn't afford to take this any further. He was sure she'd understand once he figured out some way to explain it to her.

"The lifts are going to close soon."

"What was that?" He looked over to where she'd stopped, a few feet from him.

"It's after three-thirty. The lifts close at four." She nodded toward a trail that would take them back to the other side of the mountain. "We'd better head down."

"Right." He nodded. "I guess we'd better."

He wanted to say more, and searched for words. But she'd already skied away. All he could do was follow.

When he got to the bottom she was there, with Armstrong, minus the cameraman. The producer was standing beside her with his arms crossed tightly over his chest, his lips pinched together. When he spotted Jack, he strode toward him. "I guess you think that was funny, running away from me like that?"

Jack clicked out of his skis, then bent to pick them up. "You had plenty of pictures," he said. "I wanted to ski."

"And you talked Shelly into going with you."

"He didn't have to do much persuading." She joined them, her gaze shifting away from him when he looked up. "I'm beat," she said, shouldering her skis. "I'm going back to the condo to find that hot tub."

They watched her leave, Jack's gaze locked to her backside as she picked her way across the snow.

"Don't tell me you've never noticed her cute ass before."

Armstrong's comment broke through his trance. He stared at the producer. Armstrong shrugged. "Hey, I'm a guy. I notice this stuff. Now, about tomorrow…"

"Forget it." He picked up his own skis. "No more pictures. No more video. Tomorrow I'm going home."

"You're not planning to ski? You've got a lift ticket for tomorrow."

He shook his head as he walked past. "No. I'm done."

Time to go back to the city and get his head back on work, where it belonged.

At his condo, he took a shower, then opened a bottle of beer. Every muscle ached from the punishment he'd given them on the slopes. He needed a soak in the hot tub, then maybe a massage.

Halfway to the hot tub room, he remembered that Shelly had said she was going to the hot tub. Had that been a casual comment, or a hint for him to meet her there?

He shook his head. *Don't go there, bud,* he told himself.

But she was there, alone in the tub with her back to him. He stopped, watching her. She had her hair up, and he could see drops of water beading on her shoulder. Steam rose around her in clouds, so that she looked more like an apparition in a dream than a flesh-and-blood woman.

He took another swallow of beer. He'd enjoy the view for a minute, then leave and come back later, after she'd gone in.

She reached back to get her glass of wine. He meant to step out of sight, but was frozen. "Jack?" She took a sip of wine. "Come on in. The water feels great."

He moved toward her, dropping his towel on a chair. He set his beer on the floor at the side of the tub, then eased into the water. "Oh, God, that feels good," he groaned, sinking down until he was up to his neck.

"I haven't skied that hard in years." She laughed. "Probably never. Were you determined to wear me out?"

No, I was trying to wear myself out. He reached for his beer. "You should have said something. I'm sorry."

"You don't have anything to apologize for."

"Yes, I do." His eyes met hers. "I shouldn't have kissed you."

"You didn't see me fighting you, did you?"

God, she was beautiful. Even without makeup and her hair in a ponytail, she was gorgeous. And she didn't want anything from him, or care what he looked like or didn't look like. She just wanted him. How many women could he say that about?

"Maybe instead of worrying so much about what might happen, we should just enjoy what can happen," she said.

"You're willing to risk that?"

She set aside her glass and stretched her arms over her head. "I've played it safe for most of my life. Maybe now I'm ready to live a little dangerously." She stood and climbed the steps out of the hot tub, then turned and held her hand out to him. "Are you coming with me?"

He looked up at her, at the invitation in her eyes and the soft curves of her body, and tried to ignore the way his heart was pounding. Was he ready for this? To take the next step with the one woman who always told him how she felt about things, who demanded as much honesty as she gave? Was he ready to risk his feelings with a woman who looked past his body to the man he *really* was?

The idea scared him spitless, but thrilled him, too. If he said no now, he doubted Shelly would give him a second chance. And he knew he'd regret that.

"Yeah." He grasped the edge of the tub and hoisted himself to his feet. "Yeah, I'm coming with you."

CHAPTER FIFTEEN

SOMEWHERE BETWEEN THE TOP of the mountain and the bottom, Shelly had decided to stop being afraid of things that hadn't happened yet. How much of her life had she wasted already, living in the future? *When I get promoted to on-air anchor, then life will be good. When I get done with this story, then I can take some time for myself. When my career is established, then I can focus on my personal life....*

She and Jack were here now, and despite lingering reservations, her gut told her she'd regret it the rest of her life if she wasted this opportunity.

She fumbled with the keys at the door of her condo, then felt Jack's hands wrapped around hers. "Let me get that," he said.

He held the door open for her and she led the way into the condo. The one-bedroom rental was furnished in leather and wood, with expanses of glass in the living room and bedroom that offered a view of the slopes. A single Sno-Cat trundled up the mountain, carving the run into corduroy, getting ready for tomorrow.

"Would you like a drink?" she asked, heading for the kitchen and setting her empty wineglass on the counter.

"No." He came up behind her and wrapped his arms

around her, pulling her close. His erection was a hard ridge against her buttocks. She caught her breath as he pressed against her, and felt the rush of wet heat between her legs.

He bent to kiss her neck, tracing the line of her jaw with his tongue, while his hands pushed down the straps of her bathing suit. "Were you waiting for me, there at the hot tub?" he asked, his words vibrating against her skin.

"Yes."

"Thank God."

He peeled the suit down to her waist, freeing her breasts, his breath growing ragged as he shaped his hands to her, and dragged his palms over her stiffened nipples. "I told myself on the way here that I'd take it slow, give us both time for second thoughts, but I can't," he said. "I want you too much."

"And I want you." She turned to face him, pressing against his chest, reveling in the feel of his still-damp skin against hers, at the drag of the crisp whorls of chest hair against hypersensitive flesh, at the thud of their hearts in syncopated rhythm.

He started to peel the suit down farther, but she grabbed his wrist, stopping him. "Let's go into the bedroom."

He nodded and led the way down the short hallway, to the hewn cedar bed. The fading rays of the sun reflected off the snow outside, bathing the room in a soft gray light.

She caught a glimpse of herself in the mirror on the dresser and moaned, not with pleasure. "Why didn't you tell me I was such a mess?" she asked, putting a hand to her hair, which was coming loose from its clip, wet strands curling wildly about her face and neck. Red marks from the swimsuit straps were carved into each shoulder, and a roll of pale skin swelled from the tummy-control midsection of her one-piece swimsuit.

"You look wonderful to me." He turned her away from the mirror and kissed her cheek, and the side of her mouth. "You look real, and soft, and sexy as hell."

When had a man called her sexy in a voice that was half growl, half caress? How could she not believe him?

On the strength of those words, she lowered the suit the rest of the way and stepped out of it. She resisted the urge to cover herself with her hands. If Jack wanted her, then he deserved to see what he was getting—every fold and bulge.

And speaking of bulges…her gaze zeroed in on his erection, which tented the fly of his swim trunks. "Let me see you," she said, reaching for him.

Grinning, he shucked off the trunks and stepped back.

It was probably unfair that one man could look so good. She dropped to her knees and kissed the head, then the shaft, then took him into her mouth. He was hot and hard, tasting of chlorine and salt. He pulsed against her tongue, and she felt a corresponding throb in her own sex.

He grasped her shoulders and tugged her up, to her feet. "Come here," he said, and pulled her to him once more, his lips hard on hers, his hands caressing.

They fell onto the bed, still kissing, his body across hers, his knee between her legs, pressing against her clit. She ground against him, her breasts thrust up, blatant in her need for him.

"Yes," he murmured, the word like the escape of steam from an overstressed valve. He sucked one breast into his mouth, taking in as much as he could, the stroke of his tongue and the pressure of the suction driving her to distraction. She moaned and thrashed beneath him, unable to be still or silent against this onslaught of her senses.

She felt rather than saw his smile as he moved to her other breast. He sucked hard, desire lancing through her like a knife, tension building. She thrust against him, grinding against his knee, desperate for relief.

And then he grew still, withdrawing slightly, his forehead pressed against her breastbone. "Please tell me you have a condom," he said.

"I have a condom." She had two, actually, in her makeup kit, a constant reminder of what, until now, hadn't been a part of her life lately. They'd been there awhile, but the wrapping was still intact. They would do until she could make a trip to the store. "I'll get them."

She started to rise, but he pressed her back down. "I'll get them. Just tell me where."

While she waited for him to return, she stared at the ceiling, debating pulling the covers over herself. She felt vulnerable like this, spread out naked in the middle of the bed, every ounce of her made to look wider still, pressed against the mattress.

But no, she wouldn't cover up. Jack would see all of her, including the parts camouflaged by control-top hose and underwire bras during their workdays. If he wanted her, then he needed to want her just as she was.

He returned, tearing the condom packet open as he walked. When he stopped beside the bed, she turned her head to look at him. He'd grown still, half-opened condom in one hand, staring at her.

"What?" Her voice quavered with fear and nascent anger. Was he so taken aback by her appearance that he'd refuse to go on with this? Still, she refused to turn away from that intense gaze.

"You're just so…beautiful," he said, his voice low. He knelt beside her on the bed and rested his free hand on her stomach. "So soft and…womanly."

She squeezed her eyes shut against sudden hot tears. Was he trying to make her fall in love with him? He was halfway to succeeding, his words and his touch—and the fierce desire in his eyes—capturing her heart as surely as if he'd already enslaved her body.

He sheathed himself, then nudged her legs farther apart and knelt before her. She propped herself up on her elbows and braced herself as he slid into her.

She was slick with arousal, muscles tightening around him as he eased into her. She raised her knees and thrust against him, trembling now from being poised on the edge so long.

When he reached down to stroke her clit, she thought she might come right then, but forced herself back from the edge. She wanted this moment to last, to build. She wanted something worthy of all the hours she'd spent daydreaming about them together like this.

They moved awkwardly at first, then found a rhythm of long, smooth strokes and short, hard, deep ones. His thumb moved back and forth across her swollen clit, until she was moaning and panting, tremors rolling through her like warning shocks before an earthquake.

And then she shattered, senses rent by the force of her climax. She was still trembling beneath him when a cry tore from his throat and he thrust hard against her, overtaken by his own release.

He collapsed against her, his breath ragged against her throat, elbows braced on either side. They lay with their arms around each other for a long while, not speaking, until their breathing grew even and shallow, and the last light had faded from the day.

She was beginning to think he'd dozed off, and was wondering what to do about her left leg, which was definitely asleep, when he stirred. "I'm sorry. Didn't mean to crush you." He rolled off of her.

"It's okay." She flexed her leg, then sat up. Now that her desire was sated—at least for the time being—other needs clamored for her attention. She had to go to the bathroom, and her stomach was growling. "I'm starved," she said.

"Me, too." He put his hands behind his head and grinned up at her. "Does this place have room service?"

"I don't know, but I saw a notice by the phone for a pizza delivery service."

"Sounds good." He sat up also. "You like pepperoni?"

"Canadian bacon and mushrooms."

He made a face. "Half and half?"

She laughed. So much for the instant and complete compatibility she'd naively believed in in her younger years. "Half and half is good."

She heaved herself off the bed and headed for the bathroom. "Why don't you call it in and I'll find us some more wine in a minute."

Later, they'd have to figure out what they'd do when they were back in Denver. But she'd put that off as long as she could. They deserved a few more hours of simple pleasure before the real world crowded in again, with all its complications.

"WE GOT A LOT OF GOOD footage today, though I would have liked to get more." Armstrong Brewster punched the remote control and started the tape he'd put together of Shelly and Jack at Copper Mountain, then sat back on the black leather sofa in Ed Palmer's penthouse.

"I'm surprised Jack agreed to do any of this," Palmer said from his own seat in a leather recliner. "He was dead set against it when the subject came up earlier this year."

"Now that the show is gaining momentum, I managed to convince him we should do everything we can to build on that." The television screen filled with a wide shot of Copper Mountain, then moved in to footage of Shelly and Jack skiing down the slope. They came to a stop side by side at the base of the lift and struck a pose for the camera.

The video changed to a close-up of Jack, who was smiling and talking to someone off camera. Probably Shelly. "He looks like some movie star." Armstrong chuckled. "Once we run these ads, we'll have even *more* women tuning in."

"Don't tell Jack that. He hates people commenting on his looks. Sometimes I think it would have been easier on him if he'd taken after my side of the family and been born plain."

"You think by now he'd have learned to use that handsome face to his advantage."

The camera shifted to Shelly as she clicked into her skis and prepared for another run. Armstrong frowned.

"We should have put her in a pair of black tights instead of those ski pants. Maybe she'd look slimmer."

"The pants don't do much for her," Palmer agreed. "But she's a good skier."

They watched more footage of the two skiing. "For a big girl, she's pretty athletic, I'll give her that," Armstrong said. "But let's face it—she doesn't look like the female anchor of a top-rated news show."

"There's something to be said for being new and different." Palmer rested his chin in his hand and studied the video as it shifted to a shot of Shelly and Jack waving from the lift chair.

"Tell that to all the 'new and different' news magazines that didn't make it out of their second season." The video ended and Armstrong punched the off button on the remote. "Don't get me wrong—I don't have anything against Shelly as a person. She's a damn good reporter. But so were the other women who interviewed for the job. One of them would have sold better to the viewers."

"How do you know that? We're doing better than I expected in the ratings."

Armstrong frowned. "We've had letters. Viewers who think Shelly's too fat. People who think a good-looking guy like Jack should be paired with a beauty queen."

Palmer dismissed this information with a wave of his hand. "The world is full of crackpots with typewriters."

"I just want the show to succeed," Armstrong said. "I'm looking out for your interests."

"I know." Palmer stood and clapped Armstrong on the shoulder. "Shelly was Jack's choice and this is his show. I'm not inclined to interfere with that unless something goes wrong."

"Let's hope nothing goes wrong." Armstrong stood and ejected the tape from the video player. "I feel like the show is on a roll and I don't want anything to slow us down."

Palmer laughed. "You worry too much. Nothing's going to happen."

SHELLY WOKE THE NEXT morning feeling amazing. Euphoria, or maybe some kind of sexual high, was like a balm over sore muscles and stiff limbs. Last night ranked as one of the most memorable of her life, a new standard by which all future relationships and fantasies would be measured. She rolled over to greet Jack but found the pillow beside her empty. Smiling, she slipped on a robe and went in search of him.

She found him in the living room, drinking coffee and munching cold leftover pizza, looking out the window at the empty ski runs. "Looks like another gorgeous day," she said, coming up behind him.

He turned, his smile telegraphing his delight in seeing her again. "Not as gorgeous as you."

"Oh, you are a smooth talker, aren't you?" But she let him pull her near, let him undo the tie of her robe and hold her close.

"What do you want to do today?" he asked.

"Oh, I can think of a few things." She traced her finger down his breastbone, her smile coy.

"*After* that." He nuzzled her ear.

She laughed. "Sleep? Eat?"

"How about ski? We have lift tickets."

She looked over his shoulder at the perfectly groomed expanse of snow outside the window. Skiing with him yesterday had been so magical. She nodded. "Yes. We should ski." *Who knows when we'll have a chance like this again?*

She looked up at him. "But I need a shower first."

He parted her robe farther. "Yeah. I think I do, too."

They showered together, taking turns soaping each other's bodies, reveling in the feel of slick wet skin, hard plains and smooth curves. The way he touched her, the way he looked at her, made her feel more beautiful than she ever had before.

It was after ten when they finally made it out onto the slopes. "We'll take it easy today," Jack said as they headed toward the lift. "I'm still tired from yesterday."

"Me, too." Frankly, she didn't think she could handle black-diamond runs today. She wanted nice blue cruisers, or even an easy green.

Most of all, she wanted to extend this time alone with Jack. Tomorrow, they'd be back at work, back in their familiar roles, except…except their relationship wasn't the same. They'd have to find a way to balance their new feelings for each other with the demands of the job. Not easy, maybe, but she was optimistic they were up to the task.

They reached the top of the lift and skied away from the chair. She stopped to adjust her goggles and slip her pole straps onto her wrists. The run stretched out before them, a gentle slope that still held patches of fresh corduroy. Overhead, the sky was a breathtaking Colorado blue, not a cloud in sight.

"We really lucked out on the weather, didn't we?"

She turned to address Jack, and found he wasn't beside her. He'd been waylaid near the lift by a group of female fans and was busy signing autographs.

She laughed. Even when Jack wore ski togs, his gorgeous face was unmistakable. Women might follow him, but *she* was the one he'd chosen to be with. The thought made her feel smug, and generous. "I'll meet you at the halfway point," she called to him.

He looked up and waved in acknowledgment that he'd heard her. Still smiling, she planted her pole and started down the run.

JACK CAPPED HIS PEN and straightened after signing the last of the women's lift tickets. "There you go, ladies. I'm glad you enjoy the show."

"Jack, you could sit up there and read the stock market report out loud and I'd tune in to watch you," said the oldest of the group, a fortyish brunette in a bright pink parka, Gloria something-or-other.

He kept his smile in place, wondering what she'd think if he told her he didn't view her words as particularly complimentary. But there was no point. Fans were fans, and they were entitled to their opinions. So he merely nodded goodbye and started to turn away.

"Wait. Can we get a picture?"

"I really need to be going." He shuffled back, anxious to head down the slope and meet up with Shelly.

"This won't take a minute. I have my camera right here." The tallest woman, a blonde named Millie, fumbled in her waist pack and came up with a disposable camera. "Now, Gloria, you and Debby lean in close." She motioned them over to Jack. Playing along, he put his arms around them and smiled. The shutter clicked.

"That was great," Debby said.

"One more. Okay, now, Deb, take one of me and Jack together."

As soon as Debby snapped the shutter, he started moving away. "Nice meeting you, ladies. I really have to go now." If he hurried, he might even catch up with Shelly before she'd gone too far.

Within a few minutes, he came over a small hill and spotted her ahead of him. She was skiing smoothly, approaching a group of giggling teens on snowboards. He grinned and shoved off hard on the inside edge of his right ski. He'd catch up with her and surprise her.

But as he headed toward her, one of the snowboarders broke loose from the pack and set off, never looking where he was headed. He plowed right into Shelly and she lost her balance and went tumbling.

Jack stopped and waited for her to right herself, but instead, she became tangled in her skis and poles and started to roll down the slope, a human snowball, gaining speed. "Shelly!" he shouted, and took off after her.

When he reached her, she'd come to a stop on the edge of the run, her skis and poles scattered uphill in every direction. She lay on her side, curled in a ball, her moans audible from some distance away. Another man had already stopped to help her.

Jack kicked out of his skis and knelt beside her. "Shelly? Shelly, are you all right?"

She shook her head, tears spilling down her face, her teeth clenched.

"I think it's her knee," the other man said. "My wife went to fetch the ski patrol."

"Jack, I'm sorry," Shelly gasped.

He put his hand on her shoulder, afraid to touch her for fear of adding to her pain, but unable to keep his hands completely away. "You don't have anything to be sorry about. I saw the whole thing. It was that dumb kid's fault."

She shook her head. "Everything was going so well. Us…the show…"

"Don't worry about any of that. You're going to be all right." He continued to pat her hand, numb, the world around him hazy, every part of him focused on Shelly. She was going to be all right, wasn't she? She had to be.

The ski patrol roared up beside them on a snowmobile, towing a sled. Jack moved back to allow them to work, queasy at the sight of Shelly in pain and helpless. He was helpless, too. It was worse, even, than if he'd been hurt himself. He folded his arms tightly across his chest and watched two of the patrollers lift Shelly into the sled. She groaned and the sound cut through him.

Get a grip, he told himself. But he couldn't push away the numbing fog that wrapped around him. Things were happening too fast. Last night…and now this. Too many emotions to deal with. Not enough time to figure out what was happening, how he should feel.

For a man who was used to being in control, who always knew where he was headed, this sensation of having his world tipped on its side shook him more than he'd ever let anyone know.

CHAPTER SIXTEEN

SHELLY'S MEMORIES OF THE FALL were scattered kaleidoscope images: a glance at the snowboarder barreling toward her; the shock of losing her balance and going into a slide; the lightning strike of pain tearing through her; the achingly vivid blue of the sky as she lay on her back in the snow; Jack's face hovering over her, like something out of a dream; the gray cloud of oblivion dragging her under.

"Shelly? Can you hear me? You're going to be all right. They're taking you into surgery now. I'll be right here."

When she opened her eyes again, the sky was a soft green. She frowned at it. What the heck had happened to screw up the sky so that it turned green?

"Shelly? Are you awake? How do you feel?" A warm hand squeezed the tips of her ice-cold fingers. She turned her head toward the voice and saw Jack bending over her. Everything behind him was green, too. She blinked, and the rest of the room came into focus. She hadn't been looking at the sky, but a ceiling. The ceiling of a hospital room.

Jack brushed her hair back from her forehead. "Hey there. It's good to see you awake."

"You look like hell." She hadn't meant to say it; the

words popped out when she opened her mouth. Maybe it was the shock of seeing him this way—hair uncombed, shirt untucked, dark circles beneath his eyes. Even at that, he was the best-looking thing she'd ever seen. Knowing he'd stayed here with her brought tears to her eyes.

"Hey, don't cry." He dabbed at her eyes with his shirtsleeve. "It's not that bad, is it?"

She managed a smile and he looked relieved. "That's better. I'm betting you feel like hell, but you look pretty good." He brushed his fingers across her cheek. "A little pale, but good."

"What happened?" She tried to lift her head off the pillow to get a better look around, but her skull apparently now weighed as much as the rest of her. Or else someone had tied an anvil to her head, which would explain the ache that throbbed in rhythm with her heart.

"You had a bad fall." He squeezed the tips of her fingers again. "Gave me quite a scare."

She closed her eyes, then opened them again. "So what's the damage? Will I ever dance the tango again?"

He laughed. "Backward, and in high heels." He glanced down to where she could feel her left leg swathed in bandages. "You have a tibial plateau fracture. I understand you have a bunch of high-tech metal in your knee now."

She groaned. "A fracture? Shit! Pardon my French." She turned to him, searching his face for some reassurance. "What are we going to do?"

"You're going to take all the time you need to get well, and I'm going to brush up on my nursing skills."

The thought of Jack nursing her back to health

brought a rush of warm, fuzzy feelings. Or maybe that was only the pain medication they'd no doubt given her. She licked her dry lips. "I mean, what are we going to do about the show?"

"To spout a cliché, the show will go on." He patted her arm. "I've already talked to Armstrong. We're going to bring in someone to fill in until you're back on your feet."

Ugh. The words weren't as reassuring as he'd no doubt intended. "I'll be back as soon as I can."

"The doctor says at least six weeks before you're up and about. But we'll be okay until you're well."

Right. If she had her way, she'd be reporting from a wheelchair. The image almost made her laugh. If Armstrong worried about having an overweight anchorwoman, he'd have a stroke over the idea of a reporter who was a cripple, too. "Who will you get for the job?" she asked.

"I'm not sure. Armstrong's going to make some calls tomorrow. I suggested he see if any of the other women who interviewed when you did are available."

She closed her eyes again. She had to, to keep him from seeing her panic. The three beauty queens vying to take over her slot on the show? It was her worst nightmare come to life. Once they flashed their blindingly white smiles and tossed their perfectly coiffed heads on air next to Jack's own perfection, she'd be toast. Between Armstrong and the disgruntled letter writers, she could say goodbye to her dream job.

And how long would it be before Jack started comparing her with his new co-worker? She believed him when he said he wanted to be with her now, but he was a man who was used to dating knockouts. Women like

Jessica Peabody. How could she stand up to that kind of competition?

The door to the room opened and a nurse bustled in. "I see you're awake. Wonderful!" She turned to Jack. "If you'll excuse us for a moment, I need to check her dressing."

"Sure." He backed toward the door. "I'll go get some coffee and be back in a little bit."

When he was gone, the nurse swept back the covers and inspected the bandages around Shelly's knee. "Your friend there is certainly a nice-looking man," she said. "And he's been so worried about you."

"Jack's a very sweet guy."

The nurse pulled the covers up again and checked the IV bag. "How are you feeling? Are you in any pain?"

"My head hurts." *And my heart.* But she doubted there was a medication that could help with that.

"OH, NO!" YVONNE STARED at the small article in the paper, heart pounding.

"What is it?" Daniel asked, tearing his attention from the hockey game on TV.

"It's Shelly. She's been hurt in an accident." She scanned the small notice on the back of the *Denver Post*'s Entertainment section, but the report was frustratingly short on details.

"The fat gal who used to be your friend?"

She's still my friend, she wanted to say, but was she? She and Shelly hadn't talked in weeks, and Yvonne had refused to think about finding another maid of honor. How could she get married without Shelly by her side? It seemed stupid that one disagreement could come between two people who had been closer than sisters for more than half their lives. But wouldn't a friend have called to let Yvonne know she'd been hurt? "Shelly's not fat."

Daniel laughed. "Well, she's not exactly thin, either. What happened? Somebody plow into her car?"

"It wasn't a car accident. She was skiing." She worried her lower lip between her teeth and read the few sentences a third time. "It must have been pretty bad. It says here she's expected to be off work for six to eight weeks."

"You ask me, anybody who'd strap two sticks to their feet and slide down an icy mountain ought to have their head examined." He turned his attention back to the television, where a group of dorky guys, surrounded by half a dozen supermodels, sang the praises of a local beer.

Yvonne looked toward her phone. "I should call her, see if she needs anything."

"I thought the two of you had a fight." Daniel took a long pull on his own bottle of beer, the same brand as the one in the commercial.

"We did." A stupid, petty argument. Her stomach churned at the memory. She shouldn't have let them walk away from each other, angry, that night. They'd had differences of opinion before and agreed to disagree. Why hadn't they been able to do that this time?

"Then screw her," Daniel said.

"I've known Shelly longer than anyone except my mother. I can't just drop her like that."

"Why not? She put you down for doing something to improve your life, so forget her." He focused on the TV once more. "Besides, you've got me now. You don't need her."

But I do need her. Every woman needed another woman to confide in, to laugh with. Women understood each other in a way no man ever could.

Women friends forgave each other more. Sure, Shelly stubbornly refused to accept the idea that a boob job could be a good thing for Yvonne. Maybe that was because for years she'd been so focused on accepting her own body exactly as it was. Maybe admitting this surgery was a good idea, admitting that it was okay to take drastic measures to change the way you look—maybe that would be admitting that she could do more for herself, too.

Or maybe it was only because she loved Yvonne and wanted the best for her.

She glanced toward the sofa, where Daniel was sprawled, the remote in one hand, a beer in the other. Shelly didn't like Daniel. She tolerated him for Yvonne's sake, but she didn't like him.

Yvonne could accept that. And despite what Shelly or anyone else thought, she wasn't stupid. She knew Daniel wasn't perfect, that he could be self-centered and chauvinistic and annoyingly arrogant.

But that was only one side of the man. He had another side that was sexy and generous. He was smart and hardworking and dependable. He'd be a good father, though she had no illusions about who would do the lion's share of the work associated with raising their children.

That was okay. She could deal with the negatives in exchange for all the good stuff—someone to share her life with, to come home to after work, to raise a family with. When she'd met Daniel she'd decided he could be that man, and had done everything in her power to get him to propose. Shelly might not understand that, but until this whole thing with the surgery came up, she'd been there for Yvonne.

Yvonne should be there for her now.

"I'm going to call her."

Daniel's answer was a grunt. He leaned forward and addressed the TV. "What do you think you're doing, idiot? You let that puck get right past you!"

She got up from the table and went into the bedroom. Shelly's number was still on speed dial, so she punched it and sat on the edge of the bed and waited for it to ring.

"Hello?"

At first she thought she'd dialed the wrong number. She didn't recognize the woman's voice. "Uh, I'm trying to reach Shelly Piper."

"May I ask who's calling?"

"This is Yvonne Montoya. Who are you?"

"I'm Ms. Piper's nurse. She can't come to the phone now. May I take a message?"

Yvonne clutched the phone with both hands. "Is she all right? How is she doing?"

"She's recovering well."

"What exactly happened? I read this was a skiing accident."

"I'm afraid I'm not at liberty to discuss Ms. Piper's medical condition. If you're a reporter, you may call KPRM and I believe they have an official statement available."

"I'm not a reporter, I'm a friend."

"I'll be happy to relay your message."

She left a brief message, asking Shelly to call her, and

hung up. She hugged her arms around her body, trying to squeeze out the black, empty feeling.

She lay back on the bed, remembering another time when she'd felt like this. When she was a little girl, her mother had had a boyfriend named Doc. He wasn't a real doctor, people just called him that. She'd never questioned why back then, but she thought now it might have been because he sold drugs. Her mother had always had a weakness for men who were more than a little shady.

But Yvonne had been just a kid. She knew none of that. All she knew was that Doc spent a lot of time with them. Because of him, they had a nice house to live in. He bought her presents—pretty dresses and toys—and fussed with her, even lying on the floor playing Barbies with her.

Her mother was jealous, of course. When she was with a man, she didn't want him to look at another woman, even her own daughter. She'd go to ridiculous lengths to keep a man's attention, but in the end they always left.

Doc stayed the longest—almost a year. But in the end, he left, too. Or rather, he was taken away, by cops who showed up at the house, put handcuffs on him and took him to jail.

That night, Yvonne had laid in bed, sobbing, while her mother taunted her. *You're the reason men never stay around,* she'd said. *No man wants a woman with a brat to take care of.*

But Yvonne knew Doc had loved her. Maybe more than anyone had before. Losing him had left a big empty space inside her.

After that, Yvonne's mother said they couldn't live in the house anymore. She had to leave behind the pretty dresses and the toys and move into a shelter. They'd never had such a nice house again. For a long time she missed the dresses, even after she no longer could have fit into them.

But most of all, she'd missed Doc, and having a man in her life. Someone to take care of her.

Daniel would take care of her now. Despite his flaws, he was someone she could depend on. He'd been in the same job for ten years. He'd driven the same kind of car for fifteen years. He'd lived in the same neighborhood for twenty years. And he would be with her forever. She was certain of that.

Shelly didn't understand that. She'd never needed taking care of. She was so strong. So independent. Some people were like that, but Yvonne knew she wasn't one of them. She wished she could tell Shelly that now. She wished she could find a way to bridge this chasm between them.

Daniel came into the room and flipped on the overhead light. "What are you doing lying here in the dark?" He came over to stand beside the bed. "You okay?"

She sat up and nodded, manufacturing a smile. "I'm fine. How was the game?"

"They lost. Stupid goalie couldn't block a shot if his life depended on it."

She listened with only half an ear while he ranted about the game. She washed her face and put on a nightgown, then slipped into bed beside him.

He reached for her, as automatic as he would have reached for a glass of beer when he sat down to watch the game, or his sunglasses when he picked up his car keys. She smiled at the thought. She liked the idea of being something essential to him. Someone he needed.

She snuggled closer, and his hand drifted down to cup her bottom. "Still thinking about Shelly?" he asked.

"I'm worried about her. I wish things weren't so messed up between us."

"I bet I can take your mind off her." He slipped his hand under her gown.

She arched toward him. "That feels good."

"I want you," he murmured, and pulled her close.

When it came down to it, this was all she needed. Someone to want her. Someone who would always be there for her.

"AND THAT'S ANOTHER EDITION of *Inside Story*. I'm Angela Lawson, with Jack Halloran."

When the on-air light went out, Jack turned to his new co-anchor. "You did a great job."

Angela sat back in her chair and fanned herself. "Thanks. Do you think anyone could tell I was nervous?"

"No. They'll think you've been doing this all your life."

"Thanks. And thanks for giving me this opportunity." She unclipped her microphone and laid it on the desk between them.

Jack gathered up his notes for that night's stories. "I was surprised you were available. It's been almost three months since I interviewed you."

She made a face. "There's a lot of competition out there. And I guess I'm particular. I've been doing some freelance writing and some modeling to make ends meet until the right position opens up."

"I'm sorry I can't offer you anything permanent, but this will give you some good exposure, and tapes you can send around."

"That's what I thought, too. So how's Shelly doing?"

"Pretty good. Not being able to drive or move around much is hard on an active person like her." He grinned. "When I talked to her on the phone this morning, she had just finished a session with the physical therapist, and she wasn't in the greatest mood."

Her exact words had been "This sadist actually enjoys watching me suffer. I told him when I was well I was going to do an exposé on people like him, who are paid to torture people like me."

"When you talk to her again, tell her I said hello. And let her know I'll be keeping her chair warm for her." She gathered up her notes and stood. "Meanwhile, I intend to make the most of this chance. As soon as you're available, I'd like to get together and discuss some story ideas I have."

"Let's do that Monday. I have a few things to do tomorrow."

"Great. Good night, then."

When she was gone, Jack collected the rest of his notes and made his way down the hall to his office. This was his favorite time to work, when everything was quiet. He could analyze that night's show and rough out a plan for the next episode. Mary Anne had chided him about burning the midnight oil, but this kind of work was more pleasure than chore to him.

Except tonight he couldn't stop thinking about Shelly. Between the demands of the show and her schedule of physical therapy, doctor's appointments and the need to rest and recuperate, they hadn't seen much of each other since he'd brought her home from the hospital Monday afternoon. They'd talked on the phone, but that only made him more anxious to see her, to hold her and touch her and kiss her.

That was probably all they'd be able to do for a while, considering her condition, but that was all right. He'd be content to sit with her, to continue to get to know her better outside the confines of work. He didn't know if it was because she didn't see him as a celebrity, or a handsome face and body to be pursued, or because of his growing feelings for her, but he was able to really relax with Shelly—to show the real self others couldn't see behind his professional mask.

Though he'd never have wished for her to be hurt, he welcomed the reprieve from the whole working-together-as-lovers issue. Maybe if they developed a more normal relationship first, they could avoid the problems he and Jessica had had.

He hoped so. He didn't want to lose Shelly as a lover, or as a co-worker.

SHELLY SAT IN BED, her attention riveted to the morning newspaper. The media columnist had devoted four whole paragraphs to the addition of Angela Lawson to *Inside Story. Ms. Lawson brings a young energy and multicultural perspective to the news magazine. Last night's story on Denver's Hmong community is an example of the kind of piece we hope to see more of while she's with the news magazine.*

Of course, Shelly had been working on that story before Angela came along. Would the columnist have said

the same thing if she knew an over-the-hill white chick
had written it? She tossed the papers aside and dragged
herself over to the side of the bed, grimacing as she bent
her knee. She took hold of the walker and heaved herself upright. She might be only thirty-one, but since the
accident, she felt about sixty-one. Not to mention she'd
been in a perpetual bad mood. For someone who did *not*
consider herself a weepy woman, she'd gone through
two boxes of tissues mopping up after crying jags, and
there were days when all conversation was reduced to
various moans and growling.

Then again, being housebound, in constant pain and
in fear of losing your job would probably give anyone
the most raging case of PMS imaginable. Only in this
case, the letters stood for Pissed-off and Melancholy
Syndrome.

"Good, you're out of bed."

Her nurse, Susan Bryant, whom Shelly had dubbed
Nurse Tyrant, swept into the room. The woman never
dawdled over anything, whether it was serving meals or
giving meds. She was devastatingly efficient, supreme-
ly professional, and had all the warmth of a marble
statue in a museum basement. "Come on, start walking."
She motioned Shelly forward. "You remember what the
doctor said. He wants you to take at least one hundred
steps a day."

"The good doctor has obviously never had his knee
broken by some kid who was in too much of a hurry to
look where he was going. It hurts." Her knee ached
pretty much all the time, but one circuit of the room with
the walker and she was exhausted, her whole left leg
pulsing with pain.

"It's supposed to hurt. If it didn't hurt, we'd have to worry about nerve damage." The Tyrant began making up the bed, pulling up the sheets and fluffing the pillows. So much for Shelly's plans for a nap later.

"That's the biggest load of crap I've heard in a while," she said as she continued to drag herself around the room. *Slide, thump, thump. Slide, thump, thump.* "I had an accident, I'm not doing penance."

The Tyrant shot her a disapproving look. "When I'm done with the bed, I'll help you get dressed."

"I thought I'd wear this all day." She looked down at the extra-large T-shirt and cutoff sweatpants she'd worn to bed. "This is the height of fashion for housebound invalids, didn't you know?"

The Tyrant's expression didn't lighten one iota. Shelly decided she was going to have to talk to the agency about that. If you sent a nurse to look after someone, you should at least make sure she laughed at the patient's jokes. The insurance company was paying the woman enough, she could afford to fake a chuckle or two at least.

The Tyrant gave the pillow a hard *thwak,* then walked over to Shelly's closet. "This blue pantsuit is nice," she said, taking out a steel-blue silk ensemble.

Shelly raised one eyebrow. "Do *you* wear silk to lie around the house?" she asked.

The Tyrant made a tsking sound and hung the pantsuit on the hook on the closet door, then laid out a clean bra and underwear. "Do you need me to help you undress?"

"No, thanks. I can manage." It was bad enough having to accept help getting in and out of the shower; at least she could still dress herself.

When she was alone, Shelly stripped and put on the clean undergarments, then started to hang the pantsuit back in the closet. She hesitated when she had it in her hand. It *was* a comfortable outfit. And the blue brought out her eyes. What the heck? She slipped the top over her head. Maybe getting a little dressed up would help improve her mood, which had taken a nosedive since last night's episode of *Inside Story.*

Seeing Jack with Angela Lawson, the two of them so beautiful and healthy and perfect, had made her feel like troll woman. She stared in the mirror at her limp hair and pale, naked face. Her eyebrows needed plucking and she had a new zit over her right temple. Her crow's-feet had crow's-feet and her chin had added a twin. She wasn't troll woman. She was troll woman's grandmother.

She turned from the mirror and reached for a pair of silver hoop earrings. She couldn't even take satisfaction in dismissing her replacement as some empty-headed beauty queen. Angela was obviously smart and talented. No wonder the critics loved her.

Armstrong was probably jumping for joy, too. He was probably praying Shelly's doctor would make her complete the full twelve weeks of therapy before she returned to work. By then viewers would be saying "Shelly who?" and she'd be pounding the pavement in search of a job.

The doorbell rang, startling her from her musing. Probably some survey taker or evangelist. She didn't get many door-to-door salespeople here, with the exception of neighborhood children selling stuff to raise money for school and scouts. Was it Girl Scout cookie time yet? A sleeve of Thin Mints would go a long way toward lifting her depression, she was sure of it.

"Shelly, are you decent?" Nurse Tyrant's voice sounded remarkably cheery. Shelly was immediately suspicious.

"If you mean am I dressed yet, yes."

"Oh, good." She mumbled something, apparently to whoever was at the door.

Still frowning, Shelly grabbed her walker and started her torturous way toward the door. *Slide, thump, thump. Slide, thump, thump.* Couldn't they make one of these that was self-propelled or something? At this pace it took her half an hour to cross a room.

"Hi, Shelly, how are you? It's good to see you up."

Jack stood in the doorway, a huge bouquet of roses in his hand. If Shelly had been able, she would have run and flung himself into his arms. "Am I glad to see you," she said. "I'm going stir-crazy."

"You look great."

The man was a liar, but he did it well. He came and kissed her, then kept his arm around her and guided her to the end of the bed, where he sat beside her. "How are you feeling?"

"I'll just put these in some water." Before Shelly could answer, the Tyrant hurried into the room and took the flowers from Jack's hand. Shelly stared at the nurse. She was actually smiling. Shelly peered closer. The woman was even wearing *lipstick!*

When she'd disappeared again, Shelly turned to Jack. "That's the best mood she's been in all week. Obviously, she likes you."

"She was very friendly when I called earlier and told her I wanted to stop by to see you."

That explained her insistence that Shelly dress up.

Shelly definitely owed her for that one. She might even forgive her lack of a sense of humor. "You certainly have a way with women. They can't resist you."

"What about you? Can you resist me?" His smile was wicked, sending tremors through her. He slipped his arms around her and his mouth found hers.

Despite her weakened condition, Shelly's thoughts soon turned to the bed beneath them. Would it be possible to make love if she propped her leg on a pillow or something? Of course, they'd have to send Nurse Tyrant on an errand. Otherwise, she was liable to listen at the door.

That thought went a long way toward cooling her libido. They parted and she smiled at Jack. "I think I've discovered a great new painkiller."

"There's nothing new about it." He kissed her again.

"Think I could get my doctor to write a prescription?"

"That would definitely be new."

They didn't say anything for a while after that. They were in full make-out mode, their hands inside each other's shirts, when the Tyrant returned.

"Remember, our patient needs her rest," she chided, her cheeks bright pink.

"I can rest fine on my back," Shelly muttered as she straightened her clothes and eyed the tray of cookies and coffee, and the paper cup of pills for her.

"Now I'm positive she likes you," she said when they were alone again. "I usually have to take my pills with plain water. Not even the bottled kind."

"Want me to speak to her? I could probably charm her into bringing you cookies every afternoon."

"No doubt you could, but that's okay. She's a good nurse, even if she isn't good company."

"Are you bored?"

She groaned. "Out of my head. Another few days and I'll be caught up on my reading. Considering my to-be-read stack was once as tall as my nightstand, that's saying something."

"Next time I'll bring you a new book and some movies."

"Just bring yourself. That's the best present you could give me."

"It's a deal." He sipped coffee. "Before I forget, Angela says hello."

The mention of the woman she couldn't help but think of as her replacement made her chest tighten. "Oh? How's she doing?"

"She's doing great. She jumped right in and went to work. I feel really lucky to have found someone like her on such short notice."

Gee, if he tried, could he be a little more enthusiastic? She swallowed hard. "That's great." She considered jealousy a singularly unattractive emotion, and was determined not to let hers show.

"I really miss you, though." He turned to her, his expression serious, his eyes looking into hers. "I've lost count of how many times I've started toward your office, or dialed your extension to tell you something, then remembered you were here, at home."

"I've missed you, too." She missed work, driving and wearing high heels, too, but Jack was definitely at the top of the list. "At least we can still see each other after work."

"And I intend to see as much of you as I can." His grin turned devilish. "If we can get rid of your nurse for a while, we might find out how much you can accomplish with a bum knee."

"Now, that's physical therapy I could enjoy." They kissed again, even as the pain pill she'd just swallowed started taking effect. She began to feel fuzzy-headed and dreamy, though who was to say that wasn't the effect of Jack's kisses?

"I'd better go," he said. "I don't want to wear you out."

"I'm fine." But she could hear the slur in her voice.

He patted her cheek and stood. "I'll come by tomorrow, if you like."

"I like." She grinned. "And it's the nurse's day off."

"Then I'll definitely be here."

CHAPTER SEVENTEEN

WHEN HE VISITED SUNDAY, Jack offered to take Shelly out for a change of scenery. "Yes! Get me out of here before I go crazy. I've spent the last three days watching decorating and cooking shows. Any minute now I'm liable to start knocking out walls and attempting to make French pastry, both of which I'm pretty certain would lead to disaster."

He laughed. "Have I mentioned how much I love your sense of humor?" Some women would be moaning about the rough hand they'd been dealt, but Shelly was making jokes.

"I'm serious," she said. "Yesterday I caught myself wondering if a mirrored wall would make my dining area look bigger. Like I really want more mirrors in my house."

"So where would you like to go? Maybe up into the mountains, or out to the lake?"

"Those would be nice, but…" She hesitated, looking uncertain.

"But what?"

She looked toward the calendar on the kitchen wall. "This is going to sound weird, but would you take me to the hospital?"

"The hospital?" His heart pounded and he grasped her by the shoulders. "Are you not feeling well? Is something wrong with your knee?"

She shook her head. "I'm fine. But I have a friend who had surgery Friday. I think she'd probably be able to have visitors by now."

Relief made his knees weak, but he thought he hid it well. "Sure. Sure, I can take you to see her. Which hospital?"

"Rose Medical."

Three times on the way to the car she apologized for how long it was taking. "I don't think I'll be entering any walker races soon," she said as she gingerly negotiated the curb.

"Take your time. We're not in a hurry." He hovered near her elbow, poised to catch her if she stumbled, everything in him fighting the urge to sweep her into his arms and *carry* her to the car. The only thing that kept him from acting on that impulse was the fear he might injure her somehow in the transfer, and the suspicion that Shelly wouldn't appreciate being treated as though she were helpless—even if that was close to the truth.

By the time he actually had her buckled into the front seat, she was pale and sweating. "Maybe this wasn't such a good idea," he said. "Maybe this is too soon for you to be out like this."

"No, the worst part is over. I'll be fine." She gave him a weak smile. "I'll just think of it as an extra session of physical therapy."

"If you're sure. Maybe you should just call your friend."

"No. I want to see her."

He could have put his foot down, of course, and refused to drive her. But Shelly wasn't the type to take orders from anyone, and the thought of trying to bully her into anything didn't set well with him. "All right." He settled into the driver's seat and inserted the key into the ignition. "But if you start feeling too bad, promise you'll let me know and we'll go home right away. All right?"

She nodded. "It's a deal. Thanks."

They set out toward the hospital. "What kind of surgery is your friend having? Or is that too personal a question?"

"This is the friend I told you about." She turned to him, her expression grim. "The one whose fiancé gave her a boob job as a wedding gift."

"I remember." How could he forget that night, when his fantasies of kissing Shelly had become reality? "So she went through with the surgery?"

"Yeah. I thought Yvonne had more self-respect than that."

"So your friend—Yvonne—thinks this is a good idea?"

She nodded. "Yvonne's been desperate to get married for years. She says if this will make her fiancé, Daniel, happy, then she's happy to do it."

"Obviously, you're not thrilled with the idea."

"I'm sick about it." She glanced at him again, her eyes filled with anguish. "Yvonne's been my best friend since we were kids in school. I hate to see her...demeaning herself this way."

"Does she know how you feel?"

She nodded. "That was a mistake. I thought I could talk her out of doing this. We had a big fight." She chewed her lower lip. "In fact, we haven't spoken since."

"So she doesn't know about your accident?"

"She knows. I guess she read it in the paper. She called while I was asleep or something, right after I got home from the hospital. Nurse Tyrant told her I couldn't be disturbed and took a message."

"And you didn't call her?"

She shifted in her seat. "I tried once, but she wasn't home, and I was too chicken to leave a message. I mean, what could I say? 'I hate what you're doing, but I still care about you'?"

"That sounds like a good start to me."

"Maybe I'll try it out this afternoon." She sighed. "Maybe I shouldn't even be going to the hospital, but I have to see for myself that she's all right. Do you think I'm being crazy?"

"I think you're being a good friend. She called you when she heard about your accident, so I'm sure she'll be glad to see you."

"Thanks." She flashed a smile. "You're not only a pretty good chauffeur, you make a good counselor, too."

"I'm a man of many talents, some of which you haven't discovered yet."

She laughed. "Then I'm looking forward to finding out what I've missed."

SHELLY WONDERED WHAT SHE and Jack had missed in that time between making love at Copper Mountain and him visiting her today. The accident had definitely changed things for them, forced them to take a step back, as it were, to allow things to progress at a slower pace.

Which wasn't a bad thing. She didn't know anyone she enjoyed talking with more than Jack, and it was good to get to know him outside of work. But patience had never been her strong point, and now that she and Jack had made the biggest leap of all—admitting their feelings for each other—taking these baby steps in their relationship frustrated her almost as much as her inability to get around physically.

She and Jack had spent some pleasant time together, but they hadn't talked about what would happen when she was able to return to work. The thought of trying to juggle life and work and romance all at the same time scared her, but the thought of breaking up with him felt even worse. Did Jack see them together in the future? Had he fallen for her as hard as she'd fallen for him— so hard she had to bite her tongue to keep from blurting "I love you" whenever they were together?

He turned into the parking garage for Rose Medical and found a handicapped spot near the elevators. "I don't have a sticker, but I figure if anyone qualifies, you do," he said as he switched off the engine. "Wait here."

"What for?" she asked. "If you'll get my walker from the backseat…"

"I'll get something even better." He got out of the car and jogged toward the elevators. She watched him go, admiring the way his jeans hugged his backside. Obviously, her libido hadn't been damaged one bit in the accident. When they were alone later, they might have to do something about that….

Jack returned, pushing a wheelchair. "You might as well travel in style," he said as he helped her out of the car. "Save your strength."

"Thanks." She settled into the chair. "I wasn't looking forward to trundling all over the hospital with that walker."

They rode the elevator up to the surgery floor, then asked at the desk for Yvonne. "Let me see if she's accepting visitors," the volunteer behind the counter said.

She returned in a moment. "She's in 312. Down that corridor, on the right."

At the correct room, Jack tapped on the door while Shelly reached up and clutched his hand. The thought that Yvonne might not want to see her made her cold all over. Friends were too important to give up easily. Shelly needed every friend she had just to get through the day sometimes. Surely Yvonne still needed her, too.

"Come in." The voice was tentative but definitely Yvonne's.

Shelly smoothed her sweaty palms down her thighs, then looked up at Jack and nodded. "I'm ready."

As soon as the wheelchair rolled into view, Yvonne gave a little cry. "Shelly, what are you doing here?"

Tears clogged her throat at the realization that Yvonne wasn't angry. "I had to make sure you're all right. And I had to apologize for being such a butt." She rolled to the bedside and clutched Yvonne's hand.

"Oh, honey, you're not a butt."

The waterworks started then. Shelly and Yvonne both sobbed, patting each other's hands and blurting apologies and endearments. Jack retreated to a corner of the room and crossed his arms, assuming the role of dispassionate observer, like an anthropologist studying that intriguing species known as woman.

"I can't believe we've both been so stupid." Yvonne sniffed. "I felt so horrible when I heard about your accident. Tell me about it. Are you going to have to be in that wheelchair for a long time?"

"I don't have to be in the wheelchair now. At home I use a walker, but this was easier to get around in here." She patted Yvonne's hand again. "I'm going to be fine. I had surgery to put some pins in my knee, and I'll have to have therapy and stay off my feet for a few weeks. But eventually you won't even know I was hurt. The doctor says I can probably ski again by next winter."

Yvonne made a face. "Why would you want to, after an accident like that?"

"You know me. I'm too stubborn to let anything get the better of me. And I'm certainly not going to let some snot-nosed kid on a snowboard knock me out of something I've always loved." *Including the job you love?* a voice in her head nagged, but she ignored it. "Tell me about you. How are you doing?"

"I'm a little sore, but fine. The doctor said everything went great."

If Jack hadn't been there, Shelly would have probably asked to see the results, or at least the bandages. As if fearful she might do just that, he cleared his throat. "I'll go get a cup of coffee and leave you two to talk," he said.

"Is this Jack?" Yvonne's smile transformed her face. She was suddenly the warm, easygoing person Shelly loved like a sister.

"This is Jack Halloran," she said, making the introductions. "Jack, this is Yvonne Montoya, my best friend since seventh grade."

"It's so nice to meet you, Jack. And thank you for bringing Shelly to see me. Seeing her is the best medicine I could ever have."

"I was happy to do it." He took a step back, toward the door. "Can I bring either of you anything?"

"You don't have to go. Daniel will be back in just a minute. He went to find the doctor to get him to sign the orders letting me go this afternoon." She grinned at Shelly. "He has been so sweet. He sent me those roses." She nodded to the vase of white roses that sat on a small table in view of the bed.

"They're beautiful." Shelly hoped Yvonne didn't hear the lack of enthusiasm in her voice. She still hadn't forgiven Daniel for this so-called wedding gift that was really designed to stroke his own ego.

As if summoned by her thoughts, Daniel himself burst into the room just then. "I had them page the doctor and he said he'd be down here in a few min—" He stopped and frowned at Shelly. "What are you doing here?" His gaze shifted to Jack. "And who are you?"

"It's all right, Daniel. Shelly came to make sure I'm okay. And this is her friend, Jack Halloran."

"The reporter, right?"

"That's right." Jack offered his hand. "Good to meet you."

Shelly could tell the handshake was perfunctory, dismissive even. Daniel turned his attention back to Yvonne. "I don't think it's a good idea to have you upset right now."

"I'm not upset," she said, her voice rising. Her smile slipped, but only for a moment. When it was firmly back in place she spoke again, her voice calmer. "Shelly and I are over our silly disagreement. I'm really happy to see her—and to meet Jack."

Jack came to stand beside Shelly, his hand on her shoulder. The protective gesture made her throat tighten.

"I was telling Shelly how the doctor said the surgery went really well," Yvonne said.

"He says she'll be completely recovered for the wedding." Daniel's smile was smug. "And she's going to look fantastic in a bikini on our honeymoon."

Shelly wondered if Daniel worked at being so tactless, or if it came naturally. She clutched the armrests of the wheelchair until her knuckles whitened.

"Oh, Daniel, don't embarrass me!" But Yvonne seemed pleased by his comments.

"Can I help it if I'm proud of you?" He put his hand on the top of her head, as if she were a small child, or a prize puppy. "This worked out so well, I'm thinking about giving her a nose job for our first anniversary."

Shelly rolled back so suddenly, she almost ran over Jack's toes. He avoided the collision and took hold of her chair. "I'm sorry," she muttered, so that only he could hear. "We'd better go." She couldn't sit here and listen to Daniel one more minute without either puking or screaming in rage.

"We'd better get out of here and let you get ready to go home," Jack said, already wheeling her toward the door. "It was nice meeting you."

"I'll call you," Yvonne said as they left the room.

Jack didn't say anything until they were in the elevator again, alone. "If you like, I could arrange to meet up with Danny boy in a dark alley somewhere and punch his lights out," he said.

"It's tempting, but I know it wouldn't do any good." She shook her head. "It scares me that someone I thought I knew so well would sacrifice herself for the sake of a relationship." Is that what love did to women? Is that what it would do to *her?* She glanced at Jack. "I don't understand what Yvonne sees in him, but if he makes her happy, I can't interfere. I already tried that, and it almost cost me a friend. From now on, I'm keeping my mouth shut."

"Smart woman. But I sympathize. I don't even know the couple and seeing them together upset me."

The elevator opened and he wheeled her to the car and helped her in. "I'd offer to take you to eat somewhere, but you look worn out," he said.

She nodded. She was exhausted, but it was more emotional than physical. "I'd still like to eat. Maybe you'd go for takeout?"

"It's a deal."

Maybe after eating she could muster the strength to enjoy a romantic afternoon with Jack. A few hours alone with him would do away with these silly fears she'd let creep into her head. Jack cared for the woman she was, not some woman she might be. As long as she remembered that, she'd be fine.

BACK AT HER CONDO, Shelly unearthed the menu for her favorite Chinese place and called in an order of mu shu pork, sesame chicken and crab-cheese wontons. Jack picked up the food and brought it back.

When he returned, he found she'd changed into a softly flowing caftan and was reclining on the sofa, looking more relaxed. "There's a bottle of zinfandel in the refrigerator if you want to open it," she said.

As he poured the wine and hunted in the drawers for silverware, it struck him how long it had been since he'd spent a casual Sunday afternoon like this, just hanging out with a female friend, making himself at home in her home.

He arranged the food and wine on the coffee table, then sat on the floor and began filling his plate. "You don't mind if I hang out here awhile, do you?" he asked.

"Mind? Why would I mind?"

He shrugged. "I wanted to make sure you weren't tired, ready to be alone."

"If I get tired, I'll tell you. I promise."

Her smile sent a warmth spreading through him that had nothing to do with desire, but everything to do with contentment. "Yeah, that would be nice."

They ate in silence for a while. He chewed mu shu and listened to the metronome beat of the antique clock that sat on top of the entertainment unit. From time to time he looked over at the woman on the sofa, and marveled at how in tune he felt with her, even when neither was saying a word. He'd known sexual compatibility with women before, and had worked with others as part of an efficient team, but he'd never experienced such a psychic connection with another human being.

Ordinarily, the thought would have worried him. Since his split with Jessica, he'd avoided anything that smacked of commitment. Did his change of heart mean he had fallen in love with Shelly? He studied her, trying the idea on for size. He and Shelly in love. Amazing how right it felt.

"Can I ask you a really personal question?"

Shelly's question managed to disturb his serenity slightly, like a pebble tossed into a heretofore glassy pool. He finished off the last wonton and set his plate aside. "What's the question?"

"Someone told me you used to be married to Jessica Peabody."

He nodded. "It didn't last long. We were both working at KXAS in Dallas at the time."

She dragged the end of an egg roll through a puddle of sweet-and-sour sauce on her plate. "What was that like? I mean, both of you working at the same station and everything?"

"It was...uncomfortable." He leaned back on his hands, watching her face as he searched for the right words to describe what went wrong with his marriage. "For a big city, Dallas can be a small community. We were local celebrities, so the gossip columnists dutifully reported our every move. Or at least it seemed like it at the time. And then the station decided to play up the match to boost ratings, so we were in the spotlight even more." If he and Shelly continued to see each other, would they run into the same problems? They were on public TV now, not a network. And a weekly show wasn't as high-profile as the nightly news.

Most important, Shelly wasn't Jessica. Maybe they *could* make this work. He began to hope.

"I guess that kind of scrutiny would be hard on any relationship."

He nodded. "It didn't help that Jessica and I had entirely different attitudes about all the attention. She thought it was the best thing that had ever happened, that it would make our careers. She thrived in the spotlight, while all I wanted was to be left alone to do my job."

"Easier said than done in this business." Shelly emptied her wineglass. "And in a way, I guess we ask for that kind of scrutiny when we dare to step in front of a camera."

He nodded. "I've come to accept that now. At least

somewhat. But I was younger then, and so determined to define myself as a skilled, dedicated newsman. I felt like I'd begun to make real headway, too. I'd done a couple of really gritty stories—corruption in local government and problems with a high-profile criminal case. I thought people in the industry were beginning to take me seriously. And then, practically overnight, all that work was wiped out and I was back to being 'Handsome Jack Halloran,' one half of the 'Evening News Newlyweds.' Instead of writing to praise or criticize the stories I reported, people were back to critiquing my hair and gushing about what a 'cute couple' Jessica and I were."

"The 'Evening News Newlyweds'?" She laughed. "Ouch!"

"No kidding. Some genius in the marketing department thought that one up, and insisted on using it right up to our first anniversary." He refilled both their glasses with the last of the wine. "By then, it had become clear to both of us that we wanted different things in life and we'd agreed to split up."

"Still, that must have hurt."

"Oh, yeah." Deep inside, he still carried a little of the pain from those days. He'd gone into marriage with the idea of true love and "until death do us part" and come out of it believing he'd married a woman who had seen him as little more than another rung on her career ladder. With time, he'd been able to admit that Jessica had never deliberately misled him. She'd sincerely given him all she could of herself, but in the end, Jessica looked out for Jessica. There wasn't room in her life for anyone else.

He shook off the memories and took another drink

of wine. "We were lucky enough to part as friends. That's something to be proud of, even if the marriage itself wasn't."

"And Jessica went on to work for CNN."

He nodded. "She'll do well there. She's smart and a hard worker."

"And she's gorgeous." There was no bitterness in her voice; she was stating fact.

"*And* she's gorgeous." He reached for another piece of sesame chicken and popped it into his mouth. "But those folks who talk about beauty being only skin deep aren't just blowing smoke. Jessica could be very cold and hard when it suited her. And she was so obsessed with her looks—maintaining them, displaying them, making sure she was noticed—there wasn't room for a lot of other things in her life. Even without the pressure from the outside, I think that aspect of her personality would have driven us apart eventually."

She rearranged the folds of the caftan around her. "Speaking of gorgeous newswomen, Angela Lawson's doing a great job, isn't she?"

"She's done well, for someone who stepped in at the last minute. But I know the viewers and I will be happy to see the regular anchorwoman back in her usual spot in a few weeks."

She made a face. "Don't be so sure about that. Give the average viewer a few weeks and they won't remember who I am."

Since when was Shelly so pessimistic? He got to his feet and came to sit beside her. She moved over to make room for him, though it seemed she did so reluctantly. "If that's the case, then the average viewer is a moron.

That still leaves me. And I definitely will be glad when you're able to come back to work."

"I don't know…" She looked away.

They'd been so close; he wasn't going to let her pull away from him like this. He took her chin in his hand and turned her to face him again. "What is it? Tell me what you're thinking."

She tightened her mouth into a thin line, but he kept his gaze locked to hers, refusing to let her put up walls between them. She sighed. "I've been reading reviews of the show in the papers. The press loves Angela, too. And I'm sure Armstrong loves her."

He rubbed his palm up and down her arm. "Haven't you figured out by now that I don't care what Armstrong thinks? He's a good producer, but he's not the one responsible for choosing the co-anchor. I am. And I chose you."

The worry lines around her eyes softened. "I know you did, Jack. That means the world to me." She leaned toward him, her lips parted, eyes closing. "You mean the world to me."

He kissed her as much out of relief that this uncomfortable conversation had ended as he did out of a desire to feel his lips on hers. But the heat that had been simmering between them all day flared at the meeting of their mouths. He slid his arms around her and deepened the kiss. She responded with a breathy moan that had every cell of his being focused on her.

CHAPTER EIGHTEEN

SOMEWHERE BETWEEN THE FIRST kiss and Jack starting to undress, he and Shelly ended up in her bedroom. She tugged at the knot of his tie as they sat on the end of the bed. "I want us to be together," she said. "We just have to figure out how."

"We'll find a way." He kissed her cheek. "I love you, Shelly."

"I love you, too, Jack."

He looked into her eyes, buoyed by the certainty he saw there. "What are we going to do about it?"

Her smile sent a jolt of heat through him. "Oh, I can think of a few things." Eyes locked to his, she finished unknotting the tie and tossed it aside.

They undressed slowly, working carefully around the brace on her knee. "I'll be so glad when this damned thing is out of my life forever," she said as he eased her panties down over the brace.

"You don't notice it slowing me down, do you?" He crawled up to lie beside her, reaching up to cup her breast.

"That's one thing I love about you. You don't let a few obstacles get in the way of what you want."

"No, I don't. And right now, I want you." He kissed her again, a long, deep caress of his lips on hers, his tongue plunging into her mouth, tasting her, possessing her. When they finally broke apart they were both breathless. He stared down into her eyes, which were dark with desire, and thought hers was a face he could enjoy looking at for the rest of his life.

A scary thought, that, and yet not frightening at all now. Once he'd leaped across that first chasm of his fears, everything else had been easy.

He gently nudged her legs apart with his knee and knelt between her thighs. She reached up to caress his shoulders. "It's been too long," she said.

"Yeah." He couldn't say more, all his attention was focused on maintaining control. He poised at her entrance, quivering in anticipation of plunging into her, but sensing she wasn't yet ready.

His gaze still locked to hers, he brought his thumb to her mouth, and slipped it between her lips, then lowered it to her clit.

She gasped as he touched her, her eyes widening as he traced lazy circles around the sensitive nub. "Good looks and talented hands, too. How did I luck out?"

"Shh. We're both pretty lucky." He increased his tempo, watching as passion transformed her. Eyes closed, head thrown back, she breathed in shallow pants, a warm flush spreading across her breasts and up her neck. He matched his breath to hers, his heart pounding and his hand beginning to shake as he willed her to come. *Now. Come on, baby. Now.*

She screamed as her climax overtook her, the sound fraying his control almost past the point of bearing. He entered her while her cries still echoed around them, then stilled himself for a moment, eyes closed, willing his heart to slow and his mind to focus on enjoying this feeling of being joined with her as long as possible.

She smoothed her hands down his thighs, then back up to caress his buttocks. When he opened his eyes, she was smiling at him. "Come on," she said. "I want to feel you moving in me."

"Yeah." He sank deeply into her, then withdrew slowly. By the third thrust they found that sweetest of rhythms. He stroked faster, deeper, losing himself in her, surrounded by her, overtaken by his need for her.

He came hard, holding nothing back. She sat up and put her arms around him, embracing him as the last aftershocks shuddered through him. Afterward, they lay in each other's arms, his head on her breast, her arm around his shoulder. "I could get used to this," he said after a while.

"Me, too." She stroked his hair, her fingers twining in the strands. "There's only one problem."

He raised his head to look at her. "Only one? Then we ought to be able to overcome it."

She avoided his eyes, focusing somewhere to the left, her fingers still toying with his hair as she spoke. "What's going to happen when you have to be my boss *and* my lover?"

He groaned. "Nothing's going to happen. You'll come back to the show and we'll go on like before. I'll be your coworker during working hours and your lover after hours."

"I'm not sure you can divide the day into neat compartments like that." She looked at him again, worry clouding her eyes. "Jack, you know what happened with you and Jessica."

"You're not Jessica. And I'm not the same man I was then, either. We can make this work." He'd ignore the public attention this time, focus on doing whatever it took to keep them together.

"True. But can we afford to take that risk?"

He sat up, gathering the sheet around his waist, frowning at her. "Are you talking about giving up *me* or your job?"

"Not you." She shook her head. "But you have to admit things would be easier if we didn't work together."

"You told me once that working at *Inside Story* was your dream job."

She nodded. "It is."

"Then why would you even think about giving it up? Why are you making this so difficult?"

"I'm not *making* it difficult. It just is." She set her mouth in a stubborn line.

He threw up his hands in frustration. "It figures I'd fall for an obstinate woman."

She shoved up onto her elbows. "Only because you're obstinate yourself."

He sighed. "So it's back to the same old question. What are we going to do?"

"I could find another job." She said it with the same conviction she might have said "I could cut off my right arm."

"You have a perfectly good job. Why would you walk away from it?"

She frowned at him. "I have on-air experience now, so that should make it easier. If I don't find something in broadcasting, I'll try print journalism."

"But do you really want to be a print journalist?

Didn't you tell me that your goal has always been to be a broadcast reporter?"

She shrugged again but didn't have an answer for him.

Her pretended indifference angered him. "Did you hit your head when that snowboarder knocked you over, too?" he asked.

She looked at him again, her expression guarded. "Why do you say that?"

"Because I can't believe you're actually suggesting that I give your job to someone else."

"I'm only trying to think of what's best for the show. *Inside Story* is a new show. You can't afford to take too many chances. If Angela is a better draw for viewers…"

"The show was doing just fine with you as co-anchor," he said, unable to keep the irritation from his voice. "I don't see how this accident and your *temporary* absence changes that."

"I *want* to believe it doesn't make a difference, but when I'm honest with myself, I know that ratings and viewer feedback and all those things matter. And I couldn't live with myself if I was responsible for destroying your dream."

He stared at her, confounded by this reasoning. Hadn't she been paying attention? One of the reasons he'd wanted to have his own news magazine was in order to do things the way he felt they should be done. What happened to the woman he thought understood that about him? "This isn't some network show. I don't have to play to the ratings. I don't have to have someone on camera just because she looks like a model and gets a high approval rating from a test audience."

Her eyes met his, the sadness he saw there unsettling. "If you want to survive long in this business, you *do!*"

"The show is going to do just fine, no matter what the polls or Armstrong or anyone else says about Angela." He sat up and leaned toward her. "Look, one of the things I admire most about you is the way you've never bought into that 'looks matter most' crap. And now you act like you believe it."

She shook her head. "Maybe it's not all crap. That sociologist I interviewed…"

"To hell with him. You have too much going for you to focus on what you aren't. Concentrate on everything you are and people will respond to that."

She lay back on the pillows again. "I love you, Jack. And I want to believe that's enough." Her eyes met his once more. "But do we really want to take a gamble like that?"

He wanted to lie down beside her once more, to hold her and kiss her until her doubts—and his—were burned away by passion and need. But life wasn't that simple. Problems couldn't be wished away. You had to wrestle them into submission, fight them out. He rested his elbows on his upraised knees and stared across the room, as if a solution might be written on her wall. "So you're proposing you give up your dream job for the sake of our relationship. Then what? What happens in a few weeks, or months, or years, when you start to resent being forced to make that choice?"

The silence pressed in too close around them. He waited, counting heartbeats, straining to hear any word of encouragement from her. When he'd counted to fifty, he turned to her. "Answer me."

"Resentment like that would eventually tear us apart."

That would be it, then. Another failure. He closed his eyes, fighting against the black mood that engulfed him. What kind of choice was it, to force someone to decide between love and the thing that made them who they were?

"Maybe we should never have started this," she said. "Maybe we should have left well enough alone, and been satisfied with working so well together."

"We can't go back now." But it seemed they couldn't go forward, either. He wanted to shout and beat his fists against the mattress, but he remained absolutely still, cold in spite of the blankets wrapped around them.

"I'm sorry," she said, her voice barely a whisper. "I just…I can't deal with this right now. It's too much."

She couldn't deal with thinking about their dilemma—or she couldn't deal with seeing him again? He couldn't bring himself to ask. Instead, he pushed back the covers and got out of bed. "I'd better go. I have work I need to do."

She nodded, no doubt knowing work was merely a convenient excuse, something to say instead of everything he no longer could find words for.

"I'll call you," he said, as he buttoned his shirt.

She nodded. "Good."

But there was nothing good about the way he felt as he left her apartment. He only made it three blocks before he pulled into an alley and laid his head on the steering wheel and sobbed.

UNTIL DANIEL HAD FOCUSED on the subject, Yvonne had never thought much about her breasts. Now they constantly claimed her attention. Right after the surgery, they were bruised and aching. But even after that had subsided, her new shape distracted her. Getting dressed every morning became an ordeal of finding clothes that still fit. Some of her favorite outfits had to be discarded for new ones, many of them gifts from Daniel.

Unfortunately, most of the things he had given her were too revealing to wear at the office. Even outside of work she hesitated to put on the low-cut blouses and skintight sweaters. Even in more ordinary clothes she attracted more attention these days. She felt men staring when she walked into a restaurant or passed a group of them on the street. Even her co-workers were affected; she'd had to repeat herself three times while explaining a computer problem to the IT administrator, and had finally asked him, rather pointedly, if he would stop staring at her chest and look her in the eye.

Before the surgery, she'd anticipated enjoying such attention, but the reality was disconcerting. To this point in her life when men spoke and smiled at her, she could be fairly sure they wanted to get to know *her.* Now she couldn't help thinking they were only interested in her breasts.

She even began thinking of them that way—"the breasts," as if they were some separate entity.

Daniel, of course, was thrilled with the results of the surgery, and never failed to tell her. "You look fantastic," he'd say.

At first, the compliments had thrilled her. Daniel had never been one to hand out praise lavishly. But after a while it seemed his words weren't really directed at her, but at "the breasts." He even focused on them when he spoke. And he couldn't stop touching them—fondling, stroking, pinching even. Yvonne was constantly slapping at his hands and telling him to leave her alone.

In public, he took the reprimands with good humor. "I can't help it," he'd said. "You look so great."

In private, he was less accommodating, once persuading her to eat dinner topless while he ogled her from across the table.

He brought her gifts several times a week, or rather, gifts for "the breasts": exquisite drop necklaces, low-cut silk tops and lacy push-up bras to accent her cleavage even more. Yvonne unwrapped each new present with growing dismay. "Can't you focus on something besides my boobs?" she asked in exasperation, after unwrapping a skintight Lycra top.

"You know I love all of you," he said, pulling her close. "I just appreciate your new look. That's not bad, is it?"

"It makes me feel weird," she said.

"You're just high-strung because of all the wedding preparations," he said. "You'll feel better once we're married and things have settled down."

"Maybe you're right. The wedding's less than three months away and there's still so much to do."

"You'll get it done, I'm sure." He slid his hand around to cup her right breast. "You're an amazing woman, did you know that?"

That's me, amazing boob woman. But she didn't push him away this time. If this is what he needed from her, she was willing to give it. Love was complicated, and not always easy to figure out. The important thing was to keep working at it. If you worked long enough, you were bound to get it right.

CHAPTER NINETEEN

JACK DECIDED THE BEST WAY to deal with Shelly was to wait her out. She wasn't due back at work for almost two weeks, at the earliest. By the time she got her doctor's release she would surely have figured out she'd be crazy to give up a job she loved because it *might* cause problems between them. If she tried to resign, he'd find some way to change her mind. He could be every bit as stubborn as she was when it mattered.

In the meantime, he focused on work. He had several stories he was working on, including the feature on children's beauty pageants that Shelly had begun. It was enough to distract him most of the time.

The Tuesday after his confrontation with Shelly, Armstrong walked into his office, a sheaf of papers in his hand and a smug look on his face. "Take a look at this," he said as he tossed the papers on Jack's desk.

Jack reached for the stack, but before he had a chance to look at them Armstrong sat in the chair across from him and crowed, "Last week's show garnered a twelve Nielsen share. Up two whole points. Do you know the significance of that?"

Jack studied the figures, a small thrill spreading through his middle as he stared at the number Armstrong had circled with a yellow highlighter. "It means we're finding our audience," he said. "Viewers get what we're trying to do here and they like it."

"They like Angela Lawson." Armstrong scooted to the edge of his chair and leaned toward Jack. "Have you seen the press she's getting?"

Armstrong's obvious glee quashed Jack's excitement. "I've seen some articles," he said cautiously. "Angela's a talented reporter. We're lucky she was able to fill in on such short notice."

Armstrong sat back, hands folded on his stomach. "We need to think about keeping her on a permanent basis."

Of course. Jack should have seen this coming. The producer had disapproved of Shelly from day one. Jack pretended to misunderstand. "It's a great idea, but we can't afford a third on-air person right now," he said.

"I'm not talking about adding her." Armstrong frowned at Jack. "I'm talking about keeping her on full-time instead of Shelly."

"Absolutely not." He reached for a file from the stack at the corner of his desk, ignoring the producer. End of discussion.

Armstrong didn't take the hint. "You've got to do it for the sake of the show."

Jack struggled to rein in his temper. He glared at the producer. "Are you saying I should fire Shelly? Because she had an accident that wasn't her fault?"

"Fire her because she doesn't pull in the viewers Angela does."

"That's harsh."

"That's business. You've been around long enough to know it."

Jack shook his head. "If we fire Shelly and replace her with Angela, we're going to look like coldhearted bastards to viewers. I wouldn't be surprised if ratings took a nosedive after that."

"If you let Shelly come back and get rid of Angela, more than a few viewers—not to mention the sponsors and contributors who pay our salaries—are going to think you let personal feelings get the better of good judgment."

"Personal feelings?" Jack stiffened. "What are you talking about?"

Armstrong folded his arms over his chest and looked away. "Checked the Web lately? Or the gossip rags?"

"What the hell are you talking about?" Jack sat back in his chair, heart pounding. Armstrong wasn't making sense, but then, what about any of this was logical?

Armstrong sighed, then opened his suit coat and pulled out a folded newspaper and laid it on the desk. Jack recognized part of the local alternative weekly, open to a column called "The Media Muse." Dread formed a cold knot in his gut as he read the portion Armstrong had highlighted: *According to the Web site FansofJackHalloran.com, the public TV journalist and voluptuous reporter Shelly Piper are more than co-workers. The two were spotted recently on the ski slopes in a rather...intimate discussion.* This snippet was accompanied by a grainy picture of the two of them kissing at Copper Mountain.

Jack dropped the paper as if it had burned him. "How the hell did they get that picture?"

"I take it a fan saw you two and snapped it."

Jack couldn't stop looking at the picture. He would

have sworn he and Shelly were alone then. "These people are vultures."

"Maybe so. But they're also viewers. Viewers with opinions. If you bring Shelly back, more than a few of them are going to think you're playing favorites. You won't be doing Shelly any favors, leaving her open to that kind of talk."

"Shelly is a damn good reporter, and you know it."

Armstrong nodded, his calm infuriating. "She's a good reporter. But Angela's a better fit for this type of show."

"You can't prove the ratings are because of Angela."

"I've been around long enough to know they are." His voice softened. "I know you don't want to be the bad guy here and get rid of Shelly. But think about this—if the show tanks, you and Shelly are both out of a job. What are you going to do then?"

Jack shook his head. He didn't have an answer. Armstrong looked at him a long moment, then got up and left.

Jack picked up the paper again and reread the words. He hoped to God Shelly hadn't seen this. He'd like to find the reporter and break a few teeth. Just as well the writer was anonymous.

He started to toss the paper in the trash, but hesitated. Ignoring this news didn't make it go away. If one news source had reported it, others would pick it up soon. People would talk, and everyone would be watching to see what happened next. It was the curse of living a public life—the curse that had plagued his marriage. Could he subject Shelly to that now?

Certainly they'd be subject to less gossip if they weren't working together. Then there was the ratings argument to consider. What if he brought Shelly back and the ratings fell? He was ready to accept responsibility, but that wasn't the kind of information he could keep from Shelly. How would that make her feel?

This is what happened when you started caring about someone. You worried more about feelings than facts. All he wanted was to put together the kind of news shows he'd always envisioned, with top-quality reporting and interesting, important stories. And he wanted to love Shelly without worrying about how the public saw them, or what harm their jobs might do to their personal life.

He'd told Shelly she shouldn't sacrifice her dream for his sake. Could he jeopardize his own dream for her? Did he risk poisoning their love if he did so?

He could blame her dismissal on Armstrong, or even on his uncle. It wasn't that far-fetched to believe keeping Shelly on could jeopardize underwriting for next year. Uncle Ed hadn't gotten to be a wealthy man by making poor business decisions. If he thought *Inside Story* wasn't a good investment, he wouldn't hesitate to pull the plug.

He ground his teeth together and suppressed a groan of frustration. The problem wasn't Shelly. It was how people looked at her. They were so caught up in the way they thought things *ought* to look they couldn't appreciate someone who was a little bit different.

If only he could make people see her differently. If only he could do something to take the blinders off their eyes.

His gaze landed on the folder he'd pulled from the stack on his desk. It was a press kit for a beauty pageant production company. The glossy cover had a photo of a smiling toddler, lashes stiff with mascara, lips glossy, dimpled cheeks pink with blush. *We help girls reach their potential,* touted the slogan beneath the photo.

Jack stared at the picture with a mixture of fascination and disgust. Is this how some people thought little girls should look? No wonder the world was so screwed up.

He sat up straighter. He was on to something here, he was sure of it. He pushed the folder away and pulled his computer keyboard toward him, heart racing along with the ideas in his head. He jabbed at the keys, typing in a search engine address. Maybe he *could* do something for Shelly. Something that would make a difference.

TUESDAY EVENING, SHELLY SAT at Yvonne's kitchen table, her leg propped on a chair while she attempted to wrap a little circle of lavender tulle around a miniature bottle of bubble solution. In the background, the television droned on about weather patterns in the southeast. Shelly wondered if she could use a low-pressure system and the full moon as an excuse for her own stormy mood.

"Tell me again why we're dressing up bubble bottles?" she asked as she concentrated on tying a length of purple satin ribbon into a bow at the neck of the bottle.

"We're going to hand these out to people instead of bags of rice or birdseed." Yvonne finished off a bottle and added it to the growing ranks arrayed around them. "It's neater, and more fun than pelting the couple with birdseed."

"Probably less painful if they're aiming for you, too." She wadded up an uncooperative scrap of tulle and reached for another. She didn't really have the patience for this today, but when Yvonne had called and asked for help, she couldn't bring herself to say no. "So how are the rest of the preparations coming?"

"Good. But I'll be glad when everything's done and the wedding is finally here. I never realized going into this how much work was involved."

Especially if the groom isn't any help. But she kept the thought to herself. "It's going to be a beautiful wedding," she said, remembering her lines.

"Yes, it is." Yvonne smiled. "It's going to be perfect."

There was that word again. *Perfect.* "Nothing is perfect," Shelly said. "And why would you want a perfect wedding, anyway? It's the stories about what went wrong that everyone remembers years down the road."

Worry lines formed a W on Yvonne's forehead. "We can talk about how beautiful the wedding was, and how it came off without a hitch," she said. "Screwups are too stressful."

"Maybe you're not as used to them as I am. I'm to the point now where I coast right through one mishap after another, smiling like a beauty queen surrounded by alligators."

Yvonne laughed. "Speaking of screwups, how's the knee?"

Shelly looked down at the bright blue brace around her left knee. "It's still there. I'm making progress. Not fast enough for me, of course, but the therapist says I'm doing well."

"When will you be walking on your own again?"

"I've been practicing on crutches at home. I'm hoping to convince the doctor to let me go back to work soon. I have an appointment a week from this coming Monday and I'm going to do my best to walk out of there with a work release."

"I bet you can't wait to get back to *Inside Story.*"

"I don't know if I'm going back there." She spoke casually, though the words tied her stomach in a knot.

"Why wouldn't you go back?" Yvonne dropped the ribbon she'd been holding. It fluttered to the floor and landed atop a scattering of other ribbons and tulle. "I thought you loved working on the show. What happened?"

"I fell in love with Jack." She pushed aside a trio of bottles and folded her hands on the table in front of her.

"I knew it!" Yvonne squealed, and clapped her hands together. "When I saw that story in the paper, I was hoping it was true."

"What story?" Shelly sat up straighter and tried to ignore the queasy feeling in her stomach. "What are you talking about?"

"It was in that column in the *Denver Underground,* you know, 'The Media Muse.'"

Shelly shook her head. "I didn't see it."

"I've got it here somewhere." Yvonne hurried over to the sofa and dug through a stack of papers on the floor by its side. "Here it is." She pulled out a section of newsprint and waved it over her head.

When Yvonne handed her the paper, Shelly opened it carefully, as if she feared it might explode at any moment. "There. See, it has a picture and everything." Yvonne pointed to a grainy black-and-white photo two-thirds of the way down the page.

Shelly stared at the photo of her and Jack kissing. She shifted her gaze to the column to the left of the photo. *...the public TV journalist and voluptuous reporter Shelly Piper are more than co-workers.* She groaned. "I hope Jack hasn't seen this," she said.

"Why should he be upset? It's all in fun."

"It's not fun when your private life is open to public scrutiny." She closed the paper and shoved it across the table, as far away from her as she could get it. But it wasn't so easy to push aside her worries about Jack. "Part of the reason his first marriage failed was because he and his wife couldn't make a move without having it reported in the papers. That's too much pressure to put on a relationship. It's one of the things he's worried about with us." And now that worry was a reality.

"Well, I'm happy for you," Yvonne said.

"I'd be happier if I wasn't worried about my job situation. Jack thinks we can still work together, but I think that's a really bad idea."

Yvonne looked puzzled. "But Jack's a great guy, isn't he?"

"Yeah. He's a great guy." Too great to risk losing to the pressure of public opinion, or the differences of opinion they were bound to have in the course of working together. When she was merely Jack's co-worker, she'd thought nothing of disagreeing with him over the best way to present a story or how to handle a particular issue. If she returned to work as his lover, would she start censoring herself, stifling her opinions to protect their relationship?

"Then what's the problem?" Yvonne reached for another bottle of bubbles, then stilled. "He does want you to come back, doesn't he?"

Shelly nodded. "Oh, he wants me back. He doesn't see any problem with it."

"So what *is* the problem? Is it Angela? Do you think now that's she's in the anchor chair, she won't want to give it up?"

Shelly frowned. "I hadn't even thought of that. I don't have a clue how she feels about all this. I haven't talked to her." She leaned forward, elbows on the table, chin in hand. "But you could say she's part of the problem. The show's ratings have gone up since she took over for me, and the critics apparently love her. I'm afraid if I go back, the viewers won't be too happy."

"You're worrying about something that hasn't even happened yet. You have your fans, too, you know."

"Maybe." She straightened and picked up another circle of tulle. "Anyway, I think it would be a lot better for Jack and me if we didn't try to work together anymore."

"So you're giving up your job for the sake of love." Yvonne's expression softened. "That's so romantic."

Gag me, Shelly thought. "Don't give me so much credit. I'm still looking out for number one. If I go back to the show and the ratings fall, I'll be in worse shape career-wise than I am now." And if the pressure drove Jack and her apart, she didn't want to think about how bad the pain would be. Better not to take the risk.

"So what will you do?" Yvonne asked.

"I don't know. I could probably get some kind of off-camera production or reporting job. Or maybe move to print journalism…."

"Why not get another on-air position? You've got experience now. I'd think another show would be thrilled to have you."

"Right." She shifted her bum leg. "They'd be thrilled if I weighed thirty pounds less."

"I don't think you give yourself enough credit." Yvonne reached for another bottle of bubbles and a circlet of tulle. "You're a very pretty woman, and you're a fantastic reporter. Some of the stories you've done for *Inside Story* have brought tears to my eyes."

"I *am* a good reporter." She wove a strip of ribbon between her fingers, anger at the unfairness of her situation tightening her chest. "But the truth is, it takes more than that to succeed in this business. Television is a visual medium. Looks count, whether we want to admit it or not."

"So you're not sure if you could get another job that's as great as the one you've got." Yvonne tied another neat bow. "Jack wants you back working with him. Why not stay and give it a try?"

"We're both too stubborn and opinionated, and carrying on a romance in the public eye puts too much strain on a relationship. I don't want to risk it."

Yvonne's eyes met hers, dark and serious. "If you love each other, you'll find a way to work it out."

Yvonne would do that, wouldn't she? She'd do whatever it took to keep the relationship going. But Shelly wasn't like that. She could only give in and shut up so many times before the pressure got to be too much. The resulting explosion was never pretty.

Besides, Jack hadn't fallen in love with a woman who gave in easily. "No matter what I do, I can't see it ending up good. I either risk losing Jack, or end up with a job I merely tolerate, instead of love." She tossed aside yet another shredded piece of tulle.

"You're still drawing disability, right? And you've probably got some vacation time left. You don't have to rush to decide right now."

"Right. No rush." Except the longer she sat at home, the more depressed she felt and the greater the risk that people who mattered in the business would forget about her. The next hot talent would grab the spotlight and she'd be left in the shadows.

Her gaze shifted to the television across the room. She blinked at the familiar face on the screen. "Where's the remote?" she asked, holding out her hand. "Turn up the sound."

Yvonne picked up the remote and punched up the volume. "Good evening, I'm Jessica Peabody, reporting from Denver from Rocky Flats, where debate continues on…"

"She's very pretty," Yvonne said. "Do you know her?"

"Not exactly." She sat back, frowning at the woman on the screen. "She's Jack's ex-wife."

"That's her?" Yvonne studied Jessica more closely.

Shelly nodded. Jessica looked so cool and lovely up there on the screen. Even her voice was smooth and well-modulated. People probably tuned in just to marvel at her. "It's bad enough she's Jack's ex," she said. "But she's also the kind of woman I'm competing against when I apply for other jobs. It's hard to keep convincing myself I can beat *her*."

"Women shouldn't compete like that," Yvonne said. "We should help one another more."

"Right. Like Jessica Peabody is going to help me." Women like Jessica—and like Darcy and Perky Pam and countless others Shelly had known in this business—only helped you when they thought it would somehow benefit them.

"I think the accident and all this time off has really gotten you down," Yvonne said. "You used to not be like vthis. What happened to the Shelly I knew who refused to let anything stand in the way of her dreams?"

Yvonne's words hurt. What had happened to all that optimism Shelly had once felt? The events of the past weeks had shaken her, no doubt. "Eventually, we all have to learn to deal with reality."

"Deal with it, or overcome it?" Yvonne arched one eyebrow in question, then shoved another dozen bottles of bubbles toward Shelly. "My reality right now is that we have to get all these finished tonight. So get to work."

"Yes, ma'am." Shelly grabbed a bottle and plopped it in the middle of a circle of tulle. But Yvonne's words still echoed in her head. She'd spent years fighting against others' expectations and perceptions. Was it so wrong if she was tired of the battles? Maybe the time had come to settle for something else. Something easier, even if it wasn't what she'd always wanted.

SHELLY NOTICED JACK WAS preoccupied when he came to see her Wednesday evening. Though they'd talked on the phone a couple of times since their argument, things were still awkward between them.

One day—she expected sooner, rather than later—they'd have to wrestle with questions about their future again, but for now they were in a holding pattern, each waiting for the other to make the first move. She knew she ought to be strong enough to bring it up, but she could see no easy answer, no good outcome.

Her small living room seemed too intimate now, the temptation to use sex as a substitute for talking too great, so she suggested they go for a walk. "I need to exercise my leg," she explained.

Outside on the sidewalk, the tension eased some. "What stories are you working on now?" she asked.

"I've been working on your beauty pageant story." He shoved his hands into his pockets and glanced at her, a lopsided smile tugging up the corners of his mouth. "Why didn't you warn me how creepy it is to see six-year-olds with false eyelashes and lipstick? Whatever happened to letting little girls be little girls?"

She laughed at the horror in his voice. "I warned you it wasn't all pretty dresses and cute kids."

"Next time I'll listen better."

They fell silent again. *If there is a next time,* she thought. She bet Jack was thinking it, too.

"I saw Yvonne yesterday," she said.

"Oh? How's she doing?"

"Great. A little stressed about the wedding, but I think that's normal. Of course, she's convinced herself the wedding has to be perfect. I told her there was no such thing."

"Oh, yeah?" He gave her an odd look. "If there's no such thing, why are people trying so hard for perfection? Take those little beauty pageant contestants. I'll bet every one of them believes she has to look perfect in order to win."

She frowned. "Yeah, well, that's one of the things that's wrong with beauty pageants, isn't it?" She stumbled and he reached out to steady her. She held on to his arm, reluctant to let go. It felt good to be this close to him again, at least physically. If only they could get past their difference of opinion about her job. She glanced up at him. "It's a crazy world we live in, isn't it? Beauty pageant winners have to be perfect. A lot of people think news anchors should be, too. At least the female ones."

There. It was the closest she'd come to broaching the subject with him. She waited for him to argue; instead, he looked thoughtful, and nodded slowly. "Yeah. It's a crazy world, all right."

Silence stretched between them again. Awkward. She cleared her throat. "Yvonne showed me a column in the *Denver Underground.* 'The Media Muse.'"

Jack's expression grew tense. "The one with the picture of us on the slopes?"

She nodded. "I was hoping you hadn't seen it."

"Armstrong made it a point to show it to me."

"What did he say?"

"He said people were watching us, waiting to see if I played favorites."

She felt weak. "Do people really think that?"

He glanced at her, then looked away. "Armstrong thinks so. I told him I don't give a damn what they think."

She tightened her grip on his arm. "One more reason for me not to come back to the station," she said.

"Wrong." He stopped and faced her. "You're wrong, and people who think you don't belong on the show are wrong, too."

She'd expected anger, so the excitement that sparkled in his eyes surprised her. Jack looked almost *happy* about this turn of events. "What are you so happy about?" she asked. "This is serious business. We could both end up in big trouble. The *show* could be in trouble."

"Or, we could change people's minds. Show them how wrong they are about us."

She shook her head. "Why take that chance?"

He let the smile out now, even as he shook his head. "Wait until you see the project I'm working on. You've given me a great idea."

"I'm full of great ideas." She tried for a bravado she didn't necessarily feel. "What was this one?"

"Oh, no. It's a secret."

"If it's my idea, you shouldn't keep it a secret from me."

"Watch next week's show and you'll figure it out." He stopped walking, forcing her to stop, too. "Why don't we head back to your place? I need to call it a night. I have a ton of work to do tomorrow."

I sure wish I did. The lady-of-leisure routine she'd been forced into was a drag. Part of her wanted to protest that he seemed in a hurry to leave her, but she recognized the look in his eyes. It was the real-life equivalent of the lightbulb glowing over the head of a cartoon character. Something she'd said had triggered an idea in Jack's brain. An idea for a story, or some twist to a story. She would have bet an all-you-can-eat spree at Baskin-Robbins that when he left her, he'd head for the office.

She understood the feeling, and was jealous of it. She wanted to be the one in a fever to work on a story, instead of being the one left behind, twiddling her thumbs. Jack probably would have argued that she *could* be working again, with him, but even though she was tempted, the practical nature that had always ruled her life held her back.

All she had to do was look around to realize how hard it was to sustain a relationship in their demanding profession. Working together and being an "item" in the public eye would only make things worse—and make a breakup a hell of a lot more painful. But the truth was, she couldn't stop loving Jack. She'd handed over part of her heart to him and didn't expect to get it back anytime soon.

That meant something else had to give. Yvonne hadn't been that far off the mark when she'd concluded Shelly was abandoning her career for the sake of love. She hadn't abandoned it yet, but she was definitely losing her grip. Yvonne thought that kind of sacrifice was worth it for a man. Shelly had her doubts. She loved Jack, but was love really enough these days? She wasn't sure she had the courage to find that out.

CHAPTER TWENTY

THE FOLLOWING THURSDAY morning, Jack sent Shelly a dozen roses with a note. "Don't forget to watch tonight's show."

As if she'd missed an episode yet. Though it pained her to see someone else sitting in her chair on the set, she couldn't keep away. *Inside Story* was still partly *her* show, and she wasn't ready to let go of it yet.

"Roses." Nurse Bryant beamed as Shelly arranged the long stems in a tall vase. The nurse only worked two half days a week now, helping with Shelly's physical therapy. "That handsome man of yours is definitely a keeper."

"Call me suspicious, but when a man sends flowers for no reason, he's up to something." Shelly set the vase on the dining table and stepped back to admire it, one hand on the back of a chair to steady herself.

"You *are* suspicious," the Tyrant said. "Jack sent those flowers because he's crazy about you." She looked Shelly up and down, lips pursed. Shelly could almost hear her speculating on what Shelly's particular charms must be to snare a man like Handsome Jack Halloran.

She smiled, and turned to pick up the cane which she'd recently started using in place of the crutches. "Must be my charm and personality," she teased.

"You're certainly in a better mood than when I started working here." The Tyrant fastened a length of cable to a hook on the kitchen doorjamb, in preparation for Shelly's workout. "I can't say as I blame you. What you've been through is no fun."

Sympathy from the Tyrant? "Was I really that pathetic?"

The Tyrant glanced over her shoulder at her patient. "Yes. But time to shut down the pity party and get to work. You've done really well."

Shelly sat in a chair and reached for the ankle weights that were stacked at one end of the table. "Well enough to get a doctor's release to go back to work?"

"I don't see why not."

"That's good." Never mind she didn't really have work she could go back to.

"This morning I want you to do fifteen forward leg lifts, fifteen to the side and fifteen back, without stopping."

"You're a slave driver." She stood, walked over and fit her foot in the loop at the end of the cable. The other end was attached to a pulley and more weights. The Tyrant could adjust the resistance and weight she was moving, putting more or less strain on the muscles and healing tendons.

"Haven't you heard the expression 'no pain, no gain'? I'm the one who invented it."

"I thought that was Jane Fonda, or another of those exercise gurus."

"Whoever it was, I'm sure they got it from me. Now, come on, get busy. I want to see you break a sweat."

"You should see a professional about these sadistic

tendencies of yours." She grunted and began kicking her leg out in front of her.

"I wouldn't work you so hard if I didn't believe you could do it," the Tyrant said calmly. "Now lift it higher. You have to stretch yourself or you'll never show any improvement."

"Yes, ma'am." Shelly gritted her teeth and kicked her leg higher. Anything to get that work release, and eventually be able to throw away that cane.

THAT NIGHT, SHELLY PLANTED herself in front of the television and prepared to be surprised. Maybe Jack had finished the beauty pageant story, but what was so special about that?

Angela was up first, with a segment about dropout rates in Denver schools. Shelly had to admit it was well done, with just the right mix of narrative and film, and a great ending hook that would make viewers think. And of course, Angela looked great on camera.

Shelly had always seen jealousy as a worthless emotion. Anger could motivate a person to take positive action to correct a wrong. If you were sad, you could at least indulge in a good cry that would make you feel better. But jealousy only stewed in your gut, making you sick and having no effect on the object of your jealousy.

Watching Angela on screen with Jack, Shelly felt the stewing start. So much for the calm, cool professional she'd always prided herself on being. But who wouldn't have a tough time maintaining that attitude when she was confined to her home, condemned to living in caftans and sweatpants that would fit over her bulky leg brace, relying on walking aids like some two-year-old?

Those conditions would send any self-respecting woman into the occasional temper tantrum or jealous fit.

The camera zoomed in on Jack, who stood before a larger-than-life-size mock-up of a magazine cover. A half-naked model with impossibly white teeth and amazingly smooth thighs loomed over Jack, while cover blurbs around her shouted *Get Ready for Bikini Season!* and *Flatten Your Stomach in Ten Minutes a Day!*

"Magazines like this one fill newsstands and mailboxes every month. Models like the one shown on this cover sell everything from soap to haute couture." He looked the picture up and down, then addressed the camera again, one eyebrow raised. "She's gorgeous, isn't she? Perfect, even? But does she exist? Does this perfect woman with flowing hair, smooth skin, big breasts and thin thighs, really exist?"

Cut to film of a magazine photo shoot. The model, who was indeed gorgeous and thin, was sprayed with oil, posed in awkward positions and commanded to smile for the camera. A few seconds later, the photograph of the same model was shown, pinned to a whiteboard in a studio. A dapper-looking man with graying hair frowned at the photo. "We're going to need to airbrush the cellulite. Get rid of that mole. Give her some more cleavage…."

Jack's voice again, off camera. "Sebastian Delluci is a graphic artist whose specialty is retouching magazine photos. He's worked for some of the top publications in the country."

"What we're dealing with here is fantasy," Delluci said as he hunched over a computer keyboard, eyes focused on the image of yet another young model on the screen. "Advertisers are selling a product, but they're also selling the fantasy that if you use their product, you could look this beautiful, this glamorous, this perfect." With the click of a few keys, he slimmed the model's waist, bronzed her skin and smoothed her hair. "No one looks this good in real life. But who wouldn't want to?"

Shelly leaned forward, unable to tear her eyes away from the image on that computer screen, which dissolved to a shot of an older woman, her dark hair swept back from her high forehead, fashionable wire-rimmed glasses perched on the end of her nose. A subtitle identified her as Ellen Waterford, Ph.D., professor of anthropology and women's studies at the University of Denver. "There's nothing new about certain people being held up as ideals of beauty. Nefertiti, Helen of Troy and Cleopatra were all women renowned for their great beauty. What's changed is that in today's culture these images are insidious. Everywhere we look—magazines, newspapers, television, billboards, even on the computer screen—we're confronted with these perfect people. We can't help but compare ourselves to these paragons, and we always come up short. We can't help it."

Jack's voice again. "The average American runway model is five feet, ten inches tall and weighs one hundred and seven pounds. In contrast, the average American woman is five feet, four inches tall and weighs one hundred and forty-three pounds. Twenty years ago, the average model weighed eight percent less than the average woman. Today's models weigh twenty-three percent less."

"There's a lot of pressure, particularly in certain fields such as entertainment, television, the performing arts and athletics, to conform to this idea of perfection," Dr. Waterford continued. "Adults have a tough time dealing with it, but where we really run into trouble is with children."

Switch to shots of a high school hallway, girls dressed in midriff-baring shirts and low-slung jeans primping before their lockers. The next frame showed a group of young boys working out with weights. "A 2002 study estimated that a half a million teenage boys use steroids. When Dr. Harrison Pope of Harvard Medical School tested boys as young as eleven, he found that when they were asked to choose the ideal male body, the picture most of them chose was of a body that could only be obtained through use of steroids. Anorexia, once a disorder associated almost exclusively with young women, is also a growing problem for teenage boys."

The next shot showed a group of young women playing soccer. "The news isn't all bad. The continued growth of women's sports and the popularity of female athletes like Mia Hamm, Gabrielle Reece and Lisa Leslie—" photos of each of these women flashed on the screen "—has given us another image of female perfection, a healthy version with muscles *and* curves."

"Do I think these women are sexy?" The speaker was a young man with a goatee, dressed in a T-shirt, shorts and a knit beanie. "Hell, yeah, they're sexy."

"Body image is ingrained into our psyches, part of our culture that has evolved over the years," Dr. Waterford concluded. "We're starting to make some strides. Some magazines have vowed to stop airbrushing models, and schools are becoming more aware of the need to present young people with role models of all shapes and sizes."

The camera moved in on the group playing soccer. An ordinary young woman jogged off the field and drank from a bottle of water. "Sure, I wish I looked more like a model," she said. "But I like having a body that's strong and healthy. There's something beautiful about that, too. You know?"

The screen faded to black on her smile. Shelly swallowed the sudden knot of tears. So this was Jack's surprise. She could almost hear his voice, telling her *she* was beautiful.

The surprises weren't over yet, though. The camera showed Jack and Angela again, seated in the chairs usually reserved for on-air interviews. "Tonight, we're debuting a new segment of the show where we share some of the feedback we've received from viewers," Angela said.

"Our first letter concerns my regular co-anchor, Shelly Piper, who's recovering at home from her skiing accident," Jack read. "Michael Plummer of Arvada writes, 'I've really enjoyed the stories Shelly has done. She's both beautiful and talented and I hope she's able to be back on the air soon. Please let her know a lot of us are wishing her a speedy recovery.'" Jack looked into the camera. "I'll second Mr. Plummer's sentiments. Everyone here misses Shelly, especially me. We'll be glad when she's able to join us again."

Shelly sat back, stunned. Had Jack really said he missed her—on camera? Considering how much she knew he'd hated his relationship with Jessica being a matter of public record, this had to be important, didn't it?

She clicked off the television and sat back, staring at the black screen as if it was a window into the future.

To the ordinary viewer, what Jack had done probably didn't look like much. To her, it meant the world.

She reached for the phone and punched in Jack's number.

"Hello?"

"Jack, it's Shelly."

"Shelly! Did you see the show?"

"I saw it. I thought it was wonderful."

He sounded relieved. "I hoped you'd like it."

How could she not love it, knowing he'd worked on that story with her in mind? "It was a great story, Jack. It really made me think."

"I hope it made a lot of people think. When you come back to the show, I want them to see a beautiful, real woman who's also a terrific reporter."

She took a deep breath, trying to steady her voice, which had gone all shaky with emotion. "I think it's great what you did, Jack, but you can't change people's minds with one show. You proved in that story just how ingrained this kind of thing is in our society."

"You can't use that as an excuse to hold yourself back. The show tonight changed some people's minds, I'm sure of it. And you can change minds, too, just by being you and holding your head up and doing your job. I want you doing that here with me."

She nodded, forgetting for a moment that he couldn't see her. "What we want and what we should have aren't always the same thing."

"Dammit, haven't you been paying attention?" The fierceness in his voice startled her, but the softness of his next words was her undoing. "I love you and I want you to keep doing the job you love," he said.

She shut her eyes, squeezing back tears. "I *do* love you, Jack," she said. "But don't tell me the articles praising Angela in the press haven't worried you. And what about the ratings? What have they been doing?"

He was silent for a moment. "They've come up a little. But nothing says that's because of Angela."

"And nothing says it isn't." She swallowed hard. "The two of us wanting to be right won't make it so. Don't let stubbornness keep you from making the right decision."

"Who says putting the woman I love ahead of work is wrong?"

"*Inside Story* isn't just work for you and you know it. It's your dream. Something you've worked for and planned for, something that's been a part of your thinking for so long you can't ignore it."

"I can if doing so means not hurting you."

"You'll hurt yourself. And in the long run that will hurt us. I won't let you do it."

"Then what will you do, dammit?"

"I don't know." She stared down at her left leg, the brace bulky beneath her sweatpants. "I see the doctor again on Monday and I'm hoping to get a release to come back to work."

"Then you'll come back to *Inside Story?*"

"I don't know. If I did, things wouldn't be the same between us."

"They'll never be the same. You know that."

"I know. Just…give me a little more time, okay?"

"Shelly…" His voice broke, and he tried again. "You love me. I love you. Let's focus on that."

"I wish I could, but it isn't that simple."

"So what are you going to do?" She heard the irritation in his voice. She sympathized with him wanting things to be settled between them. But that would never happen as long as they were both too stubborn to give in. Her chest hurt at the thought, and she struggled to breathe, like a passenger in a car headed for a crash, trapped in her seat, forced to wait for the impact, praying the hurt wouldn't be too bad.

"I'd better go," she said. "I'll call you later."

"Yeah." His voice was flat, without emotion, wounding her with his indifference. She blindly replaced the receiver in the cradle and blinked back tears. The conversation hadn't gone at all as she'd intended. She'd meant to tell him how wonderful his story was—how much it meant to her, how it was the best gift he could have given her. It didn't matter that he hadn't changed people's minds. All that mattered was that he'd tried.

She sank into the sofa and stared again at the dark television screen. *Don't use society's attitude as an excuse to hold yourself back,* Jack had said.

Was that what she'd been doing—holding herself back, because of what people thought? Was she the one making the big mistake here—limiting herself because she might be rejected by someone, because she might be hurt?

She swallowed, truth hitting her hard, making her tremble. She'd spent days trying to convince herself and Jack that they couldn't both have their dream jobs and each other. Had she overlooked another way out of this dilemma, all because she'd been too afraid to try?

CHAPTER TWENTY-ONE

Subject: Dinner Wednesday?
Date: April 26, 2005
From: SPiper@mailwave.com
To: Jhalloran@KPRM.org

Can we have dinner Wednesday night? I have
some news.
Love, Shelly

JACK READ THE E-MAIL, frowning. He picked up the
phone and punched in Shelly's number, and listened to
it ring. When the answering machine picked up, he hesitated, then hung up. What was this news Shelly had,
and why hadn't she called him on the phone to talk to
him about it?

They'd spoken a few times since their argument after
last week's show—casual conversations that skirted
around any mention of their future and whether or not
Shelly would return to work with him. She'd been
scheduled to see the doctor today. Had he given her
good news?

If she'd been released to return to work, they couldn't
avoid the issue anymore. Maybe that's why she'd invited
him to dinner—to argue her point in public.

He was sure she intended to try to resign. But he was just as determined to keep her on the show *and* in his life. He'd taken what some would view as a drastic step to convince her he was serious about his commitment to her *and* to the show. When Armstrong found out, he'd no doubt pitch a fit. Uncle Ed might not be too pleased, either, but Jack was convinced he could make his uncle see things his way.

But could he make Shelly see? Could he convince her he was right?

He leaned forward and hit the reply button. *I'll make the reservations. Pick you up at seven.* Shelly might think she was the one with momentous news to share, but she was in for a surprise.

JACK WAS LEAVING HIS OFFICE Tuesday afternoon when his phone rang. He stared at it, debating not answering. He needed to leave the office now if he wanted to get to the cleaners before they closed. Dinner with Shelly tomorrow night was probably one of the most important dates they'd had yet, and there were a few other things he needed to take care of before then.

In any case, he didn't have time to talk to anyone right now. Unless it was Shelly…

He snatched up the receiver. "Hello?"

"Jack, I'm so glad I caught you in," Jessica's voice trilled at him.

She was probably calling to bug him about the CNN job again. Someone like her couldn't fathom him not jumping at a chance like that. "Listen, Jess, I'm really busy right now…."

"Too busy to talk to me?"

He frowned. His ex was getting too old to play the coy innocent, though she continued to try. "Is there something in particular you needed from me?"

"God forbid I keep an important man like you from your business." She laughed. "I called to ask you about Shelly Piper."

He blinked, surprised Jessica even knew Shelly's name. "What about Shelly?" he asked, wary.

"I've seen her on your show, of course, but I'm wondering what she's like to work with. I mean, she's not a ditz or a flake or anything, is she?"

Shelly, a flake? "Shelly is definitely not a ditz or a flake. But why do you even care?"

"No need to get huffy. I merely wanted to know if she's the kind of person who's building a good reputation in this business. If she's someone I wouldn't mind being associated with."

He rubbed his temples, confused by the direction the conversation was taking. "What's going on? Why would you ever be associated with Shelly?"

"Whether you believe it or not, I still have an interest in your welfare. When I saw the show the other night and you talked about missing Shelly, I got the impression you'd become rather...attached to her."

He stiffened. "I don't see that that's any business of yours."

"Oh, my, you are in love with her, aren't you?" Jessica's voice was gleeful. "Imagine that? Mr. Untouchable has fallen for his co-worker. Again. After you swore you'd never mix business with pleasure again. I guess old habits die hard."

He gripped the phone more tightly. "I can't believe

you wasted your time—and mine—with this. I have to go now."

"Not until you answer my question. I want to be sure Shelly is good enough for you."

"You're my ex-wife, not my mother," he snapped.

"Humor me. Or is there something bad about her that you don't want to tell me?"

"Shelly is one of the finest reporters I've ever worked with. I wouldn't be surprised if she earns an Emmy nomination for some of the work she's done this season."

"An Emmy. My, my. That *is* impressive. Too bad she's a little chunky...."

"Watch it."

She laughed again. "I love it when you turn chivalrous. It's a side of you I haven't seen in a while."

"Goodbye, Jessica."

"Goodbye, Jack. And don't worry. Maybe you and Shelly will have better luck together than the two of us did."

He hung up and stared at the phone a long moment. Jessica was definitely up to something, but what? Why the sudden interest in Shelly? It wasn't as if she was the jealous type. Jessica no longer had any interest in him outside of distant friendship; she was too self-centered to focus on another person for very long.

And he certainly had no interest in Jessica. Shelly had shown him how shallow his feelings for his ex had been. The love he felt for Shelly was at times painful, but he had no doubts it was real.

His gaze shifted to the stack of newspapers on the corner of his credenza, and his chest tightened. Jessica must have seen the gossip column that mentioned him and Shelly. She'd been trolling for the inside scoop, no doubt.

Let her gossip. He was determined not to pay attention to what anyone said about him and Shelly. All that mattered was what the two of them thought and felt about each other.

SHELLY THOUGHT SHE HAD her feelings under control, so the intense longing that hit her when she opened her door to Jack Wednesday evening caught her by surprise. Another time, she might have blamed the sensation on hormones, or the effects of being cooped up in her condo too long. Now she knew love was the culprit, a love that had the power to shake up her whole world, to bring her to her knees.

Love that could change everything. The idea thrilled and terrified her.

"You look beautiful." He kissed her cheek. "I have reservations at the Ship Tavern," he said as he helped her with the beaded shawl she'd chosen to wear over a black silk pantsuit.

"Sounds great," she managed to say, though her stomach felt as if goldfish were doing laps in it. The Ship Tavern was in the gorgeous and historic Brown Palace Hotel. The combination of great food and wine and opulent atmosphere would be enough to weaken the willpower of any woman who was torn between giving in to what her man wanted and doing things her own way.

This is Jack, she reminded herself as she carefully maneuvered down the steps to his car. *He'll be okay with this.* Of course, he might be angry at first, but surely she could make him see things her way.

They got through most of the dinner pleasantly enough, though she ate without tasting much of the food, her attention riveted on the man across from her. It was all she could do not to reach across the table and touch him. The minute he'd walked in her door tonight, her longing for him had hit her like a strong, hot wind, almost knocking her back. She hadn't imagined it was possible to miss a person so much, not just physically, but emotionally. She'd wanted to close the door and lock it, and spend the rest of the evening touching him and looking at him, drowning in the contentment of being with him again.

"You look great," he said, for probably the sixth time that night, as the waiter set their desserts in front of them. "And you seem to be handling that cane like a pro. What did the doctor say?"

"He said I'm free to return to work, as long as I don't overdo it." Actually, he'd wanted her to take another couple of weeks off, but she'd badgered and begged, refusing to leave his office until he signed the consent form. Even then, she'd had to endure a lecture and agree to a long list of conditions—no driving, no working more than thirty minutes at a time on her feet, and physical therapy at least three times a week.

Jack's grin outshone the candles on their table. "That's terrific. And don't worry. We'll do whatever it takes to accommodate you. I'll talk to Armstrong—"

"Jack, I won't be coming back to work for you."

Her words froze him, a half grin still on his face. Shelly wrapped her hands around her coffee cup and tried to remain calm in spite of her racing heart.

"I must not have heard you correctly," he said after a moment.

"You heard me. I'm resigning from *Inside Story*. I mailed my resignation this morning." She'd deposited the letter in the mailbox with feelings of both dread and relief. She absolutely knew she was doing the right thing for her—she only hoped Jack would see it was the right thing for *them,* as well.

"Then I'll tear it up when I get it." He leaned toward her, his gaze burning into hers. "We've already discussed this. I'm not going to let you quit."

"Jack, let me explain."

"No, let me explain. One—" he held up a finger "—I love you. There's no arguing that. Two—*Inside Story* is my show. I make the rules. It's my dream and I want you to be a part of it. Three—I'm not going to let you be a martyr. It's a role that doesn't suit you and it's lousy for our relationship. Four—I'd rather fight you than let you make a mistake like this. Five—"

She watched him as he ticked off his reasons, waiting for him to run out of steam. "Are you finished?" she asked when he'd exhausted his supply of words and fingers.

"Yes." He sat back, arms folded across his chest, eyes burning into her.

"Will you let me talk for a minute?"

"Not if you're going to tell me you're quitting."

"I *am* going to tell you that. I'm leaving *Inside Story* and there's nothing you can do to stop me."

"What about this?" He reached into his coat pocket.

For half a second, she flashed to dozens of suspense thrillers she'd seen, where the desperate lover pulls out a gun.

But of course, Jack wasn't a violent man. And it wasn't a gun he pulled from his coat, but a box. A small velvet box. Looking at it, her breath caught.

"Will this change your mind?" He handed her the box.

She didn't want to take it at first, afraid of what it represented, scared to hope for that much. But he gently pressed it into her hand. "Open it."

With shaking fingers, she lifted the lid of the box and stared at the contents. "Jack, I don't know what to say."

"How about saying you'll marry me?"

She looked at him, then back at the diamond solitaire that glowed like a miniature sun. Somehow she found her voice. "This only convinces me I'm doing the right thing in leaving the show."

"Dammit, woman." He gripped the edge of the tabletop so hard the silverware rattled. "Has anyone ever told you you're stubborn?"

In any other circumstances, his agitation would have been comical. Now it only made her feel more nervous. "Are you saying you'll withdraw your proposal if I resign?"

He sat back. "No. I think you're making a mistake, but I love you. I want to be with you. For the rest of my life."

The warmth of his words, and the heat in his look, thawed all the icy fear within her. She set the ring box on the table between them, and raised her eyes to his. "I'm leaving *Inside Story* because I've found another job. A better one."

She almost laughed at his look of astonishment. She could hardly believe the words herself.

He sat back, eyes still locked to hers. "You got a better job?"

She nodded. "CNN has hired me as a reporter for their Denver bureau. I'll work on breaking news and feature stories. Granted, it's the bottom of the ladder there, but I can move up quickly."

He nodded, lips pursed, taking it in. "I don't know what to say. How did this come about?"

"You told me Jessica had offered you a job with CNN and you'd turned her down." She stirred cream into her coffee, choosing her words carefully. "After the feature you did about perception and body image, I realized I'd been letting my worries about what people might think of my looks hold me back. I'd been focusing on the negative, instead of all the positives I had to offer an employer."

"But what does this have to do with Jessica?"

"I called her up and asked if the position was still available and if she'd help me set up an interview."

"You called Jessica?" He frowned, more puzzled than angry, she thought. "And she agreed to help you?"

Shelly nodded. Making that call had been one of the gutsiest things she'd done in her life. "She was reluctant at first, but I managed to convince her having another woman on staff would be good for her."

Jack looked skeptical. "How, exactly, did you do that? Jessica's not one to do favors for the sake of being nice."

"So I gathered. But I promised I'd make her look good." She'd also let Jessica know that Jack wasn't keen on Shelly leaving the show. She'd reasoned that, no matter how amiable the parting, what woman wouldn't relish the opportunity to get in a subtle dig at the ex who'd turned down her offer to get back together? It was devious and bitchy and something she'd never tell Jack, but the tactic had worked.

He shook his head. "I can't believe you talked to Jessica. And she got you the interview?"

"She did." She'd done it in less than twenty-four hours, too, for which Shelly definitely owed her. "I was a little nervous what they'd think when I showed up with my bum knee and all, but I remembered what you said—to focus on what I was, rather than what I wasn't." She grinned. "Frankly, I think I blew them away." She'd gone in there knowing she had nothing to lose, an idea that had freed her to be her smartest, funniest, most creative best. That, and the Emmy rumors Jessica had conveniently brought up, had clinched the deal.

Jack laughed, the tension between them evaporating. "Congratulations. This does put things in a different light."

"Then you're not upset I went behind your back, so to speak?"

He shook his head. "Maybe a little hurt you didn't ask me for help, but I think I understand why you didn't."

"I had to do this on my own."

"I know. That's one of the things I love about you."

Their eyes met, heat arcing between them. Her earlier nervousness returned tenfold. Something wonderful was happening here. *Please, God, I don't want to blow this.*

Jack cleared his throat. "You still haven't given me your answer."

She looked down at the ring. The diamond glittered in the lamplight, a beautiful, magical thing—like her feelings for Jack. "Yes," she said.

"Yes what?"

"Yes, Jack, I'll marry you."

He got up and came around to her side of the booth, nudging her until she slid over enough that he could sit beside her and put his arm around her. She slid her arms around his neck and kissed him, their lips tasting of salty tears.

He raised his head enough to look at her, his eyes reflecting all the joy she felt. "Part of me thinks it's crazy to propose like this, in the heat of a new relationship. But I can't be cautious anymore. Not with you."

"It is crazy. But I understand." They'd come so close to giving up, to calling it quits before their love even had a chance. It was an audacious, thrilling move to go from that to declaring they wanted to be together forever. And yet it felt like the right move. The only move.

He leaned across the table and picked up his wineglass. "To happily ever after."

She wrapped her fingers around the stem of her own glass and looked at him curiously. "Is there such a thing?"

He nodded. "You make me believe it's possible."

"Then I'm going to believe in it, too." She touched her glass to his. "To happily ever after."

EPILOGUE

SHELLY STOOD AT THE FRONT of the church, tears rolling down her cheeks as she watched Yvonne and Daniel exchange vows. So far, Yvonne was getting the perfect wedding she'd always wanted. She looked like a fairy-tale princess in her white satin gown, a wreath of orange blossoms crowning her piled-up hair. And Shelly had to admit that Daniel definitely looked like a man in love as he watched his bride say her final vows.

"You may kiss the bride."

At the minister's words, Daniel and Yvonne embraced, then locked arms and almost ran down the aisle, to the applause and cheers of the congregation.

Shelly wiped her eyes and followed at a more sedate pace. On the way, she found Jack, who had a seat on the aisle. He gave her a thumbs-up sign and she smiled and glanced at the engagement ring on the third finger of her left hand. In a few months, she'd be the princess bride, and Jack would be the one waiting for her to walk into his arms, and into his life "till death do us part."

The thought added an extra spring in her step. How did one woman get to be so lucky? She was in love with a great guy, working at a great job. Though the CNN position wasn't as high profile in Denver as *Inside Story* had been, she was airing national stories an average of once a week.

Surprisingly, she and Jessica had become a great team. After one tense exchange about Shelly's weight, Jessica had apologized and dedicated herself to showing Shelly the ropes.

Of course, Shelly suspected part of Jessica's kindness was prompted by a desire to raise her own profile and thus earn a promotion, but Shelly didn't fault her for that. A woman had to do whatever it took to get ahead in this business, even cozying up to her lover's ex-wife.

She found Jack waiting for her outside the church's reception hall. "You were gorgeous, standing up there," he said, kissing her cheek.

"Right. A gorgeous green Jell-O mold." She looked down at the poofy dress with its trimming of ribbons and bows.

"I love green Jell-O. You look good enough to eat."

The look in his eyes sent heat curling through her middle. "Were you thinking impure thoughts in church?"

"Most impure. In fact, I'm getting fonder of this dress every minute. Maybe we should have ones just like it in our wedding."

"So you can lust after the bridesmaids?" She shook her head. "No green Jell-O mold dresses."

"We could skip the dresses altogether."

She shook her head. "And no tulle-wrapped bottles of bubbles or other fussy stuff."

"No fussy stuff." He nodded soberly, though his eyes danced with suppressed laughter.

She struggled to maintain a sober expression. "And I positively, absolutely will not say 'obey.'"

"I wouldn't dream of it." He pulled her close. "Maybe we should elope."

"No, I'm determined to walk down the aisle. It's a chick thing."

"Speaking of walking—" he glanced down at her legs "—how's your knee?"

"Just fine." She wore a light brace beneath her dress, but at least she was free of that hated cane. Another month or so and she'd be as good as new, except for the scar around her kneecap. She looked across the room, to where Yvonne and Daniel were standing with their parents. "Yvonne looks really happy."

"Not as happy as we'll be." He smiled at her. "They've poured champagne. Would you like some?"

"Please."

While Shelly waited for Jack to return, Yvonne made her way over to her. "Thank you for helping me through all this," she said, hugging her friend.

"It was such a beautiful ceremony," Shelly said. "You looked gorgeous."

"Your turn is coming soon."

Shelly nodded. "Don't remind me. Between the new job and wedding plans, my to-do list is as long as my arm."

Jack returned with their drinks. He lifted his glass to Yvonne. "Congratulations."

"Thank you. I'm still in a daze. Oh, wait, I'd better go."

Shelly turned to see Daniel beckoning Yvonne from beside the cake. "Excuse me," Yvonne said. "He really hates to wait."

Shelly watched her friend scurry across the room to her new husband. She had a feeling that was the next twenty years summed up in a few seconds. How long before Yvonne tired of catering to Daniel's every whim, at the expense of her own desires?

"Someone's going to see you frowning like that and think something's wrong." Jack's breath tickled her ear as he whispered to her.

She assumed a noncommittal expression. "Thanks. I didn't even realize I was frowning."

"It was closer to a glare." He sipped champagne, then nodded toward the couple who were preparing to cut the cake. "You can't stand the guy, can you?"

She looked into her glass. "Does it show that much?"

"Only to me. I recognize the way your mouth tightens at the corners whenever he's around."

The idea that he was so attuned to her pleased her. "He's my best friend's husband, so I'm trying to tolerate him."

"Maybe this will cheer you up." He reached into his coat pocket and withdrew an envelope and handed it to her. "This came this morning."

"What is it?" She examined the plain white envelope.

He grinned. "Open it and see."

She handed him her glass, then tore off the end of the envelope and shook out the single sheet of paper within. She opened it and read the words there, then read them again. "This says I've been nominated for an Emmy. For the public hospital piece."

"Congratulations."

She looked at the words again. They seemed to float above the paper, the ink so stark against the white linen sheet. "I can't believe it."

"Believe it." He put his arm around her and pulled her close. "This is only the beginning."

She looked up at him, the room fading away around her as she lost herself in his eyes. "Right." The beginning of lots of great things in her life. She just had to keep believing in herself, and in the man who was her best fan, and her biggest inspiration.

Everything you love about romance...
and more!

Please turn the page for Signature Select™
Bonus Features.

Bonus Features:

Alternate Ending 4
What Could Have Been

Author Commentary 8
A Few Final Thoughts from Cindi

Author Interview 10
A Conversation with Cindi Myers

What's Your Dieting Degree? 14
A Quiz

Sneak Peek 17
Surf Girl School
by Cathy Yardley

BONUS FEATURES

LEARNING CURVES

EXCLUSIVE BONUS FEATURES INSIDE

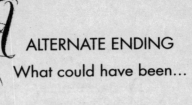

ALTERNATE ENDING
What could have been...

SHELLY STUDIED HER REFLECTION in the unforgiving glare of florescent lighting and mirrors on three sides and felt a thrill run through her. The dress was perfect. Whether it was the cream-colored satin, or the excitement of being a bride or the fact that the dress was a small size ten, she couldn't stop smiling at her reflection in the mirror.

"I think we should take it up a little more in the hips." The seamstress leaned forward and inserted a pin to take in the seam. "You want to show off those wonderful curves."

"You want to take it in?" Shelly laughed. She could count on the fingers of one hand the number of times she'd heard that phrase in her life.

"It's gorgeous!" Yvonne clapped her hands together and beamed. "Jack is going to be thrilled."

"I'm thrilled." Shelly turned to admire her reflection once more. She looked good. Glowing, the way brides were supposed to look. And thin. Who'd have thought?

"I want to know your secret," Yvonne said. "You've really trimmed down."

"Fall in love with a man whose idea of a good time is a fifteen-mile bike ride or rock climbing or climbing a fourteener." Since getting together with Jack, she'd been more active than she ever had in her life. And she was having a blast. Why hadn't someone told her before that exercise didn't have to be drudgery?

"Or go to work with a woman who's determined to convert you to her macrobiotic diet." Jessica's idea of a great lunch was a tofu wrap with organic yogurt. She always packed enough for two and insisted on sharing. To her amazement, Shelly had learned to love edamame and sprouts. And despite her model looks, Jessica had turned out to be a good mentor. She'd showed Shelly the ropes at CNN, and, unlikely as it had seemed at first, the two had become friends. Recently, she'd been promoted to the Washington bureau, leaving Shelly to cover Denver on her own.

"You're going to look great for the wedding photos." Yvonne brought the veil and helped arrange it on Shelly's head. "The *Post* is going to cover it, right?"

Shelly nodded. "And the *Rocky*. And *5280* magazine. Jack's ready to run away to Vegas."

"And miss seeing you in this dress? I don't think

so." Yvonne stepped back to admire the veil. "Gorgeous."

"Thanks." Shelly grinned at her reflection. If she was any happier, she might float away. The thought of walking down the aisle and becoming Mrs. Jack Halloran had her giddy. She caught Yvonne's eye. "Any advice for the bride to be?"

Yvonne shook her head. "You'll do fine. You and Jack are perfect for each other."

Shelly reached up to remove the veil. "You and Danny seem happy." Despite her misgivings about Yvonne's choice of a husband, things seemed to be going well.

"We are happy." Yvonne stepped forward to unzip the wedding gown. "We're talking about starting a family soon."

"Really? And Danny's for that?"

"Oh, yes. He's excited about the idea."

"Is he still talking about giving you a nose job for your birthday?"

Yvonne made a face. "I told him one cosmetic surgery was enough."

"Good for you."

"I think it surprised him when I said no, but he was smart enough not to press the issue." She laughed. "Like I told you before, a successful marriage is all about compromise."

"Maybe so." Shelly turned back to the mirror and smiled. She and Jack would probably do their share of compromising. More than likely, they'd talk out their differences the way they always had, both of them stubbornly clinging to their point until they either outmaneuvered each other or made their way to middle ground.

But beneath their stubbornness, there was a lot of love and respect. No matter what happened, they loved each other, just the way they were. They brought out the best in each other, and were stronger together than either one of them was separately.

Fat or thin, she knew Jack would be there for her. For better or worse. In sickness and in health. Happily ever after. An absurd notion, really, but one she was ready to embrace with her whole heart. As long as she and Jack were together, she could believe anything.

THE END

Author Commentary
A few final thoughts from Cindi

Learning Curves was a special book to write
because the characters really came to life for me.
Shelly was a woman after my own heart, strong
and insecure, struggling with so many of the
issues we all struggle with as women: insecurities
about weight and appearance, wondering if
Mr. Right is a myth or if our dreams are too
impossible to obtain. But Shelly overcame her
doubts and mustered up faith in herself, no
matter how fragile it was at times.

Like many of us, Shelly was a naturally big
woman who compounded her problem by
refusing to exercise or watch what she ate.
Originally, I envisioned the ending of the book as
a way to show that she'd finally gotten her weight
under control along with the rest of her life.

But Shelly herself had other ideas. As the book
progressed, I came to feel that the focus
shouldn't be on her size, but on her crises of

confidence. Shelly's weight didn't matter nearly as much as her ability to look past her imperfections to her own strengths.

So I decided (or Shelly decided for me) that her getting the new job and winning an Emmy was far more important than fitting into a less-than-size-ten wedding gown.

I'll admit this was a hard book to let go. I still think about Shelly and Jack and Yvonne and Daniel and wonder what they're up to. I hope you've enjoyed their story as much as I have.

Author Interview:
A conversation with
CINDI MYERS

Is there a pivotal life lesson you can share with our readers?

It's up to us to make the life we want. If we're not happy about some aspect of our life, we have the power to either change that aspect, or change our attitude toward it. Knowing that can be very empowering, I think.

What's the one thing you don't have enough of that you wish you did have more of?

Money. It sounds so trite and greedy, but freedom from financial worries gives you so many more options in life. That said, I do try to be content each day with what I have and not stress too much about what I don't have.

How did you begin your writing career?

When I was eight years old, I read all the Little House books and decided I wanted to be a writer. I wrote my first story on a Big Chief tablet. It was about our Siamese cat who slept in the sink. I wrote stories all through school, sold my first short story at age nineteen and wrote for magazines and newspapers for ten years or so before trying my hand at novels. I sold my first book, a historical romance, in 1997.

Do you have a writing routine?

Sort of. The only thing routine about it is I try to work steadily on a book straight through to the end. And I usually write five days a week, taking weekends off to decompress and do things with my husband and housework. When I'm working on a project, I keep the file open on my desktop or laptop all the time. I work four or five hours a day actually parked in front of the computer, but if I think of something while I'm cooking dinner or something, I can run to that open file and get it down.

When you're not writing, what do you love to do?

In the winter, I love to ski. It's one of the reasons we moved to Colorado. In the summer we hike and camp a lot. I'm also a quilter and almost always have some quilting project going. And of course I love to read.

Do you believe in inspiration or plain old hard work?

I tend to think inspiration without the hard work is useless, since nothing will come of inspiration without the work to hone the idea and get it down on paper. Hard work and perseverance get the book done. But inspiration is one of the wonderful gifts of writing. That moment when the brilliant idea suddenly appears, seemingly out of nowhere, makes all the hard work worthwhile.

Is there one book that you've read that changed your life somehow?

The Bible would be first. After that, there's a book called *Write for Your Life*, by Lawrence Block (now out of print), that really changed how I looked at my writing and at my life. And it helped me develop the attitude espoused in the answer to question one. (And then there were those Little House books, which started me on this whole writing journey.)

What are your top five favorite books?

This is so hard to pick! But I'm going to go with some I have read and re-read and enjoyed over and over through the years:

1. Morning Glory by LaVyrle Spencer

2. Pride and Prejudice by Jane Austen

3. The Lady's Companion by Carla Kelly

4. The Sound and the Fury by William Faulkner

5. Saint Maybe by Anne Tyler

What matters most in life?

People. Your relationships with them, the love and laughter you can share with them, the opportunity to help them and be helped by them. All my books, whether they're hot stories for Blaze or emotional women's fiction, have this underlying theme that people matter—all of them.

Does size matter?

Only the size of your heart, and your capacity to love and be loved. Everything else is window dressing.

Marsha Zinberg, Executive Editor, spoke with Cindi in the summer of 2005.

What's Your Dieting Degree?
by Cindi Myers

1. Which one of the following is not a diet?
   A. Atkins
   B. Perricone
   C. Pritikin
   D. Somersizing

2. What's the calorie count of 1 cup of 1% cottage cheese? How about an ounce of dark chocolate?
   A. Cottage cheese 163, Chocolate 140
   B. Cottage cheese 135, Chocolate 160
   C. Cottage cheese 100, Chocolate 150

3. You and your significant other both go on a diet. After starving for a week, you lose three pounds. He gives up his coffee break muffin but eats normally the rest of the day and loses 7 pounds. You:
   A. Accuse him of cheating.
   B. Realize men have faster metabolisms and refuse to compare yourself to him.

C. Contemplate if a jury would rule justifiable homicide if you gave in to your desire to strangle him.

4. To cut calories you have:

A. Eaten sandwiches without mayo.

B. Eaten salads without dressing.

C. Chewed only sugar-free gum.

D. Refused to lick envelopes.

5. True or False?

You would seriously consider giving up sex in order to eat dessert every day without gaining a pound.

Answers:

1. They're all diets, each named for its inventor. Somersizing is named for actress Suzanne Somers.

2. A. Now who's going to choose cottage cheese over chocolate?

3. If you answered B, you're too rational to really be on a diet.

My advice: never go on a diet with the man in your life.

4. If you answered D, I think you've *definitely* been on too many diets.

5. Sex or chocolate? Hmm...hold on, I'm still thinking.

Scoring:

If you answered all five questions correctly, you have a Ph.D. in dieting and you should treat yourself to a hot-fudge sundae. Go ahead, I dare you!

Four answers correct means all the study and practice you've put in qualifies you for a master's in dieting. Lighten up a little by finding a few more extracurricular activities to take your mind off food.

Three correct answers and you've earned your bachelor degree. Add an extra olive to that martini.

Two or fewer answers correct: Are you a man? From another country? You obviously haven't been on too many diets. The rest of us either envy you or hate you—we're not sure which.

Here's a sneak peek...

Surf Girl School
by
Cathy Yardley

A novel of sand, sun and sex appeal!

Allison Robbins's Guide To Surf Like a Pro:

1. Find surfboard, beach and hot instuctor (Sean Gilroy fits the bill).
2. Learn to surf (six weeks should do it).
3. Avoid imagining surf instructor without a wetsuit (difficult).
4. Relax, and become one with the beach.
5. Return to work as ultra-driven ad exec...and surf queen extraordinaire (or maybe not?).

CHAPTER 1

"WE ARE GOING TO LAND the Kibble Tidbits account, or we are going to die trying!"

Allison Robbins nodded vigorously at her boss Frank's vehement statement. She noticed that everyone else at the conference table at Flashpoint Advertising was also nodding in agreement.

"I don't have to tell you how big this account is," Frank said, pacing around the conference room table like Patton rallying the troops. "We're talking millions of dollars in media placement, more millions in brand advertising development and creative development and direct mail. Their parent company? Only one of the largest fast-food restaurant chains in the United States!"

Allison tried not to think about the fact that one of the largest fast-food restaurant chains in the United States also had a dog food product. There wasn't any correlation.

Probably.

Frank continued, undeterred. "And, if we land this

part of the account, the Kibble Tidbits dog food product, there's a good chance we could get the whole damned shooting match!"

Frank gestured to Allison, and she stood up. Her heart was beating fast as usual whenever she had to make a presentation. She had enough adrenaline in her bloodstream to bench press a school bus.

"Frank's asked me to pull together some notes on how we're going to attack the proposal," Allison said. "Gary? You want to run the slides?"

Gary, her assistant, instantly had the laptop and projector running like clockwork. Before they hit the lights, though, she noticed several people rolling their eyes and sneering ever so slightly. She didn't blame them, she supposed…it was the day before Thanksgiving, it was three o'clock, and a lot of them hoped to go home early. Beyond that, she knew she didn't have their unswerving support.

It hurt a little, sure, but she knew it.

The fact was, if they managed to land this account, Frank was going to be promoted to vice president. That meant there would be an account supervisor position open for the taking by one of the very account executives sitting around this table. Every single one of them was aware of it.

And Allison was going to have it, or die trying.

Everyone also knew that Allison was probably first in line for the job, she thought, clicking on her laser pointer, which only added to their resentment. That hurt just a touch more.

Her heart was still dancing wildly in her chest, but she pushed the sensation aside. She was next in line for a damned good reason. She was the best at what she did. Period. End of sentence.

"They've been saturating the market with some feel-good stuff, but more of today's consumers are getting more health conscious—not just for themselves, but for their pets...."

She started to run through the slides, her voice never wavering. The slides were very convincing, and she noticed lots of people taking notes. The slides ought to be convincing. She and Gary had been here till midnight getting them done.

"In addition to that, we're going to suggest a direct mail campaign to veterinarians, and maybe a coupon to the consumers themselves..." She paused. "Gary? Could you check the thermostat? It's getting a little hot in here. I'll bet they cranked up the heat again."

That's when she noticed everyone looking around at each other. She felt like she was on fire.

"Not too low," Marianne, one of the other execs, said hastily. "Actually...honestly, I'm a little cold."

"Really?" Allison realized that a couple of people were nodding, and to make matters worse, they were all staring at her. She took a deep breath, or as deep as she could manage, and tried to ignore the heat rushing through her. It was nothing. Probably just a little…well, she was only twenty-nine, so it wasn't a hot flash. Maybe something she ate. "So, to continue. What we're recommending…"

Her heart suddenly pumped faster, demanding her attention. *What the heck…?*

"Allison?" Frank asked, when she paused noticeably. "You all right?"

She struggled to focus, reined herself in. "Sure. Anyway, it's all there in the handouts." She wasn't going to be able to continue. The feeling threatened to overwhelm her, and she forced herself to keep her voice steady. "You don't need me to walk you through it. Especially when most of you probably have turkey and pumpkin pie on your minds, not dog biscuits."

She got a polite businesslike laugh, and she realized that Frank was still staring at her curiously as she went back to her seat. She sat down because she was afraid she'd fall back. It felt about a million degrees in there. Worse, she was starting to find the atmosphere absolutely cloying. It was like breathing fog. She looked longingly out the hermetically sealed window.

Just one deep breath…

"Great job, Allison. Of course, that's what I expect." Frank walked to the front of the room. "I also expect everyone to be putting in overtime on this one. Whatever it takes. So enjoy your turkey or pie

22

or whatever…because come Monday, we go to war. You can go ahead and go home early, if you like."

His eyes said *but not if you want to get the promotion*.

They all thanked him…and then filed out, going to their respective offices. Nobody was leaving, Allison felt quite sure of that.

Allison felt her head start to pound in tempo with her heart.

Frank hung back, staring at her. "What the hell was that about?" he asked, as Gary packed up the projector and laptop. "You didn't even go over your presentation, after all that work." He squinted at her. "And you look sort of pale."

"Frank, I *am* sort of pale," she said, laughing it off. Or trying to. All she wanted to do was rush outside and take some gulping breaths, but she forced herself to get up slowly, steadying herself. "I'm in here at six-thirty, don't leave until eight. When do I have time to tan?"

"Well, make sure you're not coming down with a cold," he said, with a grumpy note of concern.

"I will," she said. A cold. Maybe that was it. The flu…

"Because I really need you on point for this. We can't afford to screw this up."

"Of course." Like she didn't know that?

He waited a second, just to let her know that he

was serious, then he left. She walked slowly back to her office. She felt nauseous.

Gary was putting the laptop away, but he stood up. "What happened?" he repeated Frank's question, but unlike Frank, his voice rang through with real worry.

"Nothing," she said. "Can I ask you a favor?"

He looked at her, frowning. "Your wish, my command, yada yada. What do you need?"

"Did you bring your car?"

He blinked at her from behind his wire-rimmed glasses. "Um, yeah. What, do you need me to pick something up?"

"More like drop something off," she muttered, grabbing her briefcase from behind her desk. "Come on. I'll tell you on the way."

They walked to the parking lot at a fairly decent pace. She could see some people glancing at her, obviously wondering if she were leaving early. She kept her expression schooled, and ignored the desire to hold Gary's arm for support, letting him talk about her schedule, the upcoming presentations…the works.

When the doors opened to the outside, she took in a deep, explosive breath.

Gary glanced around, then put a steadying arm around her waist. "Whoa. What the hell?"

"Anybody looking?" No matter how hard she breathed, she still felt like she couldn't get enough air.

"No." Now his voice crackled with worry. "What's going on?"

"You're taking me to the hospital," she whispered. "Slowly. Something's wrong."

If anyone could look casually panicked, it'd be Gary. She almost laughed at the war of emotions on his normally impassive face. "You got it."

She got into his car, barely grinning at the way he sedately pulled out of the parking lot...and then gunned the engine when they were out of sight of the building.

"What is it? What's happening?" Now that they were safely out of earshot, Gary's voice rang out like a very high-pitched trumpet. "You looked awful. I thought you were going to pass out."

"I feel like I can't breathe," she said, finally leaning back against the cushions. "My heart's beating like a wild woman."

"Does it hurt?"

"Well, it's not what I'd call *comfortable*," she snapped.

"Do you think it's a heart attack?"

"I don't...well. Hmm." She tried to remember what it had been like when her father had his three heart attacks. The problem was, she'd never actually been there when he'd had them. All three times, he'd been in his office at work.

That probably wasn't a good sign, she thought, gnawing at her lower lip.

She rolled down the window, tried to take deep breaths as the beginning of rush-hour Los Angeles traffic zoomed around her. They pulled into the emergency room with a squeal of tires. Gary practically carried her to the door.

"I am not completely incapacitated here," she said.

"At least you feel well enough to bitch at me," he said, with his usual straight face.

In a shorter amount of time than she would've expected, she was shuttled off by a nurse practitioner. "So? You've got chest pains? What type? What time, exactly, did they start?" the woman asked.

"A little squeezy, and my heart's beating like crazy. They started about an hour ago."

"Have you had any heart problems before? Any heart attacks?" She handed Allison an aspirin, which Allison stared at. "Take this."

Allison did as she was told. "No heart problems personally, but attacks run in the family."

"Feel nauseous? Dizzy?"

"A little of both," Allison admitted.

"Lie down. Breathe this." The nurse put the tubes of oxygen in Allison's nose and then started unbuttoning Allison's shirt, sticking her with EKG pads. "Are you taking Viagra?"

Allison was so surprised, she sat up, strangling herself on the oxygen hose. "Am I taking *what?*"

"Are you taking anything like Viagra?" the nurse repeated impatiently.

26

Allison couldn't help it. She let out a burst of nervous laughter. "Do I look like I have erectile dysfunction to you?"

"Gotta ask it, whether you're male or female. Okay. Just lie back and let me check this out."

Allison did, focusing on her breathing.

"Ms. Robbins…have you been under any stress lately?"

"Well, sure. Who isn't?" That probably shouldn't have come out as defensively as it did.

"Are you regularly under pressure?"

"Only when I'm awake," she tried to joke, then thought about the last nightmare she had—a client review where she was giving a presentation in nothing but granny panties and a big grin. "Okay. Sometimes when I sleep."

The woman nodded knowingly. "Well, I can't say this conclusively, and the doctor's going to want to talk to you, but from everything I've seen, you aren't having a heart attack."

Allison slumped back against the gurney. "That's a relief."

"But I will say one thing," the nurse added. "You seem to be having the mother of all panic attacks."

"FIVE…FOUR…THREE…two…one!"

Sean Gilroy watched, amused, as his surf buddies and their families surrounded a vat of boiling peanut oil. His good friend Mike was wearing a big black apron and a welder's mask, and he was slowly lowering the turkey into the oil. There was a ragged cheer when the whole bird was submerged.

"Whooo!" he yelped, stepping back and taking a triumphant, Rocky-esque stance. "We have turkey! I repeat, we have turkey!"

"Thank God for that," Sean's sister, Janie, said, holding her baby daughter on her hip. "I was worried that maybe we'd just have French fries for Thanksgiving."

Sean chuckled. "You've been spending too many holidays with that traditional family of your husband's," he said, tugging at her ponytail like he did when they were kids. "'Bout time you returned to your surf roots."

She smiled. "I know. It's been a while since I hung out with you and the Hoodlums."

"Graduating from college, getting married, two kids in two years," he said, stroking his niece's face and feeling a little goofy grin cover his face, even as he felt a little pang. "Hell. It's not like you haven't been busy. Besides…I'm always here, kid. You know that."

"You can say that again," his friend Gabe said, with feeling.

Sean's eyebrow went up, with a little grin. "Commenting on my lifestyle, buddy?"

"Just saying what everybody else says, bro." Gabe's lightning-flash smile showed that he meant no malice in the statement, but there was still a look of concern in his eyes. "Next year, you might want to think about shaking things up, that's all."

"Shaking things up how?" Janie asked, curious.

"Like maybe a new girlfriend," Sean's friend Ryan interjected, popping the top of a Negro Modelo beer. "Dude, you've been single for the past two years. When a guy doesn't have a girl for that long, there's a chance he might, you know, explode." He took a sip of beer. "Just thinking about it freaks me out."

Mike walked up, popping the front of his welder's mask off his face. "Yeah, but you're not Sean," Mike pointed out. "He's a lot more surf-Zen than you are."

"So what, that makes him a monk?"

"No, it just means that he's not ready to nail every girl that walks into the surf shop," Mike responded, glancing nervously at the turkey. "Of course, if we're voting for what Sean can change next year, I'd say replace that piece-of-crap pickup truck of his. Creaking around in that would make me nuts." He grinned. "But I'm not that Zen, either."

Sean shook his head, listening to them bicker. He let them keep gibing as he walked out toward the surf, taking a sip of his beer. He was going to eat too much tonight to go for a night surf, which was too bad. He'd been surfing every day for the past month, despite the cold November temperatures of the water. He was just too restless lately. For somebody that people described as Zen, he wasn't feeling serene and calm lately. The problem was, he had absolutely no idea *why* he was feeling so wound up. He'd been going along, perfectly fine, doing the same job, in the same city and the same apartment for—he quickly did some mental math—about sixteen years.

So why was he feeling so restless *now?*

Gabe walked next to him, also looking out at the water, watching as the sun set into the Pacific. "What's going on, buddy?" he asked, and now there was no joking…his voice was all concern.

"The usual," Sean replied. "Been slow down at the surf shop, and Oz is going progressively balder by tearing his hair out." Oz, his boss and the owner of the shop, was a notorious stress case. "Otherwise, the surf's been great if sorta cold. So my life's pretty much normal."

"Are you still happy at the surf shop?"

"I love working at the surf shop," Sean said. "You know me."

"Yeah, I know you." Gabe's voice sounded a little resigned. "If you wanted a new job, or a change, you know…the offer's always open. You could come work at Lone Shark."

Sean shifted uncomfortably, staring at the ocean, watching the last sliver of the crimson sun disappear into the waves. "I love you like a brother, Gabe," he said, in a low voice. "Which is why there is no way in hell I'm going to work for you."

Gabe sighed impatiently. "Look, it's not like a

handout. It's just…I've known you since high school, and that's how long you've been working at Tubes, for Oz." He shook his head. "Sometimes a guy can get bored, doing the same thing."

Sean took a deep breath. *Or restless.* "I know surf stuff. I like helping people choose their gear, talk waves. I like teaching kids in the summer," he said. "I like the community. And besides, I feel like I owe Oz."

"I know he took you and Janie in when you were kids," Gabe said. "But you're, what, thirty-three now? And he doesn't pay you nearly enough, you know that."

Now Sean felt really uncomfortable. "Yeah. I know that. But he lets me live over the shop. It's a trade-off." Before Gabe could keep going, Sean put his hand up. "I appreciate your worrying about me, man. But, well, it just feels too much like a handout, and I don't need a favor. I can take care of myself."

Gabe looked at him, frowning, then shrugged. "Can't blame a guy for trying."

"Yeah, well…you're acting like your sister." Sean grinned. Gabe's sister Bella was a notorious buttinsky. "And your wife would kick your ass if she found out."

"If I found out what?"

Charlotte, Gabe's wife, walked up, her expression curious. Sean had known her for years, too, but it was still amazing to see the two of them together. They'd been married for three years now, and it still seemed like they were in perpetual honeymoon mode. They got razzed about it by the rest of the Hoodlums, their rowdy bunch of surf friends. But Sean knew better. Gabe and Charlotte were like peanut butter and jelly, a perfect match.

His restlessness shifted a little. Maybe he did need a girlfriend.

"We were just talking, honey," Gabe said, nuzzling her neck. "No biggie."

"Really." Her voice said she wasn't buying it one bit. Then she glanced at Sean, even as her arms went around her husband's waist. "You okay? Did you eat anything?"

"Waiting for the turkey," he said. "But everything looks great. You guys keep pulling together a great party. Thanks for inviting me."

"You're not just a friend…you're family," she said, sincerity rich in her voice. She'd lost her parents at an early age, so she knew what it felt like to be alone. Sean was grateful he had Janie and her family, but he knew what she meant—the Hoodlums were his family, had been for years. "You sure you're okay? You've seemed a little out of sorts lately."

Sean laughed, even as he wondered just how restless he'd been, if people were starting to comment on it. "What, am I wearing a sign?" he asked, a little embarrassed.

"Oh. That's what Gabe was bugging you about, I

get it." She reddened a little. "Well, we were just…you know."

"I know," he answered, chucking her under the chin. She was like a little sister, too. "Don't worry about it."

"Uh-oh," Gabe said, noticing that Mike was back at the vat. "I'd better make sure that they don't maim anybody or start anything on fire. We'll talk later."

"If we have to," Sean said, with a little grin to show he was kidding. Still, as he watched Gabe and Charlotte walk away, and saw his friends all gathered again around the turkey, he realized that he still felt weird. Like all the surfing in the world wasn't going to solve it. He was lucky to have his friends, his job, his place to live. He'd always loved his life. He just wasn't sure what was missing.

He took one last look at the surf, hearing the crash of the waves in the growing darkness. His life wasn't perfect, he admitted. But at times like this, it was pretty darned close. And for now, that'd have to be enough.

"HAPPY THANKSGIVING," Allison said, with as much cheer as she could muster.

"Happy Thanksgiving, dear," her mother replied. "I can only speak for a minute—they're going to serve dinner soon."

Allison shifted the phone to her other ear. "That sounds nice," she said, looking down at the remnants of the deli turkey sandwich, sitting on a paper plate by her open laptop. "How's Dad enjoying the Bahamas?"

"He's been thinking of investing down here. You know how he is," her mother said, with a tone of tolerant amusement. "Just like your brother, always on the lookout for some kind of deal."

"Once a venture capitalist, always a venture capitalist," Allison said. "I take it Rod never made it down to the islands, then?"

"No. He's in the middle of some deal with a company in…let's see, Norway? Sweden? Someplace cold that doesn't celebrate Thanksgiving." Again, that small laugh, with the boys-will-be-boys-and-businessmen brand of humor.

"And Steffie?" Allison asked.

"Are you crazy? She's studying for finals!"

Steffie, Allison's younger sister, was in UCLA law, and working hard on becoming the top student. Allison sighed. She really should've known better than to ask.

Her mother cleared her throat. "And what about you, dear? We were hoping that at least you could have joined us for this holiday."

Allison felt a little spurt of anger, and quickly quenched it. "I'm working on this promotion. If we land this account, I'll be account supervisor. Before I'm thirty." Which would be in March. Not that she was thinking about that too hard.

"Well, that'll be nice," her mother said, a little diffidently. "Still, you might've taken just a few days to be with your parents. I mean, they could probably spare you."

"It's not a merger with a European conglomerate," she said, her voice even, "and it's not editing *Law Review,* but it's still important, Mom."

There was a pause on the other end of the line. "You're the one who chose advertising, Allison," her mother said, and even over the thousands of miles, Allison felt her mother's rebuke like she was in the same room. "I'm just saying, it's not quite as rigorous. If you're feeling inadequate, you've only yourself to blame."

Allison swallowed hard, but took the comment quietly.

"Oh, here's your father. They're serving dinner. I trust you'll be at the house for Christmas?" Her mother's voice was a study of forced cheerfulness. "Even your brother will be there."

What, he's not doing a deal with some African company that doesn't celebrate Christmas? "I'll be there," Allison said, keeping her own voice cheerful in response. "Love to Dad."

"All right, dear. Goodbye."

Allison hung up her phone, then threw it on the couch. She looked at her living room. There were papers everywhere. There were remnants of her Thanksgiving feast next to her laptop with the presentation slides. The television was on, the volume turned low. They were playing *It's a Wonderful Life* on cable, and it was her favorite part, when Donna Reed got caught naked in a hydrangea bush.

"This is a very interesting situation," she quoted right along with Jimmy Stewart, and she giggled, a little hysterically.

The thing is, it wasn't a very interesting situation. It was a sad and vaguely alarming one.

Panic attack.

She hadn't mentioned it to her mother, for obvious reasons, but she sat on her couch, trying to will away the incipient touches of squeezy pain starting to clench at her chest. She had too much on her plate to succumb to panic attacks, of all things. Her family didn't *do* panic attacks. Just like they didn't *do* failure.

The doctor at the hospital had tried to prescribe anti-anxiety medicine, and a bunch of other kinds of pills, but Allison had turned them down. She had tried pills like that before, back when she was in college. Of course, then it had just been lower-level stress, and she had felt weird going into the doctor for something so stupid, but she'd gone at her roommate's insistence. Unfortunately, the medicine had made her dizzy and loopy, unable to focus.

So she'd done the only thing she could. She moved out on her own. No roommate, no pressure to go to the doctor. She still stressed out, and she'd lost a lot of weight that semester, but she'd managed to pull it off with a 3.85 grade point average.

The fact that her mother had shown off her brother's dean's-list 4.0 grades was not helpful, admittedly. But the point was, she'd made it through just fine.

Allison picked up her plate and headed off to the kitchen, where a pumpkin pie from the grocery store was thawing out on the counter. She methodically washed up her dishes, then looked at the pie. Then she grabbed a fork, taking the whole pie to the couch. "Happy Thanksgiving to me," she said, with a firm nod…then dug in.

An hour later, with a sick but happy feeling of satiety, Allison stretched out on her couch. She managed to rough out a lot of the presentation, but she knew that there were going to be about seven thousand more drafts, if her boss had any say in it…and of course, he did. It was too important for him not to get obsessively involved.

The thing was, if she kept having panic attacks, she wouldn't be able to work. At all. And that scared her more than anything.

She frowned, replaying the conversation with the doctor in her head.

"What can I do, other than drugs, to prevent these…" she'd winced, not even wanting to say the words "…panic attacks?"

The doctor was not happy with her comments,

and he'd frowned fiercely. "There's only one way to prevent these, really," he said, and from the tone of his voice, he didn't sound very confident. "You're going to need to relax."

"Relax. Just…relax." Allison tensed up immediately. "Uh…"

"Which I can see," he said, dryly, "that you're completely incapable of doing at this point."

She bristled, even as some part of her brain said *he's got your number there, kid.* "I can…I mean, I'm sure…"

"What are your hobbies?" he asked, throwing her off.

"Hobbies?"

"Yes. You know, what do you do when you're not working?"

"I…er…" She thought about it. *Eat. Sleep. Shower. Repeat as necessary.* "Um…"

He sighed, impatient. "What was the last movie you saw? The last book you read? The last time you spent time with a friend?"

"I've been busy," Allison hedged, feeling her face redden. "So you're saying I need to get a life."

He frowned so fiercely, she thought he was going to blow a fuse. "I'm saying if you keep working this way, next time, it might not be a panic attack," the doctor warned, even though he'd kept his voice gentle. "Next time, it might really be a heart attack, Ms. Robbins. Believe me, you don't want that."

Allison sighed, just remembering the exchange. Reluctantly, she leaned over, shut down her laptop, put her work into neat, respective folders and tucked the whole lot of it into her briefcase. She'd have enough time to work on it tomorrow, anyway, since a good chunk of the office would still be on vacation the day after Thanksgiving. Hopefully, it'd be nice and quiet, at least.

Then she pulled out a large piece of paper. Panic attacks, like anything else, were just a problem—a challenge. She could handle challenges. In fact, she lived on them.

First thing to do was to brainstorm. She pulled out her felt pens. On the TV, *It's a Wonderful Life* had moved on to *Funniest Holiday Moments,* so she changed the channel, not even paying attention to what was playing. Then she started scribbling away, with the single-minded determination that made her one of the best advertising execs on the West Coast.

Hobbies, she wrote in fat letters.

She realized, with some distress, that she didn't have a lot of friends to hang out with. Most of the people that she had been friends with in college had drifted away, gotten married, moved. The friends she had now…well, *friends* was a loose definition. They were people from work. She barely had coffee with them, unless it was somehow related to a work project. Besides, they were people who were more than likely vying for the same job she was, now that she thought about it. Approaching any of them to join her in a hobby was probably not going to happen.

Social life, she wrote on a different corner of the large paper. Then, biting her lip, she added *Friends* to the list. Might as well work on that, too. "In my copious spare time," she said ruefully to herself.

She looked back at *Hobbies,* then started listing things randomly. Skiing. Skating. Swimming. Painting. She kept adding things, getting as blue-sky as possible. She always told the people she worked with to think big, and then they'd come up with how to get there. There was always a way, she was a firm believer in that. Dream it, and you could do it.

She figured this wasn't any different.

After an hour, she looked at her sprawling list. It didn't cheer her up. On the contrary, she actually felt hints of the panic creeping back.

How am I going to have time to do any of these things? I barely have time for the whole eat-sleep-shower thing!

She took a few deep breaths, and a few more forkfuls of pumpkin pie. She took a few more deep breaths. *Just pretend it's a client project,* she told herself. And slowly, logically, she forced herself to focus.

She needed something she could do locally. She crossed off *skiing, camping* and *European travel* immediately.

She needed something that incorporated exercise,

if at all possible—the doctor had mentioned that exercise would also help, and she was all about multitasking. So she crossed off *poker*, the art-related stuff and *museum-visiting*.

She needed something that wouldn't stress her out more than she already was. She scratched off *bungee jumping, skydiving* and *hang gliding* with a silent breath of relief.

She stared at the options she had left. She lived in Southern California. Sure, it was winter, but all things considered, that didn't mean much. She should probably choose to do something outdoors. She *was* pretty pale, as she'd mentioned to her boss. So something involving sunshine, she thought with a smile.

And maybe the water. She'd loved the beach when she was a kid, she remembered, even though she never had time to enjoy it. And now, she only lived ten minutes from the sands of Manhattan Beach. When was the last time she'd actually looked at the ocean, now that she thought about it?

So what could she do that involved the water?

"I feel like I just got hit on the head by a sledgehammer," a girlish voice said from the television.

Allison looked up, startled…and then abruptly started laughing.

Gidget. The classic-movie channel was playing the movie *Gidget.* Allison watched as a diminutive and driven Sandra Dee tackled the sport of surfing with the same single-minded focus that had apparently made her valedictorian, or something. Now there was a woman who knew what she wanted, and knew how to go after it.

Allison felt herself grin. She looked down at her list...and sure enough, there it was.

With a fat felt-tip pen, she circled one word in red and leaned back, feeling better than she had in hours. She had her answer.

Surfing. She could hardly wait.

...NOT THE END...

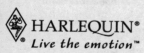

SHOWCASE

**Two classic stories in one volume
from favorite author**

FAYRENE PRESTON

**In one house, secrets of past and
present converge...**

SwanSea
Legacy

Caitlin Deverell's great-grandfather had built
SwanSea as a mansion that would signal the
birth of a dynasty. Decades later, this ancestral
home is being launched into a new era as a
luxury resort—an event that arouses passion,
romance and a century-old mystery.

PLUS, exclusive bonus features inside!

Available in November 2005.

SHSL